STAIN OF A NATION

STAIN OF A NATION

TWO-GUN WITCH
BOOK TWO

BISHOP O'CONNELL

Charlotte, NC

FALSTAFF
BOOKS

WWW.FALSTAFFBOOKS.COM

For "The Boot" and Dennis Morgan, who believed in me before I believed in myself.

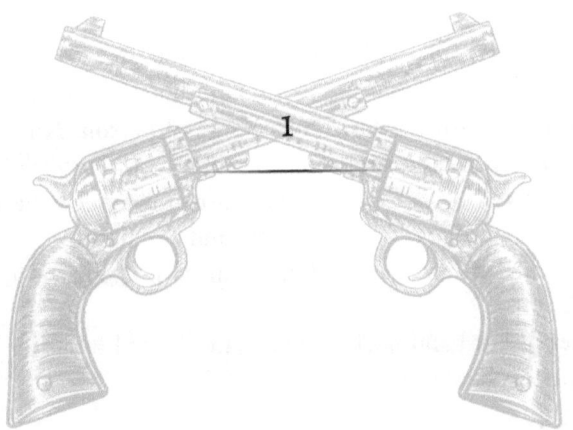

1

Margaret stared out the window, watching the Iowa plains roll by. The monotony of the landscape and gentle swaying of the train threatened to lull her to sleep, the growing soreness in her nether regions from sitting on a hard wooden bench for too long notwithstanding.

"You alright?" Wilfred, seated on her left, asked in what passed for a whisper on a train.

"I'm fine." Margaret forced a smile to veil the lie.

Wilfred gave her a level look, glanced down at her lap, and then back at her face.

Margaret furrowed her brow and followed his gaze. At some point she'd begun rubbing at her right leg, the underdeveloped one, without even realizing.

She straightened and her expression turned to mock reproachful. "It's possible I'm reconsidering my thoughts on coach seating."

Wilfred cracked a smile. "Yes, ma'am, my ass is a mite sore, too."

She stifled a chuckle.

He pulled out his pocket watch, checked it, and then tucked it away. "Fifteen minutes."

Margaret's heart rate increased, but she made sure to keep her expression neutral. She nodded and patted her pocket for the hundredth time to make sure the charm was still there. Just like the other ninety-nine times, it was. She swallowed back the anxiety and took a few slow breaths. Once her heart rate slowed, her smile slid away, and she shook her head.

"What is it?" Wilfred asked.

"I was just wondering what George would say if he could see me now." She sighed.

A warm grin settled on Wilfred's face, and he shrugged. "Now, I ain't known you nearly as long as he did," he said. "But even a fool like me can see you got a wholesome heart. You're a good person. No matter what you do—and I seen you do some feats of note—you always try and do the right thing. Now, as he had sense enough to marry you, he weren't no fool. So, I suspect he'd just say, 'I love you, and be careful.'"

Margaret turned her hand, taking Wilfred's, and gave it a squeeze. "Thank you."

He squeezed her hand back, winked, and leaned in closer. "Now," he said, "let's rob this here train."

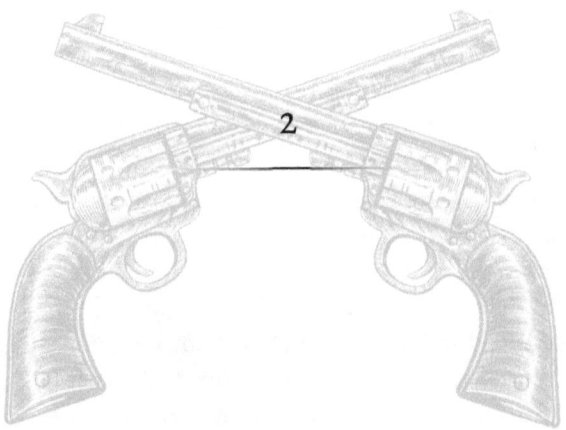

2

W ilfred stood and adjusted his coat, calm as could be. Margaret passed him her cane and, with his help, got to her feet.

"Pardon me," she said to the couple seated in front of her as she braced herself on their seatback.

The gentleman gave Wilfred a sideways glance but touched the brim of his derby and nodded at Margaret. A politeness she was certain he wouldn't have shown if he knew she was Black too.

Once steady, she took her cane back from Wilfred, and with him close on her heels, they made for the front of the passenger car. Few of the—all white—passengers paid them any mind as they went by. The men, who were all siting nearest the aisle, scooted away. Even if Margaret had been naïve enough to believe it was out of politeness, the women who shifted their handbags away would've disabused her of such a notion.

We're robbing the train, ma'am, not you, she thought to herself, and smiled.

The couple seated nearest the car exit turned to each other and back as Margaret took hold of the door handle. The woman opened her mouth to say something, but a sudden blast of air and the roar of the engine drowned her words.

Margaret stepped out onto the small platform, turned to face the door, and gripped the railing behind her. Wilfred joined her and closed the door behind him. She looked over her shoulder. The mail car had a platform similar to the one she and Wilfred stood on, if a bit smaller, with matching iron handrails, separated only by a length of chain.

Her gaze went to the open space separating the two cars' respective platforms. Apart from the coupling—which looked too small to hold the massive train cars together—there was nothing between her and the speeding ground. She tried, unsuccessfully, not to imagine falling into that gap and being mangled by the train's undercarriage and steel wheels.

Her heart started pounding.

The only blessing was the lack of soot and ash spewing from the stack, and what little there was, the wind blew to one side.

Wilfred tapped her arm.

"It'll be fine," he said, practically shouting to be heard.

Margaret nodded and forced herself to calm, with mixed results.

Wilfred drew a small metal disk from inside his coat and passed it to her. "If you'd be so kind. We don't want no surprises coming from behind us."

Still gripping the railing with one white-knuckled hand, Margaret took the charm with the other. Just as he'd instructed, she pressed it against the door, close to the latch. She drew in a slow breath, focused, and sent a trickle of magic into the talisman. It warmed for just an instant before vanishing into the door. Half a blink later, the seam between the door and its frame vanished as the two pieces fused into one.

"I'll get the chain on the mail car," Wilfred said and held out his hand. "If I may?"

Margaret passed him her cane with a shaking hand.

He gripped the railing and leaned out over the open space, reaching with the handle of the cane.

Stomach tightening, she took hold of his coat as the train jostled.

After what felt like a week, Wilfred managed to unhook the safety chain on the mail car's platform, leaving a gap in the railing.

"Ready?" he asked, removing the chain on their side.

Logically, she knew the chain wouldn't stop her from tumbling into the gap, but its removal sent a fresh wave of near panic through her.

"No," she said, but forced herself to take a step to the edge of the platform, clutching the handrails on either side in a death grip. Likewise, she knew full well that the gap between the two platforms was only a few feet, but standing there, it seemed closer to fifty or sixty.

Holding tight to one railing with her left hand, she—very slowly and

4

very carefully—reached into her blouse with her right and took out an amulet Wilfred had crafted for just this occasion. She took several slow breaths, but her heart wouldn't stop pounding. Try as she might, she couldn't focus enough to channel any magic.

Wilfred came up behind her and—gently but firmly—put his hands on her hips. "We practiced this," he said into her ear. "I made that charm, and you checked it three times. It'll work. Even if it don't, I got hold of you. I promise, I ain't gonna let you fall. Just don't look down."

She looked down.

The track sped by so fast she couldn't see the individual ties. However, she could very clearly see the claw-like coupling and large steel wheels. Rather vivid images of them cutting her into gruesome pieces rolled through her brain again.

She glared at him over her shoulder. "I wouldn't have if you hadn't said it!"

"In that case, be sure to look down," he said through a smile.

"You think you're funny, but you're really not."

He laughed. "Maybe not, but you ain't scared no more, are you?"

Margaret opened her mouth to argue, but he was right. She scowled. "I'll concede you're clever, but not that you're funny."

"Fair enough."

Margaret turned back to the chasm-like gap between the cars, focused on the amulet, and activated it. A shiver of warmth spread from it. The heat ran along her arm, down her torso, into her legs, and finally her feet. Like every time she'd tried it before, a tingling settled into her toes, and the taste of mint filled her mouth.

She swallowed and put a tentative foot forward, still gripping the iron rail.

Her foot came down on what should've been empty air but, thanks to Wilfred's crafting, was as solid as the platform under her back foot.

Relief surged through her, loosening the knot in her stomach, if not untying it entirely.

A few quick, shuffling, steps across the solidified air—never once looking down—and she stood on the mail car's platform, holding the railing with white knuckles.

Once she started breathing again, she looked to Wilfred who tossed her the cane. She caught it and watched as he took a step back and readied himself.

The recently eased knot in her stomach tightened up once more.

Wilfred, being a crafter, couldn't use charms, which meant making the jump on his own.

Granted, it wasn't a giant leap, and he had long legs, but even a slight misstep and—

She pushed the thought away and focused on him, willing him to make the jump easily. Even so, she readied herself to offer whatever help, however limited, she could if needed.

He blew out a breath, charged forward, planted a foot on the edge of the platform, and leapt.

Time slowed, and he hung in the air, eyes wide, jaw clenched, and both hands reaching out.

After a small eternity, his leading foot landed on the platform, and his strong hands grabbed onto the railing.

Margaret pulled him the rest of the way, or at least tried. It was unlikely she helped much at all. They both put their backs to the mail car and slid down onto the small platform.

"And here I was worried that might be unnerving," Wilfred said.

They both laughed, quietly, and Margaret gave him a playful shove.

"Never doubted you for an instant," she said.

"Me neither," he said through half a grin. "Mind, it won't bother me none to never do that again." He nodded at the car's wall. "You best get to work. I'll just sit here, taking in the scenery and breeze. Not waiting for my heart to ease its pounding."

"Of course not," Margaret said and patted his hand.

Wilfred was the first man she'd ever met who didn't mind anyone seeing him scared or unsure. She wondered how much of that came from being in chains. Pride wasn't exactly a prized attribute at slave auctions.

They'd been friends for near on a year now, but it still astounded her that someone could see—much less experience firsthand—horrors beyond imaging, and not just survive, but come out still capable of compassion and hope. More than that, he was practically overflowing with kindness and caring.

As always happened when she considered Wilfred's past, thoughts of her mother rose up. Even before the consumption made more than a few words impossible, her mother rarely talked about life before the Railroad got her north. Margaret never learned the particulars of what her mother had survived, not that she'd ever wanted details. The scars on her mother's back and the hardness in her eyes said enough. As remarkable as Wilfred's kindness was, so too was how Margaret's mother only ever

6

looked at Margaret—the result of a gruesome, violent, and recurring violation—with love, pride, and joy.

Margaret shook her head, bringing herself back to the here and now. She had to focus on the task at hand.

Not the time or place for that sort of thinking.

She untied her hat, handed it to Wilfred, and carefully got to her feet, steadying herself with both hands. Unlike passenger cars, the mail car didn't have doors at the ends. Instead, for security, it had a pair of slightly bigger sliding doors on just one side.

Very slowly, she peeked around the edge of the car.

From this angle, she couldn't tell if both doors were open, but at least one was. She could just make out the shoulder of a—presumably—large man in a suit leaning against the open doorway.

Margaret drew back out of sight.

"Door is open," she said. "One guard is at the doorway. A Pinkerton from the looks of him."

Wilfred nodded, set Margaret's hat to one side, removed his own, and then pulled a small leather bag that hung from his neck down inside his jacket. He slipped the bag's cord over his head, passed the pouch to her, and got to his feet.

"I'll keep a watch." He drew a mundane revolver from an inside pocket, and went to stand at the car's edge, occasionally peeking out around the corner.

Margaret opened the pouch and removed the small hand glass, roughly edged in silver. She placed the back of the mirror against the mail car's wall and traced her right index finger over the delicately etched runes, pushing magic into the charm as she did. Her reflection faded away, replaced by a clear view of the inside of the train car.

Two men in postal uniforms worked at small desks built into the walls. Sacks of what she presumed was mail hung from various hooks. Boxes of varying size were stacked on the floor and high shelves, secured with leather straps.

She shifted to get a better view and clearly saw the Pinkerton standing at the doorway. A gun hung from his hip, but Margaret couldn't tell if it was a spell iron or a mundane shooter. Two more men, similarly dressed and armed, sat inside the car on stools attached to the flooring. Apparently one of them had just told a joke, because all five men shared a laugh.

Margaret stopped, deactivated the charm, and it returned to a normal, if scratched, mirror. She tucked it back into the pouch, slipped the pouch's cord over her head, and pulled out the charm in her skirt pocket. It was the dial off a small safe, set on a wooden disk. A magnet had been glued to the back, Draven's idea, so it would stick tight to the car's steel cladding. She turned the dial with her right hand, pouring magic into it. She spun it right to the two, then left around to the three.

Wait, she thought. *Was it guards first, then workers?*

She closed her eyes and thought back.

No, workers first, then guards.

Right?

She honestly wasn't sure, so she decided to go with her first guess. Not that she suspected it would matter much. She doubted any of them would prove much of a challenge for Talen.

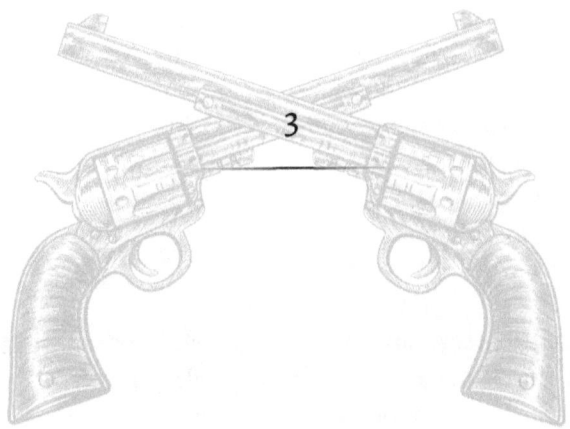

3

Talen paced back and forth in the confines of the Cumulus's bridge. The airship's control room—she still didn't understand why it was called a bridge—only had enough space to allow her a couple of steps before she had to turn and go back the other way. Like most elves, she'd never been overly fond of enclosed spaces, but until now, not being able to properly pace hadn't been one of the key reasons.

Draven stood, stoic and unreadable. Even after all these months, the dwarf still looked outsized by the huge ship's wheel, and a bit ridiculous on the raised platform that gave her a clear view through the glass window.

Not that Talen was fool enough to ever say that aloud.

"I don't like it," Talen said, her gaze shifting from the train far below and ahead of them to the charm in her hand. "Something must've gone wrong. We should activate the masking charms and drop down."

"Calm yourself," Draven said. "Just give them some time. Also, I'd appreciate if you didn't wear through my decking."

Talen stopped pacing and came to stand beside the dwarf. "I should've gone, not them."

"I recall us all having this discussion," Draven said, one side of her mouth pulling up and arching her moustache. "A few times."

Talen didn't return the smile. "I shouldn't have agreed."

"You've got a limited number of glamour charms," Draven said

9

without a trace of impatience. "And even if you used one, it wouldn't have lasted long enough."

"I know," Talen said.

"It had to be Margaret—"

"Because the guards might shoot Wilfred on sight," Talen said. "And that might well have happened if Margaret didn't pass like we hoped. Either or both of them could be bleeding out right now. And here we are, floating safe, having the same argument I should've won before."

"If anything happened, Margaret would've signaled you."

"Unless they shot her first," Talen said.

"She passed for white most of her life," Draven said. "Around some of the worst sort."

"She could've fallen off the damned train."

"A less charitable sort might mistake your concern for a lack of trust."

Talen stiffened, and the rush of anger almost got the best of her. Rather than replying, she took a breath and let the ire pass.

"Reckon that sort could," she said once she'd calmed down. "Just don't know as I'd ever forgive myself if something happened to either of them."

"The burden of family," Draven said through a broad smile, side-eyeing Talen.

Talen could only sigh and nod.

Family. Who'd have thought it even possible?

Weren't so long ago the very notion of having another family seemed laughable at best. Suggesting it would include a couple humans, much less a dwarf, would've resulted in significant blood being shed. But here they were. Life was a hell of a thing.

"Sorry," Talen said.

"No need."

"I don't take to waiting so well."

"Might be I picked up on that," Draven said, stroking her bare chin.

The gesture was just habit, but it reminded Talen of what Draven had given up. She was beardless, a sect of dwarves that had cut their beards and broken away from their king in protest. What had once been a united people were now split, one on each coast. The schism had come when the Dolomite—the dwarf king—had joined with the US Army in slaughtering the Oceti Sakowin and the elves. Only the expanse of the Great Plains now kept it from becoming an actual war.

Once, Talen had painted all dwarves with the same brush, but Draven had become a sister, earning both trust and respect. "Well, I'll try and muster a bit more patience from—" The charm in Talen's hand chirped and the dial started turning. "Thank the mothers!"

Draven let out a belly laugh.

"What?"

"Just recalling a joke," Draven said and pushed a lever forward. In response, the Cumulus's four fans pivoted, and the airship began to descend.

"What is it?" Talen asked. "I could use a laugh."

Draven passed Talen a pair of goggles. "I think you need be a dwarf to see the humor. Go activate the mask before we get too close."

"Yes, that famous dwarven humor," Talen said, sparing half a grin.

"You saying we ain't funny?"

"Perish the thought."

Draven chuckled as Talen slipped on the eye protection and left the bridge.

Once outside, she went to the extensively engraved, six-foot diameter wooden disk set into the deck just in front of the bridge. She bent down and touched her fingers to the control charm. It was inlaid with gold, silver, and a dozen other metals, with thin copper wires running from its edge like sunbeams along the deck to the fifty sub-charms placed all over the outside of the airship.

As she wasn't a crafter, she didn't pretend to know much about charms, aside from using them. But until Wilfred had suggested it, she'd never even heard of interconnected charms. Leave it to him to come up with such an ingenious solution.

They'd spent better than a month—and a thousand dollars—collecting the needed components, and it took him about as long to put the thing together. Unfortunately, this one use would likely burn the thing out, which meant they didn't get to test it. Wilfred had been the only one disappointed, no one else doubted his skills.

"Here we go." She focused intently, and poured magic into the massive charm. Typically, channeling magic was like breathing, almost effortless. This time, it felt more like trying to fill the sails of a ship with nothing but her lungs. After a moment, the carved symbols slowly filled with blue spellfire. A dull pain started between her eyes, and she was literally getting short of breath from the required concentration. It was taking more out of her than any other charm she'd used, which made sense as she was actually activating fifty of them.

But still, damn.

After a very long moment, the magical inertia built up enough that it took less and less effort. The strain, thankfully, began to ease. Another few seconds passed before she could sense that all the sub-charms had activated. As she got to her feet, her head spun. She wobbled and stumbled but managed to catch herself before falling.

"You alright?" Draven asked through the glass pane of the bridge.

"Fine," Talen said. "That was just a bit of heavy lifting."

"Did it work?"

Talen smiled. "Sure looks it."

The airship's egg shaped, woven metal—and usually—dull gray gas bladder was invisible. Well, not really. According to Wilfred, making something as big as the Cumulus invisible would require a small army of charms and twice as many casters. However, masking it to seem as whatever was on the other side of it, though not as effective, was simpler.

The lightness in her head passed, and Talen went to the deck edge and glanced over, just to make sure the rest of the ship was similarly disguised. It was.

"That man is a damned genius," Talen said as she reentered the bridge and pushed the goggles onto her forehead.

"No argument," Draven said.

The train steadily grew larger as they descended. Talen took up Draven's spyglass and took in the iron monstrosity. She couldn't see Margaret or Wilfred, but they should be hunkered down and out of sight. Odds were she wouldn't see them until just before she jumped.

Thankfully, she also didn't see any sort of ruckus. No flashes of gunfire and no spells being thrown about. The anxiety clawing at her guts eased up a bit, and she turned her attention to the mail car.

"Move a little to the right," Talen asked.

Draven turned the wheel, and the Cumulus drifted a bit.

The metal-covered train car's door closest to the engine was open, the suited arm and shoulder of a Pinkerton guard just visible as he leaned in the doorway. Turning her attention to the car itself, she studied the roof.

"How long?" she asked, returning the spyglass to its holder, and then checking the loads in her spell irons.

"Couple minutes," Draven said, all humor gone from her expression. "The fireman on that engine knows their job, so I'll be able to get you close without worry of the soot fouling my engines. Even so, it's going to be a leap."

Talen nodded and holstered her irons, making sure to secure them tight with leather straps. "Should be fun."

Draven chuckled. "We have very different definitions of that word. Just make sure you're not having so much fun that you tumble off."

"That would be a mite embarrassing, wouldn't it?" Talen said, smiling as she left the bridge and headed below.

As she made her way to the front hatch, a couple of thuds sounded from down the stairs—Gaoth shuffling in his stall.

Her heart twinged. "I told you, next time," she shouted to the horse.

As much as she would've loved to board the train on horseback, the others had talked her out of it. A quick getaway was easier and surer by air. Add to that, it'd be terrible dangerous for Gaoth. Even if you ignored the bullets and spells, train tracks weren't the best terrain for a horse, especially at full gallop. Even an elf-raised horse could trip on a stray tie or spike. She'd tried explaining all this to the horse, but he'd been as stubborn as ever. In the end, it had taken half a dozen apples to soothe his wounded pride.

A faint snort sounded.

"You're not getting any more damn apples," she said, as she slipped the goggles on and braced herself. Once she felt secure, she pulled the lever to open the hatch.

The wide brass and wood doors at the front of the ship slid wide and a hard blast of air, reeking of coal fire and grease, hit her in the face. She lifted the kerchief over her mouth and nose and went to fetch the crane.

Like she'd done with the rest of the Cumulus, Draven had excitedly tried explaining how the thing worked. Talen hadn't followed, and honestly didn't much care neither, but she'd let the dwarf go on a bit. Eventually though, she'd had to ask Draven to skip the intricacies and just explain how to operate the damned thing.

The crane rolled easily along tracks set into the floor, right up to the hatchway. Just as she'd been told a dozen times or more, Talen inserted the six metal pins that would keep the crane from tumbling out of the ship. Lastly, she took a coiled cord from a hook on one wall, connected one end to the crane, and the other to a receptacle on another wall.

"Should be hooked up," Talen shouted through the speaking tube.

"It is," Draven answered. "I'm seeing the power draw. Once you signal, I'll give you a five count before I reel Margaret up."

"Got it."

"You got about thirty seconds," Draven said. "Good luck."

Talen returned to the hatch, steadied herself against the opening, and eyed the approaching train. She smiled when she saw Margaret and Wilfred, both waving from the rear of the mail car. Talen wondered briefly what it must look like from their angle. Did she appear to be standing on blue sky? Or was there a big doorway floating there?

Putting the thought aside, she focused on the task at hand. A quick scan of the rest of the train didn't show anyone moving about. If the engineer or crew noticed anything peculiar, they weren't doing nothing about it.

She checked the buckles on the harness Draven and Wilfred had made, finding them good and tight. Satisfied, she grabbed the crane's hook with one hand, released the spool lock with the other, and then pulled some line free.

Forty feet to go.

Still watching the train, she reached back and looped the hook into the ring on her harness. A gentle push of magic activated the charm, and the two pieces became as one.

Thirty feet.

She tugged the hood up over her head—both to contain and hide her green hair—and buttoned it tight. Drawing long, slow breaths, she forced calm. Her gaze followed the gentle sway of the train, and her body shifted to match the rhythm.

Twenty feet.

She jumped and landed as light as she could, rolling once, and came up on her knees, left hand gripping the edge of the cupola. Reaching back, she deactivated the hook's charm, drew it free, and magically attached it to the train's metal roof.

The rushing air and engine noise drowned out nearly every other sound, but she decided it best to assume someone had noticed her arrival. She focused on the markings covering her body, channeled magic into them, wrapped herself in shadow, and crept to the edge of the roof near where she'd seen the open door.

It was unlikely anyone on the train would have a charm that could penetrate her shadow cloak, but best not to risk it. Closing her eyes, she laid flat on the roof and pressed one ear to the warm metal. It took some effort to focus past the ambient noise, and even then, she couldn't make out what they were saying, only feel and hear their hard-soled shoes on the steel floor. It didn't seem like they were hurrying about with any kind of panic or concern.

Hopefully, they'd assumed the thump was from a piece of unburned tender thrown out of the stack. And why wouldn't they? It weren't as if anyone had ever been fool enough to try to rob a train before.

Spotting the doors was easy, as the car had curved ridges over each, she presumed to route rain. That did not, however, tell her if the doors were open. Peeking over the lip of the roof, she confirmed one still was, but whoever had been standing in it a minute ago had gone.

She crawled along the roof until she lay between the edge and the rain trough. With her left hand, she got a firm grip on the ridge. With her right hand, she undid the leather strap securing her right-hand iron and drew it. Still wrapped in shadow, she made a small prayer to her mother and then swung herself over the edge and into the car.

As it happened, the guard that had been standing in the doorway only went a step or two inside. As such, he was perfectly positioned to get an invisible boot to the face.

He toppled against the far wall, kindly making room for Talen. She followed him along and slammed his head against a riveted iron seam twice more.

Before the now unconscious man could fall to the floor, she slipped her left arm around his neck and spun, putting his limp form between her and the remaining guards.

They gaped in utter bemusement.

Talen kept low, dropped her cloak, and took aim with her right-hand iron.

"What the—" one said, fumbling to draw his shooter.

Talen poured magic into her iron, lighting the runes and sigils with blue spellfire, and pulled the trigger.

A blast of kinetic force hit the man just above the heart, sending him spinning back into the two cowering postal workers.

Despite the tight quarters, his compatriot managed to duck to one side and draw down.

Talen hefted her human shield and surged forward.

The Pinkerton hesitated.

Talen didn't.

She rolled her iron's cylinder to a fresh load, poured magic into it, and fired.

The point-blank force blast hit the guard just below his sternum. The shot damn near folded him in half, and he almost kicked himself in the face. An instant later, he slammed against the iron wall, which did a fine job unfolding him with only slightly less violence.

She rolled the cylinder and turned her spell iron on the two mail workers, both of whom were huddled in a corner, faces buried in their hands.

"Please, don't kill us!" one of them said, still not looking up.

"I got a wife and kids!" the other said.

Talen shoved her shield to one side, making sure to slam his head against a polished railing from which a dozen or so mail bags hung.

His skull bounced off it, and he fell to the floor in a heap.

"You heeled?" Talen asked, pitching her voice lower and giving herself a more western lilt.

"No, sir!" one worker said. "Ain't neither of us got any sort of shooter—"

"Well, that ain't exactly right," the other said, sheepishly.

"Oh, you shouldn't have lied to me," Talen said to the first.

"No!" he shouted and started to weep. "I didn't. I swear!"

"He didn't," the second said. "We got nothing on us, but there's a couple Colts in a locked box at the other end of the car." He pointed with a shaking hand. "You can check."

"We don't carry when there's Pinkerton's riding with us," the first said.

Both were sniffling now, and neither of them had looked up even once.

"Fine," Talen said, and holstered her right-hand iron.

"Thank you, sir!" they both said.

"We won't give you no trouble," the first said.

"No sir," the other said. "We ain't even seen you, so we can't tell no one nothing."

"I believe you," Talen said. She drew her left-hand iron, lit the sigils, and fired.

A pulsing golden orb shot from the barrel, hit the floor between the men, and exploded into a shimmering cloud that quickly settled over both men. An instant later, they slumped forward, going limp and quiet.

Talen rolled the cylinder to a new chamber, holstered the iron, then bent low to check the mail workers. Both were breathing slow and deep. The one on the left started to snore.

"Sweet dreams," she said and straightened back up.

One by one, she heaved the Pinkertons unceremoniously out the open door. Once the trash had been cleared away, she went to the rear of the car and pounded on the back wall four times. After pausing for half a heartbeat, she pounded three times more.

Six knocks came in reply.

While Wilfred and Margaret let themselves in, Talen set to work inspecting the various crates stacked around the car. She didn't bother with the safe, not because they weren't going to take any gold it might have in it. Rather, it'd be warded to hell and back, which meant Wilfred would need to clear the protections first. Truth be told, she didn't much care about the gold at all, but the others had all said it would be useful, and Draven suggested it'd provide a nice cover from their real aim.

Talen didn't know what difference it made if anyone knew they were searching for filled bounty crystals, and none of the explanations had made much sense to her, but she went along with it anyway.

While checking a fourth crate's shipping label—still not what she was looking for—a hissing sound from the back of the train made her glance up over. A roughly door-shaped line appeared on the far wall. A second later, it turned dull red. A couple of hard thuds—and a shower of fine rust flakes—later, and the cutout section fell into the car with a loud thud.

Margaret and Wilfred stepped through the opening and into the mail car.

"Shh," Talen said, putting her finger to her lips, then pointing at the unconscious mail workers. "They're sleeping."

Margaret and Wilfred exchanged a look.

"Did she just make a joke?" Margaret asked.

"I believe she did," Wilfred said. "Attempted one at least."

"That's what, three jokes this week?"

"Four, actually," Wilfred said. "Reckon we should be worried?"

Talen glared at them both. "I'll give you something to fret on."

Margaret and Wilfred chuckled.

"Enough fun," Talen said. "Clock is ticking on that charm. Get the roof open."

"You been through these here?" Wilfred asked, pointing to a couple crates.

Talen nodded and helped him stack a few. She climbed up, checked the height to the ceiling, and then helped Margaret join her. Wilfred put his hands on Margaret's waist, steadying her.

"You good?" Talen asked Margaret.

"I am," she said.

Talen braced herself, putting both hands against the ceiling, and nodded. "Do it."

Margaret took out a wand-like charm made of old and rotting wood. She took a breath, and the symbols carved on it began to glow. In a slow, steady motion, she dragged it in a circle on the ceiling.

Talen moved her hands as needed so that she'd be at the center of the circle. After a moment or two, red rust appeared and rained down as the piece came free. It was heavier than Talen expected, but not overly so. Rather than setting it down, she pushed it onto the roof. Once the opening was clear, she pulled herself up enough to have a look. The bay doors—and nothing else—hung over head. It was damn strange, seeing into the ship but not the ship itself.

She ducked her head back in. "We're good. I'll fetch the hook." She nodded at Wilfred. "See what you can do about the safe."

He nodded back.

"Check the rest of the crates," she said to Margaret.

"Will do."

Talen climbed onto the roof and made for the hook. She deactivated it, crawled back to the hole, and dropped into the mail car, hook in hand.

"I think I found it," Margaret said.

"Show off," Talen said and went to stand beside Margaret who was studying a seemingly plain crate. "How do you know this is it?"

"All the others have manufacturer logos or names," Margaret said, pointing at the various other boxes. "These two are the only ones that don't have any markings at all."

"Huh," Talen said.

"Also, they're the only ones that don't have a return address," Margaret said, tapping the white label on the top.

"And that's unusual?"

"I've never seen one without one," Margaret said. "Seems strange, unless it's a government shipment, and they don't want it to appear as one."

Talen chuckled. "Never would've thought of that. Good work."

Margaret grinned.

"We best open it up and make sure though," Talen said.

"Careful," Wilfred said, from the safe. "If anyone sees someone was in it, wherever it's headed might get warned to expect a visit." He paused and glanced over. "Where is it going anyway?"

"New York," Margaret said. She tried the lid, but it didn't budge. "It's nailed tight. Do you see a hammer or something we can use to pry it open?"

"No need," Talen said and drew a bone-handled knife from her belt.

Making sure not to damage the blade, she used it to lift the top just enough to get her fingers under, and then easily pulled it free.

"Well, ain't that a thing," Talen said.

Inside, scattered through a liberal amount of straw and wood shavings, were dozens of crystals. All of them were inky black, each a testament to a stained who'd been stopped.

And all of them were broken.

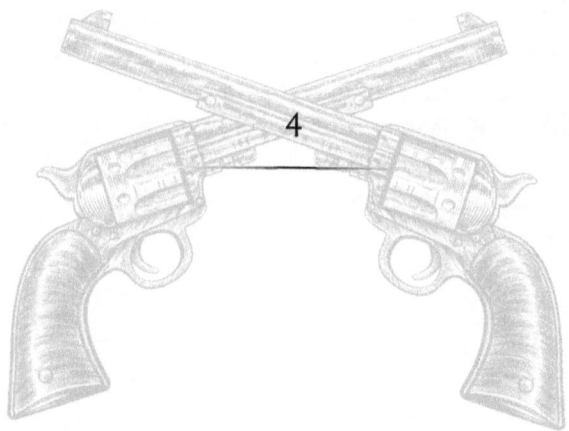

4

Margaret took a step back. "Is it safe? Can the corruption—I don't know—get out and infect us?"

"I wouldn't think," Wilfred said, now standing behind Talen and Margaret. "Shouldn't work like that." He looked to Talen. "You're more sensitive than any of us, you getting anything?"

Talen shook her head. "You have to choose to let dark magic in. It can't just sneak in when you ain't looking." She knew that to be true, but something about this felt off. Bizarrely, the crystals weren't shattered, or even broken into multiple pieces. They were all split in two, damn near down the middle. Even so, her stomach turned a bit sour.

"Do you think maybe these are damaged?" Margaret asked. "Like, they were dropped or something, and they're being sent to be repaired or destroyed?"

"Mind, I don't know much about bounty crystals," Wilfred said, "but I know enough about crystals in general to say those were broken that way on purpose."

"How do you know?" Margaret asked.

"Crystals don't break like that," he said. "Not on accident. The force wants to move through the lattice structure and shatter the whole thing. Getting them to break into two pieces, with no flakes or the like, well that took some doing."

"Why would they go through all the trouble?" Margaret asked.

"I got no idea," he said. "Reckon we can ask whoever they're bound for."

The sour unease in Talen's gut grew and started to wriggle. She didn't think it was the dark magic leaking out. After all, dark magic didn't work that way. At least, it wasn't supposed to. But then, Elizabeth Tuller had done plenty that stained weren't supposed to be able to do either.

Talen had learned to trust her instincts, and they were screaming at her to get the hell away from these crystals.

"Something about this is wrong," she said. After a moment she replaced the lid, carefully lining up the nails to the holes they'd been in before. "It's past time we get gone. You finished with the safe?" she asked Wilfred while she used the handle of her knife to hammer the lid back down.

"Uh, yeah," Wilfred said, exchanging a look with Margaret. "Fancy wards, but whoever made them was sloppy." He held out another charm, a metal circlet with three small wheels set evenly around it. "Just need Margaret to pop the lock."

Margaret accepted the magical lock pick and set it in place. "Shouldn't take but a moment."

"Good," Talen said, putting the crates back where Margaret had found them as the picks whirred and spun. "We need to get the gold and go."

A loud click sounded from the safe.

"Lord have mercy!" Margaret said.

Talen's right hand went to her spell iron, and she spun around. "What is it?"

Margaret stared into the open safe and the two iron-strapped wooden boxes inside. "Are those filled with gold?"

Talen bit back the curse on her tongue and let out a breath.

Wilfred bent down, and with a great deal of effort, removed one of the boxes and set it on the floor. "I can lift one," he said, "and maybe lug it a bit, but not much more. So, I suspect they are."

"How much do you think it is?" Margaret asked.

"Can't say for sure 'til we get them open," he said. "By weight, I'd guess it's got to be north of fifty-thousand."

Margaret's eyes widened. "Dollars?"

"This is a discussion for when our thieving is done," Talen said. She moved to the safe, took hold of the second box and pulled it out. Wilfred was right, it was heavy, but not unwieldy. She set it down on the floor beneath the opening, then stacked the first on top of it.

"It is a good thing I'm secure in my manliness," Wilfred said. "Were I not, such a display might make me feel a mite inferior."

"If you feel the need, you're welcome to heft them onto the roof," Talen said.

"No ma'am," he said, grinning. "As I said, I'm quite secure, thank you."

"Give me a boost?" Margaret said, then looked to Wilfred. "Unless you'd prefer to do it."

"I'm being attacked from all sides," he said.

Margaret laughed.

Talen didn't. She just wanted to get the hell away from those damn broken crystals. Right now. The only thought that competed with the overwhelming wrongness of them was the frustration that she couldn't explain or define the wrongness.

She made a stirrup with her hands for Margaret. "If it's all the same to you, I'd like to go."

Margaret's laughter died, and her smile vanished. She nodded, hefted a booted foot into Talen's hands, and braced herself with one hand on Talen's shoulder. "Ready."

Talen hefted her easily, nearly tossing her through the opening.

Margaret scrambled onto the roof.

"Your turn," Talen said to Wilfred.

"What's going on?" he asked as he put a boot in her hands.

"Since Boston, I'm a mite less confident in how dark magic does and doesn't work," she said. "I got an ill feeling just now, and I'd just as soon be gone and moving toward getting some answers instead of more questions."

Wilfred nodded. "Heard and understood," he said. "Just making sure there weren't something else."

"Other than you're being too feeble to lift a bit of gold, no." Unfortunately, the joke didn't ease her disquiet none. She'd never had Wilfred's skill with that.

"You're the muscle. I'm the brains." He winked. "And the beauty."

Despite herself, Talen smiled and heaved him through the opening and onto the roof. After handing him Margaret's cane, she set to looping the hook and line through the gold box handle on one, underneath, and then back up through the other handle. She lifted the load by the cable and held it for a moment or two, just making sure it wasn't going to slip loose. Satisfied, she turned back to the opening.

Wilfred appeared at the edge and reached down, offering her a hand.

She took it, and he hauled her up.

"Looks like we've been noticed," he said, once she clambered to her feet, pointing ahead of them.

Talen turned and saw two men—engineer and fireman if she recalled correctly—gaping at them from the engine. They pointed and were, seemingly, arguing about what to do.

"Do we need to worry?" Margaret asked.

Talen took hold of the cable tied to the gold crates. "Well, I don't reckon they're going to climb over the tender car to try and get to us, but if they got shooters, they might take a pot shot or two." She grunted and hauled the crates onto the roof, hand over hand.

"You mean as we ride up?" Margaret asked, helping Wilfred slide the boxes away from the opening while Talen set to freeing them from the crane.

"I'll make sure they're otherwise occupied," Talen said, drawing her right-hand spell iron. "But probably best if you two go together with the gold."

"Can the crane hold that much weight?" Margaret asked.

"I'll stay behind," Wilfred said, pulling out his mundane shooter and turning to Talen. "We'll both leave when she sends the hook back down."

"I recall Draven saying she tested it for a thousand pounds," Talen said. "So, unless one of you had a horse or two for lunch, I reckon you'll be fine."

Wilfred opened his mouth to argue.

Talen's last bit of patience snapped. "Damn it," she said, turning to him full on. "With the gold, you won't be able to loop the line around yourselves. That means it'll just be your own grip that keeps you from falling, and I'd feel better knowing you've got four hands holding rather than just two."

Wilfred looked from Talen to Margaret and back a couple of times.

"Add to that, whoever goes second ain't gonna have no one covering them. I'll be the harder target, and harder still on my own." She pinned each of them with a hard stare. "So, please, just do as I ask."

"Come on," Margaret said, stepping onto the boxes.

"Be careful," he said, joining Margaret.

Talen let out a sigh of relief and gave him a single nod.

They stood near as they could to the center of the box. Wilfred took hold of the line with one hand, wrapping the other around Margaret, holding her tight. Margaret did the same.

While they got situated, Talen replaced the spent loads on her iron and rolled the cylinder to the desired spell. "You ready?" she asked.

"No," Margaret said through a forced smile. "But go ahead."

"See you soon," Wilfred said.

Talen poured magic into her iron, lighting the runes with spellfire, aimed high, and pulled the trigger. A sparkling red star shot from the barrel, arcing up and in front of the airship. Before it had reached its apex, Talen rolled to another chamber and leveled the iron at the train's engine.

Five seconds later, the line went taught and jerked upward once before becoming a slow, steady pull. Wilfred and Margaret wobbled but held tight. Another moment later and they were rising, slow and steady. They twisted and turned as they rose but seemed to be holding on okay.

Talen pushed aside her still nibbling anxiety about the crystals and the second guesses about just leaving the gold behind. Instead, she focused on the task at hand and hurried to the front of the mail car just as the crack of a gunshot sounded through the deafening noise of the wind and steam engine.

Talen spotted one of the two men holding a mundane revolver, taking aim at Wilfred and Margaret.

She poured magic into her iron and fired.

A sphere of bright blue energy leapt from the barrel, struck the shooter in his shoulder, and exploded, sending him spinning. Bright sparks and thick white smoke filled the small space behind the engine. As the cabin was mostly open, the starburst wouldn't last long. Which was why she hadn't used another sleep spell. Hopefully though, it would be enough time for Margaret and Wilfred to get clear. Even so, she rolled her iron to another chamber, knelt to steady herself, and took a more careful aim.

As the smoke and sparks started to clear, she fired another starburst. This time the shot must've gone all the way into the cabin because a massive gout of sparks and smoke belched out over the tender car.

The bright white, sparkling cloud caught the wind and came right at Talen.

She turned, ducking low, and covered the back of her neck with her arm. Putting the ensorcelled leather of her coat between the spell and as much of her exposed flesh as possible. The sparks wouldn't hurt her, but a stray finding its way down her back as she was hanging from the hook would be a mite inconvenient.

When the smoke passed, she glanced up and saw the crane had drawn back into the belly of the Cumulus. At least that meant Wilfred and Margaret were out of the line of fire. Now all Talen had to do was wait for them to unhook the boxes and send the line back down.

As if fate had heard her, the crack of another gunshot rang out, this time from the other direction. Something pinged off the roof of the mail car, sending up a flash, just a couple feet from her.

A suited man on the roof of the passenger car worked the lever on his repeating rifle and sighted it on Talen.

"Damn it." Must've been more Pinkertons stationed throughout the train. "At least he ain't got a spell iron."

As soon as the words left her lips, she regretted saying them.

A second man clambered onto the roof of the passenger car, drew a spell iron, and came to join his partner.

One of these days she'd learn to stop tempting fate.

At least he was down wind. No chance she'd be lucky enough to have a spell fly back in the caster's face, but shooting into a strong wind did make hitting what you were aiming a lot harder.

Downwind however, was another story.

Unfortunately, they were standing on a carload of innocent people. If she had time to meet them, she suspected she'd be less concerned about a good portion of them, but there just wasn't the time. That meant she wouldn't risk setting it on fire or throwing a bolt of lightning through it.

Sometimes having a conscience was damn inconvenient.

Talen watched the men close and waited. When the one with the spell iron twitched, she rolled over the cupola, catching herself with her free hand, and coming to a low crouch.

Before she'd gotten her feet under her, another shot ricocheted off the roof, and a blast of invisible force tore a section away.

"*Shanzi fetsuian!*" she said and fired.

A cloud of frozen air and ice crystals erupted from the barrel. An instant later, a thick fog exploded from the subzero blast. She knew the spell wouldn't last long enough to do much damage, and certainly not freeze the men solid.

That was why she'd aimed for where they were standing instead.

The frigid cloud passed as one of the Pinkertons slipped and landed on his ass. The train shimmied, and he slid, scrambling desperately for purchase on the ice-covered train car roof, toward, and then over, the edge.

The other was nowhere to be seen.

He might've fallen off too, but Talen didn't trust her luck enough for that.

She chanced a quick glance back at the engine, but neither of those two men could be seen. Apparently, they'd decided they were going to sit this one out. That was when she spotted the hook slowly descending from the Cumulus. Margaret stood in the doorway, shouting into the speaking tube.

Something moved in her peripheral vision, and she turned just in time to see the second Pinkerton—or rather his head, arm, and spell iron—poking over the edge of the passenger car.

He sneered and lit his iron.

Talen leapt straight up. With her free hand, she reached for the hook, still a few feet away. She caught hold of it, pulled her legs up above her head, and looped them around the line.

A crackling bolt of lightning arced from the Pinkerton's iron and passed through the empty air between Talen and the mail car.

As anyone with half a brain would guess, it preferred the massive, steel-covered train car to the dangling elf.

A blinding fountain of sparks exploded up and a boom of thunder split the air.

Talen's goggles and hood served a purpose neither had been designed for, and she managed to hold on to the hook. Ignoring the loss of senses, she brought her legs down fast, kicking out and twisting them. This motion set her to swinging and spinning, and, hopefully, making her a harder target.

Since a blast of fire didn't swallow her, and she wasn't knocked into next week by a force shot, she figured it must've worked.

The *whump, whump, whump* of a dwarven rail gun sounded distantly through the ringing.

A soft hand closed over Talen's, and an arm slipped around her waist.

"I got you," Wilfred said through the droning buzz, and gently pulled at her.

Talen let out a breath she didn't know she'd been holding and felt herself hauled onto the solid flooring of the Cumulus. An instant later, she felt more than heard, the doors slide shut.

"She's in," Margaret said into the speaking tube.

Wilfred said something, but Talen couldn't make it out.

Someone, maybe Draven, said something back and the ship tilted as, presumably, it began to climb high out of reach of any rifle or spell iron.

Talen lay back on the floor, eyes still closed. She let out a sigh. When the whine in her ear finally subsided, she opened her eyes, but everything was blurry.

"You alright?" Margaret asked.

"Reckon I will be in a bit," Talen said. "Wilfred, you're a smart man, can I ask you something?"

"Go on."

"How hard would a mule need to kick someone in the head to make firing a lightning bolt at a goddamned train car seem like a reasonable notion?"

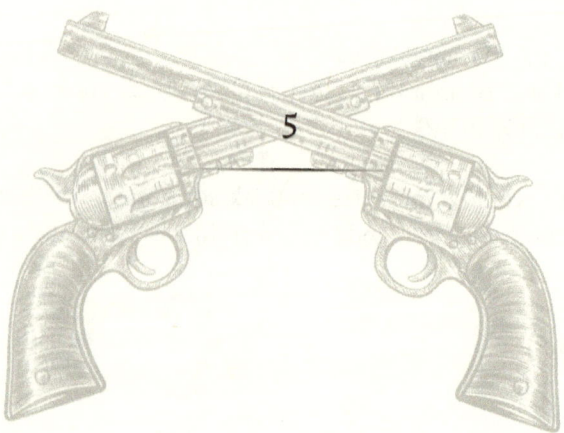

5

It took a little while for Talen's vision and hearing to return to
normal. She passed the time lavishing attention on Gaoth, as was
his due. She mostly switched off feeding him slices of apple and
brushing him down. Much to his chagrin, Talen also gave an apple to
Wilfred's mare, Elise, and Margaret's massive plow horse, Joseph.

"Don't give me that look," Talen said as she fed the last slice to Joseph
and stroked his muzzle. "You've had more than either of them already,
and Joseph is twice your size."

Joseph huffed.

Talen and Gaoth both turned to him.

"And apparently is much smarter than he's let on," she said.

An hour or so later her hearing and vision returned to normal, but the
wriggling disquiet from the train still fouled her insides. It hadn't even
eased a little. Talen tried to put it out her mind and made for the galley.

She always hated leaving the horses in their stables. It wasn't that they
weren't well cared for. Draven's spindles—the mechanical spider-like
creatures that maintained the ship—did a good job keeping the stalls
clean, and Wilfred and Margaret doted on their horses almost as much as
Talen did Gaoth. Neither was it because the stables were small. They were
twice the size of most others Talen had seen, though in fairness, Joseph
would make the biggest space feel cramped. It wasn't even that they didn't
get plenty of time to run about outside, because they did.

She just didn't like seeing the animals inside at all.

Not for the first time, she thought about letting them go, to run wild and free. Gaoth would probably do just fine for himself, but odds were Elise, and especially Joseph, would get caught and no telling how they'd be treated. That of course entirely ignored the selfish aspect of it. Gaoth was her best friend, and despite having made a new family, she wasn't sure she could bear going on without him.

Talen put that thought aside as she stepped into the galley, but finding it empty, returned to the stairs and headed for the bridge. A name she still found odd, though she'd never ask Draven about it until there was an hour or two to spare for the explanation.

She found all three of her friends on the bridge, looking over one of Draven's maps.

"I'm sorry," Margaret said, "but the label didn't have a street address, just the name H. Gable, Niagara, New York."

"You sure there weren't nothing else?" Wilfred asked.

"I'm positive."

"So am I," Talen said. "She showed me the label and that was all it said."

"Well," Draven said, "without more, I can't get you any closer than the town itself."

"I reckon there was twenty or thirty crystals in that crate," Wilfred said.

"Sounds about right," Margaret said.

"That was just from Sioux City," Wilfred said. "We followed the fella from the magistrate's office to the train station." He nodded at Margaret. "Well, you did."

"What are you getting at?" Talen asked.

He shrugged. "I don't claim to know how many places they got to deal with used bounty crystals. But seems to me, we ain't going to be looking for some small operation with just a couple people working it."

Margaret nodded. "Reasonable to assume they'd need a sizeable building."

Draven laughed. "We can get away with circling the town a couple of times, but more than that and people are going to get suspicious."

"Any chance you can work up a charm?" Talen asked.

"I reckon I probably could," Wilfred said. "Mind, I'd need to know what you're expecting it to do."

"I've seen some Red Right Hand men with eyepieces," Talen said. "They could see through my shadow glamour. Could you make one, or something like it, that can see the crystals? Or maybe the corruption inside them?"

Wilfred's brow furrowed, and he turned to one side, considering. "Might be I could, or something near it. Couple of problems though."

"Oh?" Talen asked.

"First," he said, "I'd need some of them crystals, which we ain't got none of. But, even if we got a hold of some, I'd need at least a week just to figure out how I'd go about building it."

"How long for us to get there?" Talen asked Draven.

She tapped the map. "It's about eight-hundred-fifty miles. We stay high enough to ride this tail wind for all it's worth, we could be there in twenty-two hours or there abouts. More realistically, probably twice that."

"That's still a little shy of a week," Margaret said to Wilfred.

He laughed. "It is a bit."

"No chance you can get it done faster?" Talen asked.

"Might be I could shave a day or so off," he said, "once we actually get a crystal, that is."

Talen swallowed her frustration. "I don't reckon we can just sit in town for a week without drawing attention, and I can't go walking around town asking for directions."

"We can," Margaret said, nudging Wilfred. "Both of us. Word is, Harriet Tubman herself bought some land from Seward in New York."

"That is a fact," Wilfred said. "She runs a boarding house, and still helps them who need it to get into Canada. Though she's officially retired. That said, just cause some towns were for abolition don't mean they see us as equals. We still need to be mindful. I do at least."

"I'm sorry," Margaret said. "I didn't mean—"

"Nothing to apologize for, it's just how the world is," he said, then looked to Talen and Draven. "You expecting to use all that gold we got from the train?"

Talen shook her head. "As I ain't got much need or want for gold, I planned on letting you all decide how to use it."

"Half would keep us fed and flying for some years," Draven said, nodding at Wilfred and Margaret, and then smiled. "I suspect the General could do quite a bit with the other half."

"General who?" Margaret asked.

"That was a nickname John Brown gave Mrs. Tubman," Draven said.

"You have any idea where she settled?" Talen asked.

"Auburn," Wilfred said.

"That's about a hundred or so miles east of Niagara," Draven said.

Talen nodded. "Alright then, once we learn what we can, we'll make a donation."

Margaret's eyes went wide. "Wait, are you saying we're going to meet Harriet Tubman herself?"

Wilfred shrugged but couldn't hold back a smile. "We already have."

"Few times," Draven said, a matching grin settling on her face.

"I only met her once," Talen said, the hint of her own smile pulling at one corner of her mouth.

"Are you making fun?" Margaret asked.

"Never," said Wilfred.

"Perish the thought," Draven said.

"I don't have fun," Talen said. "You know that."

All the others laughed.

"Well, I'm going to be at least a little giddy about it," Margaret said. "And I will make no apologies for it."

"Nor should you," Draven said.

"She is a miracle," Wilfred said. "I've seen some truly impressive things in my time, large beyond describing. But not many can compare to meeting her. God alone could've managed fitting so much in so small a woman."

"Tell me about her," Margaret asked, smiling wide and eyes bright.

Talen went to leave the bridge.

"You alright?" Draven asked.

"I'm still feeling a bit off," Talen said. "I'm going to head below and rest."

Everyone looked at her.

"What?" she asked.

"I don't recall as I've ever seen you feel even 'a bit' off," Wilfred said.

"Do you think it was the broken crystals?" Margaret asked.

Talen shrugged and opened her mouth to brush off their concerns.

"Broken?" Draven asked. "What do you mean broken?"

Margaret explained what they found.

"Well, no wonder you ain't feeling right," Draven said.

A sliver of cold fear wound down Talen's spine, adding an icy edge to existing unease. "What are you talking about?"

"Mind, I can't say for sure," Draven said, "as I haven't seen how humans make their crystals. But I was there when the elementals made a new one and transferred the corruption from the one in your belly."

Talen's hand moved absently to the crystal, set there by a greater elemental—a physical manifestation of immense magical power—after she'd been shot with a stain-tainted bullet. Elementals were beings so vast they were almost beyond understanding. Dwarves, through centuries of study, had a better understanding than most. But even their knowledge amounted to drops of water in the ocean.

"We took the opportunity to examine them both," Draven said. "Before we destroyed it, I mean. It ain't just happenstance that the crystals are that size and shape."

"How so?" Margaret asked.

"And why haven't you mentioned this before?" Talen asked, holding back her fear fueled anger.

Draven shrugged. "I figured you all knew more about the crystals than I did. It seemed little more than a bit of curiosity."

"Well, that doesn't appear to be the case," Talen said. "Why is the size and shape so important?"

"Dwarves don't do magic like you and humans do," she said. "But that don't mean we don't understand how it works. It's ain't nothing but a transfer of energy. The crystals are just containment vessels. Stained magic, like any caustic material, needs to be contained correctly."

"Caustic?" Margaret asked. "Are you saying corruption is like an acid or something?"

"It's corrosive, ain't it?" Draven asked. "Eats away at a soul and mind?"

Talen nodded. "Never thought of it that way, but yeah."

"Like a boiler, or a dwarven furnace," Draven said, "you need to design it to specific tolerances."

Talen's mind was beginning to wander. Without anything to focus on, the foul queasiness—and rising fear—were harder to ignore.

"Not that I don't enjoy the minutiae," she said, forcing a calmness to her tone that she didn't feel. "But would you mind coming to the point?"

"She don't actually enjoy the minutiae," Wilfred said.

Talen shot him a look, and his smile faltered.

"Sorry."

"By breaking the crystals, even cleanly," Draven said. "They won't be as effective as containment vessels. It'd be like thinning the walls of a boiler or the reactor below. It might not cause a catastrophic failure, but there'd be an impact. Excess heat from the boiler, a milder sickness than you'd get from direct exposure to earth fire."

"Since you're more sensitive to corruption," Margaret said, "makes sense you'd be the one to feel it."

"Lucky me," Talen said. "Do I need to worry?" Though she was already worrying plenty.

"Can't say for sure," Draven said. "If it works like my examples, you didn't spend a lot of time around it, so I'd think it should pass."

Wilfred and Margaret looked from Draven to Talen and then to each other.

"I ain't gonna drop dead right here in front of you," Talen said. "I'm just feeling ill is all."

"I wasn't thinking that," Margaret said.

"Won't lie, I sort of was," Wilfred said and smiled. Until Margaret elbowed him in the ribs.

"That isn't funny," she said.

"Well, I'm going to adjust my previous plans," Talen said. "I think instead of going below, I'm going to lay out on the deck and see if I can do some healing."

"We can land in a nice green spot, or a lake if you need," Draven asked.

"Nah," Talen said. "Don't need that much energy, I should get what I need from the sun."

Margaret looked as if she wanted to say something but was restraining herself.

"I'll keep my clothes on," Talen said. "Damn humans and your weird notions."

Wilfred raised his hand. "I'm not bound by such narrow thinking."

"Wilfred!" Margaret said.

He sighed but never stopped smiling.

"If I'm not up and about by nightfall, come poke me with a stick," Talen said and left the bridge.

The hard focus of three sets of eyes pressed into her back as she walked across the deck. They were only showing concern, but even after all these months together, Talen still hadn't quite adjusted to having others fret after her. All the same, she had to admit that it wasn't entirely unpleasant.

Once she reached the—what had Draven called it? Bow? Prow? Something like that—the very front of the ship, Talen found a sun-soaked spot, removed her coat—and nothing else, since she'd promised—and laid down. She closed her eyes, drew in slow breaths, and started her healing prayer. Focused on the markings that covered her torso, she whispered the incantation. The magic spread out from her, a request for help. As they were in the air, there wasn't much in terms of energy, but the sun offered more than enough for what she'd need.

Her senses expanded out, but also focused on her own body. A strange miasma clung to her. It wasn't corruption, she'd never forget that sensation, but it was, well, foul and fetid. Like the stink of something rather than the thing itself.

Thankfully, the energy gifted to her from the sun seemed to slowly burn it away. However, it did little to remedy the unease weighing on her.

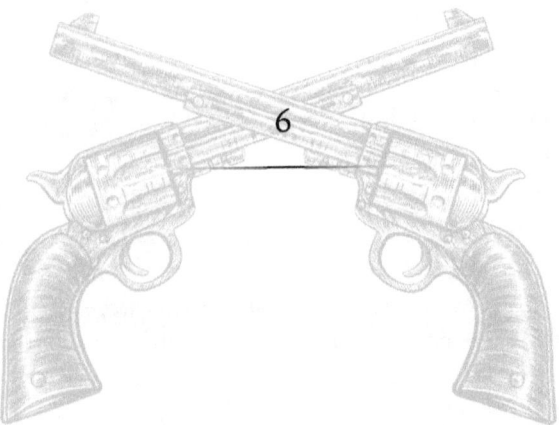

6

Talen finished her healing prayer not long before sunset, feeling clean and refreshed. She still worried a bit about the notion she could be poisoned, so to speak, by the corrupt magic leaking from the crystals and what it would mean if they found more. But the filthy, sick feeling that had been plaguing her was gone. In fact, it was as if she'd spent the last few hours soaking in a hot spring. She slipped on her coat and went to the bridge.

It was empty; Draven's metal hook held the ship's wheel steady.

Must be suppertime, she thought and made her way below.

Draven, Wilfred, and Margaret sat together at a table talking and laughing over bowls of what smelled like Margaret's vegetable soup.

Talen stood in the doorway, not hiding, but not quite not hiding, and watched them for a minute or two. The smile that made its way onto her face still felt a bit strange, though less so than when this unlikely family had formed. She'd come a long way in that time. There were still plenty of wounds that wouldn't scar over for some time, but her soul felt less tattered now. What really did her ragged heart good though, was seeing how well her friends were doing.

Margaret still mourned her husband and the life she'd lost when Tuller had marked her falsely as a stained. Talen had more than once heard her crying alone in her room late at night. But every day Margaret smiled a little more often and more sincerely. Without the weight of having to pretend you're something you ain't, Margaret—and Draven too —were finally free to just be, and, well, happiness looked good on them both.

Even Wilfred, who'd always been quick with a joke and an open ear, seemed more at ease. He'd found a measure of peace before he and Talen had first met—and loved—years ago. But if you're human, and not a white man, making peace usually means compromising, and it's always the person with the darker skin that's expected to give the most. Now, he too was free to just be.

It pained Talen to think back to when they'd first met, and how blind she'd been to that truth. Elves tended more toward the reddish brown of redwood bark, or dry earth, but they damn sure weren't seen as white. As such, she'd known even then how bent humans were on hierarchy, and how often that came down to color of your skin, and what was between your legs.

But Wilfred had always been so sure of himself and incredibly kind. It was almost as if he'd found a way to exist above it all. Of course, he hadn't. It'd just been a necessary façade. One of the many compromises he'd had to make in his life for a small measure of peace. Unfortunately, Talen hadn't figured that out until after they'd parted ways. It was the only lingering regret of their time together. Not that Wilfred had ever, or would ever, begrudge Talen for that. It just wasn't who he was.

And yet, despite the warmth, joy, and a bit of serenity they'd all managed to carve out for themselves, Talen still felt a shadow looming over her. A foreboding that'd haunted her since taking on Elizabeth Tuller. She had no sensible reason to believe it, but she just knew that Tuller hadn't been some aberration, just the first of some new, terrible sort of stained.

"Feeling better?" Margaret asked.

Talen snapped out of her reverie. "Much." She stepped into the galley and went to get herself a bowl of soup.

"Everything okay?" Wilfred asked.

"Sure," Talen said and took a seat between him and Draven. "Why do you ask?"

"You were out there for a good while," he said. "I was starting to worry is all."

"Nah, I just needed a good cleaning," she took a sip of the soup and gave Margaret a side-eye. "Would've been done a mite quicker if I'd stripped down."

"I recall being entirely supportive of that idea," Wilfred said.

"For entirely selfless reasons, of course," Margaret said, narrowing her eyes, but the hint of a smile tugged at the corners of her mouth.

"Not entirely, no," he said, scratched at his head, then shrugged. "But a good three or four percent."

Draven turned to the others, eyebrows drawn together. "What is it with humans and nudity? You seem to be ashamed of your bodies and obsessed with them at the same time."

"It's not shame, at least not with me," Margaret said. "Though after I got sick and my leg stopped growing, plenty of people thought I should be." She leaned back in her chair and let out a sigh. "I just see my body as the most precious thing I have, apart from my soul of course. As such, I only share my body with those I feel deserve such a gift."

"Ain't gonna lie," Wilfred said, "that's a damned sight better reason than any preacher ever gave."

"It is a good reason," Talen said and took another mouthful of soup and swallowed it. "I had no idea you thought so highly of yourself though."

Draven, Margaret, and Wilfred all looked at her for a long moment.

Talen opened her mouth to apologize for her bad joke.

"You'd think eventually, one of her jokes would have to be funny," Draven said.

Wilfred and Margaret started to chuckle.

Talen narrowed her eyes and glared but couldn't keep herself entirely from smiling. "What's the plan for finding this facility?" she asked.

"We ain't come up with much in terms of good ideas," Wilfred said.

"I figure we'll fly over the town a few times," Draven said. "Big as this place ought to be should make it easy to spot from the air."

Talen nodded. "And it'll at least give us a place to start looking."

The others exchanged a look.

"By which I mean you two," Talen said to Wilfred and Margaret. "I'm stubborn but I ain't stupid."

Wilfred opened his mouth.

Talen pointed at him. "You keep quiet, now."

He chuckled. "I didn't say a word."

"Either of you know anything about this town?" Talen asked Wilfred and Draven between spoonfuls of soup.

"I never made it up this far north," Wilfred said. "I was only a conductor a couple of years, mostly got folk to Quaker depots." He nodded at the dwarf. "Or to folk like Draven who handled long distance transport. Otherwise, I just worked different stations and safe houses."

"I've been over Niagara plenty of times," Draven said. "But I only ever set down on the Canadian side. Don't make much sense running folk all the way up north just to have them cross a bridge at the end." She took a sip from a cup. "Falls are a sight to see though. Between the river and the falls, there are three old and powerful elementals there."

"Make sense," Talen said. "An elemental made the crystal in my belly. Only seems logical they'd be involved somehow in making bounty crystals too." She lifted her bowl and swallowed the last of her soup. "Don't reckon they'll be able to help us with directions."

"Not likely, no," Draven said, and smirked. "Though if they'd give them to anyone, it'd be you."

Talen ignored the quip. "Then I guess we fly over and see what stands out." she nodded at Wilfred and Margaret. "You two can check out anything that looks hopeful. If you come up with nothing, maybe ask around a bit, but don't draw too much attention. Just in case."

"And when we do find it?" Margaret asked.

"Wait for nightfall and go for a visit," Talen said. "All of us."

"Seems almost too simple," Margaret said.

"Don't mean there ain't still plenty to go wrong," Wilfred said. "Flies always seem to get in the ointment."

"Especially now that someone said it," Draven said.

The following day was spent sailing over Michigan and into Ontario, Canada. In the late afternoon Draven landed in a quiet and remote wooded area so the horses could get some exercise. While Wilfred and Margaret tended to Elise and Joseph respectively, Talen saddled Gaoth, who was near vibrating with excitement. She'd barely got settled when he took off, running down various trails. Talen enjoyed standing on the deck of the Cumulus and feeling the wind on her face and in her hair, but it was a poor substitute to the way it felt on Gaoth's back. The horse's powerful muscles churned underneath her, a silent language between them, telling her which way to lean or shift her weight.

As he tore down trails that would've tripped up any other horse, deftly avoiding roots and rocks, Talen smiled and whooped like a child dancing in the rain. She ducked some branches, let others slap against her leather coat. Sometimes she'd snatch leaves and eat them on the go, enjoying the different tastes of even the familiar breeds of trees.

After an hour or so, she reluctantly urged him back toward the waiting airship. As expected, his pace and gait weren't nearly as exuberant as it had been on the way out.

"I know," Talen said, patting his neck. "I wish we could run all the way back to California, but we got important work to do."

Gaoth sighed and bobbed his head.

"I couldn't do this without you, my friend," she said, bending forward and kissing his crest. "I know it ain't easy for you, spending so much time on the ship, but I promise it won't last."

Gaoth snorted and swished his tail.

Talen patted him again, proud of him for putting on a brave face.

It pained her to lead him back up the gangway and into his waiting stall. After she'd refreshed the hay, he happily crunched the apple she offered him, and then lowered his head to hers. Talen pressed her forehead against his and stroked his muzzle.

"I love you too," she whispered and after a few more moments, grudgingly headed up to the bridge.

Wilfred was manning the wheel, giving Draven a chance to get a few hours of sleep. It had been a big surprise when the dwarf had agreed to show him how to operate her beloved airship. Though she'd made it clear only Wilfred would ever be allowed to pilot the craft without her there.

"Margaret in her cabin?" Talen asked as she came to stand next to him.

"She couldn't use her cane much while walking Joseph, and I think her leg was starting to bother her."

"I'll mix her up a tea that might help," Talen said.

He arched an eyebrow. "Might be a leg rub could ease her aching as well."

Talen gave him a level look. She adored Wilfred, but even he could fray her patience.

His grin faltered but didn't vanish. "I wasn't implying nothing untoward. I do recall you got a gift for working out aches and pains."

"I also got a gift for causing them," she said.

He nodded. "That is a fact."

She let out a sigh. "When she and I met, I admit there was some attraction on my part. Supposing she ever gave even a hint that she were so inclined—"

His grin returned to full force.

"Which she has not," Talen said, without a trace of humor or teasing in her voice. "She's still mourning George, and I reckon will for some time. We talked about all this before, and I hope we won't need to again."

Wilfred's smile melted away. "I don't mean to harp on it. I admit that I might enjoy teasing you about it a bit, but mostly I just think you'd be good for each other."

Talen shrugged. "Maybe one day. Maybe not. Won't change how I see her either way. Besides, I reckon we're plenty good for each other as is."

"I can't argue with that," he said.

They shared a long, comfortable silence, watching the eastern sky darken.

"What about you and Draven?" Talen asked.

Wilfred's brows drew together. "I'm sorry?"

"You know she's sweet on you, right?"

"She's what now?"

Talen looked at him for a moment, waiting for a wink or grin, but neither came. She laughed. "You really don't see it, do you?"

"I, uh, um." His mouth opened and closed several times, but only sputtering sounds came out.

"Are you speechless?" Talen asked. "I don't recall as I've ever seen you at a lack for words."

"Are you being serious?" he asked.

Talen's grin shifted to a warm smile, and she put a hand on his broad shoulder. "You're the only one she lets fly this thing."

"She let Margaret take the wheel more than a few times."

"While practically standing on her shoulder," Talen said. "And never more than a few minutes."

His brow furrowed. "I suppose I hadn't thought about it before."

"We both know you ain't got any hang ups about being with someone who ain't human," Talen said. "I asked you that more than once when we shared a bed."

"I don't deny that," Wilfred said, eyes on the horizon.

Talen leaned against the back wall. "And from what you told me about others that shared your bed, it ain't the moustache that's the problem, so I reckon it must be the height difference?"

He scratched at his head and shrugged. "I suppose that would be a concern. I am twice her size."

"Uh huh. But?"

"But, well, I just never seen her that way."

Talen stepped over and kissed his cheek. "And I suspect Margaret ain't never seen me that way neither."

Wilfred's expression turned sheepish. "I believe I get the point you're trying to make. I apologize and shan't speak of it again."

"Thank you," Talen said. "I'm going to make Margaret her tea. You want me to bring you some coffee?"

He smiled. "I'd be much obliged."

She patted his back and left him to the twilight sky.

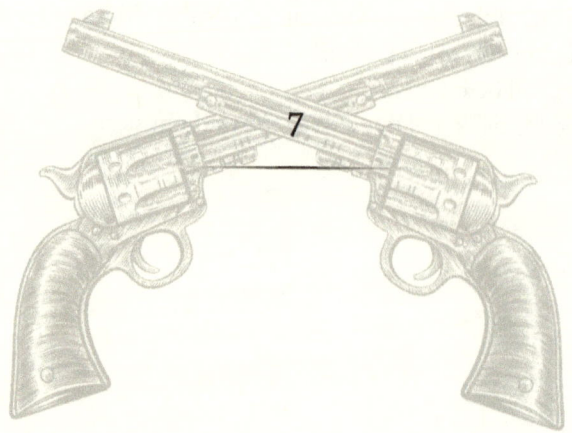

7

T hank you," Margaret said, accepting the cup of steaming tea. When she caught a whiff of it, her expression soured. "I think."

Talen chuckled. "It works a mite better than it smells."

"One would hope," Margaret said and took a sip. "Oh, Lord have mercy!"

"Don't sip," Talen said. "Drink it all fast, including the dregs."

"Now you tell me," Margaret said. "Do I want to know what's in it?"

"Nothing terrible. Some pepper seeds, lavender, some roots I don't know the human name for. It'll ease the pain and help you sleep."

Margaret pinched her nose and tipped the cup back, downing the entire thing in a couple of swallows.

Talen accepted the empty mug. "Well done."

"At least the taste doesn't linger," Margaret said.

"Shouldn't take long before you feel the effects, so best to settle in."

Margaret did, sparing a kiss to the photo of George sitting on the bedside table, before smiling at Talen. "Thank you."

"Sleep well."

Talen blew out the lamp and left the cabin, closing the door behind her, and then made her way back to the galley. It was a quick thing to brew some coffee. Draven had rigged up some way to have near boiling water on demand. She'd explained how, but Talen hadn't really paid much attention.

She delivered Wilfred his coffee but didn't linger. Instead, she went out to the frontmost part of the deck. The early spring night had a chill to it, but Talen didn't mind. It reminded her of home. She lay back on the narrow bench Draven had installed—just for Talen no less—and stared up.

The dark blue sky was shifting to black, and there were few clouds to hide the shining stars. After a bit, her eyes drifted closed and she drew in long, slow breaths, savoring the taste of the air. Unfortunately, there wasn't much to be heard over the hum of the airship's engines, but Talen had come to find it oddly calming. The hard, wooden bench wasn't as comfortable as the bed in her cabin, but she'd never much cared for sleeping indoors. It felt confining, and unnatural.

She woke to a bright and clear sky above her and a shimmering lake below. The blue reached from one horizon to the other, with just the barest hint of land. While she'd always felt a connection to the land, she couldn't deny the serene beauty of the sky. There was a clean feeling out here, above it all. She knew it was just an illusion, but that didn't stop her from taking a moment to savor it.

The rest of the day passed in the tedium that had become the routine of life aboard an airship. Despite Draven's mechanical spiders doing a fine job, Talen tended to the horses. This included not just grooming and feeding, but also keeping their shoes and hooves, as well as all the tack, in good repair.

Draven kept the ship on course, regularly checking and adjusting their heading based on winds from whatever direction. Wilfred and Margaret were the only ones with any cooking skill, so they saw to the meals, though Talen usually tidied up after.

Otherwise, the general cleaning duties, including the brass and wood of the ship were shared.

Talen had little aptitude for mechanics and as such was banned from helping on most repairs or upkeep of engines, furnace, or really anything with moving parts. At least until something heavy needed lifting or moving.

The familiar chores were almost meditative. The comfort of the routine nearly let Talen forget about the darkness that wanted to swallow the world, and that so many were eager to help it along.

Nearly.

They reached the Town of Niagara in early afternoon. Wilfred, Margaret, and Talen stood at the rails as Draven made several circles of the town proper. The falls were utterly majestic, she had to admit. Though not as tall as some she'd seen, it was an order of magnitude larger in the volume of water that moved over them. Her wonder was short lived though. On either side of the broad river and breathtaking falls, the land had been cleared of trees and just about everything else. In place of the living, verdant natural beauty were wide roads, homes, and factories. The countless—and ubiquitous—chimneys and stacks spewed foul black smoke into the clear sky.

She looked to her friends, both of whom stared with wide-eyed wonder, and very deliberately kept her mouth shut. At times, she almost envied their ability to become so fixated on a single beautiful leaf that they never saw the rotting, dying tree.

While they marveled, Talen turned her attention to the town itself. Unfortunately, she had no idea what a facility for processing bounty crystals would look like, or how it would look any different than the other brick and wood boxes. Some of the structures were larger than others, but that didn't mean much to her. The fetid, foul, grimy stench that haunted every human city wasn't helping.

"See anything?" Wilfred asked.

Talen shook her head. "Though unless it had a sign that read 'bounty crystals' I don't imagine I'd know if I did."

"I see a few buildings worth getting a closer look at," Margaret said.

"Oh?" Wilfred asked.

"Those right there," Margaret said, pointing to half a dozen large buildings with several tall stacks each, all of them belching filth.

"What about those?" Wilfred said, gesturing to a couple closer to the river.

Margaret shrugged. "Might be, but they're a fair distance from the railroad depot." She motioned to it. "If they get and send out crystals via rail, it seems reasonable to take the spots closer to it."

"Make sense," Wilfred said. "Sounds like we got a place to start looking." He turned to the bridge and waved him arms, signaling Draven to set down.

The airship turned and started to descend toward the river, north and downstream of the falls. The steep cliffs on either side of the wide river looked precarious, but Draven swore there were trails up to town, on both sides of the border. She'd also said there'd be fewer prying eyes to notice an elf well past the treaty line.

Talen tried to spot the aforementioned trails, but the lower they went, the worse she felt. It was as if the stench of the city, and the foulness it undoubtedly poured into the river, was reaching a clawed hand down her throat, and lashing at her guts. Before now, she hadn't thought anything could've been worse than her time in Chicago.

"You alright?" Wilfred asked.

"I'm fine," Talen lied, gripping the railing tight.

The Cumulus touched down on the river and moved toward the shore before dropping anchor.

Talen's stomach knotted, and she doubled over. It took all her willpower not to retch.

"You are clearly not fine," Margaret said, stepping closer. "You look like you did when you saw those broken crystals, only worse."

It took Margaret's words for Talen to recognize the core of this all-consuming revulsion.

"It's corruption," she said between slow breaths.

"What?" Wilfred and Margaret asked, nearly as one.

Talen closed her eyes. "It's like the whole damned city is stained." She shook her head. "No, it's like everything around me is stained. The people, the city, the river, even the dirt, all of it."

"I think maybe I feel it too," Margaret said. "I would've probably just ignored it if you didn't say anything."

Wilfred narrowed his eyes. "I reckon I'm getting it too. Not a stench like a stained was about, but a guts-deep feeling that something ain't right."

Talen nodded.

"We need to get you away from this place," Margaret said.

"I'll tell Draven," Wilfred said.

Talen reached out, eyes still closed, and got hold of his shirt. "No. There's something terrible happening here, and we have to stop it."

"You look like you're about to lose every meal you ever had," Wilfred said, putting his hand over hers. "You ain't in no shape to do nothing. We got to get you out of here."

"He's right," Margaret said. "We'll find another place to set down and then Wilfred and I will come back. If it's too far to walk, we'll take the horses."

"No." Talen said, struggling to wrestle back the wrongness trying to swallow her whole.

Common sense told her to get away, as far and fast as she could, but the shadow warden in her wanted to find the corruption and burn it out.

On instinct, she started a healing prayer, but stopped. No telling what she might find if she reached out. But then she had to do something. Tightening her focus, Talen reached out for the only thing she knew wouldn't be touched by the corruptive influence, the sun.

At least she hoped.

There was a thumping of Draven's heavy boots as she hurried across the deck. "What the hells is wrong with her?"

"Corruption," Margaret said. "I know she's more sensitive than us, but I don't know why it's affecting her so strongly."

Because it's everywhere.

"You feel anything?" Wilfred asked.

"Dwarves don't sense corruption," Draven said. "We're not sensitive to..."

"What?" Wilfred asked.

"I hadn't really noticed before, but I am feeling anxious," Draven said. "And ain't no reason to be."

"What is going on here?" Margaret asked.

"I don't rightly know," Wilfred said. "But I don't like it none."

Thankfully, Talen found the sun burning bright and pure as ever.

She started pulling her clothes off.

"Wh—What are you doing?" Margaret asked.

"I don't reckon it's the time to worry about what's proper," Wilfred said.

Talen squeezed her eyes tight, blocking out everything but the pure magic of the sun. Someone helped her out of her coat. Someone else, or maybe the same person, took her holsters as soon as she'd unbuckled them. The rest went quick enough, and in a few moments, she'd stripped down and lowered herself to the deck.

The sun wasn't as high as it could be, nor as bright as in summer, but it didn't matter, and she couldn't think of anything else to do.

Time slid away, and existence shrank until it was just her, the corruption doing its best to sink into her very soul, and the burning purity of the sun running along her markings.

Inch by inch, the foul magic's taint shrank back from the light.

Panic and fear gave way to anger and a righteous indignation.

This foulness will not stand!

The fire gathered in her belly, slowly building until it blazed like a small star. The fetid miasma around her evaporated, burning away, and revealing the life it had been choking out.

Once confident she could hold the foulness back, Talen opened her eyes.

Margaret, Wilfred, and Draven were all looking down at her, mouths open, but squinting back against a near blinding light.

Talen lifted her head and looked down to find the source of the radiance. The crystal in her belly was shining like the sun itself.

"Holy shit," she said.

"How are you doing that?" Margaret asked.

"No idea," Talen said.

"Reckon you might want to cover up," Wilfred said, offering her a hand up. "Before someone comes to see what's happening."

"Or an airship mistakes you for a light house," Draven said.

Talen accepted Wilfred's hand, and he hauled her to her feet. She got dressed as quick as she could. Despite the relief at no longer feeling the corruption, it was a damned odd thing having a warm light shining from her belly. The light danced over the deck as she slipped on her trousers, as if there was a lantern set in her middle. Which, she supposed, was the case.

The heavy cotton of her shirt only diminished the illumination enough that her friends could open their eyes fully.

Thankfully, her leather coat did the trick. Mostly. When she moved, stray light would shine down on her legs and feet, so she pulled the coat tighter. Once she cinched it with her belt, the light show vanished entirely.

Her friends all looked at her in bewilderment.

"Seems that crystal does more than contain corruption," she said.

"You reckon?" Wilfred said.

"What did you do?" Margaret asked.

Talen shook her head. "The same healing prayer I've used a thousand times before, but since everything around me seemed stained, I only reached out to the sun."

"Looks like it obliged," Draven said. "And then some."

"Well, you do look better." Wilfred chuckled softly. "But I reckon it'll make stepping into shadows a mite challenging."

"Do you think bounty crystals could store pure magic as well?" Margaret asked. "Or is it just those made by an elemental?"

Draven shrugged. "Or that one specifically."

Talen arched an eyebrow. "I suspect them questions are, uh," she glanced at Margaret, "rhetorical? That right?"

"It is, yes. Do you have an idea how long the crystal's power will last?"

"Not a one. This is all new to me," Talen said. "And while I appreciate the effect, I do hope it ain't permanent."

"Probably best to assume it'll fade in time," Draven said. "Which means we ought to get a move on and find out what's going on here."

"Agreed." Talen let out a breath, still adjusting the crystal's effect. It reminded her of wearing gloves, not exactly a numbness but certainly distancing. "It seemed to get worse the closer we got to the river, so I'm guessing the place we're looking for will be on the river."

"And upstream," Draven said.

Talen nodded.

"I didn't see anything on the river." Margaret turned to Wilfred. "Did you?"

"I did not."

"I suppose we can move upstream and see where the sensation fades," Margaret said.

"My thinking exactly," Draven said.

Talen barely managed to keep from flinching. "Except I ain't about to purge this crystal. Assuming I even can."

"We might not be as sensitive," Wilfred said, "but we can feel it. I reckon it won't be as precise, but it'll be a damned site safer for you."

"That's the plan then," Draven said. "I'll keep us low and close to the river 'til we near the falls. Assuming we don't find the source of all this, we'll try farther upstream."

"Maybe you ought to head below," Wilfred said to Talen.

"What? Absolutely not." The fear and panic that erupted inside her had no logical basis, but that didn't stop it from coming. She trusted her friends, but the notion of not being involved, being incapable of helping in fact, sent shivers of helpless terror through her; a feeling she did not enjoy.

"Maybe he's right," Margaret said. "Down here, there isn't really anyone to notice you, but south of the falls is level with the town."

"And there ain't no mistaking your green hair," Wilfred said.

Talen wanted to object, but she knew they were right. The plan had always been to wait for nightfall for just that reason. Even so, it didn't stop the unsettling send of powerlessness. Reluctantly, she nodded. "Yeah, alright."

"No need to go below," Draven said. "You can join me in the bridge. Unless someone's got a spyglass, they ain't seeing you in there."

Talen followed and watched Wilfred and Margaret through the glass as Draven worked the controls. The Cumulus lifted a dozen feet or so from the water then turned south and proceeded at a leisurely pace.

"Any theories?" Draven asked, eyes focused on their path.

Talen shrugged. "Not one that makes much sense. You know more about elementals than me, and everything I thought I knew about dark magic and corruption says this sort of thing ain't possible. But Elizabeth Tuller showed me that humans got a talent for doing the impossible."

Draven grunted her agreement.

Talen glanced over. "What about you?"

"I'm thinking about how when you had just a sliver of corruption an old one set a crystal in your belly to trap it."

"Well, I did have to ask for help," Talen said. "Indirectly anyway. But I doubt an old one would've noticed so small an amount of corruption on its own. It'd be like Wilfred noticing a flea egg on his arm."

"Reckon you're right," Draven said. "But this place is so stained that it damn near put you down, and there are three elementals here." She shrugged. "They ain't old ones, but they're still mighty powerful entities. Don't it seem that between the three of them, they'd be able to contain corrupt magic the same way?"

Talen narrowed her eyes. "Then why ain't the river filled with crystals?"

"That is the question."

"You sure the elementals are still alive?" Talen stepped up next to Draven. "Or active, or whatever word suits."

"They're still here," Draven said, eyes narrowing. "I can feel them. So why aren't they doing nothing about this corruption?"

Talen shrugged again. "I got no idea. Hell, I can't even figure out how any elemental made crystals could be of any use to humans."

Draven's eyebrows drew together. "What do you mean?"

"Well, they'd be filled with corruption, right? That's why they form, ain't it? To capture corruption, and you can't use a crystal that's already filled."

"There was room enough in yours for Tuller's stained soul."

"You ain't wrong, but wouldn't any made here be full up from all the corruption?"

Now Draven shrugged. "Could be they figured a way to collect and clear them out. Might be that's what's fouling the river."

"You said the elemental transferred what was in mine. They didn't clean it. You reckon humans figured out how to do what an elemental couldn't?"

"Humans are full of surprises."

Talen threw up her arms. "That is a fact. All the years I was collecting bounties, I didn't never hear of cleansing a crystal. But then I hadn't never heard of no one using crystals to power a damned leviathan neither." She deliberately didn't let herself think about the human-made version of the dwarven war machines that had slaughtered her people and the Oceti Sakowin. As a further distraction, she thumped her head against the wall, hoping it might knock some questions into answers. "And even if you're right, we're back to the question of, with so much corruption, why ain't the river full of crystals they ain't got to yet? Also, what the hell are the broken crystals for?"

"Sure hope we start finding some answers cause these questions are piling up," Draven said as they neared the roiling mists. She pulled a lever, and the Cumulus began a slow climb, rising above the upper level of the falls.

Wilfred and Margaret came into the bridge.

"Well?" Talen asked.

"The feeling never faded," Wilfred said. "In fact, could be I'm mistaken, but I think it got worse."

Margaret nodded. "That's how it felt to me too."

Talen absently touched the crystal in her stomach, grateful for the protection from the corruption's influence, and recounted the conversation she and Draven just had.

"Maybe it's too much corruption for the elementals to deal with," Margaret said. "They're containing what they can, but the excess is running down the river."

"That's as sound a theory as any," Draven said.

"Which means," Talen said, "that whatever is happening, it has to be close to the elementals."

Draven nodded.

"Why do you say that?" Wilfred asked.

"Because if the source was happening upstream," Draven said, "and the overflow reached the falls, they'd be covered in crystals. Probably enough to disrupt the flow of the water."

"But we circled the falls and didn't see nothing," Wilfred said.

Margaret narrowed her eyes. "How big are elementals?"

Draven furrowed her brow. "What do you mean?"

"Would the elemental of the river stop at the edge? Or would its reach extend past the shoreline?"

"A bit past maybe," Draven said. "Why?"

Margaret drew in a breath, clearly trying to put her thoughts together. "Like Wilfred said, there isn't anything at the falls or at the river's edge. The nearest building was at least a hundred feet away."

Talen's mind churned "So, if we assume the place we're looking for is also the source of the corruption, it's got to be hidden."

Draven chuckled. "My only concern with that notion is that it makes sense."

Talen arched an eyebrow.

"Ain't nothing else about this that makes a lick of sense, so I'm a bit wary of that which does."

Everyone nodded.

"Some rivers run underground," Wilfred said. "Could it be someone set up operation out of sight that way? Or maybe even dug tunnels to bring the river closer to town?"

"Yeah, that might work," Draven said.

Talen leaned against the wall and sighed. "Meaning this place could be anywhere in the city and we're right back where we started."

"Maybe not," Margaret said.

Talen looked up and saw her staring intently out the window. "What do you see?"

Margaret nodded at the relatively small island separating the two falls. "Which elemental would have influence there?"

Draven narrowed her eyes and seemed to consider it for a moment. "Can't say for certain, but I'd expect a fair share of overlap. Could be all three."

"If you needed elementals to make crystals," Margaret said, "and wanted to get the most output possible, wouldn't a spot where three of them had influence be the best spot?"

Draven turned from Margaret to the island and back. "It would, yeah, but I don't see nothing except trees and a wooden walkway to the mainland."

"Me either," Wilfred said.

"Not there," Margaret said and pointed to the mists. "There."

"I don't see nothing but spray," Wilfred said.

Talen took a step closer to the window. Almost entirely concealed by the mist was a spire of some sort. "What the hells is that?"

Draven turned the ship's wheel and moved the Cumulus closer to the mid-point between the falls. Barely visible through the vapor was a tall wooden spire, reaching from the base of the cliff to the top.

"Is that a tower?" Draven asked.

"No," said Margaret, smiling. "It's a staircase."

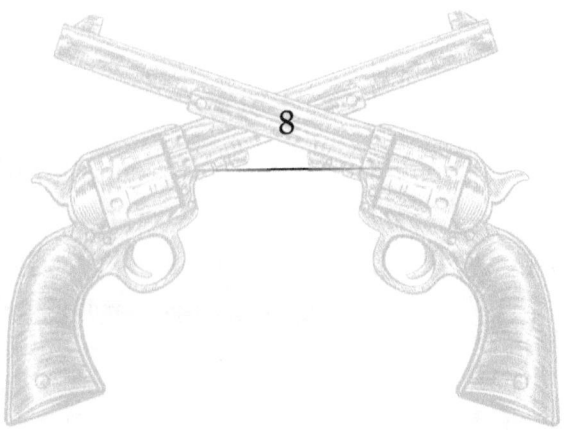

8

From above, the island looked to be maybe half a mile long and a quarter mile across. A sliver of land that split the river, with falls on either side. Trees covered most of the small island with footpaths crisscrossing it, and a narrow bridge connected it to the mainland. After a few minutes, Draven found a spot clear enough to set the Cumulus down. It didn't actually come to rest on dry ground, rather she lowered the craft until it floated a foot or so off the rough earth. The gangplank took care of the rest. Thankfully, the immediate also seemed clear of people.

The unease and anxiety that accompanied the sense of helplessness returned, but Talen beat it back with vigor. Unfortunately, her efforts only quieted the apprehension, rather than silencing it entirely.

"Keep your eyes open and your wits sharp," she said to Margaret and Wilfred. "Stick close to each other."

Wilfred grinned and holstered his revolver. "Yes, mother hen."

Talen gave him a level look and then turned to Margaret, passing her the shortened and Draven-modified repeater. "If you run into trouble—"

"Fire twice into the air." Margaret slid the repeater into its leg holster and pulled on a long coat to hide the weapon. Once composed, she gave Talen a soft smile and put a hand on her shoulder. "We'll be careful. I promise."

Talen glared at Wilfred and motioned toward Margaret. "She's in charge."

He arched an eyebrow. "You going to threaten to put me over your knee if'n I don't mind her?"

"That'd just get you riled up," Talen said, hiding even a trace of humor.

Wilfred's eyes went wide.

Margaret's cheeks flushed.

Draven laughed.

Wilfred cleared his throat. "Well now," he said to Margaret. "I do believe that's our cue to depart."

"Agreed," Margaret said, taking up her cane.

Draven's mirth settled into a quiet chuckle.

Talen watched Wilfred and Margaret go, right hand reflexively resting on her spell iron.

Before long, the trees hid them from sight.

"They grow up so fast," Draven said from behind Talen.

"I swear by my mother, I will toss you over the falls."

"Drink?"

"Please."

Time dragged by slower than a lame snail traversing a river of molasses.

Talen and Draven sat in the darkest part of the cargo bay, staring at the trees beyond the bay doors, passing a bottle of belly burner between them. The only sound was the roar of the falls and creaking of the Cumulus's anchor lines as the wind nudged it back and forth. The smell of the spray, the trees, and damp earth almost made up for the stench of the nearby city. Even so, something about it felt not quite right.

Desperate for a distraction, Talen's mind latched onto an incident from months ago. As part of a large and complex ploy, stones had been created for use in charms. They would, after some time, make the person using the charm appear stained, even though they weren't. Draven had presented that evidence to the Granite Lord, the leader of the beardless dwarves.

"Been meaning to ask," Talen said. "You heard anything from the Granite Lord?"

Draven shook her head. "Not a peep."

"He sounded sure those stained crafting stones would make a difference in things between the dwarven kingdoms," Talen said and took a sip from the bottle.

"The number of beardless did go up quite a bit once word got out," Draven said. "But the Granite Lord said diplomacy takes time, and we ain't a quick-acting people under the best of times."

Talen almost said 'unless it involves murdering elves for gold,' but she didn't. Her friend and the other beardless had reacted just as quickly in disapproval, and Draven especially didn't deserve a comment like that.

"I reckon," was all Talen said instead.

"Could be no one wants to make another rash action, considering what happened last time," Draven said, as if reading her mind.

Talen looked at her friend, but didn't meet her eyes, as she passed the dwarf the bottle.

"I know you wouldn't say it," Draven said, accepting the whisky. "So I figured I'd say it for you."

Talen opened her mouth.

"And don't you apologize," Draven said and took a drink. "You and yours didn't do a damned thing wrong."

After that, they sat in silence. Wasn't much else to say. A week or two passed—or could've been just a half hour—and Talen decided to check the crystal in her stomach. It still burned bright as the sun.

"Might be a good time to see if you can still wrap yourself in shadows," Draven said. "Be good to know now rather than when you need it."

"Reckon you're right." Talen stood, passed Draven the bottle of whisky, and focused on the markings on her face, neck, and arms. Almost before she'd finished the incantation, the shadow cloak wrapped around her.

"Looks like it works just fine," Draven said and took a sip from the bottle.

Talen stood there, dumbfounded for a moment. The shadow cloak hadn't felt this strong in years. Moreover, while it normally wasn't overly taxing to maintain, just requiring a bit of concentration, now it damn near seemed to stay up on its own. She reached down and touched her belly, feeling the crystal through her coat. Still holding the shadow cloak, she undid her coat and opened it. When she lifted her shirt, she found the elemental's gift still shining, but the light had turned blue.

"You see this?" Talen asked.

"I don't see a damned thing."

Talen turned and looked around the hold. The light from the crystal, though it still burned bright, didn't seem to actually illuminate anything.

"Well, that's a hell of a thing." Talen let the shadow cloak fall.

"What is—ahhh!" Draven covered her eyes as bright white light suddenly flooded the interior of the ship.

Talen tucked in her shirt and closed her coat. "Sorry about that."

"You had it exposed while you was hidden?" Draven asked.

"I did."

"And here I thought that was an impressive trick before."

"Did the light look any dimmer to you?" Talen asked.

"Before or after it blinded me?"

"Uh, either?"

"You reckon maybe it's storing power that you can draw on?" Draven asked.

"Might be. Reckon it could work like that?"

Draven shrugged. "We just assumed it was made to contain stained magic and corruption, since that's what it does best. But I don't see why it'd be limited to that. Mind, I don't know much about magic, but a barrel will hold clean water as easily as foul." She took another swig from the bottle. "Course until we know for sure, I wouldn't rely on it."

"Sound advice," Talen said.

After a long silent moment, Draven offered up the bottle. Talen sat once more, accepted the whisky, and they resumed their waiting.

Half the bottle later, Wilfred and Margaret returned. Talen almost sprinted off the Cumulus to meet them when they came into view, but Draven had reached over and took hold of Talen's hand.

"You think it's likely that there's someone lingering just outside, waiting for an elf to show?" Talen asked quietly, reluctantly staying put.

"I think we're going to be stirring up enough trouble as is," Draven said, "and there ain't no reason to take unnecessary risks."

Talen glared but didn't say anything until Wilfred made to help Margaret up the gangplank.

"I told you. I'm fine," Margaret said to him. "How many times will it take before you listen?"

"Clearly at least once more," Wilfred said, ceasing his attempts, but staying close enough to step in if needed.

"Did you find anything?" Talen asked, getting up to clear a spot for Margaret to sit.

Margaret nodded, silently accepted the seat, and absently rubbed her leg. "We did indeed. It's a staircase alright. Leads down to the lower river shore and, after a bit of a hike, to a cave behind the smaller falls."

Draven's eyebrows lifted. "You don't say?"

"But that ain't what we're looking for," Wilfred said.

"That cave isn't deep enough," Margaret said. "It seems to be a novelty for visitors."

"But?" Talen asked.

Margaret smiled "There is a second cave midway down the stairs. The lower cave is natural, but the upper is clearly man-made."

Talen appreciated the detailed retelling, but the seemingly extraneous information strained her patience. "Why mention the lower cave first, or at all, if you had to pass the upper one on the way down?"

Margaret's face fell. "I'm sorry. I thought you'd want to know everything, and it seemed logical to save the pertinent information until the end."

An angry kick from Gaoth wouldn't have hit as hard as the wave of shame that washed over Talen. "No, I'm sorry." She opened her mouth to explain the feeling of helplessness, the frustration that went with it, and the anger of the situation. However, that would've just been an attempt to excuse away her rudeness. Instead, she said, "Please, go on."

Margaret's expression softened, and a smaller version of the previous smile returned. "We tried to get a look inside the upper cave."

"Didn't get too far though," Wilfred said. "Just a chain and some signs shooing folk away at the entrance, but near as soon as we stepped in, a fella showed up and told us to get."

"We decided it wasn't worth risking any trouble to go deeper, but..." Her brow furrowed, and her mouth twisted. "There is something going on there. You can feel the corruption. It's like with the river, but more intense." She shook her head. "It's somehow easy to miss if you're not looking for it, but when you do, you can't not notice it."

Wilfred nodded and grinned. "That and the fella had an apron with a crystal in the pocket."

"Reckon we'll have to wait for a visit until after nightfall," Talen said.

"We should probably leave and come back," Draven said. "An airship parked on the island is like to draw enough attention as is. Lingering about after sunset is sure to bring someone poking about."

"We did overhear some people talking about it," Margaret said.

"Best not to dally then," Draven said and hurried up the stairs.

Talen went to the bay doors and pulled the lever to close them. As they slid shut, she could just make out the sounds of people and distant movement in the trees. Luckily, the doors sealed, and the ship started rising before anyone got near enough to see.

"Care for some supper?" Wilfred asked.

"I could eat," Margaret said. "Give me a hand, please."

"You still shining like the North Star?" Wilfred asked Talen as he helped Margaret to her feet.

"There's actually been an interesting development in that regard," Talen said and filled them in as they headed to the galley.

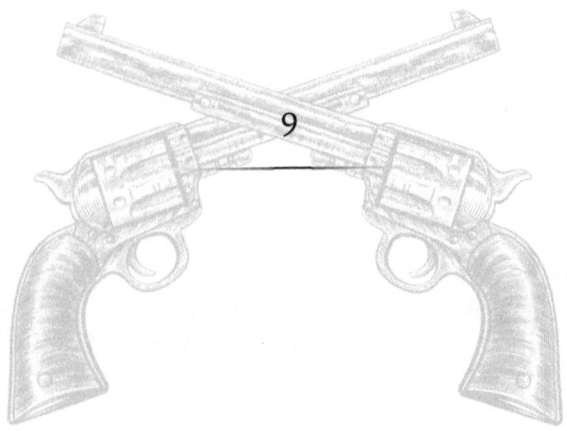

9

S everal hours later, Draven piloted the Cumulus just a few feet above the river at the bottom of the falls, well below the island's cliff edge. Heavy clouds hid the sliver of a moon and the stars. Much of the town had long since gone dark and quiet.

Talen checked the loads in her spell irons and slid replacements into the loops on her gun belt, trying not to think about what they might find. As a dwarf, Draven knew more about elementals than Talen, but she did know they were beings of magic. That made them sacred, and even just her imaginings of what humans might be doing stirred anxiety and anger in equal measure.

"We're not going to hurt anyone, right?" Margaret asked, checking her repeater.

"Not unless we have to," Talen said. "If they're stained, or they come at us, and we have to defend ourselves, I mean."

"Or they're too stupid to run before this goes off," Wilfred said, putting the finishing touches on his spell bombs.

"I thought you said they weren't dangerous," Margaret said.

"They ain't," Wilfred said. "But when they fill the chamber with stone, if anyone is inside, they'll be stuck. Won't be no getting out."

Talen put a hand on Margaret's shoulder. "Which means, if anyone is there, we'll make sure they're out before the bombs go off."

Margaret nodded.

"If they're really are using elementals like we think," Talen said, "they ought to be mighty grateful it's us and not the dwarves."

"Don't misunderstand," Margaret said. "I have no problem defending myself, or one of you, I just—"

"We're nearing the falls," Draven said through the speaking tube. "Call it two minutes."

Talen walked over to the tube. "Got it," she said into it and then turned back to Margaret. "And you ain't got to explain to us, little sister."

Margaret smiled, holstered her repeater, and pulled on her coat.

Wilfred slid the four spell bombs into a satchel and slung it over his shoulder. "Ready."

Talen led them back down to the cargo hold.

A minute or so later, Draven joined them, dwarven pistols on her hips.

"You're sure the ship will be here when we come back?" Talen asked.

"We ain't in the water, so currents aren't an issue," Draven said. "There's a bit of wind because of the falls, but I dropped our anchors. So, unless a hurricane blows through, in which case we'll have bigger problems, my girl ain't going nowhere."

"Alright," Talen said to the trio. "Everyone knows their job, right?"

"Yes, ma'am," Wilfred said and gave a little salute.

Talen narrowed her eyes.

"Yes," Margaret said.

"Aye," Draven said.

"Let's get to work then."

Draven opened the bay doors and extending the gangway.

Talen wrapped herself in shadow and made her way through the mist and dark to the enclosed staircase. She made to open the door at the bottom of the stairs, but the wet air caused it to swell and stick. The moisture waterlogged the wood so bad she damn near pulled it off the hinges getting it open.

The others tailed a few seconds behind. The darkness and uneven terrain slowed Margaret and Wilfred more than Draven, hence the reason she brought up the rear, just in case someone slipped.

Once everyone neared the doorway, Talen stepped in and began climbing the metal stairs. What looked to be self-recharging crafter lights hung every ten feet or so, filling the chamber with a soft glow. She guessed the smooth white stones gathered sunlight during the day and shone it back out at night. The question was, why would the stairs need to be lit?

Obviously, because someone uses them after the sun has set.

Staying a dozen paces ahead of the others, she laid a hand on her right-hand spell iron, and moved slowly, keeping a keen eye ahead.

Thirty or so feet up, she came to the upper-cave entrance: a rough-cut rectangle about the size of a door. Nothing but a waist high chain and a sign that read "authorized access only" barricaded the way. The entranceway only ran a dozen paces before splitting into a "T." The cavern had also been furnished with crafter lights hanging at regular intervals, filling the stone chamber with a warm glow.

The familiar calm before a fight settled over Talen like a blanket as she removed the chain and stepped inside.

Water seeped through the stone walls and dripped from the ceiling.

She crept down the hall, each step purposeful so as not to slip on the slick stone floor. With each breath, the musty air settled on her tongue, tasting of moldy, citrusy minerals.

When she reached the split in the tunnel, Talen put her ear to the stone, closed her eyes, and listened. The sound of the others coming up the stairs and the falls themselves made hearing anything else just about impossible.

Just about.

A very faint, rhythmic tapping sounded under all the noise. Not hard, like hammering nails, but purposeful. And also very careful.

Like maybe breaking crystals?

She drew her right-hand iron, stepped around the corner, and checked the tunnels in both directions. Each passageway went straight for forty or fifty feet, with openings—roughly door-shaped—every ten or twelve feet.

A wan glow shone from crafter lights, filling the otherwise empty tunnels.

Talen glanced over her shoulder as the others entered the cavern. As agreed, they waited just inside, weapons out but pointed at the ground. Draven stood at the front, Wilfred watching the staircase. Talen tapped the barrel of her spell iron on the cave wall three times. When they nodded, she turned back and made her way down the leftward tunnel.

At the first opening, she stopped and peeked inside. Though unlikely anyone had the means to see her, she didn't want to take any chances.

It wasn't another tunnel, but rather a round chamber, maybe ten feet across. Liquid dripped from the ceiling, feeding a pool that occupied almost the entire floor. Around the edge of the basin, just under the water's surface, lay dozens of broken bounty crystals.

The wet, citrusy taste of the air here also had a faint, rancid, fetid edge to it. Talen wrinkled her nose, more than a bit unsettled. Being so close to the broken crystals and not feeling anything, despite tasting them, just felt wrong.

More troubling though were the clean, new crystals forming around some of the murky, dark, broken ones. The new crystals seemed small, not... well, ripe was the only word that came to mind. However, she could almost see them growing before her eyes.

Talen just stared for a few heartbeats, a slimy, wriggling disgust and smoldering indignation slithering through her insides.

She and Draven had discussed how new bounty crystals would be made, and something like this had been one theory. However, seeing the desecration with her own eyes was so much worse than she'd dared to imagine.

The filthy, voyeuristic feel to the sight couldn't be ignored. Like staring at an open wound, where someone continually carved away the new flesh, instead of allowing it to heal.

A righteous fury swallowed the writhing disgust, but Talen bit it back, gripped her spell iron a little tighter, and went to check the next chamber.

Save the anger for later.

Inside it, and each successive chamber, she found the same defilement. With each room, the rage grew harder and harder to hold back.

It also became clear that the tapping sound—which she'd almost forgotten about amid her rising ire—originated from the chamber at the very end of the tunnel.

The seething indignation focused on that sound, burning away all thoughts of caution. She strode into the final room, spell iron up, hoping someone would give her cause to gun them down without breaking her promise to Margaret.

This chamber, easily three times the size of the others, contained not a single pool, but half a dozen smaller ones.

Suspended just above the water of each, hung people.

Or what might have once been people, all of them naked, and most so emaciated they could've been mistaken for corpses, save for the slow rise and fall of their chests as they breathed.

The rage died like a campfire buried by an avalanche, and that cold chilled Talen's blood. Unbidden, memories of the stained crafters Elizabeth Tuller had imprisoned under her factory rose to the forefront of her mind.

Thankfully, it didn't smell of death and filth like Tuller's prison, but that was the only reprieve from the horror.

Heavy chains and leather bindings held each of the creatures to platforms that sat on some sort of mechanism. Just below, a collection of clean crystals reached out of the water, like fingers, toward the captives. It took her a moment to realize the contraptions must adjust to keep the stained, just out of reach of the forming crystals.

Shock and disbelief clashed against wrath and disgust for emotional supremacy.

It took another moment for Talen to recover enough to notice the source of the tapping. A human man, sporting a leather apron and long gloves, knelt next to one of the abominations. He seemed entirely unaware of her presence as he used a small, pointed hammer to break a clean, full-sized crystal from beneath the captive. After a quick inspection, he placed the harvested bounty crystal into a satchel next to him.

The anger and revulsion won the fight for control.

Talen stepped from the shadows and poured magic into her spell iron. A flood of power like she'd rarely known answered her call, and the runes lit up like a noon-day sun.

The man cried out as he jumped, or tried to, and cover his eyes at the same time. He stumbled, slipped into the pool, and bumped against the captive stained.

The pitiful creature groaned and writhed impotently in response, rattling the chains.

The man recoiled in horror, rolling away.

"Are you alone?" Talen asked through a clench jaw, with all the warmth of a glacier. "Answer quick or you're a dead man."

"What?" he asked, shading his eyes, and turning away from Talen's burning spell iron.

Pounding footsteps sounded down the tunnel and Talen glanced back to see her friends coming. With a monumental effort of will, she managed to ease up the flow of magic. The spell iron dimmed enough to let the others see what she'd found.

"Mother of God," Margaret said.

"What in the hell?" Wilfred asked half a blink later.

"Sacred stones," Draven whispered, as she scanned the room.

"Are you alone?" Talen asked, her voice a low growl. "You got to the count of one to answer before I start pulverizing limbs." Crushed bones ain't fatal, she almost said to Margaret.

The man just stared at her, blinking rapidly as his mouth opened and closed. It took half a moment for him to say anything. "You're an elf!"

Talen pointed her spell iron at his left leg. "One—"

"I'm alone!" He raised his shaking hands. "Please, I'll do whatever you want. Just don't hurt me."

Talen opened her mouth to speak, but Draven stepped in front of her, one of her dwarven pistols aimed at the man's head.

"How dare you?" she said in a low tone, her voice shaking with barely contained fury.

"What? No!" the man said, cowering back from her. He looked from the dwarf to Talen, and then finally to Wilfred and Margaret. "They're not people! They're stained!"

"Even if that were all you were doing," Draven said, glancing at the still forms above the pools. "It'd be cruel and foul enough a thing to do." She took a step closer to him. "But what you're doing to the elementals is nothing short of profane!"

Talen didn't speak. Not because she didn't have plenty of choice and impolite words ready to spit at this *juarchian*, but because Draven's grievance was bigger.

"The elementals?" the man asked, his brow furrowing. "No, you don't understand, they create the crystals naturally as a response to—"

"You bleed naturally in response to a blade," Draven said. "Does that mean you wouldn't mind if I opened you up?"

"We're not hurting them!" the man said, almost in tears. "I swear. It's like an oyster making a pearl. It's a natural process!"

The fire burning in Draven's eyes and her utter stillness sent a ribbon of cold fear trickling down Talen's back. In a sudden moment of clarity, her rational mind overtook the screaming desire to punish someone for this violation of magic. On reflection, she looked over at Margaret, and found her sister as terrified as Draven was furious. Despite how much, a rather large, part of her might like to see this play out, she stepped forward. Slowly, she laid a hand on Draven's arm, and gently pushed down.

It didn't budge.

Draven turned her wrath-filled gaze on Talen, but otherwise remained still as a statue.

"I ain't saying your anger ain't warranted," Talen said to her friend. "I feel it too. But your rage is blinding you." She glanced back at Margaret. "And we made a promise."

Draven said nothing for a long moment. Neither did she give in to Talen's efforts.

"Trust me," Talen said. "I know what carrying the weight of choices made out of anger feels like. I promise you that this desecration will not stand, but this ain't the way."

Draven drew in a slow breath and, reluctantly, lowered her pistol.

"Thank you," the man said.

"Oh no, don't go thanking me." She reignited her spell iron and aimed it again at the man's legs. "You got a long ways to go before you're out of this storm."

The man turned to Margaret and Wilfred in obvious desperation.

"They the ones you need to sweet talk," Wilfred said.

"What's your name?" Margaret asked.

"Thomas."

Maragret swallowed. "Well then, Thomas, I suggest you answer their questions. If you do, honestly, you won't be hurt. You have my word."

Talen's gaze met Margaret's.

Her sister didn't say anything, but she didn't have to.

Talen let out a breath. "I'm going to be charitable and assume you got no idea what you're doing. So, like my friend said, you got a chance to walk away from this. I suggest you take it."

Thomas swallowed and nodded. "I'll tell you anything you want to know."

"How many places like this are there?" Talen asked.

"Ten," the man said. "Mostly around the Great Lakes, but there's also some in the Smoky Mountains, the Blue Ridge Mountains, and the Everglades."

"Where do you get the stained?"

Thomas shrugged, but averted his eyes. "I, uh, don't know. I never asked. I mean, they're just stained."

Talen wanted to slap the stupid out of him, but reminded herself that most humans didn't understand pure magic or corruption. "They're also alive," she said, more than a little patronizingly. "They're living, breathing embodiments of dark magic, and you got them gathered up together."

Thomas's brows drew together. "There's no danger—"

"Oh no," Wilfred said. "Best not go telling an elf what's what when it comes to magic."

"It's the only way to make the crystals," Thomas said. "And we need the crystals to stop the most dangerous stained from hurting people."

"I swear by my mother you got a level of willful ignorance that's almost impressive," Talen said. "You don't need crystals to stop stained. My people were killing them long before yours came up with bounty crystals." She took a few more slow breaths in an attempt to ease the frustration and anger Thomas seemed intent of stoking. "But that don't matter right now. What are you doing in the other chambers with the broken crystals?"

"It's a new discovery," he said, almost giddy. He nodded at the bound stained. "This was the only method of crystal creation initially. We put stained near the elementals and the crystals start forming. When they're the right size, we harvest them and—"

"We figured that part out," Draven said, her voice still tight with anger. "She asked about the other chambers."

"It can take weeks to make crystals this way," Thomas said, again nodding at the stained around him. "A researcher at a facility in Michigan found that if we used a full bounty crystal, either those from collected bounties or those spoiled from one of our stained having touched and broke it, the same growth would happen in a matter of days."

Talen and Draven exchanged a look of disgust.

"It's safer for everyone," Thomas said, brow furrowed. "Not only is it more efficient, we don't need to use living stained." He gestured around him. "With this method, when stained died, production would slow until they were replaced. Add to that, if a stained made contact with a crystal, not only would the stained likely die, the crystal would fill and become unusable. Broken crystals don't have either issue. There is no stained to die, and the corruption is inside the broken crystal, so it can't corrupt clean ones."

"And you don't see any problems with this new discovery?" Draven asked.

Talen recognized the desire to slap Thomas in her friend's expression.

Thomas frowned. "No. How could it be a problem to get more—"

"Not the harvest amounts, you dolt," Draven said, clearly exasperated. "You're exposing the elementals to corruption they can't contain. What you reckon happens to it then?"

Thomas opened his mouth, his expression blank. "I don't—huh?"

Talen didn't know how much longer she could hold off smack him. "You got corruption running down the river, *shanzi fetsuian.*"

"No, that's not possible," Thomas said. "It's contained in the crystals!"

Everyone swore under their breath, except Margaret, who let out a long sigh.

"You ain't too bright, are you?" Wilfred said.

"Think about it," Margaret said with what Talen considered near saint-like patience. "If it was truly contained, then how could it get the elemental to make new crystals?"

Talen couldn't be sure, but there appeared to be a glimmer of understanding in Thomas's eyes. "And how long you think, before all this corruption starts to hurt the elemental?"

Thomas laughed. "What? We can't hurt an elemental!" The laughter died abruptly when he spotted Draven's cold glare. He lifted his hands. "I'm sorry, but elementals are massive, even the small ones. We're tiny in comparison. Miniscule. To use your analogy, it's like a mosquito taking your blood."

"You do know folks get sick and die from mosquitoes, right?" Wilfred asked.

Thomas shrugged. "My point is, we can't possibly impact something so large. You might as well say we're melting the ice caps or killing the ocean."

"If there was money to be made doing it," Talen said, "I'm sure you'd find a way to do that too."

Thomas opened his mouth.

Talen leaned forward just a bit. "I'm telling you corruption is spilling out. When I got close to the river, it felt like it was tearing my guts out. I've been hunting stained since before your grandpa's grandpa, and I ain't never felt nothing like that."

Thomas stared at her, his mouth working, but no words came out.

"Did any of you geniuses ever think to ask the elementals for help?" Draven asked.

Thomas came back to himself. "Communicate? With an elemental? Are you serious?"

"You see something unserious about me in this moment?"

Thomas swallowed. "Um..."

"You also could've asked the dwarves for help. Sacred stones, at the least, you could've asked us to help dispose of the used crystals."

Talen wanted to give this *juarchian*, Thomas, the benefit of the doubt. But even Margaret had to see this level of ignorance could only be willful.

"They'd never do that," she said. "It's the same reason he don't believe me about the corruption in the river. They'd have to admit humans ain't masters of creation. That maybe someone else knows something they don't."

Thomas opened his mouth again.

"Shut it," Talen said, her patience expended. "We're putting you out of business."

"What? No, you can't!" Thomas said.

"We can, and we will," Talen said. "And you'd best thank your lord and savior it's us. I promise you, we're a damned sight more friendly than the dwarves will be when they learn what you're doing." They might be slow to act about the stained crafting stones, but Talen suspected this sort of desecration would light a fire under them.

The color drained from Thomas's face.

Talen stepped closer and bent down. "As someone with personal experience, I can tell you, you don't want to be on the wrong side of a leviathan."

Thomas swallowed again and might've pissed himself a bit. Or it could've been water from when he fell, Talen couldn't be sure.

She turned to Wilfred. "You got enough to fill this place up?"

"And then some."

"Best get to putting them in place." Talen turned back to Thomas. "He ain't going to stumble across anyone else, right?"

Thomas shook his head.

"I'll be well and truly unhappy if you're lying to me, Thomas," Talen said and drew her left-hand iron. "And you do not want to see me well and truly unhappy."

"I'm alone. I swear."

"Go on then," Talen said to Wilfred and turned to Margaret. "You go and help him."

Margaret didn't move; she just held Talen's gaze.

"We all made a promise," Talen said. "It still stands."

"Okay," Margaret said.

"Come on," Wilfred said, and the two of them left the chamber.

"You going to kill me now?" Thomas asked, his lower lip quavering.

"Not if you don't give us a reason." Talen motioned at Draven with her head. "Much as either of us might like to."

"Though I'd suggest you find a new occupation," Draven said. "And right quick."

Thomas nodded repeatedly. "Yes, sir. I will."

Talen tapped Thomas's head with an iron, just hard enough to get his attention. "She's a ma'am, you twit."

Thomas looked from Talen to Draven, who was straightening her long mustaches, and furrowed his brow. "Yes, ma'am?"

"Better," Talen said. "But before you get, you got work to do."

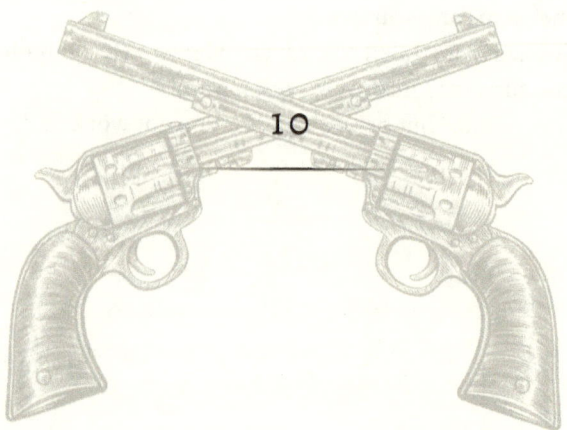

10

After Wilfred and Margaret set the spell bombs, they joined Draven and Thomas loading the broken crystals into crates. While they did that, Talen took care of the stained. Unlike those wretched monstrosities that Tuller had locked up, none of these moved or made a sound. If they were conscious at all, they didn't show it.

A single force blast into the chest, crushing their ribcages and hearts, was thankfully enough to end each stained. That done, Talen set to removing the chains holding them to the platforms. Normally, she'd just burn the bodies in place and be done with it, but these elementals had been abused quite enough already. Not even Draven could say for sure what destroying the bodies would do, but Talen decided it best to do it someplace else. Neither of them much liked the idea of hauling stained bodies, but it had to be done.

With grim resolve, she hefted a body over each shoulder and made her way to the staircase.

"Can't I at least harvest the rest of the crystals that are ready?" Thomas asked Draven as he filled a crate with broken crystals. "It would be a waste not to collect them. They're already—"

"Open your mouth again and you'll be helping me instead of them," Talen said, pausing at the chamber's entrance.

Thomas looked over and when he saw the bodies, he paled. After that, he went back to work and didn't speak again.

Neither did anyone else.

Talen made it a point to avoid Margaret while hauling bodies. Wilfred had seen his share of dead, some mighty gruesome, and no doubt, so had Draven while working on the Railroad. Not to say Talen didn't think Margaret could handle it. She'd faced plenty of hardships and wasn't some fragile thing that might crumble. However, Talen didn't see a need to add to Margaret's burden. Especially not when it could be helped.

It took the better part of an hour to get all the crystals and the bodies into the hold of the Cumulus.

"You two go on and get cleaned up," Talen said to Margaret and Wilfred as they stood at the foot of the gangplank. "I'll see to the charges and Thomas here." She could sense him tensing. It might've been a little cruel, but she didn't bother saying anything to ease his mind.

"I'll have the ship ready to go soon as you get back onboard," Draven said.

Talen nodded and looked at Thomas. "Alright, back up the stairs."

She had him lead, and when they reached the entrance to the facility, she drew her right-hand iron.

"You said you wouldn't kill me!" Thomas said and fell to his knees on the stairs. "You promised! Please, I did everything you asked!"

She scowled at the sniveling little man. "Get to your feet. I ain't going to kill you. I keep my word." She motioned up the stairs. "Get out of here."

"You won't shoot me in the back?"

Talen lit her iron. *"Juarchian*, you don't get moving, I'm going to shoot you in the face. Now go on! Get!"

Thomas hurried up the stairs, glancing back every few steps. She didn't know if he'd run for the law, but if he did, it'd take him twenty minutes just to get to town. By the time anyone came to investigate, the Cumulus would be long gone.

One by one, she fired the special charges Wilfred crafted into each of his spell bombs. After a second or two, watery mud began to pour out. Once the liquid hit the floor, it hardened instantly into stone. It started as a slow trickle, but the flow quickly began to increase.

As usual, Wilfred had come up with a brilliant solution to a problem. In this case, how to render the facility unusable without causing damage to elemental or surrounding area.

By the time she set off the last bomb, the opposite tunnel had nearly filled in. Less than a minute after that, she'd made it down the stairs and was back on board the Cumulus.

"Let's get out of here," she said into the speaking tube.

"We're gone," Draven answered back as the ship began to lift into the air.

"Considering the cargo," Talen said into the tube, deliberately not looking at the corpses, "I'm going to leave the bay doors open."

"I'd certainly appreciate that."

"Any patch of open ground will do to burn the bodies, so long as we're well away from any towns or such."

"I'll find a spot right quick."

Talen went to the open bay doors to enjoy the fresh air and darkened scenery passing by. Despite her best attempts to resist, she kept glancing over her shoulder at the bodies stacked near the opposite wall. A few of the corpses stared at her. Or rather their heads had fallen in such a way that they faced her. She'd tried not to pay them much mind when she put them down or carried them out. Even so, a twinge of what might've been pity sounded in her heart.

Most of the stained she'd ever dealt with had been the worst kind; violent, angry, and cruel. Likely had been before any dark magic touched them. The corruption had amplified that. But like the tortured things under Tuller's factory, these seemed different. They didn't look danger-ous. They looked... well, sad, pitiful even. The more she thought about it, the more it made sense. It didn't seem possible to capture anything but a freshly corrupted stained, or someone that had turned to the dark out of desperation.

Hell, one of the dead, a girl with filthy dark hair, couldn't have seen more than fifteen years.

The stairs behind Talen creaked.

A moment later Wilfred's familiar footsteps sounded on the decking.

"How the hells does a kid turn stained?" she asked. "And why do I care so much?"

"You know why," Wilfred said and came to stand next to her. "And you always cared. You just forgot after your sisters were murdered."

"They're just stained," Talen said, trying to convince herself, and unable to turn away from the dead girl's empty eyes. "They invited dark magic in of their own free will."

Wilfred lit his pipe and puffed a couple times. "Not everyone what makes a bad choice is a bad person. Sometimes folks is just hopeless."

Could this child have been saved if someone had gotten to her in time? Could the darkness have been purged?

Talen finally tore her gaze from the dead girl and focused on Wilfred.

He didn't look away from the view, but his ever-present smile had vanished.

"You sound like someone speaking from experience," Talen said. "But you ain't no stained."

"No, I ain't," he said. "But I was sorely tempted on more than one occasion."

"You never told me that." But she'd suspected.

He chuckled. "Not exactly my proudest moments." He glanced at her and then away. "And knowing how elves, you in particular, viewed stained, I didn't reckon it a topic worth discussing."

Talen's heart twinged with pain. "You really didn't think you could tell me?"

"At first?" he asked. "Hell no." He shrugged. "After, well, I suppose it was more that I didn't want you thinking less of me."

Talen touched his cheek and turned his head until he looked at her. "I couldn't ever think less of you. And I'm sorry I never made that clear."

His smile returned, if briefly, and he put his hand over hers. "Not sure you could've."

"Why?"

"I believe they call it the human condition."

"Or being a dumbass?"

He chuckled again. "Six of one, half a dozen the other."

Talen laughed and stepped a little closer, just enjoying the silence with her dear friend. Even so, a question wriggled in her mind.

"I know you're too polite to ask," Wilfred said a moment later. "So, I'll just tell you. Yeah, I saw slaves turn to the dark." His brow furrowed. "Not near as many as you'd think, but more than a few." He took a final puff on his pipe and then tapped it on a bulkhead, knocking the ash and embers into the night. "As you'd expect, the white folk were quick to add a susceptibility to corruption to the long list of reasons why we needed to be in chains."

Talen didn't say anything.

His expression hardened. "Can't trust the negro with magic, you know. They're more prone to the temptations of corruption! Their violent, simple minds, ain't enough to resist it."

Talen reached over and took his hand.

"They never asked if chains, beatings, and all the rest might, just might, push a man to breaking."

A cold pain pierced Talen's heart. "I can't quite condemn them for something I've done."

His brows furrowed and he turned to her. "What the hell are you talking about? The only other non-Black folk I ever heard of that hated slavery more than you was John Brown."

Talen let out a breath. "Wish I'd have known more about him. I'd have liked to lend a hand. But that ain't what I mean."

"Go on then," he said. "You certainly have my undivided attention."

"The bounty crystals."

"What?"

"I never asked where they came from," Talen said. "For a while, I convinced myself it was because I was naïve, that I wanted to believe maybe humanity had gotten something right and was fighting the dark too." She shook her head. "Truth is, I didn't ask because I didn't want to know. It was something that made my life easier, and wasn't hurting no one I knew."

Wilfred just stared at her for a long moment. "How, in all creation, do you see that as the same thing?" He shook his head. "I swear, I ain't never met no one as eager as you to shoulder blame. I'm talking about people, and I'm being mighty generous calling them people, who justified keep me and mine in chains. You didn't think to ask questions about something that didn't seem at all questionable."

"That's just an excuse," Talen said. "Mind, only person I'll put down faster than a stained is a slaver, or a sympathizer, but that don't mean I'm innocent. I didn't look because I knew I wouldn't like what I found."

"Damn, but you elves sure have mastered guilt," Wilfred said. "It's like an artform."

"What's that supposed to mean?"

"You think a murderer is the same as someone steals food?"

Talen opened her mouth to answer.

"Both are guilty of a crime, means they're the same, right?"

Heat surged through Talen, born from frustration. "That ain't what I meant!"

"It is what you said though. The two ain't the same, and you know it, but you can't let a chance to climb onto the Cross pass you by."

The truth of his words, even if she didn't know what he meant by cross, sent her frustration running like a spooked deer. Though it only nourished the shame. Try as she might to find something to say, she couldn't think of nothing.

Wilfred sighed. "I know it comes from a good place, but the fact you don't seem able to forgive yourself, ever, for anything, does get a might aggravating at times. Hell, you can't even put down the guilt of what your mother's mother did." He shrugged. "Reckon humans are just as bad, though we're the opposite. We don't even feel bad for what we ourselves have done. Hell, most can't even stop ourselves from finding all kind of excuses for why we weren't even responsible."

The weight of Wilfred's words left her speechless for a bit. "I confess, I ain't exactly sure how to feel just now. You're right, which makes me ashamed, but then I feel guilty about being ashamed."

"Your people might've done some mighty terrible things, but you sure as hell ain't never done nothing to compare with them that kept me and those like me in chains. Truth to tell, it pisses me off that you'd think that for even a moment."

"I am sorry."

His grin returned, if a somewhat less than usual, and he leaned into her. "I know. Just don't do it again. That's my friend you're talking about."

Warmth poured from her heart. "I'll do my best, though I can't promise I won't stumble. Not everyone can be as saintly as you."

He nodded and smiled. "That's a fact. And yet, somehow, I manage to remain so very humble about it all."

Talen laughed, reminded, once again, why she'd fallen in love with Wilfred, and why she loved him still.

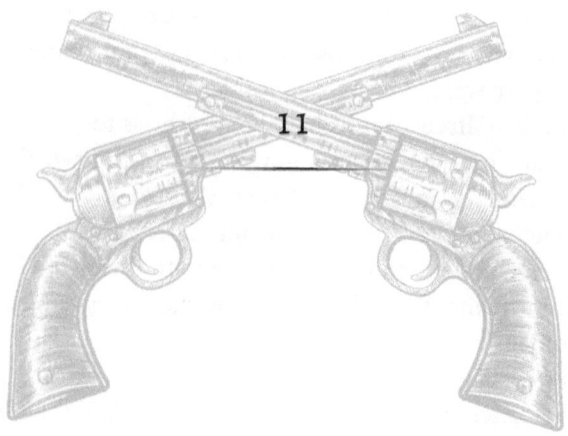

11

After an hour or so, Talen had the sudden desire to check on Margaret. She'd no reason to think Margaret wouldn't be fine, but after the events of the evening, Talen just needed to see for herself.

As expected, Margaret was sleeping soundly in her cabin. Silent as the night itself, Talen slipped in, pulled the blankets up to Margaret's neck, and departed just as quietly.

Before closing the door, Talen took a moment to watch Margaret sleep. Despite the ever-present fear of losing this new family, just as she'd lost her first, the immense gratitude of having a family of her choosing, one that had also chosen her, entirely outshined that fear.

When she returned to the cargo hold, Talen found Wilfred exactly where she'd left him.

"She sleeping?" he asked as Talen stepped up next to him.

"She is," Talen said.

"You sound relieved."

"I am." Talen let out a sigh. "Though I'd never say it to her. I just…" she shrugged. "It ain't that I think she hasn't got the stomach to deal with the bodies, but…"

"She shouldn't have to?" Wilfred asked.

Talen nodded.

"No one should." He took a pull from the whisky bottle Talen and

Draven had shared earlier and then offered it to her. "Reckon wanting to spare her from it could be seen as patronizing, but I'm willing to take the risk."

She accepted and took a drink. "Me too."

They shared the whisky and the silence for another hour or so until the Cumulus began to descend.

"I think I found a clear spot well away from anyone," Draven's voice said over the speaking tube.

"Has to be long past midnight," Wilfred said. "Even if anyone was about, I don't expect they'd be up and looking."

Talen went to the tube and spoke into it. "Don't expect we'll be long."

"Take your time," Draven said. "We got four or five hours before we get to Auburn, and I'd just as soon not come knocking on Mrs. Tubman's door at the crack of dawn."

Once the airship was close to the ground, Wilfred extended the gang-plank. He and Talen stepped off and surveyed their surroundings. They were at the base of a modest hill, surrounded by trees just starting to bud. The woods were so crowded that the clearing was only just big enough for the Cumulus.

"She's one hell of a pilot," Wilfred said. "Put a dollar on the ground and she could land that thing on the eagle's beak."

"The tip of it at that," Talen said and toed the ground, checking the moisture level. Last thing she wanted to do was set the woods ablaze.

"How's it look?" Wilfred asked when he saw what she was doing.

"Evening moisture on the surface, but it's dry below," she said. "I'd feel better if we dug down a bit and put some stones around the edge as a wind break."

"As you see a damn sight better than me at night," Wilfred said, his ever-present smile almost entirely absent. "I reckon I'll get to the digging."

Talen understood, she felt the weight of the grim task ahead too. She nodded and set out to find some rocks while Wilfred returned to the ship to fetch a shovel.

It took near on another hour of looking, but Talen found enough good-sized stones to form a respectable windbreak. The last few had to be dug out, but she didn't mind the extra effort. She set down the final stone with a grunt and wrangled it into place, forming a circle about eight feet across. That done, she grabbed a second shovel and set to helping Wilfred. He'd managed to clear about half the circle down six inches or so.

"Those are not stones," he said as she set to work.

"Beg pardon?"

"You might call them stones," he said and tossed another shovel full of dirt over the rock wall. "The rest of us would call them boulders."

"The biggest ain't even two feet across."

"And weighs what, six hundred pounds?"

"Give or take."

He bent down and picked up a fist-sized stone and held it out to her. "This is a rock." He walked over, set it on the wind break, and gestured at the larger rock. "That is a goddamned boulder."

"That," Talen said, nodding at the smaller stone, "is a pebble."

He glared at her and set back to work, but he couldn't hide the hint of a grin on his face. "Now you're actively trying to make me feel insecure. And that just ain't nice."

"Your digging is quite impressive."

"Thank you. Was that so hard?"

They both chuckled, but neither could muster much more than that. Talen knew if they allowed themselves anything more, it might shatter the wall of cold indifference they both hid behind. If that happened, they'd have to think about the fact these corpses used to be people, one a child, and the terrible circumstance that had led them to becoming stained.

Together they cleared the rest of the circle in short order in silence. When they'd finished, Talen helped Wilfred scramble over the rock wall, and then passed him her shovel. He took it wordlessly, meeting her eyes for a lingering moment.

Talen nodded her thanks for being there to help with this dark deed and the comfort his presence always provided.

He replied in kind and carried the shovels back to the storage rack.

Talen went to the stack of bodies, lifted the young girl, and without looking at her face, gently carried the child to what would be her final resting place. Once she'd set the girl down, Talen closed the nameless child's eyes and set to retrieving the remaining corpses.

When the dead were in place, Talen checked—yet again—to make sure fire loads were ready in each spell iron.

"Want to say any last words over them?" Talen asked.

"Words ain't never been my talent," Wilfred said.

"That's bullshit. Your words might not always be fancy, but you're one of the most eloquent people I ever met."

"You never told me that before."

"Didn't think I had to," she said. "I just figured you knew it."

"Well, I didn't, and it's mighty nice to hear."

That took Talen a bit off guard. "I apologize. Reckon it's easy to take those that mean the most to us for granted." Her defenses against the overwhelming awfulness of the task almost collapsed. Almost.

"Reckon it is," Wilfred said, his voice breaking a bit at the end.

Talen gave him a moment to steel himself again. "So, got any words?"

"Can't think of none." He let out a breath. "Don't know what made them turn to the dark, or what they'd done after, but I hope they find some peace now." He turned away and covered his eyes.

Talen's hands had started to shake, and tears spilled from the corners of her eyes as she looked at the young girl one last time. Careful not to pour too much magic into them, she lit both irons.

"Here's hoping."

She drew in a steadying breath, closed her eyes, turned her head away, and fired both barrels. Even so, the bright flash of light stung her eyes. A second flash came half a blink later as the fireballs hit the bodies and exploded. By the time Talen could bring herself to look, the bodies were already almost unrecognizable, and the sickly-sweet smell of burning flesh filled the air.

They waited together in silence for another minute or two, making sure the bodies would keep burning. Once Talen felt satisfied, they both turned and went back to the Cumulus, neither saying another word.

"It's done," Talen said into the speaking tube as Wilfred retracted the gangplank and closed the bay doors.

The airship's rotors spun up, and it began to rise into the air.

"We'll be in Auburn in four or five hours," Draven said. "I'd suggest some sleep if you can manage."

Wilfred gave half a smile, though he appeared to have aged a few years in the last hours.

"I'll be in the stables," Talen said into the speaking tube, but eyeing Wilfred.

He nodded once, turned, and climbed the stairs.

A bone deep weariness had settled over Talen, both physical and emotional. Not tired so much as utterly spent. As she headed for the stables, she lifted her shirt to check the crystal in her belly. It might've just been the exhaustion, but she thought it seemed quite a bit dimmer.

Having neither the desire, nor the wherewithal, to consider what that might or might not mean, she tucked her shirt back into her trousers.

Joseph and Elise were lying down, dreaming horse dreams. Gaoth, awake, gave her a baleful look as she approached. As she neared though, his expression softened.

"I'm sorry," Talen said, wrapping her arms around his neck and hugging him tight. "I know you would've liked to get out for a spell, but—"

Gaoth turned, nuzzled his cheek to Talen's back, and chuffed.

"Thanks, old friend," she said. "I promise I'll make it up to you."

Gaoth nudged her with his head.

Talen took the hint and climbed onto his back, turned round, and lay down, with her head at his neck, her legs hanging off. Gaoth's steady heartbeat was like a balm for her soul, and sleep took her almost before her eyes had closed.

The smell of coffee drew her from the darkness. Talen opened her eyes and turned her head to see Margaret offering a steaming cup.

"Thought maybe you might need some help waking," Margaret said.

"What time is it?" Talen asked, sitting up and then sliding off Gaoth.

"Couple hours past sunrise."

"Much obliged," Talen said, accepting the cup and took a drink.

Margaret smiled, but it was tinged with sadness. "You're welcome."

The coffee had an acidic taste to it, though it had nothing to do with a failure in the brewing. Rather, it was the bitter taste of knowing she'd hurt Margaret, even if it had been out of love.

"Obviously, you're wondering why we didn't wake you last night?"

Margaret stiffened a bit, taking up what Talen thought of as her 'proper lady' posture. Her tone shifted to match. "Not at all." She tapped her cane on the floor. "Obviously my infirmity means I wouldn't have been useful with a shovel or carrying bodies, right?"

"Bodies are heavy, both physically and emotionally," Talen said.

Margaret's brows drew together. "You don't need to shield me. I'm not some delicate flower that will wilt away at—"

"It ain't about shielding you." Talen thought about it a moment, then shrugged and nodded. "Okay, it is a bit, but not because I see you as any sort of weak or frail. I hope that by now you know I got nothing but respect for you, and no doubt of what you're capable of."

"Then why?"

"Because it was a terrible foul thing that needed doing," Talen said. "And I wouldn't put a task like that on someone I actively disliked." She thought about it for a second and took another drink. "You and Wilfred do pretty much all the cooking, right?"

Margaret stared at her. "What has that got to do with anything?"

"Just answer me, please."

"I suppose we do," Margaret said, more than a little impatient. "I haven't really thought about it."

"Is it because you think I can't? Or that it's beyond me?"

"No, of course not. But as I've got so much experience, it seems a good way for me to do my part."

"Same thing here."

Margaret opened her mouth, presumably to argue, but stopped herself. Her brow furrowed as if considering Talen's words. "I suppose I see what you're saying. Though that was rather a winding path to get to the point."

Talen laughed. "Reckon I always did favor the trail with the most to look at. But we got there eventually, didn't we?"

Margaret smiled and nodded.

Talen put a hand on her sister's shoulder. "Wilfred and I got a lot of experience with things like needed doing last night. More than either of us care to think about, and I expect I speak for both of us when I say, I hope like hell you never get near as much."

Margaret put her hand over Talen's. "I understand. Thank you."

Talen shrugged and returned Margaret's smile. "You're my sister."

Margaret might've stood a bit taller, and dabbed at her eyes. "You hungry?"

"I reckon I could do with some food."

Margaret looked from her to Gaoth and back. "Can I ask you something?"

"Go on."

"How do you not fall off in your sleep?" Margaret asked, unable to hold back a laugh. "I don't think I could sleep on Joseph's back, and he's twice as broad as Gaoth."

Gaoth snorted.

"No offense," Margaret said.

Gaoth bobbed his head and shook out his mane.

"Yes," Talen said, stroking his neck. "You're the finest example of horse in the world."

Gaoth lifted his chin.

"Come on," Talen said, leading the way to the galley. "There ain't room in here for us and his ego."

Draven and Wilfred were already there, the latter finishing a breakfast of fried potatoes and beans.

"Morning," Draven said, over her steaming cup.

"Not sure what to think about being the last to rise," Talen said and went to get herself some food.

"Not by much," Wilfred said.

Talen filled a bowl with beans and the last of some greens she'd collected a few days ago, and refilled her cup. "You want some more coffee?"

"Much obliged," Wilfred said and slid his mug toward her.

She topped it off and looked to Draven and Margaret. "You going to eat?"

"Already did," Draven said.

"Me too," Margaret said and sat at the table with a cup of tea.

"Well ain't we just dragging behind today?" Talen asked Wilfred as she sat next to him.

"Does appear so, don't it?" He managed half a smile, despite the bags under his blood-shot eyes.

"Ain't no one keeping score on the matter," Draven said.

"And you both had a late night," Margaret said, stirring her tea.

"About that," Wilfred said.

"We already discussed it," Talen said.

"Never mind then." He finished off his food and swallowed a mouthful of coffee.

"Where are we?" Talen asked, and started her own breakfast. The greens tasted a bit rank, their texture way too soft and a bit slimy. She'd eaten worse though, so she just mixed them with the beans, made a note to forage, and set to finishing her bowl.

"I put us down in a lake a few miles south of town," Draven said. "Ain't no one about, and this section don't appear to be a popular spot for fishing or the like."

"Anyone know where Ms. Tubman's house is?" Wilfred asked. "I figure not a good idea to go asking about with boxes of stolen gold and an elf in tow."

"I hadn't thought about that." Margaret turned to Talen. "Will you use one of the glamour stones?"

Talen shook her head. "If I can help it, I'll never use another in my life." She took a drink of her coffee to clear the last of the slightly rancid greens taste from her mouth.

"Maybe you won't need to do anything," Margaret said.

"Supporting abolition don't mean they're fond of elves," Talen said. "I ain't going to hide, but I'll tuck my hair under my hat and keep my head down. If someone gets looking too close, I'll use the shadows and get gone."

"I don't know for sure," Draven said, "but I got an idea of where her farm is. It's south of town, and the reason we're settled where we are. Reckon we go, introduce ourselves, and if she's inclined to accept the donation, we'll fetch the gold and bring it round on our way out of town."

"What about after that?" Margaret asked.

Wilfred's brows lifted. "You was the most excited to meet Moses, now you're asking about what comes next?"

"I still am." Margaret shrugged. "I just don't expect a long visit. She's a hero, not a tourist attraction."

"We make for the Granite Halls," Talen said. "Get word to the dwarves about the bounty crystals and how they're made."

"Aye. Last I heard, diplomacy was progressing between us and the bearded, but slow. This news ought to bring to the two sides back together a mite quicker, common cause and all that. Won't be like we were, don't expect we ever will be, but I'm betting it'll damn sure stop any cooperation with the Dolomite and the US government."

"Do you think your people will attack the crystal farms?" Margaret asked.

Everyone looked to her.

"I'm not defending them," Margaret said. "But I don't believe most of them involved really understand what they're doing. They don't deserve to die because of it."

"According to the fella at the falls," Talen said, "all the places they make the crystals are on the eastern side of the divide."

Draven nodded. "The Dolomite is arrogant, but he ain't stupid. It'd take a leviathan weeks to cross the plains, and he wouldn't risk them in the open for so long. For his part, I don't believe the Granite Lord would just attack, even if he could without risking injury to the resident elemental. He'd give the workers a chance to leave."

Talen shuddered as the memories of running from the leviathans tried to rise up from the darkest of her memories and drag her down into it.

"Reckon this might be a discussion to have with the Granite Lord himself," Wilfred said, and pressed his foot to Talen's under the table.

That simple touch was enough to ground Talen back in the here and now. She wrestled the darkness back into the shadows, where it belonged, finished off her coffee, and picked up her bowl. As she did, she gave him a slight smile and barely perceptible nod. "Let's get moving. I, for one, am looking forward to a nice ride."

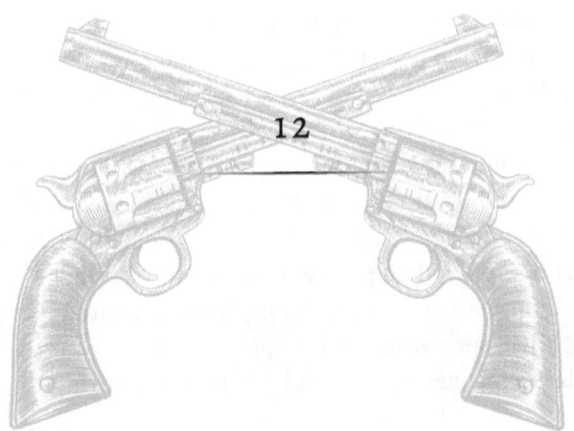

12

Once all the horses were saddled and led from the ship, Margaret activated the protection charms Wilfred had crafted. The first was meant to keep anyone from noticing the Cumulus at all. Should that fail, and someone tried to climb on board, they'd get increasingly intense shocks until they left. If neither of those worked to deter the would-be intruder, Draven's spindles would step in. Talen hadn't ever seen what they could do, and she'd be content if it stayed that way.

That done, Wilfred and Talen helped Draven get settled onto Joseph, behind Margaret. The draft horse's broad back would've proved uncomfortable for the short-legged dwarf, but she'd crafted a special seat to make it bearable. The other horses weren't really an option as Draven—though half his height—weighed more than Wilfred. Dwarven strength and endurance didn't come from a lack of muscle mass.

Joseph set the pace, slow and easy, and Elise happily walked alongside him. Gaoth however, wasn't quite so content.

Talen pulled her hat down low, turned up her collar, and drew up alongside the others.

"He's chomping at the bit to run," she said. "I'll ride ahead and scout things out."

"If you find any trouble, you get back to us," Wilfred said.

Talen narrowed her eyes. "Yes, Pa." Without giving him a chance to reply, she urged Gaoth into a gallop. He happily obliged and sprinted down the lakeside path, chewing up ground as if he were flying.

As much as she loved her friends, and having them in her life, the world often felt cramped on the Cumulus. Even standing on the deck somehow seemed to confine or restrain her. As Gaoth carried her at speed, the world felt open and expansive once again. She sucked in lungful after lungful of the crisp, clean morning air, finding it almost intoxicating, as if she could in fact, truly breathe again.

However, even Gaoth couldn't outrun the ever-present specter of being spotted by a human. It hung in the air, just above and behind her. The Eldar Treaty, the agreement that bound her people, dictated that any elf found east of the Mississippi river could be shot on sight.

She leaned forward, moving with him, but made sure to keep her right hand close to her spell iron. As it happened, she needn't have worried about people seeing her as the chill of the early spring day kept folk indoors.

After an hour or so, Talen, and a much happier Gaoth, rejoined the others. While they'd covered only a few miles, Gaoth had done at least three times that. They sidled up next to Elise and settled into a slow walk.

"Didn't come across no one, I take it?" Wilfred asked.

"Not a soul," Talen said. "Saw a few farmhouses in the distance, but weren't no one about. And even if there was, without a spyglass, I doubt anyone could've made me for an elf."

"Ground is probably still too hard to plant," Wilfred said.

"If you want to let Elise run for a bit, I'll stay with Margaret and Draven."

"Nah." He patted the mare's neck. "She can run like the wind if needs be, but we both done enough running in our time. A nice, easy walk is just fine by us."

Gaoth snorted.

Elise bumped him and snorted back.

"You tell him, girl," Wilfred said.

Gaoth glanced back at Talen.

"Don't look at me," she said. "You started it."

Gaoth sighed and turned his attention to the road.

They rode in silence for a while after that. Talen closed her eyes and took in the crisp, fresh air. The rhythmic clopping of hooves and swaying of Gaoth lulled her into a trance-like state. In the stillness, her mind turned back to the stained they'd burned. Specifically, the dead empty eyes of the girl.

Talen's whole life had been about destroying stained, but she'd only ever encountered the cruel and violent sort. Until Boston, at least, when she'd seen what other form they could take. How many others out there had turned to the dark because they had no other choice? Was there any saving them? Everything she knew said that once someone went stained, there wasn't no coming back.

If anyone had asked her even six months ago, Talen would've said there was no point in saving a stained. They'd turned to the dark once and likely would again if given the chance.

Now though, things were different.

Elven lore masters and shadow wardens had been studying dark magic and its corruptive influence for centuries but none had ever really considered saving a stained. Or if they had, she'd never heard about it.

What about the bounty crystals though? They drew out dark magic. If a bounty crystal were used on someone newly stained, would it work? Of course, if it did, she couldn't imagine anyone sparing whoever was left behind. Not least because by that point, they'd had to have committed murders, or worse. She'd never personally seen anyone come out of a collection alive, but then she'd never dealt with someone that wasn't stained to the core.

And yet, she couldn't help but wonder how many lost and desperate could be given another chance if the crystals could work.

Obviously, the way they were made was unacceptable, but what if a new method could be found? Surely between the elves, dwarves, and humans, they could think of something.

Of course, that would require them all to work together, and how likely is that?

"You alright?" Wilfred asked.

Talen blinked a few times as she came out of her reverie and opened her mouth to tell him about the foolish notion she'd been pondering, but Draven shifted in the saddle and drew Talen's attention. She looked from Margaret, to Draven, and back to Wilfred and chuckled.

"What?" he asked.

"Just thinking about unlikely events," Talen said and smiled. "And maybe daring to hope."

Wilfred's ever-present grin grew. "Daring to hope? Well, ain't you come a long way?"

"Nah," Talen said, putting on a stoic face, but winked at him. "But we all got moments of weakness."

"I think we're getting close to town," Margaret said.

Through some trees, Talen spotted a small farm: a sizeable wooden house and barn set off to one side. Beyond that, trails of smoke rose from unseen chimneys in a cluster that could only mean a city, if a small one. The smell, as of yet, wasn't too bad.

She pulled her hat lower, and her hand drifted to her spell iron on instinct. Anxiety took hold of her stomach in an icy grip as she glanced about for any impending danger.

Wilfred, apparently noticing the change in her demeanor, moved his coat clear of his revolver. "Keep behind us," he said and urged Elise forward until they were even with Joseph, at least partially obscuring Talen from view.

It helped, a little. Talen gripped the reins tighter and shifted in the saddle, ready to run or fight as needed.

It wasn't long before the smell of woodsmoke and cooking food reached her. Just beneath those came the less pleasant scents that accompanied human lodgings, but Talen ignored them. Her gaze never settled on anything for long, moving from one spot to another for threats of any kind. The war between the states was done, but it seemed reasonable there'd be guards or sentries about to watch for those might be holding a grudge against Harriet for the work she'd done.

Either they were well hidden, or there weren't any.

Even so, Talen's hand never moved away from her spell iron.

She only got more on edge as they turned down a narrow lane that led to the farm house, a hundred feet or so from the increasingly wide and well-traveled road.

In contrast, Margaret nearly vibrated in the saddle from excitement.

Draven shifted a little in her seat, but otherwise didn't show any care one way or another.

Wilfred kept glancing back at Talen, but he was sitting a little taller in the saddle. "Best hang back," he said. "I'll go and knock. If this ain't the place, I'll ask if they know where we can find her."

Talen nodded and brought Gaoth to a stop. He glanced around and pawed at the ground with a hoof, sensing Talen's unease.

A ways off, hidden from view, someone was chopping wood and whistling a tune that, after a moment, Talen recognized as "John Brown's Body."

Wilfred, Margaret, and Draven continued up to the house. He dismounted, passed the reins to Margaret, and started for the front door.

Before he could make it more than a couple steps, a curtain at one of the windows moved and a someone peered out. The glare made it hard for Talen to see any details, but they appeared to be Black, which eased Talen's nerves, though only just. Black folk might be more amenable to elves in general but that didn't mean they all were.

Head bent forward, she continued to scan the area, but just with her eyes, moving her body as little as possible.

The door of the house opened and a short Black woman stepped out. She wore a long dress of simple print, an apron, and a kerchief around her neck. Despite having only seen the woman once, and years ago at that, Talen instantly recognized Harriet Tubman. There was no mistaking those keen eyes. A moustachioed man, a foot taller than Harriet, and of an age to Wilfred, came out a moment later and stood next to her. Both of them looked from Wilfred to Talen in the distance, eyeing her for a long second, before turning back to Margaret, and then to Draven.

Harriet said something to the man Talen couldn't quite make out. He only nodded.

"We get all sorts of travelers," Harriet said. "Never had a dwarf, bearded or otherwise, though." She waved Talen forward. "Never had no elf come by neither. Come on up. Ain't no one here gonna give you no trouble. All are welcome in my home."

It didn't surprise Talen that Harriet had seen her for an elf. You didn't survive all she had by being oblivious. Even so, it didn't help ease her anxiety. Talen sucked in a steadying breath and urged Gaoth forward.

"Mrs. Tubman," Wilfred said, removing his hat and fretting it. "It's been better than ten years, so I don't reckon you'd recognize me, but we met in Philadelphia."

She narrowed her eyes. "Your face does seem familiar. Though I met lots of folks over the years, so don't take it badly that I don't recall your name. Don't make no never mind though. Get off them horses and come on inside out of the chill."

"Thank you, kindly," Wilfred said. He helped Margaret down while Talen slid from Gaoth's back.

"Keep an eye out," Talen said to Gaoth and then went to join Wilfred helping Draven from her seat.

"This here is Nelson Davis," Harriet said. "He's a boarder and helps around the house."

One corner of Nelson's mouth turned up but settled back down with a look from Harriet. He cleared his throat and nodded to Wilfred and the others. "Pleasure. Your horses need hay or rest? I can take them to the barn if needs be."

"Thank you, kindly," Wilfred said. "But that won't be necessary."

As Talen approached, the smells of hearth and home washed over her: baked goods, smoked meats, burning wood, sweat, and dirt.

"Mr. Davis," Wilfred said as he stepped inside and offered his hand. "I'm Wilfred Berkof."

Nelson and Harriet shook his hand.

Margaret joined them. "I'm Margaret Jameson," she said with barely contained glee, offering a little curtsey. "And, if I may say, it's such an honor to meet you, ma'am."

Harriet smiled. "I ain't a queen or nothing, child. Don't need to bother with none of the fanciness with me."

Draven scraped dirt from her boots and plodded in.

"Draven, ain't it?" Harriet asked, brow furrowed.

"Aye," she said, a wide grin spreading across her face. "I wasn't sure you'd remember me."

Harriet chuckled. "Ain't like to forget the only dwarf I ever met, much less piloting the only airship I ever been on." She glanced at Nelson for just an instant. "I expect that's the craft you saw this morning."

"Likely was," Draven said. "As we wasn't sure which house was yours, it seemed rude to stir things up by parking it right outside your door."

Nelson chuckled. "That surely would've caused talk in town."

Talen stepped inside, closed the door behind her, and only then, removed her hat and shook her hair out. She gave a nod to Nelson and Harriet. "I'm Talen."

"I remember you too," Harriet said. "Might be we only met the once, and so brief that I didn't get your name, but I remember you." She walked over and offered Talen her hand. "I make it a point not to forget them that helped me when I was in need."

Talen accepted and shook Harriet's hand, more than a little taken aback to be remembered. It might've also delighted her, and made her more than a little proud, but she didn't let it show.

"You never told me you crossed paths with an elf," Nelson said.

"I did a lot of living before I met you, Nelson Davis," Harriet said. "I expect there's plenty I ain't told you. Now go fetch some chairs for our guests. They got something mighty important to tell us."

"Yes ma'am," he said and went into the kitchen.

Talen looked to the others, but got only shrugs. They were obviously as confused as her. Her brain spun, trying to come up with a polite way of telling Harriet she was mistaken.

"I was expecting you," Harriet said and gestured to a couch.

"Thank you, ma'am," Wilfred said and motioned for Margaret to sit. "Did you say you was expecting us?"

"I did," Harriet said as Margaret sat and set her cane to one side. "Though I wasn't sure until just now when I saw Talen's face."

Talen didn't know what to think, much less say.

Wilfred looked to her, but she had no more clue than him. He sat down next to Margaret.

"Might I ask how you knew we was coming?" Despite her best attempts, Talen couldn't stop herself from wondering if maybe Moses had gone senile.

After a couple of trips, Nelson brought enough wooden chairs for everyone and they all sat.

"God told me," Harriet said.

Talen bristled at the mention of God, but held back from saying anything. Most of her experiences with the overly religious were unpleasant, but she reminded herself who this was. Other humans had used their god to keep Harriet and her people in chains for generations. If there was a human god who'd speak to and guide someone like Harriet Tubman, Talen would give that god a chance.

Harriet touched her head. "When I was just a child, an overseer threw a weight at a slave that'd run. I stepped between them and that weight broke open my skull. Had headaches ever since, but I also hear the Lord clearly through the hole left behind. I get visions, and they rarely led me wrong. A week ago, I saw a train. It was filled with folk I helped to freedom, my family included." She nodded at Draven and then to Talen. "A dwarf worked the engine, and a two-gun witch stood atop the train, protecting them all from a descending darkness like a guardian angel sent by the Lord himself."

Talen wasn't quite sure how she felt about the comparison, so she kept her mouth shut and let Harriet continue.

"I know the Railroad got quieter since the war ended," Harriet said. "We all had hope it weren't needed no more, and lots of them that supported it thought their work was done."

"Quiet don't mean gone," Draven said.

Harriet narrowed her eyes and grinned. "You right about that, Ms. Draven."

Draven's mouth fell open and her expression went slack for a half a blink, and then she sat up a little straighter, practically beaming.

The sublime joy of being seen for who she was poured from Draven and filled Talen's heart with warmth and joy.

Nelson glanced from Draven to Wilfred, brows drawn together.

"I didn't know for a long while neither," Wilfred said softly.

"But," Harriet said, silencing them each with a look, "I also know the wheels are still turning. I know good people do good work, helping get folks away from bad places."

"I didn't mean no offense," Nelson said to Draven. "Never met no dwarf before."

Draven waved it away.

"I ain't been a conductor since the war," Harriet said. "But I still do what I can. If you got folk in need of help, you'll find it here."

"You misunderstand," Talen said. "It ain't Railroad business that brought us here."

Harriet furrowed her brow. "Well, I know you ain't here to rent a room or have a meal."

"No ma'am," Wilfred said.

"Not that we wouldn't be proud to stay here," Margaret said. An instant later, her eyes went wide, as if surprised she'd spoken out loud. "I'm sorry, I didn't mean to suggest that, well, um, it's just that—"

Harriet leaned over and patted Margaret's hand. "Take a breath, child."

Margaret did, then wiped at her eyes and turned away. "I'm sorry, I don't mean to—"

"You got nothing to apologize for," Harriet said.

"And you ain't the first to get a bit teary meeting Moses," Nelson said.

"Thank you," Margaret said. "It's just that meeting you is, well, your story is what gave my mama the courage to run."

Harriet squeezed her hand and offered a handkerchief. "You a child of the Railroad?"

"Yes. Thank you," Margaret said, wiped at her eyes again, and took another breath. "But I wasn't born until after she was settled in Boston."

Harriet lifted her chin. "Your mama must be mighty brave. Running ain't easy, even without a baby in your belly."

"She was, yes," Margaret said.

Harriet's expression softened. "She with the Lord now?"

"Consumption took her when I was six."

"Well, I might not know you well, Margaret," Harriet said and looked to the others. "But you can tell a lot about someone by those they keep company with. So, I know enough to say, I expect she's awful proud of you."

Margaret mouth opened, but nothing came out. A moment later, she let out a small sob, and wiped at her eyes. "Thank you."

Talen wiped at her own eyes with one hand and put the other on Margaret's arm.

"I'm sorry," Margaret said, a laugh breaking through another sob, as she wiped her eyes again.

"Hush now," Harriet said. "Ain't nothing to apologize for. You hear?"

"Yes, ma'am."

"Good." Harriet looked to the others but still held Margaret's hand. "Now, you all are Railroad folk in one way or another, but this ain't Railroad business?"

"Not as such," Wilfred said. "You see, we, um." He turned and fretted at his hat. "Well, we came into, or rather acquired—"

"We robbed a train," Talen said, her patience exhausted.

Wilfred coughed and eyed at her.

Margaret's mouth fell open.

Nelson stared at her.

Draven and Harriet started laughing.

"I don't expect we're going to offend her sensibilities telling her we robbed a train," Talen said to Margaret and Wilfred.

"I do appreciate your directness," Harriet said, still chuckling.

"We didn't rob it for the gold," Talen said. "Probably best not to involve you in that part of things."

"Yeah," Wilfred said, rubbing his brow, "because that's the troubling part."

"Point is," Talen said, "we got some gold. More than we'll ever need, and we figured you'd know how to make sure it went to some good use."

"One thing I learned over the years," Harriet said, sporting half a grin, "the Lord do provide in ways you ain't expecting."

"Ain't no worry about no one coming after it?" Nelson asked.

Harriet gave him a look.

"Just wondering how quick we'll need to put it to use is all," he said.

"Not a chance," Talen said. "It was bound for banks several states over. Though I expect you'll need to figure out creative ways to store it."

Nelson's brow furrowed. "How much are you talking about?"

"Fifty-thousand dollars," Talen said.

Nelson and Harriet both froze for a long, silent moment.

"Did you say fifty-thousand?" Nelson asked.

"Or there abouts," Talen said. "We're keeping a couple bags, so maybe only forty."

Wilfred gave her a withering look, though Talen genuinely didn't understand why.

Margaret likewise seemed distressed.

Draven's laughter returned as a rumbling chuckle.

"Why are you staring at me like that?" Talen asked. "I ain't said nothing we ain't talked about and agreed to."

"But you don't just tell folks you're giving them stolen money," Wilfred said.

"Especially not someone like Harriet Tubman," Margaret said.

"Hush now, both of you," Harriet said. "Firstly, I ain't no saint. I just done what I knew was right. Second, you and I both know laws don't make something right." She pinned Wilfred in place with her gaze. "We both lived under laws that would've bound us, all our kin, and all our children's children in chains."

"Yes, ma'am," Wilfred said. "That is a fact. I just didn't want to assume nothing."

"Well, you still ain't, so there you go," Harriet said sternly, but with the hint of a smile. She closed her eyes, looked up and put her hands together.

Nelson did the same.

"Praise the Lord," Harriet said.

"Gonna be able to help a whole lot of folk," Nelson said.

"I'll be able to build that home for the elderly," Harriet said.

In that moment, Talen realized that her tension and anxiety had vanished. Not just her unease at coming to a human town, but even the long, lingering bits that she'd been carrying for years. She wasn't sure when it left, but it did feel a little strange, as if she'd put down a heavy load she hadn't even realized she'd been carrying.

"He got the right of it though," Nelson said. "We'll need to figure out a good place to keep it. Ain't like we can store it at the bank."

"Hiding things ain't never been a problem," Harriet said and looked to the group. "Bless you. God bless you all for this."

"Obviously it wasn't possible to bring it on horseback," Talen said. "But we'll fetch it back to you once we leave."

"I got a wagon," Nelson said. "Me and Harriet's brother John can follow you back to the airship and load it up there."

"Best bring some shooters with you as well," Talen said.

"You said no one would be looking for it," Nelson said, his smile fading away.

"That ain't what I mean," Talen said.

"Even good people can turn bad when gold is involved," Draven said, her tone flat, but the words landed with the weight of someone who knew the shame of that statement.

"Won't be a problem," Nelson said.

"Looks like y'all staying the night after all," Harriet said.

"How do you figure?" Talen asked.

"You expect I'm just going to let you all be on your way without feeding you and putting you up?" Harriet asked. "Even if this weren't a boarding house, and you hadn't just gave us a load of gold, my mama raised me to tend to guests."

"I didn't mean nothing," Talen said. "We wouldn't want to impose."

Draven said. "We got food and quarters on the ship."

"If you don't want to put me out, you won't refuse my hospitality," Harriet said, her tone leaving no room for argument or discussion.

"If you do," Nelson said, "you'd be the first ever told her that."

Harriet gave him another hard look.

Draven and Wilfred nodded. Margaret's eyes seemed ready to leap out of her head and dance around the room.

"I guess we're staying," Talen said.

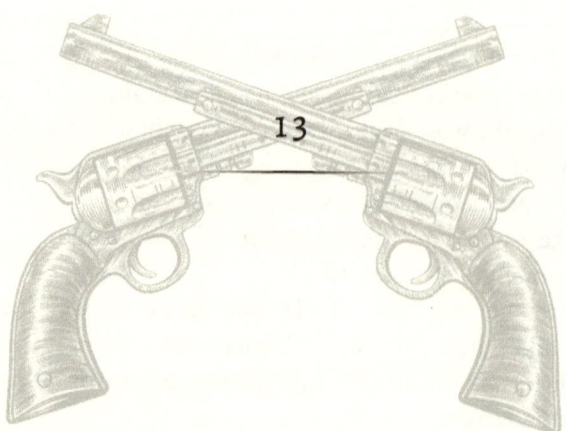

13

Nelson went to get Harriet's brother, John and the wagon, while Harriet showed Talen and the others to their rooms for the night. Each had a single bed, a dresser and mirror, a side table, and a wooden chair. Though small, the rooms were larger than the quarters on the Cumulus. Talen debated asking to stay in the barn with the horses, but decided against it for fear of offending Harriet's generosity. By the time they'd decided who would sleep where, Nelson had returned with John.

As they headed outside, Talen noticed Margaret was leaning heavy on her cane and favoring her bad leg.

"No reason for all of us to go," Talen said to Draven and Margaret. "Why don't you two stay behind and lend a hand finding a place for the gold?"

Margaret hesitated and looked ready to argue, but Draven spoke up.

"Good idea," she said. "I've done enough time in the saddle."

Harriet met Talen's gaze and after a moment, nodded subtly. "Come on, child," she said to Margaret, "I'll put on some coffee first and you can tell me more about your mama."

Margaret wasn't a fool and probably saw through all this, but accepted the offer with a smile and turned to Harriet. "It'd be my honor."

As Harriet led Margaret and Draven to the kitchen, Wilfred and Talen went outside.

A large, powerfully built man, stood next to Nelson. Both of them held mundane rifles at their sides, and behind them was a small wagon pulled by a gentle-looking, speckled mare.

Nelson made introductions and after Talen tucked her hair into her hat, they all set out for the airship. They made small talk, but Talen was happy for Wilfred to do most of it. She figured John and Nelson meant well enough, but based on her experience with humans, eventually they'd start asking questions and she just wasn't in the mood to satisfy human curiosity about elves.

Gaoth got antsy a few times, eager to run free again, but, much to his chagrin, Talen kept him reined in. Thankfully, without Joseph setting the pace, they reached the Cumulus in less than half the time it'd taken to get to Harriet's house.

"I thought you said your ship was sitting in the lake?" John asked as they rode along the shoreline.

Wilfred smiled and pointed at the Cumulus, now easily visible, less than a mile ahead. "She's right there."

Nelson and John exchanged a look, glanced where Wilfred had indicated, but his wards had them blind to it.

"I know my eyes ain't what they used to be," Nelson said, "but either that craft of yours is a tiny thing, or you got eyes like an eagle."

"What he is," Talen said, speaking up for the first time since they set out, "is a master of his craft."

Wilfred tipped his hat to her.

"And mighty proud of himself as well," she said.

Wilfred explained the wards to them, and with some effort and focusing, Nelson and John managed to see past the magic. Both their eyes widened and they gaped for a moment before breaking into laughter.

"I heard tell of some marvels of magical crafting," John said, "but I ain't never heard of someone hiding something that big in plain sight."

Wilfred beamed at the praise, and Talen let him have it. She would, however, be sure to give him a hard time about it later. And from his expression, he knew as much, and expected nothing less.

When they reached the Cumulus, Talen slid from the saddle and deactivated the charms.

Nelson and John took in the craft, and Talen couldn't blame them. Living on board made it easy to take for granted what a feat of engineering brilliance it was. It looked like a cross between a sailing ship and a flat bottom river boat, but fully enclosed, and covered in as much brass as wood. Instead of a paddle wheel, four metal rings—two on each side—stuck out of the ship, narrow windmill blades in each.

"Sit tight," Talen said after a minute of them gawking. "I'll fetch the gold."

"Reckon it'll go faster if we help," John said. "Four of us can get it done in one trip."

Talen ignored him and headed into the cargo bay.

"Y'all ain't never spent time around elves, have you?" Wilfred asked.

"No, sir," Nelson said. "No time at all."

Talen cleared away the scattering of sundries used to conceal the gold boxes, hefted one onto each shoulder, and carried them out to the wagon.

When John saw her, his brows furrowed. He passed his rifle to Nelson and scurried into the back of the wagon.

"Let me help you," he said, reaching out.

Talen turned so he could reach.

With a grunt of surprise, John lifted and set the box down just behind the seat.

"Careful," Talen said, "they're heavy."

John's face split with a smile, and he started laughing. "That they are, though ain't nobody ever guess by how you're toting them."

Talen let herself grin and passed him the second box. In a matter of minutes, she'd reset the wards on the Cumulus, and they were riding back to Harriet's house.

They arrived to find another wagon sitting off to one side, empty.

Talen pulled her hat low and reached for her spell iron.

Wilfred's hand slipped into his coat, doubtless for his shooter.

"Ain't no cause for worry," Nelson said. "We get folks through all the time. Don't mean there's trouble about."

"You'll forgive me being overly cautious," Talen said. "Seeing as it's legal to shoot me dead just for being here."

"You're a guest of my sister," John said, climbing from the wagon. "If someone wants you, they got to get through us first."

Talen didn't quite know what to say to that. She understood Harriet's family knew well what it was like to be hunted and hated. Even so, it still was an odd feeling for strangers to come to her defense.

"I'll go see what's about," Nelson said and clambered out of the wagon. "I'm sure it ain't nothing to fret over, but wait here all the same."

He left his rifle and went into the house.

Talen's index finger tapped the handle of her spell iron as she glanced about for anything amiss. Nothing stood out to her, and all her instincts said there wasn't anything to fear, but while rashness might cost your life, caution cost nothing but time.

A couple minutes later, Nelson emerged from the house. He walked with ease, though his face was stony. "Got a new boarder," he said. "Came in on the Railroad. Harriet is getting the girl settled and your dwarf friend is talking with the conductor that brought her here."

Wilfred and Talen exchanged a look. Both were obviously curious about the details, but they also knew it wasn't any of their business. Add to that, if someone was escaping something that required the Railroad, the last thing needed was a couple of strangers nosing about.

"Let's get the wagon unloaded," Talen said.

"Reckon the barn is good a place as any," Nelson said. "At least it'll do for now."

Over the next half hour or so, they stashed the eight bags of gold coins in various spots under loose floorboards in the barn. While Talen set to breaking apart the iron-strapped boxes to be added to the firewood pile, Wilfred tended to the horses, including Joseph whom he brought in from outside. Once that was done, John made his goodbyes, and the others returned to the house.

Inside, they found Harriet and Margaret in the sitting room, a young Black girl sitting on the sofa between them. The child—she couldn't be much into her teens—bore the same harried and exhausted look Talen remembered seeing on many of the Railroad's passengers.

The girl was also clearly terrified, despite being well away from wher-ever she'd left. She sat with shoulders and arms in, as if trying to make herself as small as possible, and her gaze never lingered on one thing for more than a second. She kept a white-knuckled hold on a small cloth bag with one hand, the other held Harriet's.

In a chair across the room, a white man of an age to Harriet, sat quietly next to Draven and sipped a cup of coffee. He smiled at Wilfred and Nelson, and when he saw Talen, stood.

Talen arched an eyebrow. It took her a moment to remember Margaret had told her that human men would stand when a woman came into the room. She hadn't understood the point then, and still didn't, but she kept quiet about it.

The girl shrank back a bit.

"We got everything squared away," Nelson said to Harriet.

"Thank you," Harriet said without turning to him. She patted the girl's hand. "It's all right, Cordelia. These are the folk we was telling you about."

"They're the ones who saved me," Margaret said in a soft tone. "That's Wilfred, and that's Talen."

"Pleasure to meet you, miss," Wilfred said through his most disarming grin.

"Cordelia," Talen said but didn't make any sudden movement, lest the poor kid jump straight out of her skin.

Draven caught Talen's eye, and the dwarf seemed as troubled as Talen had ever seen.

"Mr. John Haddox here," Harriet said, motioning to the white man, "he was kind enough to bring Cordelia up from Pennsylvania."

Haddox put his hand over his heart. "Just doing as the Lord asks of us all."

"Amen, Mr. Haddox," Harriet said then gave Cordelia a kindly smile. "You look like you could use something to eat, child."

Cordelia's eyes widened, and she swallowed.

Harriet winked. "I thought so. You know, when I finally got to a safe place, hunger hit me like it never did before. And the food never tasted so good."

The whisper, of a hint, of a ghost of a smile crossed Cordelia's face.

"Nelson," Harriet said, "would you take Cordelia into the kitchen and make up a plate for her?"

"Be happy to," Nelson said and held out his hand.

Cordelia looked from Harriet to Margaret and back.

"You know, I could use something to eat myself," Margaret said. "Would you mind if I joined you?"

Cordelia's shoulders relaxed just a bit, and she nodded.

As sorry as Talen was for Cordelia, she was just as grateful Margaret had been here when the girl arrived. If there was a kinder, gentler soul than Margaret, Talen couldn't imagine such a person.

"After that, I'll help you get settled in your room so you can sleep in a proper bed," Margaret said. "How does that sound?"

"Thank you," Cordelia said so softly it was barely audible.

Margaret pulled herself to her feet, took up her cane, and offered her free hand to Cordelia. "Come on, sweetie."

Cordelia took Margaret's hand and as they left the room with Nelson, Margaret glanced back to Talen, her expression grave.

Talen didn't know what was going on, or if it related to what Cordelia had escaped, but whatever it was, it was bad enough to unnerve both Margaret and Draven.

Once Cordelia, Nelson, and Margaret were gone, Harriet stood. "Why don't we all get some air and leave them to eat in peace?"

Talen and Wilfred both looked to Draven who nodded and got to her feet. Everyone filed out, following Harriet a short way from the house.

"That child looks fit to die of fright from her own shadow," Wilfred said.

"You don't know the half of it," Draven said.

Talen turned to Harriet. "I reckon this is where you fill us in?"

"It is," Harriet said and let out a breath. "Been times I got a vision, and thought I knew what it meant, only to learn down the line I had it wrong. That's what happened with the one I told you about."

"Well, the Lord works in mysterious ways," Haddox said. "But also toward good."

Talen bit her tongue. If their god worked toward good, he was taking his own sweet time about it.

"Amen, Mr. Haddox," Harriet said and then turned to Talen. "While you and Wilfred was gone, Miss Draven and Mrs. Jameson told me that elves have a special dislike for stained and dark magic. Is that so?"

Talen narrowed her eyes, the unease that had fled earlier now began to creep back. "It is. Though it's more of a sacred duty to protect magic."

"Ah," Harriet said, nodding. "Now, sacred duties. That's something I like to think I know a thing or two about. Seems we got something in common."

"I take that as a compliment," Talen said. "But, if you don't mind, I'm still mystified as to what's going on, and I'm not especially keen on that feeling."

"Apologies," Harriet said and turned to Haddox. "Mr. Haddox, would you be so kind as to enlighten our friends here?"

"Of course," Haddox said. "As you could see, Cordelia doesn't speak much, so this was all relayed to me from Mrs. Ellen Craft, from whom I took charge of the girl."

Talen narrowed her eyes. "Second-hand story?"

"I have no reason to question Mrs. Craft's veracity," Haddox said.

"Just hear the man out," Draven said. "Trust me."

"All right," Talen said. "Go on."

Haddox doffed his hat. "Thank you, ma'am."

Talen bit her tongue again but couldn't hold back the mildly exasperated sigh.

"Cordelia and her family are from a small town just on the border of Georgia and Tennessee called Aspen Hill," Haddox said. "It was, and still seems to be, home to those loyal to the Confederate cause."

Talen wanted to shake the man and tell him to get to the damned point, but she didn't.

"Maybe you should speak to the nature of the town," Draven said, "rather than its history."

"Yes, of course," Haddox said. "My apologies."

Talen wanted to shout that she'd had enough apologies, and ridiculous etiquette, but she managed to resist. For now.

Haddox swallowed. "Well, the entire town, or the vast majority of its populace, are stained."

It took Talen a moment or two for the weight of those words to settle in. "What did you say?"

"According to Mrs. Craft," Haddox said, "the entire town is stained."

"That ain't possible," Talen said. "That many stained in one place..." She shook her head. "There wouldn't be a town for long."

"Mrs. Craft said they weren't like any stained she'd ever encountered before," Haddox said. "Had the smell of corruption, the eyes, but not the madness."

Talen tasted bile and memories of putting down Elizabeth Tuller fought to rise up with it. The roused memories were washed away by a barely controlled panic. It was like standing on a redwood's highest branches and hearing a crack. At the same time though, the idea of so many stained gathered together woke a righteous indignation in her. A rage instilled in her at childhood that demanded corruption be destroyed.

"Tell her about the charms," Draven said.

"Oh, yes, of course," Haddox said. "Apart from being stained, they employ truly terrible magical wares in their attempts to maintain control over the recently freed peoples." He shook his head. "Stones that strip a person of their free will. Others that make their speech unintelligible, or even draw the very life from one person and give it to another."

Talen's blood turned to ice. The world spun around her, and she couldn't find anything to grab hold of. Even the fury, that had just moments ago stood untouched by fear and hesitation, faltered.

Haddox kept talking, but she couldn't make sense of his words. All she could do was turn over what this meant. Bad enough to find a human crafter with geas stones, but from what Haddox was describing, someone had also made babble and siphon stones. Such cruel and malicious magic had been banned by the elves for centuries, but it seemed humans just wouldn't be outdone. Humans might not have invented cruelty, but they sure seemed determined to perfect it.

The notion of an entire town of stained seemed more and more believable.

That got Talen to thinking about Elizabeth Tuller and her strange control of corruptive magic. She racked her brain trying to recall the lessons she'd learned as a child about the detestable crafts. She, like all elves, had been taught the good and the bad of their history. Specifically how, in their war-born bloodlust, they'd crafted truly cruel and appalling charms. They'd learned, almost too late, that using magic for sadistic purposes twisted the magic, turned it dark and corruptive.

Once her people realized their error, all the detestable crafts were forever banned. Additionally, as penance, the shadow wardens were created and tasked to seek out corruption and destroy it.

It was her people's mistake and, as such their burden, their responsibility.

But now, humans seemed determined to take that mistake to a new level.

"Talen?" Wilfred said, plainly not for the first time.

Talen came back to herself, but cold dread still clung to her. In that moment, she understood exactly the source of Cordelia's state.

"You alright?" Harriet asked. "You look as though someone walked across your grave."

"It's much worse than that," Talen said and turned to Haddox. "I need you to tell me everything you know. Don't matter how small or insignificant."

Talen listened intently as Haddox went over every detail Ellen Crafter had passed along to him. The importance of the information outweighed any sense of propriety, so she prodded him along when needed.

In short, Aspen Hill had embraced dark magic as true magic. They believed this truth bestowed upon them by God, and branded as forbidden by Godless abolitionists, whom they equated as tools of the devil. Once entirely dependent on slavery for their livelihoods, the town had suffered doubly from the war and then emancipation. Through loopholes, they'd found ways to once again shackle those who couldn't flee, or those who wandered too close. They made their own detestable crafts, fashioned as chains to keep people enslaved.

"According to Mrs. Crafter," Haddox said, "they even found a way to animate the dead as mindless servants."

Talen's brows drew together. "Necromancy? Plenty have tried that before, but I ain't never heard of no one succeeding." She didn't mention that some of those who tried were her ancestors.

"I only know what Mrs. Crafter told me," Haddox said.

"In a twisted way, it would fit," Wilfred said.

"What do you mean?" Talen asked.

"Being a Christian means believing that Jesus rose from the grave," Wilfred said. "If some stained figured out how to raise the dead, those who wanted to believe it could see it as proof that its use was ordained by God."

Talen had no words.

"I, for one, can't imagine how anyone that calls themselves a Christian would believe such things," Haddox said.

"Wouldn't be the first time folks turned the Word to suit their beliefs," Harriet said. "Plenty used the Good Book to keep us in chains."

"I confess I wasn't sure I believed those details," Haddox said. "But from your reaction, I think perhaps I was mistaken."

All this information, and the implications, churned in Talen's head. She supposed it was inevitable that humans would figure out their own detestable crafts. They were clever and when they set themselves to a task, weren't easily dissuaded. Which is why the very notion of humans with such terrible magics at their disposal left Talen shaken. Tuller had been bad enough. This could be magnitudes worse.

They all stood in silence for a long moment.

"I assume you want to do something about all this?" Draven asked, breaking the silence.

"You're damned right I do," Talen said. The righteous indignation that had been quieted, now answered the call for action. It redoubled, a burning sun in her soul, melting away the fear. These revelations might've left her feeling lost at sea, but what she had no doubt as to what needed doing. She had a duty as a shadow warden. "I'm going to visit Aspen Hill and see for myself what's what there." She looked at Harriet. "I'll get out all those I can, and if Mrs. Crafter has the right of it, then I'm going to burn that town, and everyone in it."

"We," Draven said. "We'll get those people out."

"Surely you're not in favor of destroying an entire town?" Haddox said to Harriet and turned to the others. "Obviously those in peril and bondage must be helped, and if there are stained, they must be dealt with, but—"

"Mr. Haddox," Harriet said, wearing an amiable smile, "I thank you for bringing Cordelia and word of this to me. Would you like to rest before departing?"

Haddox, utterly bemused glanced from Harriet's pleasant expression to Talen, Wilfred, and Draven. None bothering to look at all pleasant. "Um, no thank you," he said. "I'll be fine."

"Well then let me help you to your carriage," Harriet said.

"Pleasure meeting you all," Haddox said as Harriet, politely, escorted him away.

"Safe travels," Wilfred said, through a smile that vanished as soon as the words were out. He turned to Draven and then Talen, holding her gaze for a minute. "Reckon we should step into the barn so we can talk privately."

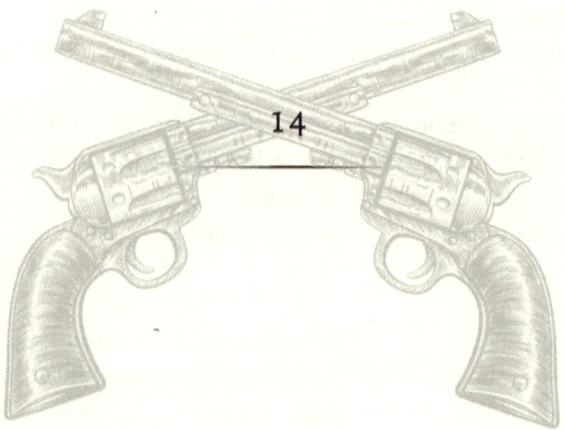

14

As soon as Draven closed the barn door, Wilfred wheeled on Talen, fire in his eyes. "What was that about?"

"What?" Talen asked, taken aback. It had been some time since she'd seen him angry. Worse, she wasn't sure what she'd done.

"You planning on going down south on your own?" he asked. "What? You just figure the rest of us would take our ease somewhere, sipping lemonade and eating cakes while you play General Sherman?"

Talen gaped for a moment. "Are you really angry that I said 'I' instead of 'we?'" She looked from Wilfred to Draven but found no help there. "I just didn't want to speak for either of you, nor Margaret for that matter."

"You sure about that?" Draven asked.

Talen furrowed her brow, genuinely mystified. "What else could it be?" She turned back to Wilfred. "You said more than once that the only way you'd go back south was in a box. I didn't want to volunteer you for something you might not be up for. I sure as hell wouldn't blame you if you didn't want to go."

"You think I'd let you go alone?" he asked.

"I know you'd have my back if we stood at the gates of hell," Talen said. "But I also know I ain't got no notion of what going back would be like for you."

Wilfred's expression softened.

Talen looked back to Draven. "And you were even more angry than

106

me when you learned how bounty crystals were made," she said. "I thought, might be, you'd want to get word to the Granite Halls about it."

Draven fixed her eyes on the floor.

"What in hellfire has gotten into you two?" she asked them both. "I thought we'd made a family on the Cumulus. You think I'm so eager to ride away from that?"

Draven shrugged. "A blind man could see you ain't one for being cooped up on a ship."

"And you rode away before," Wilfred said, a little sheepishly.

Talen swore an oath in Elven that would've made her mother blush and let out a long breath. "First," she said to Draven, "I don't know as I'll ever grow accustomed to sleeping indoors, or not riding Gaoth every day, but I ain't going nowhere. You're nearest thing I got to family now."

Draven nodded. "Same."

"And you," Talen said, turning to Wilfred. "I'd say things was a mite different when last I rode off, wouldn't you?"

He scrunched his face up and licked his lips before speaking. "When you left then, you said it was because you had a duty to your people. Ain't that what this is too?"

Talen's irritation began to wane.

"You said that geas stone was forbidden magic," Wilfred said. "And from the look on your face when Haddox was describing the other wares, I'm guessing they was too."

Talen ran a hand through her hair and let out another breath. "Technically, we didn't come up with all the detestable crafts, but we used them. I don't know that these are them, but it damn sure sounds like it." She met his gaze. "I'd hoped you know that I would've asked you to come with me last time, if I didn't know you had important things to do of your own. Now it seems the two are the same. But like I said, I don't want you to feel like you got to go back south for me. I know it was damned hard for me to go back to the Dakota territory after Whitestone Hill."

He narrowed his eyes. "I reckon I can't argue with the truth of that."

Talen put a hand on each of their shoulders. "I'm sorry I didn't choose my words better, but make no mistake, ain't no one I'd rather have with me for this, or any other job. That said, I ain't never going to speak for you, or Margaret, when you can damned well speak for yourself."

"I reckon we can forgive you then," Wilfred said, the familiar smile returning to his face.

"I reckon," Draven said.

The irritation rose again, but she fought it back and narrowed her eyes. "So charitable of you both."

The door to the barn opened and Harriet stepped inside. "Am I interrupting?"

"No, ma'am," Wilfred said. "We was just clearing up some confusion."

"Don't ma'am me," Harriet said and walked over. "Mr. Haddox has taken his leave."

"I expect we'll be taking ours as well," Talen said.

Harriet's brow furrowed.

"Not that we don't appreciate the offer to stay," Talen said. "But I reckon you understand how circumstances have changed."

Harriet nodded. "I do. If I may, I'd ask a favor of you before you go."

"Anything," Wilfred said.

"Name it," Talen said.

"Of course," Draven said.

The three of them exchanged a glance.

Harriet chuckled. "As terrible as all this is, it does my heart good to see folk stepping up when it's needed." She looked to Draven and Talen. "Especially when it really ain't your fight."

"With respect," Talen said, "it sounds like maybe it is."

"And if it's their fight," Draven said and nodded at Wilfred and Talen, "it's mine too."

"If y'all can make a family together," Harriet said, "might be there's hope for humans figuring out a way to live together too."

Talen didn't say anything, mostly because she couldn't bring herself to hope that big, or dash Harriet's with well-earned cynicism.

"So, what's the favor?" Draven said.

"Stay long enough to talk to Cordelia," Harriet said. "It'll do her good to see someone is going to help. Also, I know firsthand, she'll have a list of names of folk for you to be on the lookout for. If you're of a mind to."

Talen nodded. "Of course. Least we can do after all the girl has been through."

"Much obliged," Harriet said. "I expect she's done eating by now, and if she ain't sleeping, you can talk to her. If she is, I'll get a chance to get you something to eat."

Wilfred grinned. "Thank you, ma'am."

Harriet eyed him.

"Mrs. Tubman," he said.

"Come on," Harriet said through a hint of a smile.

They all followed her back to the house. Cordelia had decided to get some sleep, but only if Margaret agreed to stay with her. Harriet took the opportunity to make up a meal of biscuits, smoked pork, smoked chicken, fried potatoes, and carrots. Wilfred tried to help, but she shooed him away, saying when she needed help, he'd know it.

When Nelson came in to see what she was doing, he too was shooed off to do some chores.

Talen only had a couple bites of the meats, though they were delicious, and instead enjoyed the carrots. Wilfred and Draven ate as if they were afraid someone was going to take it from them.

"Ain't you eaten nothing this month?" Harriet asked.

"Nothing this good," Wilfred said after swallowing back a mouthful of food.

"I'll tell Margaret you said that," Talen said.

He blanched. "Don't be mistaken, she makes a mighty fine stew and soup, but it's been a long while since I had fresh biscuits and smoked ham."

Draven didn't pause her eating to comment.

Talen offered her meat and potatoes to Wilfred, who gladly accepted.

"Not to your liking?" Harriet asked, brows lifted.

"Not at all," Talen said. "My people just ain't big meat eaters is all. These carrots are amazing though, how'd you make them?"

Harriet shrugged. "Just some honey, butter, salt, and pepper." She brought over the dish and scooped some more onto Talen's plate. "Trick is not to cook them too long so they ain't mushy."

Talen almost declined, but it would've been rude to refuse the hospitality. The roles and responsibilities of guest and host had ancient origins, and elves took them both very seriously. This meant it was her duty, as a guest, to eat every single one of the delicious carrots. She figured it best to err on the side of politeness and also eat any leftover as well.

Draven was on her third plate, Wilfred on his second, and Talen eating the last carrot when Margaret joined them.

"Took her a bit to fall asleep, but she's out hard," Margaret said.

"Even when you ain't physically running," Harriet said and motioned for Margaret to sit, "it still feels like you are. Likely been a while since that child slept in a real bed too." She set a plate down in front of Margaret. "Now you eat up."

"I'm fully capable of making up my own—"

"Hush now," Harriet said. "Apart from being paying boarders, you're my guests."

"Well, this looks wonderful. Thank you," Margaret said and tucked in. After a couple bites, she smiled at Harriet. "Delicious, thank you so much."

"My pleasure, dear," Harriet said. "Now I reckon y'all got some things to discuss, so I'm going to see to some chores around the house. Help yourself to seconds." She nudged Draven. "Or fourths."

Draven chuckled. "I reckon I just might."

"Nice to know my food is appreciated," Harriet said and left.

Margaret ate a few bites, swallowed, and turned to Talen. "So, when do we leave for Aspen Hill?"

Talen took up the dish of carrots, and after a nod from the others, emptied it onto her plate. "Harriet asked us to talk to Cordelia before we left. Get some names of family and such to be on the lookout for. You sure you want to come along?"

Margaret's brow furrowed. "Of course. Why wouldn't I?"

Draven and Wilfred grew very attentive to their meals.

Talen gave them a sideways glance, fork midway to her mouth. "Ain't saying you wouldn't. I just want to make sure you thought this through. You ain't never been south before, and add to the usual trouble you'll find there, this is a town full of stained."

"I know," Margaret said. "Well, I don't really, but I understand it won't be like Chicago or Boston."

"That is a fact," Wilfred said.

"But you're going?" Margaret asked him.

"I am."

"Then so am I," Margaret said.

Talen nodded. "Okay, but I want you to know there's going to be killing, lots of killing. I aim to see the town burned to ash and the stained put in the ground."

Margaret considered for a moment before speaking. "I don't have your experience with violence," she said to Talen. "And while it might seem I'm opposed to it, I'm not. I don't like it, and I wish it weren't ever necessary, but I recognize that sometimes it is." She drew in a breath, as if considering her words. "From what Haddox said, these people fought to own people, or supported those who did. People like Wilfred, me, and my mother. Worse, they still think they should be able to, and they're actively working to find ways to do it. It saddens me, but I understand people like that can't be helped, they can only be stopped."

"I didn't mean to imply you weren't capable of violence, just making sure you knew what was in store."

"I doubt that I do," Margaret said. "Not really, and I don't know that I'll be much help with my gun, but I'm still going because it's the right thing to do. There are people that need help, and if I can, I'm going to."

Talen nodded again. "Good enough."

Margaret smiled, and they both went back to their food. Talen was reminded again why she loved and respected Margaret so much. And Wilfred and Draven, come to that. Everyone in their rough-and-ready family filled a different role, and Margaret was, without a doubt, the heart.

This set Talen to thinking about, and thus missing, her mother again; not that she ever stopped. Really, it just drew attention to the hole in her heart she could sometimes ignore. This in turn reminded her how long it had been—far too long—since she'd prayed to her. An error she planned on fixing in short order.

"You know just the four of us can't take on an entire town, right?" Draven asked, between bites. "Even with the Cumulus, and as good as you are, there ain't no beating their numbers. Even if it's a small town, we're likely talking about hundreds."

"They ain't soldiers," Talen said. "Which will be to our advantage."

"Some of us aren't soldiers either," Margaret said.

"But you ain't stained neither," Talen said.

"That's an advantage?" Margaret asked. "Doesn't that make us a lot easier to kill?"

"Stained don't go down easy, that's a fact," Talen said. "But they ain't unkillable. They also ain't usually one for planning, or restraint. All the same, I reckon we might get some help from them that's been put back in chains."

Wilfred swallowed a mouthful of food. "Not all of them."

"I don't expect all," Talen said. "Not even most. I know bondage ain't just about the chains, it gets into your head too. But I reckon there'll be some that are just chomping at the bit to take up arms."

Everyone looked at Draven.

Draven stared at her plate as she wiped it clean with a biscuit. Once she'd sopped everything but the enameled flowers on the dish itself, she popped the biscuit in her mouth, and slowly chewed before swallowing.

"We're gonna need us an arsenal," Wilfred said, still eyeing Draven.

She took a long drink of water, let out an exaggerated sigh, and looked around.

"You enjoying this?" Wilfred asked.

Draven chuckled. "Can't think of much better a use for my weapons than taking down slavers or stained, let alone both together."

"How much of an arsenal are we talking?" Talen asked.

"I ain't never taken a purposeful inventory," Draven said. "Never seemed a need before." She thought about it for a moment. "As far as dwarven-made, apart from my personal weapons, I got four different rail rifles. I also got plenty of human-made that I've improved." She started counting fingers. "Reckon it's a dozen repeating rifles, six double-barrel shotguns, and two dozen revolvers of various make."

Wilfred laughed. "That all?"

Draven shrugged. "I stopped collecting when I took up with you all."

"So, assuming we find people to use them, we got the arms," Talen said.

"How do you reckon we get into the town?" Wilfred asked. "Ain't like we can just land in the town square and start asking around."

"Ain't much we can do without knowing the lay of the place," Talen said and turned to Draven. "Don't suppose you happen to have a map of the place?"

Draven chuckled. "I do have a fine collection, some with impressive detail, but even my magnificence has its limits." She took a drink of water. "But I can probably draw up something good with a few passes of the town."

"And I'm sure an airship circling overhead won't be suspicious to no one," Wilfred said.

"I didn't say it'd be an easy thing to do," Draven said.

"I recall us having a similar discussion while planning the train job," Talen said. "I also recall you coming up with a fairly brilliant solution then."

"My brilliance ain't never been a subject of debate," Wilfred said, extending his pinky as he lifted his cup of water for a drink.

Margaret laughed with a mouthful of food, and Wilfred gave her an injured look.

Talen bit back her own laughter at Wilfred's reaction.

"No!" Margaret said, covering her mouth. "I wasn't suggesting you weren't brilliant, I just—"

Wilfred waved a hand. "I know you didn't."

"He just ain't used to getting laughter from his jokes," Draven said.

"Et tu, Draven?" Wilfred asked, putting a hand over his heart.

The other laughed, but Talen furrowed her brows, utterly lost.

"It's Shakespeare," Margaret said when she noticed Talen's confusion.

Talen arched an eyebrow. "That don't help it make sense. What the hell has a spear got to do with it?"

"He was an English playwright," Margaret said. "In the play Julius Caesar, the titular character is betrayed by several people, including Brutus, someone he thought was his close friend. He says 'et tu, Brute' which is Latin for 'you as well, Brutus?'"

Talen just looked at her, utterly mystified how a simple turn of phrase could have such a long and complicated origin. As much as she adored Wilfred and Margaret, humans could be incomprehensible sometimes.

"And you really didn't need a lecture on English Literature," Margaret said. "Sorry."

Talen opened her mouth to dismiss Margaret's worries.

"Don't you go apologizing for being well-read and cultured," Wilfred said and nodded at Talen. "She's just jealous she ain't as refined as you and me."

"Ain't the word I'd use," Talen said, eyes narrowed into a faux glare.

"Sophisticated?" Wilfred asked and took a tiny sip of his water. "Distinguished, perhaps?"

"Her maybe," Talen said, motioning at Margaret. "I think maybe a better word for you would be pain in the—"

"That would be four words," Wilfred said.

Margaret and Draven both laughed.

"I think we've wandered off topic a bit," Draven said.

"Perhaps." Talen turned to Wilfred. "Don't forget I know where you sleep." She tried to glare, but Wilfred made a ridiculous face and she couldn't hold back a chuckle.

"To answer your original question," Wilfred said, his tone serious again. "I did check the masking charms on the Cumulus. Like I figured, a goodly number were burned out, though not as many as I'd thought."

"Can you replace them?" Talen asked.

"Not without buying more supplies and spending a week or two crafting," Wilfred said, and then narrowed his eyes, and began to chew on his lower lip.

Talen knew him well enough to not say anything. He always told you first why it couldn't be done, but if you just let his mind work—

He opened his mouth.

"There it is," Talen said.

"What?" Wilfred asked.

"You just figured out some work around, right?" she asked.

He looked at her with a mix of confusion and surprise. "Well, maybe, but—"

"We never doubted your brilliance," Talen said and turned to Draven.

"Hold up now," Wilfred said. "If I rearrange the charms that didn't burn out, I can probably get the ship itself hidden. No, wait, the gas bladder would still be—"

"So, we do it at night," Talen said. "Most of the town will be sleeping anyway, and those that ain't likely won't notice a dark gray, giant egg-looking thing hanging in the sky."

"Yes, but—" Wilfred said.

"It'll be a full moon in a couple weeks," Draven said. "Not ideal, but, by design, the bladder don't reflect much light. Plus, if we get lucky, there'll cloud cover, which is of a similar color."

"Well, okay, but—" Wilfred said.

"You can see well enough on a dark night like that?" Margaret asked.

Wilfred threw up his hands and turned his attention back to his plate.

Talen winked at him. She had to admit, being on the other side of the playful teasing could be fun.

"Dwarves are born and raised underground," Draven said to Margaret. "We don't need much light to see." She pulled her goggles from her jacket and turned the frames until the lens went dark. "It's bright noon-day sun that presents a problem for me."

"Oh, that makes sense," Margaret said.

"So how long do you need?" Talen said to Wilfred.

"I'm allowed to speak now?" he asked.

Anyone else might've wondered if he took genuine offense, but Talen recognized the exaggerated tone. As such, she decided to play with him just a bit more.

"I'd have thought such a refined soul could pick up on subtle social cues," she said.

Wilfred stared her in silence, with no expression, for a few heartbeats.

Talen returned the level look, something she had much more experience with.

"Touché," he said after a moment and settled back into his chair, a slight smile tugging at the corners of his mouth. "I'll need a couple days to move the charms around. That's assuming none of them were damaged when we set down at the falls or here."

Talen nodded. "I reckon Harriet can help us find a safe place to hold up while we get the work done." She turned to Margaret. "Cordelia seems to have taken a shine to you, and you got the lightest touch. You okay with staying here and seeing what she knows?"

"I'm not going to push her," Margaret said.

"I wouldn't ask you to," Talen said. "She's been through enough already. Might be all she can tell you is the names of her kin. But, if she's up to it, and can tell you something about the town and the people, all the better."

"Sounds like the start of a plan," Draven said.

"I'll go talk to Harriet," Talen said and got to her feet.

"I'll join you," Wilfred said and made to stand.

Talen decided to get one more shot in and put a hand on his shoulder. "You stay and eat your fill, or as near as you can without eating her out of house and hearth. I know you ain't a fan of Margaret's soups and stews, and that's all we'll have when we leave here."

Wilfred's eyes widened.

"You don't like my soups and stews?" Margaret asked.

"No, I did not say that!" Wilfred said.

Talen grinned to herself and went outside to find Harriet.

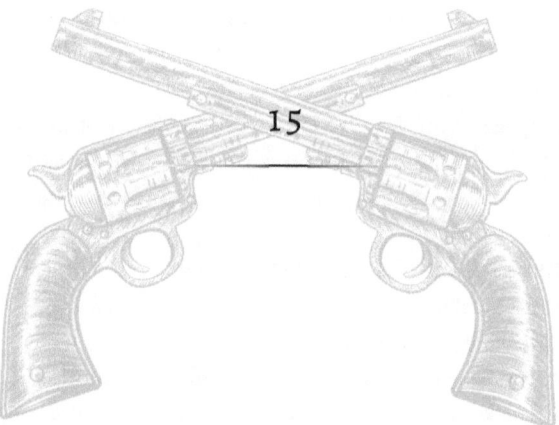

15

Harriet directed them to a small clearing on her land, onto which Draven put down with hardly a leaf disturbed. For the next two days, Talen, Wilfred, and Draven inspected charms and moved them around as needed. Wilfred broke those burnt out but still salvageable for later use. Harriet—with Margaret's help, under the guise of learning new recipes—ensured no one missed a meal. She even made it a point to have a variety of vegetables for Talen. It was strange, in a nice way, to have a human outside her circle give such thought to her preferences. Part of her wanted to dismiss this kindness as Harriet just tending to a boarder, but Talen quickly put that thought aside. It might be born from well-earned cynicism, but it insulted Harriet's obvious kindness.

On the second night, as everyone else slept, Talen lay awake, staring at the ceiling. As she often did when this happened, she saddled up Gaoth and took him for a ride. The night had an invigorating chill. As Gaoth made his way through the darkened woods, the only sound his hooves on the soft earth, Talen's mind began to wander.

What would they find at Aspen Hill? Did Mrs. Crafter have it right, or would they find this to be another instance of human exaggeration? The extent of the stained populace was secondary, of course. Getting the innocent people out, and safely, was the primary concern. Talen had little doubt as to the veracity of the stories about people held in bondage. When it came to cruel treatment, humans tended to understate the truth.

This train of thought led to worry about the charms for hiding the Cumulus and concerns over whether or not they'd work. She didn't have any doubts about the quality of the workmanship, even when Wilfred doubted himself, she never did. Rather, the charms were inherently fragile, and by Wilfred's own words, they'd already taken a beating.

Her contemplations went to their logical conclusion: the crystal in her belly and the magic it stored. It seemed that whenever she used magic, the crystal would supplement her own power with its stores. While such a boost could prove useful, in the right circumstances, it might also complicate things. Especially with more delicate wares, such as the aforementioned charms. Would she burn them out just trying to activate them?

The obvious solution was to have Margaret power them up when needed, but Talen still thought it prudent to get better control of the crystal and its power. After all, what would happen if she overcharged one of the loads for her spell irons? Would it make a pistol shot, like artillery? Or would it explode in the barrel? Even if she assumed the best-case scenario, something she never did, the wise choice would be to save that extra power for when it was really needed.

Presumably she could refill the crystal, but she'd only managed that with her healing prayers. That magic was sacred, and as near to holy as anything her people had. Magic, especially healing magic, wasn't to be used frivolously or for convenience. Power gifted to you, even by a source as plentiful as the sun, was to be treated with the reverence and respect of any gift. Besides, she'd gotten along just fine without the crystal's added energy before. No reason to rely on it now.

If she were honest about all of this, though, a part of her wanted to purge the crystal and release the energy back into the world around her. It was in part because, while it might've saved her from being overwhelmed by the corruption at the falls, it also left her essentially blind to it. Dark magic's stain might be anathema to her people, but not being able to sense it left her unnerved. Add to that, she had no idea if the crystal would work against a stained again, as it had with Tuller, if it was already full up. Granted, Tuller hadn't been just another stained, but she'd gone down like any other stained when touched with a crystal.

Not that Talen was keen on using it that way again. It'd nearly killed her after all. But, in the end, it'd also been the only thing that had stopped Elizabeth Tuller.

Ever aware of her state of mind, Gaoth came to a stop in a secluded clearing, looked back at her, and chuffed.

Talen eyed the horse for a long moment. She didn't know if he could actually read her mind, though if asked to wager one way or the other, she'd bet that he could. He could certainly read her heart.

"All right," she said and slid from the saddle. "I get the hint."

She walked to the middle of the clearing, drew both spell irons, and focused. As expected, the instant she began to channel magic, the crystal released its own. The runes and sigils on her irons burst to life, filling with bright spellfire that damn near blinded her. She cursed and doused the irons.

Gaoth whinnied.

She glared at the horse, and though she might be imagining it, she'd have sworn he smiled at her. Though she loved Gaoth deeply, he could be a mite exasperating.

After taking a deep breath, Talen tried again, carefully controlling the flow of power. Again, the crystal opened and a flood of additional magic surged forth. It was like trying to hold back a flash flood with her bare hands.

It took a couple hours of failure, and more than a little extra concentration, but eventually Talen figured out how shunt the crystal and draw only on her own power. She spent the next few hours after that practicing, over and over again, making sure she had it down pat. Mind, she was calm, and no one was shooting at her. Could be it wouldn't work so well when it mattered most, but this was the best she could do.

Satisfied, she holstered her irons and walked back to Gaoth.

Her hand drifted to her belly, fingers pressing against the crystal.

Gaoth looked at her, mouth full of dried shrubs. He chewed a couple of times, then spit it out.

"You wouldn't be so picky if you didn't know there was oats waiting back at the farm," Talen said, as she stroked his neck.

Gaoth shoved his muzzle into her coat pocket.

"Hey, that ain't how I raised you," she said, pushing him away. "If you want the apple, ask for it. Use your words."

He sighed and chuffed.

"All right, near enough." She smiled, pulled the apple from her pocket, and used her knife to cut it into pieces before feeding them to him.

He chomped happily but eyed her.

"I know it's mealy," she said. "Ain't been no apples in months, so just be glad you get any."

As he chewed the last bits, Talen rubbed at the crystal and wondered, yet again, if she was making the right choice. By keeping the crystal full, was she disrespecting the magic? She didn't know.

Her mother would know.

And I would too if I wasn't putting off praying to her, she thought.

Talen genuinely didn't know why she hadn't been more diligent about it. There were still some lingering thoughts of being unworthy of her mother's love and wisdom, but somehow, she knew that wasn't the reason.

Gaoth finished his apple, so Talen put that thought aside, saddled up, and they went back to Harriet's place.

The next day they got an early start and finished the charms just before sunset. After supper, Talen, Wilfred, Draven, Nelson, and Harriet stood in an evenly space circle around the Cumulus.

"Just about ready," Margaret shouted from the deck above them.

Talen had told Wilfred about her experiments the night before, and during the brief discussion, suggested it would be safer for Margaret to work the charms. He'd agreed, and while he'd been interested in her musings on the crystal, ultimately, he didn't understand her choice not to use it. He couldn't, really. Humans saw magic differently. However, being Wilfred, he didn't need to understand. If she had a reason to not want to use it, that was good enough for him.

"Okay, I'm starting," Margaret said.

Talen looked over the ship's hull and the dozens of charms placed around it but didn't see any change. "Slow and easy," she said. "Take your time."

"I know," Margaret said.

"And don't push yourself," Wilfred said.

"I know!" Margaret said, her tone more than a little impatient.

Talen and Wilfred glanced at each other and kept quiet after that. After several long seconds, sections between the charms turned seemingly translucent. It took another minute or so, but soon the entire underside of the craft was wrapped in the magical cloak. To those on the ground, the gas bladder hung on its own, the lines running down to nothing but open air.

Margaret's disembodied head and shoulders appeared, which was both disconcerting and amusing.

"Did it work?" she asked a little out of breath.

"I don't see nothing," Nelson said.

"Me neither," Harriet said.

"All good here," Draven said.

"Looks good here, no gaps," Talen said.

"I'm calling this test a success," Wilfred said, a broad smile on his face. "Go ahead and shut it off."

Margaret's floating head vanished again.

A minute or two later, the Cumulus reappeared, quite suddenly compared to how it had vanished. Soon after, the gangway lowered, and Margaret stepped off.

"Well done," Talen said to her.

"Thanks," Margaret said, grinning, and breathing heavy. "Never worked my magic, um muscles I guess, that hard before."

"Couldn't have done better myself," Talen said.

Margaret laughed. "You're a liar, but I appreciate the gesture."

"That was about the most amazing thing I ever did see," Nelson said, as he and Harriet approached. "Or even heard of."

Harriet nodded. "The Lord has surely blessed you with a gift for crafting."

"Thank you, ma'am, I just try and do good with what the Lord gave me," Wilfred said.

Talen bit her tongue, again. She never liked how humans seemed to credit their god instead of their own hard work and dedication. Wilfred did indeed have a natural talent for crafting, but he'd also worked damned hard learning his trade. It probably wouldn't bother Talen as much if humans also credited failures to their god, but those they relegated to themselves. If anyone asked Talen, she'd say their god seemed a petty and fickle sort, and hardly worth such devotion. But then, no one ever did ask—

A shadow moved in the trees and caught Talen's attention. Instead of looking hard in that direction, she focused and listened for anything about. It took a moment to get past the sounds of those around her, but Talen thought she could make out another four or five people in the woods. It might've been animals, or maybe neighbors coming to visit, but

Talen suspected friendly visitors would come up the road, and they wouldn't be surrounding them.

"Come on, child," Harriet said to Margaret, taking her hand. "You need to sit for a spell and get something to eat."

"I think I need some water," Margaret said, letting Harriet usher her along.

"Of course," Harriet said. "Nelson, get the girl some water."

"Yes, ma'am," he said and hurried ahead of them into the house.

Talen put a hand on Wilfred's shoulder, stopping his pilgrimage to Harriet's table, and nodded to Draven to wait.

"Y'all coming?" Harriet asked, looking back.

"We'll be along directly," Talen said. "Just need to check the *rollers*."

Wilfred and Draven immediately tensed, recognizing the old code word for slave catcher.

Harriet's expression went stony, and she gave a single nod. "Best hurry along, I ain't gonna keep it warm for you."

"No, ma'am," Talen said and forced a laugh.

"Where?" Draven asked, calmly opening her coat, and resting her hands on her belt, inches from the handles of her pistols.

"Four or five of them," Talen said just above a whisper. "All around us but probably coming in from the woods to the south." She looked to Wilfred. "You heeled?"

"It's in the house."

"All right, you head inside, nice and easy," Talen said. "Make sure Cordelia and the others are somewhere safe, and back up Harriet however she needs."

He nodded.

Talen turned to Draven. "We'll board the ship. Once I'm out of sight, I'll step into the shadows and see who's about. Hopefully I'm just spooked and it ain't but some deer or the like."

"Don't take too long," Wilfred said, his usual, easy smile firmly in place, and started toward Harriet's house. "I ain't promising to save you nothing."

"You don't save me nothing and you'll be walking," Draven said, as she and Talen went to climb up the gangway.

As soon they were inside the ship, Draven drew both her pistols, turned to face the open doorway, and took aim, ready to gun down anyone who came into view. Talen wrapped herself in shadow, turned on her heel, and sprinted from the Cumulus, silent as the night.

Once she reached the tree line, Talen drew her knives as she ran, careful to avoid any low-hanging branches, loose rocks, or twigs that might give her away. It didn't take her long to spot the first of the mysterious lurkers. He was human, naturally, of middling years and dressed in rumpled, filthy clothes. The fact he carried a spell iron disturbed her, but not as much as the old leather glove covering the hand holding it. The faint scent of blood drifted on the air. Thankfully, he didn't have an eye piece, but that didn't mean his compatriots didn't, so Talen crouched down low within lunging distance and watched.

The old fear that rose up whenever she crossed paths with the Red Right Hand—religious zealots and magic purists who felt it their holy duty to butcher elves—made an appearance and started chewing on her innards. It wasn't as powerful as before Boston, but it hadn't faded entirely neither. After a moment, she pushed the dread down with anger and vitriol, which had only grown stronger in the last several months.

Once her head was clear, Talen debated risking it and running for the house to warn Harriet and the others, but something gave her pause.

Why hadn't they attacked?

If they were here to bring down Talen, they wouldn't have given her a chance to see them coming. Which meant they were here for something—or someone—else and hadn't spotted that Talen was elf.

Could they be here for Cordelia?

Might be. Them showing up so soon after her seemed a bit much for a coincidence. Talen didn't know if slave catchers were still a thing after the states' war. Weren't supposed to be slaves anymore, but Aspen Hill sure sounded—as was often the case— like humans had just found a clever new word for it.

Could also be that these Red Hands were confederates looking to do Harriet some harm. New York seemed a long way to come for one woman, even one as well-known as Moses herself. That led back to Cordelia, but who would hire Red Hands to find and capture a child? And why? It had to be someone in Aspen Hill, and as Red Hand stalkers didn't come cheap, someone with power and money. That answer seemed to fit the detail, and it wasn't as if the Red Hand hadn't worked for a stained before. They might not have known Elizabeth Tuller had been stained herself, but they knew damned well she was dabbling in stained magic.

A thought wriggled its way up that turned her blood to ice.

What if these Red Right Hand were stained themselves?

As if Red Hand weren't bad enough on their own, she really didn't like the thought of one gone stained, much less a whole pack of them.

She started chiding herself for not returning the stored magic in the crystal back into the world. If she'd done the right thing, she'd know for sure if any of these stalkers were stained. Was that mistake going to cost Wilfred, Margaret, Harriet, or Cordelia their lives?

Just like all those who died at Whitestone Hill? Or at home—

Her hands started to shake, so she gripped her knives tighter, and tried to focus on the here and now. She put up a wall to keep the memories back. This wasn't the time for self-pitying or second guessing. There was work to do.

If she didn't pull herself together, people she loved might die.

More people I love.

The gentle warmth of the crystal in her belly offered a bulwark against the rising fear. Adding that to the ever-present pyre of righteous indignation that burned at the center of her soul, she washed away the fear and self-doubt. It was time for doing, not thinking. She had plenty of questions. What she needed were answers. Unfortunately, only the Red Hand had any right now, which meant she'd need to take at least one alive.

She swore silently to herself, and then set to studying the first stalker. He had his back to a tree but was looking over one shoulder intently. Talen followed his gaze and spotted another human. They exchanged some hand signals, which Talen didn't know, and then the second Red Hand turned away and gestured toward the darkness. Luckily, Talen's eyes were better than the stalkers', and she spotted the third Red Hand. Unfortunately, she couldn't see who he gestured to. However, if they kept to the spacing of the first three, she had a good idea where the last would be and that they were surrounding Harriet's house.

Looking back to the first stalker, she made a calculated guess that he was the leader. That being the case, if she took him out quick and quiet, the confusion would buy her some time. Clearly these boys weren't expecting a fight before they were ready.

Talen sheathed one of her knives and waited for her moment.

As soon as the second stalker turned his attention from the first, Talen made her move. She covered the distance between them in an instant, covered the stalker's mouth, pinning him to the tree, and drove her knee into his crotch so hard the large maple creaked and shook. His eyes went wide with shock and pain, and the telltale swirls of black tendrils of stained magic that danced in the whites.

She drove her knife between his ribs, twisting the blade back and forth half a dozen times, doing her best to turn his fetid heart into a shredded lump of meat.

He gasped for a breath that wouldn't come and jerked, staring right at her—but not seeing—in confusion.

"Let the dark magic mend that, *juarchian*," she whispered.

When the darkness drained from his eyes, she lowered him to the ground, face down. That's when she saw the torches he carried.

The bastards were planning on burning Harriet's place down. Rage flared at the thought of Wilfred and Margaret trapped inside. That's when she reminded herself that they were far from helpless. Add to that, they had a woman who'd survived a life in chains, a ninety-mile journey to freedom, and then countless trips back into slaver territory. All before fighting in the states' war.

Talen took comfort in these facts. With renewed surety, and still wrapped in shadow, she hurried toward—what she hoped—was the other end of the stalker's line.

Despite being cloaked in magical shadow, Talen kept low and to mundane darkness. She passed four more Red Hands, all with spell irons drawn but dark.

"George?" someone, presumably the second stalker, whispered harshly behind her.

She still had a couple dozen paces between her and the fifth Red Hand, the last in the line.

"Damn it, George," Red Hand two said. Heavy boots tromped over leaves and twigs in what he probably thought was quiet. "If you're taking a piss, I'm gonna split your—what the hell?"

Talen focused on Red Hand five's throat and drew her second knife.

"Boys they're onto us!" Red Hand two shouted. "Light em up!"

Red Hand five turned to the source of the shout and lit his iron.

In the corner of her eye, Talen saw the unmistakable flicker of the other spell irons lighting up.

The crack of mundane shots split the air.

Talen closed her eyes, bent low, set her shoulder, and charged the last couple of yards.

Bright blue light shone through her eyelids, an instant before she plowed into Red Hand five. Her shoulder sank into his soft midsection, driving the breath from him, and they both hit the ground.

His iron went dark, and he gasped for air.

Talen drew back with her knives and opened her eyes.

His widened, and like his compatriot, oily black tendrils roiled in the whites as he looked frantically for his attacker. Realization dawned in his tainted eyes, and he swung his spell iron in a desperate attempt to pistol whip his invisible attacker.

"There's a leaf—"

His shout died as Talen dodged his clumsy blow and slit his throat with one knife, so deep only his spine kept her from taking his head off. She buried the other in his chest, slicing up his heart. She turned her face away to avoid the spray of blood, but a few drops landed on her cheek.

In her periphery came the dancing blue light of a spell iron.

"Jimmy?" someone said from behind her. "Holy shit!"

Talen spun to find a tall, lanky Red Hand staring right at her, spell iron leveled. He wore a leather eyepatch over his left eye, and at its center was a glittering red jewel.

His right eye went wide. "Leafer!"

Magic spat from his spell iron.

Talen rolled twice to her right, and then back to her left, narrowly avoiding the kinetic blasts that tore deep furrows in the earth.

The stalker tried to keep a bead on her to fire again, but he was just barely too slow.

She sprang forward and slashed out for the closest part of him, his arm. Her knife sliced through the flesh just below his blood-stained glove, deep enough that he'd be dead if he didn't get it tended to... and wasn't stained.

He didn't drop his spell iron, or even lose enough concentration for it to go dark.

Thankfully, she did manage to knock it wide.

Before he could draw down on her again, she stepped close, inside his reach, and drove a knife into his belly over and over.

He grunted, wobbled, and clubbed at her with his iron.

The bastard was strong, but Talen shifted, taking the blows at an angle so they didn't break her shoulder. She was still going to be bruised all to hell though.

It soon became obvious that the blade wouldn't be enough to put him down, and the moment she stopped, she'd be in worse trouble. She needed to get away from him, draw her spell iron, and fire it, before he could put her down with his own.

Unfortunately, even Talen couldn't move that fast.

Buying for time, she drove an elbow into his face, and got a satisfying wet snap of breaking bone.

"Leafer bitch!" the Red Hand spat. Saliva mixed with blood spattered Talen's face.

More cracks of mundane gunshots sounded, followed by various shouts, but Talen couldn't place where it came from or who was doing the shouting.

Neither shots nor shouts seemed to distract the Red Hand a bit. Not even the broken jaw—which had already started to shift back into place— bothered him.

"*Dani orin!*" Talen said and tried to drive a knee into his groin, but only caught his thigh.

"Talen!" Draven shouted from behind the Red Hand. "Down!"

Talen twisted, dropped to the ground, and then tumbled to one side.

The stalker leveled his spell iron at her and a series of whumps sounded behind him.

His face vanished in a cloud of red mist.

He stumbled forward a step or two, his spell iron flickering before it went dark, and he fell to the ground.

The scene was so unsettling, it took Talen a moment to come back to herself.

"*Terisan ut marrin!*" she said, looking at the foul viscera settling to the ground. Her stomach twisted and threatened to join it. Good thing she'd moved far enough away to avoid being showered by it.

Draven emerged from the darkness, dwarven rifle at her shoulder. She spotted the body, put another slug into his back, right through his spine, and then scanned the area.

"Talen, you here?"

"I am," she said, letting her shadow cloak fall away.

"Well, on your feet," Draven said, offering her hand. "I heard at least three more moving on Harriet's house. Wilfred and them are keeping the bastards behind cover, but it ain't going to be long before they decide to put some fire spells through the windows and set the place ablaze."

Talen took just long enough to curse herself for dawdling and took Draven's hand.

The dwarf pulled her up with as much effort as lifting a small stone.

"This one had an eyepiece," Talen said, sheathing her knives and drawing both her spell irons as they crept around to the front of the house. "Safe to figure the others might as well."

Draven nodded. "They know we're behind them, but I don't think they know how many we are."

Talen gestured at the dwarven rifle. "We get close enough, I don't reckon any sort of cover will keep them safe from that thing."

Draven chuckled and patted the weapon. "Well, Wilfred here won't blow through a boulder, but he'll chew through a good-sized tree with a few shots."

Talen stopped and looked at Draven. "You named your rifle Wilfred?"

Draven flushed. "You ain't going to tell him, are you?"

"Hell no," Talen said through a grin. "Wouldn't be no living with him if I did. Now come on, hopefully there's only the three you heard."

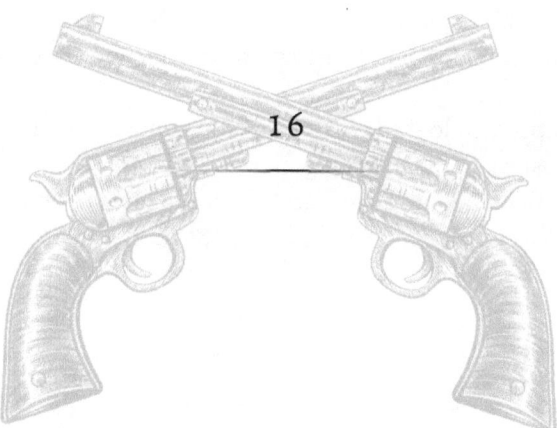

16

Talen and Draven swung wide so as not to get pinned between the Red Hand and Harriet's house. The mundane gunshots had gone mostly quiet, but the duo did their best to keep low and stay quiet as they moved from tree to tree. Draven had a natural advantage in the former, but her heavy boots and solid frame were about as quiet as a landslide.

Something moved behind a large oak ahead.

Talen stopped and held up her hand.

Draven stopped just beside her, crouched low, and lifted her rifle to her shoulder.

Talen listened. She wasn't sure, but it sounded like there were only two, though from the stench, it could've been a couple dozen.

Draven said there were three left, but Talen had only counted five total. She'd killed two, Draven dropped the last, which meant by Talen's count, these two should be the last. But what if Draven had it right? That'd mean one unaccounted for, probably lying in wait until he had a clear shot.

"Listen here, Tubman!" someone shouted from behind the tree. "You and yours ain't got to die today. We ain't here for you, we just want the girl you took in. Send her out, and we'll be on our way."

"Lord don't take to liars," Harriet shouted back, seemingly unperturbed. "So, you best get on back where you came from 'fore I send you to Him to answer for your evils!"

"I ain't no liar!" the man said. "Hand on the Bible!"

"We ain't really though, right?" a second Red Hand asked, in a whisper. "Let em go, I mean?"

"Hell no," the first said. "We'll drag the lot back with us. Plenty will pay to see Tubman strung up."

Rage rose up in Talen's belly, and she felt a deep need to see these men die in terrible ways. Fury wouldn't do no one no good though. She needed a level head to think this though and figure the next move. At least she knew they'd come for Cordelia, though she still had no notion as to why.

These weren't just graybacks with a grudge, they were Red Hand stalkers. Sure, they was also stained, but they seemed to have most of their wits and sense still. A fact Talen found more than a little disturbing.

Question was, why would a pack of Red Hand chase a girl across the country? Or why would someone hire them to? Had to be mighty important for them to move so quick as to arrive just a few days after Cordelia.

Talen pushed those questions aside. The answers could wait until the shooting was done. First, she needed to know exactly how many were left, and where they were.

Talen turned to Draven and opened her mouth to whisper a rough plan.

"Why ain't we just kicking in the door and dragging the girl out?" asked the second Red Hand in a low whisper. "They ain't been shooting nothing but bullets. We got the Preacher's blessing. Bullets ain't but a mosquito bite for us now."

That caught Talen's attention.

"Because they ain't all inside the house you nitwit," said the first, just as quietly, but clearly impatient. "Or did you forget someone took out George, Frank, and Jimmy?"

"You don't know they're dead. George has been yapping about finding some sweet, young Yankee girls since we left."

"George is a bigger idiot than you, but Frank and especially Jimmy wouldn't look for fun 'til the job was done."

"If anyone is out there, Billy will find them. I want to do me some killing. I say we light the house up. When they run, we grab those we want and kill the rest."

There was a smack.

"Because paper burns, idiot," the first said. "You want to wind up hanging from the dark ash because the Preacher's book went up in a fire?"

Preacher's book? Talen hadn't seen any book. But she had seen Cordelia holding on to a cloth bag when she first arrived. In fact, thinking back, had she ever seen the girl not holding tight to it? Talen hadn't thought much of it at the time, those fleeing chains rarely had any possessions to speak of, which made them all precious.

At least Talen knew they wouldn't burn Harriet's place without getting a hold of the book first, which was something. That might buy some time.

Talen leaned in close to Draven. "There's two behind that tree," she whispered and motioned to it.

Draven nodded.

"There's a third out there looking for us," Talen said. "They're here for Cordelia, or something she has."

Draven's expression turned cold and hard. "Ain't going to let that happen."

"Damn right," Talen said. "I'll go hunt for the third. You stay here and watch these two. If they move, or give you a clear shot, aim for the head or heart."

"Can't promise I won't take off arms or legs first, but I get your meaning," Draven said and sighted down her rifle. "You just make sure the third don't get the drop on me."

Talen patted Draven's shoulder. "I've got your back covered, sister. That's a promise."

Draven didn't look away, but one side of her mouth pulled up into a smile.

Talen stepped back into shadows, leveled her spell irons, and turned in a slow circle. Normally, a stained would've just charged at them by now, but these stained were Red Right Hand stalkers. Admittedly, one of them seemed about as sharp as a tree stump, but the magical rot apparently hadn't eaten away at their sense of self-control.

Might be the third Red Hand rot went up a tree in hopes of sniping, Talen thought as she moved slow and careful, scanning the trees. The oaks and maples were all big enough to hold a grown man, but they were still mostly bare. Wouldn't find much cover there, and besides, Talen doubted any human could've made the climb without her noticing the ruckus.

The more she thought about it, the more this felt like a trap. The two behind the tree could be the bait, and they might not even know it. She'd seen that ploy used before, especially with Red Hand. Get lured in with what seemed an easy target, only to wind up in the crosshairs yourself.

Talen looked around, taking in the sightlines. That seemed to fit. The two bickering idiots were behind solid cover from Harriet's place. The third stalker, Billy, would have to be set up somewhere farther away from the house, ready to put one in the back of whoever was stupid enough to take the bait.

The upside to a trap like that, for Talen at least, was Billy would have to be using a mundane rifle, and her spell-lined coat could stop mundane bullets; even a spell shot or two if she were lucky. Spell irons were plenty useful, but they were for close up killing.

Unless they had some new kind of spell iron rifle.

That thought, however unlikely, was also mighty unpleasant, so Talen pushed it away, turned, and went back to Draven.

"I reckon I know where he might be," she whispered. "When I take him down, I'll be sure to make a ruckus. Might be these two will give you a clean shot."

"I'll be ready," Draven said, still as a statue.

Talen moved as quickly and quietly as she could, keeping behind cover, and making sure to keep plenty of distance between herself and the most likely line of fire.

A couple hundred yards later, she reached a small marsh, but still hadn't seen any sign of the sniper. She swallowed the bitter taste in her throat and fought back the rising anxiety. Cursing silently, she turned and looked all around. The far side of the marsh would be outside range of a normal rifle, and even with a Sharps, the shooter would have to be damned skilled to hit someone in the quickly failing daylight.

Odds were better she'd missed him, but how? The trees had all been empty, and even if he'd gotten lucky and been on the far side of a good-sized tree, she should've been able to smell him. Even humans who bathed regularly and didn't wear blood-soaked gloves were hard to miss. All of these Red Hand stalkers stank of every mile they'd crossed to get here.

Could he have run off?

Maybe when he saw his friends go down, he decided it wasn't worth it anymore, and went rabbit. Tell the idiots he's going to find those that killed the others, and just keep going. Not typical for a Red Hand, but that didn't mean it was impossible. No telling how the rot might've addled his brain.

Once again, Talen cursed herself for keeping the crystal in her belly full. If she'd just emptied it out, she'd have been able to track this Red Hand just by the stench of his rotten soul.

After another heartbeat or two, she chided herself for wasting time, and headed east a hundred yards or so before heading back north toward Harriet's place. This time, she moved slower, spell irons ready, and focused more on the sounds and smells.

As if to add to the anxiety and pressure, there came a new round of shouts between the two idiot Red Hands and Harriet. Talen couldn't make out what they were saying, but she could detect the impatience and knew they weren't going wait forever. Hell, it was a small miracle they'd waited this long. Might be if they charged the place, that Draven could take their heads, but they might also decide to just start putting force blasts, or worse, through the walls and windows.

With some effort, and a few slow breaths, Talen managed to block out the mental noise and distractions. As she walked—still cloaked in shadows—she listened for any sound that stood out, and even the faintest hint of blood or human stench on the air.

Nothing. Not a damned thing.

In fact, the harder she tried to focus, the more there seemed to be to sift through.

"*Terisan ut marrin,*" she muttered under her breath and went back to Draven.

The dwarf still knelt, rifle at her shoulder, unmoved as a statue.

"I can't find him," Talen whispered, "and we're out of time. I'm going to put those two down. Watch my back."

Draven nodded.

Talen gripped her irons and crept forward, low and quiet; she still didn't know if either nitwit had an eyepiece. Once she got a clear view and saw neither did, she put a tree to her back and leveled a spell iron at each idiot's head.

Thankfully, the impatient one was kind enough to turn his profile to her and give her a better target.

Between heartbeats, Talen slipped out of the shadows, poured magic into her irons, and pulled both triggers.

The first idiot shifted.

Raw kinetic force spat from both barrels.

The left blast hit home. A foul smelling, red and black, pulpy mist sprayed the ground an instant before he crumpled.

The right blast, too high, turned a chunk of the tree into splinters.

"Son of a bitch!" the lucky bastard said, twisting and sliding low. At the same time, he lifted and lit his spell iron, taking aim at Talen.

She'd already rotated both cylinders to fresh chambers, changed position, and leveled both.

While he adjusted his aim, she pulled both triggers.

Half a blink after the magical circuit closed and her irons spat fire, an invisible boulder, presumably chucked by a giant, slammed into her back.

There was a flash of pain, a distressing wet snap, and she was thrown through the air like a ragdoll.

When she hit the ground and tumbled, the world went white with pain for an instant, and then black.

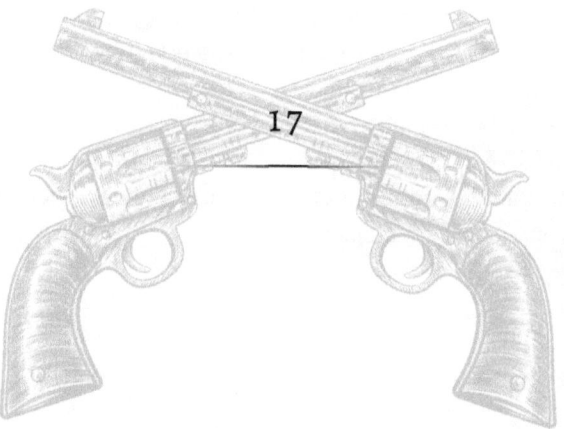

17

T alen opened her eyes. Above her, the budding trees swayed gently under a deep indigo sky filled with glittering stars. It was such a serene and beautiful sight, that she just let herself enjoy it for a heartbeat or two. Distantly, something gnawed on her brain, something important, but she couldn't seem to recall what it was. The smell of cooking meat further added to the confusion and—was someone screaming?

When she tried to move, it came back in a rush of blinding, excruciating pain from her right side.

"*Terisan ut marrin!*" she shouted and settled back down, sucking in short breaths.

Well, guess the sniper was out there. Damn it all anyway.

When the pain faded to simply unbearable, and doing her best to keep her right side still, Talen turned her head one way and then the other to get an idea of just how bad a situation she was in.

A dozen feet away on her left lay her spell irons, both of them, a few feet apart. Further back from them, just at the edge of Talen's vision, was Harriet's house. Several shapes were peering out the windows, weapons in hand, but no one made a move to leave the safety of the home.

To her right, and some distance away, lay a burning body.

Well, don't that just figure.

Gritting her teeth against the pain, Talen shifted enough to reach one of her knives. Blade in hand and working herself up to move and fight should the need arise, she watched the smoldering form.

Despite how much she might wish otherwise at the moment, she was a long way from dead, and she damned sure wasn't going to meet her end at the hands of this stained jackass.

After several very long seconds, the body didn't move.

"Thank the mothers," she said and exhaled. While grateful, she was a little surprised. She'd given him two barrels of fire, but there'd been plenty of instances when she'd had to finish a stained with—

That's when a blackened, burnt hand twitched. A second later, a low growl sounded from the should-be corpse.

He shuddered and began to get to his feet.

"I really got to learn to keep quiet," Talen said, gripped the knife, and sucking in a breath.

Draven stomped past Talen, calmly planted a heavy boot on the charred bastard's back, put one of her pistols to his head, and pulled the trigger twice.

There were two muffled whump sounds, the front of what remained of the stained's head exploded onto the ground, and the body went limp.

"Ain't gonna lie," Talen said, letting her head fall back again, "I'm giving the idea of switching to dwarven pistols some serious consideration."

Draven chuckled and knelt down at Talen's side. "As if I'd give one to an elf," she said and winked. "How bad a shape are you in?"

"Tip top," Talen said. "You get the sniper?"

Draven nodded. "He'd covered himself with mud and such, but I saw the spellfire and put him down. Sorry I didn't get him before he got you."

"Crafty bastard," Talen said. "That explains why I didn't smell him, even though I must've damn near stepped on him if he was close enough for a spell iron."

"It was a rifle," Draven said and thumbed at a long gun hanging on her back.

Talen let out a breath. "Help me up."

Draven looked at Talen's right arm and arched an eyebrow. "You sure you ought to be moving?"

"No, my right shoulder and arm are broken, maybe crushed, and I got several days of healing ahead of me, but I ain't gonna drop dead."

"You might wish you had," Drave said and reached out for her.

"Already do." Talen took the offered hand, gripping it tight. She drew in a few quick breaths, clenched her teeth, and nodded.

Draven hauled her to her feet easily in a slow, smooth motion with almost no jostling.

Talen still screamed through clenched teeth and while she apparently blacked out for a bit—between blinks, Margaret, Wilfred, and Harriet had appeared—she kept to her feet.

"We get that arm in a sling, and it'll ease some of the pain," Harriet said, removing her scarf and looked to Wilfred and Draven. "You two make sure she don't fall over. Margaret, you help me get her arm in here."

Talen didn't take well to being fussed over, but she kept her mouth shut—though she did mutter some choice swears—and did what she was told. Wilfred and Draven held Talen upright while Margaret slipped the sling over her neck. Once the length was to her liking, Harriet gingerly slid Talen's arm into it. As soon as the weight was taken off her shoulder, the pain eased considerably.

"You gonna need a doctor for any hope of that arm healing right," Harriet said.

"I'll be fine," Talen said. "Just need a week or so in the sun."

Harriet furrowed her brow.

"Elf magic," Talen said. "Meanwhile, we got to have a talk with Cordelia."

"She's not in any shape—" Margaret began but went quiet when Harriet touched her arm.

"I ain't gonna let you interrogate that child," Harriet said.

"I don't recall saying nothing about interrogating," Talen said. "I said talk with her."

"She's scared," Harriet said. "And a child."

"She should be scared," Talen said. "I sure as hell am. Only a damned fool wouldn't be. Now, I'll be as gentle as I can with her, but we need to know why someone is so set on getting her back." She pointed at the smoking corpse. "These weren't just Red Right Hand stalkers, which would be trouble enough. These were stained Red Right Hand. Something I ain't never seen before. Hell, not long ago, I'd have said it was impossible, but here we are. They were of the belief that she's got something they want—or something the person what hired them wants. We got real lucky with this lot, might not be next time."

"Next time?" Margaret asked. "What do you mean next time?"

"Anyone that can send a pack of stained Red Hands don't use that kind of power for small reasons," Harriet said, "and they ain't like to stop 'til they get what they want."

"Merciful God," Margaret said. "They're going to keep hunting that poor girl?"

"What could she have anyone would want so bad?" Wilfred asked.

"That's what we need to find out," Talen said and looked to Harriet. "I want to help her, but to do that, I need to know what they're after and why."

"It's got to tie back to the stories Haddox told about Aspen Hill," Draven said.

"Yes, it does." Harriet let out a breath before turning and heading back to the house. "Come on, then."

"I'm not saying you're wrong," Margaret said as they walked, slow and gingerly. "I'm just saying to keep in mind this is a child."

"Did you hear any of what I said?" Talen asked.

"I did," Margaret said, "but I also know you can be a little, um, plainspoken, when you get focused on something."

"Plainspoken?" Talen asked.

"I believe she means you can be an insensitive ass at times," Wilfred said. "Though I didn't know it could be said that politely."

"That's not what I said," Margaret said.

Wilfred eyed her.

"Not exactly."

It took a bit for Talen to get back inside and settled into a chair. When Margaret and Harriet led Cordelia into the room, Talen had put a decent dent into a bottle of whisky that Nelson had given her to help with the pain. The girl looked even smaller than before, trembling, and ready to bolt. As ever, she held tight to her cloth bag.

Talen opened her mouth to put the girl at ease, or at least try.

"You hurt bad?" Cordelia asked, staring at Talen's sling.

"Not so bad that I won't heal," Talen said, forcing a smile.

The girl made a face and worried at her bag. "I'm sorry."

"You ain't done nothing that needs apologizing for," Talen said.

"But it's all my fault, ain't it?"

"Absolutely not!" Harriet and Margaret said, at about the same time.

"Did you shoot me?" Talen asked.

Cordelia shook her head.

"Did you hire them Red Hands?"

"Well, no, but they was after me," Cordelia said. "If I wasn't here, this wouldn't have happened."

"It would've," Harriet said. "It just would've been somewhere else. The Lord sent you to us because he knew we could help you."

Talen made to object, but she stopped herself after a look from Margaret. "I can't speak to that," she said instead. "But I'll tell you something, Cordelia—"

"Delia," she said. "Ain't no one calls me Cordelia except Mama when she's cross with me."

"Delia," Talen corrected herself, "thinking you're to blame for what others do is a powerful lie told by bad men to ease their own guilt and shame, and to control you."

The girl furrowed her brow.

"They tell you things like, if you'd just done as you was told, they wouldn't have had to hit you," Talen said.

"Or if you hadn't run, they wouldn't have had to sell your kin down the river," Harriet said. "Only the hand that holds the lash decides if there will be a beating or not."

"Couldn't have said it better," Talen said and turned back to Delia. "You understand what we're saying?"

"I suppose," Delia said, staring at the floor. "But what if you did do wrong?"

Talen felt Harriet and Margaret's glare boring into her.

"We know you took something when you ran," Talen said.

Delia still didn't look up, but she did flinch back a little.

Margaret put a hand on the girl's shoulder. "It's okay, sweetheart."

"Ain't thieving wrong?" Delia asked. "Don't the Bible say not to steal?"

"It does," Harriet said. "It also says thou shall not kill, but the Lord knows I done killed." She lifted Delia's face and met her eyes. "I don't regret a one, and I know the Lord don't begrudge me neither. Cause every last one of them meant for me, you, and every Black soul to be either dead or in chains. And we both know there ain't no difference. Ain't no sin in killing the man who means to kill you or yours. You hear?"

"Yes, ma'am," Delia said.

"You do what you did to protect yourself or someone else?" Harriet asked.

"My pa," Delia said.

"You know when I ran, I did it alone?" Harriet asked.

"Everyone knows that," Delia said.

"Well, it ain't the whole truth," Harriet said. "I walked plenty of miles on my own, but lots of folk helped me along the way. More helped me when I got to Philadelphia. I didn't do what I did alone, and neither do you, child."

Delia looked around the room, lip trembling, and tears spilling from her eyes.

Talen's heart broke for the girl, and in those wet eyes, she saw herself. She'd never spent a day of her life in chains, but she knew the weight of duty. Delia felt responsible for her family, and Talen felt the same obligation regarding her people's past, and also for her found family's well-being.

"Let us help you," Talen said.

Delia opened her bag, pulled out a worn, leather-bound book, and held it out. "It's Preacher Thompson's crafting journal."

Harriet took it from Delia and handed it to Wilfred who opened it gingerly, as if it might spit dark magic in his face.

Talen didn't much blame him.

Wilfred furrowed his brow and turned the first page. "I ain't never seen nothing like this."

The sound of the pages struck Talen as oddly familiar, then she smelled it, and her blood ran cold. "Delia," she said, careful to keep her voice calm. "Did you try to burn the book instead of taking it?"

Her brows lifted and her eyes went wide. "I surely did! A few times. Even left it in the fire all night. Next morning it was sitting on the ashes, not even scorched."

"Let me see it," Talen said to Wilfred.

He passed her the journal. The moment she saw the pages and the text, Talen recognized it. While her soul turn to ice, a sudden, blinding fury ignited in her, one that screamed for blood and pain. When she got enough control over it to remember there were others in the room, she looked up. Everyone stared at her, eyes wide, bodies stone still.

"*Shanzi fetsuian*," she said in a low growl and gripped the book. "These pages are torn from the *Malihane Carid*. It weren't enough they slaughtered and burned us, the sons of bitches looted the ashes too!"

No one spoke, they just kept staring.

Delia had cowered back a bit.

Talen forced herself to calm. "I'd thought some human crafters had just figured out how to make their own versions of the detestable crafts, the *Malihane Carid*, but it turns out they didn't have to."

"What are the detestable crafts?" Harriet asked.

"They're just what the name says," Talen said. "They're magic so terrible and foul it was forever banned, by the elves at least. We used them during the Eldar War, when we fought—and exterminated—goblins, trolls, ogres, and a dozen other Eldar races."

"Ain't never heard of it before," Harriet said.

"It was more than fifteen hundred years ago," Talen said. "And it ain't exactly our proudest moment."

"If they was banned, why didn't you destroy how to make them?" Delia asked.

"They're artifacts of our darkest times," Talen said. "Sacred reminders of how far we fell. We kept them to remind us, so we never let it happen again." Anger and sadness roiled for supremacy in her heart. "Bad enough they stole the pages, but that they actually went and recreated what was in them…" The rest of her words were lost to tears.

"I'm sorry," Delia said.

"Don't you apologize," Talen said and held up the pages. "You didn't steal these from my people, and you're not the one crafting foulness. You did nothing wrong. In fact, you stole them away from those who did, and brought them back to my people. I thank you for that."

Delia looked away. "But that ain't why I did it."

"The Lord works in mysterious ways, child," Harriet said.

It took every ounce of willpower for Talen to keep silent. Humans, most if not all in service to their god, had been the ones who'd taken the *Malihane Carid* from the elves after raping, killing, and burning them. Not always in that order. Their god damn sure didn't get any goodwill from Talen for returning stolen pages but not the people.

"Whether you meant to or not, you still brought the pages home," Talen said. "You set out to do one right thing and did another at the same time."

Delia smiled, though just a little.

That smile served as a balm to the freshly reopened wounds on Talen's ragged soul.

"The man who had these," Talen said. "You said his name was Preacher Thompson?"

Delia nodded. "He ain't the mayor, but he might as well be. Ain't nothing happens without his say so. Even General Forrest don't argue."

"General Forrest?" Wilfred asked, exchanging a look with Harriet. "As in Nathan Beford Forrest?"

"Who's that?" Talen asked.

"One of the foulest men to ever wear the gray," Harriet said. "And that's a high achievement."

"What's he doing in Aspen Hill?" Wilfred asked.

Delia shrugged. "Don't much know. He came to town shortly after Preacher started using them stones to make people work. Brought lots of men with him too. All of them was soldiers, but now they ride around in white robes and hoods. Call themselves knights or something. They run off any Union soldiers that come to town and round up Black folk who don't do as they're told."

"You happen to know how many there are?" Draven asked before Talen could.

There was no way of knowing if they were actual soldiers or not, or if they were, if they'd seen any fighting, but it did make things more complicated.

"They wear them hoods, so I don't know," Delia said. "But when they came for my pa, there was a dozen of them."

"A dozen to get one man?" Margaret said. "Sound like cowards to me."

"Bullies always are," Harriet said.

Talen, Draven, Wilfred, and Margaret all exchanged a look. Talen figured they had the same thought: cowards are boldest in groups.

Talen caught a glimpse of Delia watching them.

"There's too many for you, ain't there?" she asked, tears welling at her eyes.

"Ain't no one said any such thing," Talen said, and though it hurt like a dozen different hells, she leaned forward. "I won't lie. I don't know if we'll able to save your pa, but we'll save all we can, and I promise that every one of those rotten souls will pay. If I have to do it myself, I'll see it done. You hear me?"

Delia nodded and wiped at her eyes.

"We're going to need your help though," Margaret said.

No one said anything.

Talen looked to Wilfred and Draven, but they didn't seem to know where Margaret was going either.

"What can I do?" Delia asked.

"We need you to tell us as many names as you can," Margaret said.

"Family, friends, and anyone else who needs our help getting away, and where they live."

"That's all?" Delia asked, her face scrunching up.

"That's all?" Margaret seemed taken aback.

Talen smiled inside, finally understanding Margaret's intention.

"Don't you know how important that is?" Margaret asked. "Without that list, we won't know if we found everyone. We'd never know if we left someone behind, and we don't want to do that."

Delia narrowed her eyes, clearly uncertain.

"You can help me too," Draven added. "I make maps, and if you tell me about the town, I can make one for us to use. That would be mighty helpful!"

Delia looked at everyone.

They all nodded.

"We need your help, Delia," Talen said. "I don't know as we'll be able to do it without. Will you help us?"

The girl sat up a little straighter, and a fire lit behind eyes. "Yes, ma'am. I surely will."

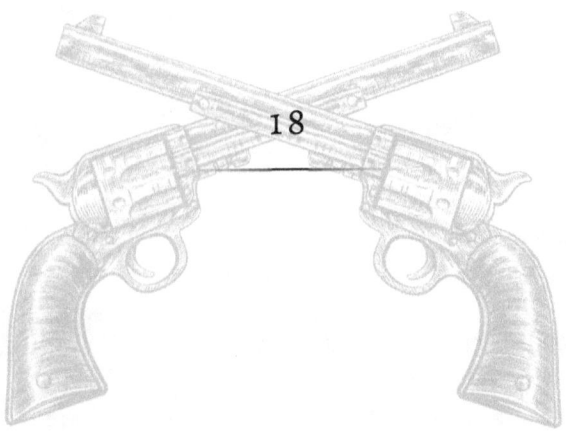

18

Margaret, Harriet, and Draven went with Delia to get the names and start drawing out the town map. Wilfred stayed behind, and when everyone else was gone, sat down next to Talen.

"I won't ask how you're doing," he said.

She ran her fingers across the pages. Each was marred with countless notes, in some cases directly over the flowing Elven script. The clumsy block letters were a harsh and brutal contrast. They seemed to be translation notes, and of course were in iron gall ink, which meant the paper would deteriorate before the sacrilege faded. It was a twisted sort of poetry that the pages were literally stained.

An inferno still churned through her guts, and though it had quieted some, she knew it just waited for the chance to rain hellfire and pain on those who'd violated her people.

Again.

"It's never enough, is it?" Talen asked without looking up, her voice quavering at the edges. "Can't stop at settling. They got to claim the land they promised to others. Not enough to enslave. They also got to brutalize and torment." She gripped the book as tears spilled down her cheeks. "Ain't enough to butcher a people to near extinction, they also got to shit on what those people hold sacred."

"I have to cling to the notion it ain't all folk," Wilfred said, uncharacteristically dour. "For my own sake and sanity, and to hold any hope for the future, I got to believe some just got a great big emptiness in them. They try and fill it with money or power or piles of stuff." He shook his head and shrugged. "But ain't nothing ever going to fill such a void. I reckon they feel terrible empty, and when they see others who ain't, they turn mean."

"*Anamara gani,*" Talen said.

Wilfred furrowed his brow. "Don't think I ever heard you say that word before."

"Soulless," she said.

"I cannot argue with that," he said and went quiet.

Talen had always appreciated that Wilfred was ever ready to offer a joke, or a smile, or just talk about nothing, if that's what you needed. But he could also share a silence. Unlike so many others, he could just be there without making any demands, not even conversation. If he wasn't sitting at her injured left, she'd have reached over and taken his hand, so she just moved her leg to touch his.

He pressed back against her.

Slowly, the vast, cold wasteland of sadness was swallowed by the smoldering fury. The mothers used to say, *if you seek vengeance, you might not find it, but you'll always find your own grave.* Even so, Talen permitted herself some rather vivid imaginings of all the terrible things she'd like to do to this Preacher Thompson. When the thoughts turned dark enough that the delight also scared her, Talen drew in a breath and let the thoughts slip away.

She didn't bother trying to quash the rage. Anger wasn't the problem. It could serve good as surely as kindness and mercy. The trick was not letting the wrathful fires grow so wild and hot that they consumed her soul. Her people had made that mistake before, which was how the detestable crafts had come to be in the first place.

She gripped the pages tighter.

No, she wouldn't—couldn't—let this desecration drive her to turn her back on what she and her people held most dear. She'd see Preacher Thompson in the ground. He, and all the strained in Aspen Hill—along with anyone fool enough to stand by them—would die. But she refused to let them drag her down with them.

"The magic must preserve," she whispered. The familiar phrase did nothing to soothe the pain in her heart, or quench the burning fury, but it did shelter her soul from the heat.

"Pardon?" Wilfred asked.

"Just reminding myself what's important," she said.

"I ain't never worried about you losing sight of that," he said.

She half-smiled. "I surely have. More than once."

"Just cause you find yourself in the dark don't mean you wandered off the path," he said. "And even if you did, it don't mean you can't find your way back."

Inwardly she smiled, but outwardly she turned to him and frowned. "There are times your endless hope and optimism can chafe."

He grinned broad and sincere. "We both know you're lying."

She chuckled, winced at the pain it stirred, and then cursed in Elven.

"Lots of words there I don't know," Wilfred said, "but plenty I do. Soon as the sun is up, we'll get you outside to get some healing."

"That's hours to go," Talen said. "I ain't keen on just sitting here 'til that happens."

"I can ask Harriet if she's got some laudanum or such."

"Much as that sounds like a delight"—Talen shook her head—"I need to keep my senses in case anyone else comes for Delia."

"You don't reckon that Preacher sent another pack of Red Hand right off, do you?"

Talen almost shrugged, but thankfully stopped herself. "Don't rightly know, but as bad as he wants these pages back, I wouldn't put it outside the possible."

"Senseless from laudanum or not," Wilfred said, "you ain't in any shape to put up a fight."

"That is why I plan on getting started healing right now," she said. "Help me up."

He hesitated for just a moment but then rose and gently eased her to her feet. "Don't you need the sun to use your healing magics?"

It hurt like a dozen kinds of hell, but after a bit, the screaming, inde-scribable agony eased just enough for Talen to think straight.

"It ain't necessary, though it does make things a mite easier." She very gingerly and cautiously patted her belly where the crystal sat, making very sure not to move any other part of her body, lest she pass out. "I'm hoping since that's where I got this power from, maybe I can use it 'til the sun rises."

"Reckon it's good you held on to it then."

"Reckon it was," Talen said and headed for the door. "Now come on. I'll need help getting outside and stripping down."

Wilfred didn't move. "Maybe I should go fetch Margaret instead."

Talen turned on him, a little too quickly. Every inch of her screamed in protest and her vision went white for an instant. After a couple of heartbeats, her mind clawed out of the spike pit of agony and she cursed herself before glaring at him.

"Or maybe Draven or Harriet could—"

"Mothers' sake! What is it with you lot and nakedness?" she asked, more impatiently than she'd intended. But then she didn't have any wherewithal to spare for niceties.

Wilfred opened his mouth.

"You done seen me naked plenty of times before," she said, before he could answer. "I got the crystal in my belly and a few more scars, but otherwise, ain't nothing new."

"I just—"

"You know I don't give a good goddamn about propriety or whatever you want to call it. You want to believe there's something shameful about your bodies, or sex—not that this has a damned thing to do with sex—that's fine, but don't hold me to it."

Wilfred stood silent for a bit, his expression serious. "You done, or can I say my peace now?"

The fire in Talen's belly died down, but her patience was frayed beyond measure. "Go on then."

"I'd have thought you know me well enough to know this ain't got nothing to do with shame or the like," he said. "You're right. I have seen you plenty of times, and I might crack wise about to tease you and Margaret, but things between us was more than a bit different then. Just cause I know things have changed, and I accept that, don't mean I don't still got lingering feelings for you. I expect I always will. I ain't the sort to stop loving someone."

The impatience and frustration withered away entirely.

"But as things are different," he said, "I don't rightly know where the line is. And not just for you, but for me as well. I don't want no confusion or misunderstanding, or for you to think I see something that ain't there." He took a moment, as if considering his words. "I expect Margaret sees things like you say, but I ain't her. And I reckon I'd just appreciate if you remembered that sometimes it ain't just about you."

Up until that moment, Talen hadn't realized that, compared to the pain of being a complete saphead, her shoulder wasn't that bad.

"It ain't exactly been my best day," she said. "But all the same, it don't mean I ought to take it out on you. I'm sorry."

"Apology accepted," Wilfred said and headed for the front door.

Even though they went at a snail's pace, each step still jostled her shoulder and sent fresh waves of agony through her.

"Might be we're moving slow enough that the sun will be up by the time we get you to a good spot," Wilfred said.

"Remind me to kick you in the ass once I'm feeling better."

"I will not."

After a bit, they found a spot not far from the Cumulus that Talen figured would serve well enough. The trees were still just budding so the sun should shine through them, and the clearing ought to provide several hours of unobstructed light for her.

"Ground looks awful damp and cold," Wilfred said. "You want me to fetch a blanket from the ship?"

Talen shook her head. "Best if I'm in contact with the earth. I'll be fine." She unbuttoned her coat with her good hand and then motioned to the sling. "Help me off with this."

He gingerly took hold of it, one side in each hand. "You ready?"

"Nope, and don't expect I will be, so let's just get it done."

Wilfred carefully lifted the sling, moved it over her head, and slowly let her arm drop to her side. Next, he took her coat and gently lowered it down her arms.

It never ceased to amaze her that such a strong man, who'd lived such a brutal life, could also be as tender and gentle as a summer breeze. Not that it kept it from hurting like the blazes. But she gritted her teeth, squeezed her eyes shut, wept, and focused on keeping upright.

After what felt like an eternity of agony, the coat was off.

"Thank you," Talen said between gasps, her voice shaking. "Give me a moment to get myself straight before we do the shirt."

"Of course." Wilfred neatly folder her coat, laid it on a nearby rock, and then stood patiently.

Time lost meaning as she dug herself out of the miles-deep pit of all-consuming misery, with nothing but her bare hands.

"All right," she said, tears still running down her cheeks. She reached out with a shaking hand. "Lend me your shoulder so I can kick off my boots."

147

"You sure you don't want to sit and have me pull them off?"

Talen shook her head, barely. "I don't want to move no more than I have to."

He stepped closer.

Talen gripped his shoulder, and he put his hand over hers. Trying hard to move her body as little as possible, Talen stepped on the heel of each boot to get her foot free, then carefully stepped out of one, and then the other.

The cold damp ground chilled her bare feet, but it was also a comfort. It'd been too long since she last laid with the earth, even just slept on the ground. She added that to the list of things she needed to correct.

With Wilfred's help, they got her out of her shirt, which wasn't fun, but not nearly as painful as slipping out of her coat or the sling. He turned away as she undid her trousers and nudged them until they fell at her feet, and she stepped out of them. Without looking at her, he bent, picked them up, and after folding them, added them to the coat and shirt on the rock. She did not make any snide comments about it.

"Help me down to the ground," she said.

He kept his eyes on hers, which felt more intimate than if he'd just looked at her body, but again she kept her peace. With more than a little pain, they got her down on her back on the bare earth. With quite a bit of pain, Wilfred extended her busted arm out and pushed her fingers into the ground as best he could. The ground wasn't frozen, but it was hard packed.

Tears streamed down Talen's cheeks, and she feared she might crack her teeth from gritting them so hard. After a while, her body settled, the torment subsided, and she managed to take in a full breath. The cold night air in her lungs and the ground at her back soothed her heart and mind. A calm and sense of peace spread through, almost strong enough to quiet her screaming body. Almost.

"You good?" Wilfred asked, crouched down beside her, still not looking past her neck.

"Good as can be expected. Thank you."

"None needed."

"I don't just mean for this."

He smiled. "I know."

"For Margaret's sake, best tell everyone but her and Draven to keep clear from here until the sun sets, and I'm back inside."

Wilfred chuckled. "I will do." His face turned serious. "You need anything, you holler. Hear me?"

"I will do."

He rose and made his way back to the house without another word.

Talen closed her eyes, focused on the markings that covered her body, and whispered the healing prayer. The magic spread out from her, a plea for help to the earth and all the living creatures nearby.

Unfortunately, the trees were only just waking from their winter hibernation, and with the sky dark, there was little energy to spare. So much came from the sun, and most life used that energy to make more life energy. It wasn't just dark; it was dark at the end of the darkest part of the year. Likewise, the only animals this close to a human town were the horses, some deer at the very edge of her senses, and a colony of rabbits. Even the unimaginably small life that resided in the dirt was only just waking from its torpor.

The power available was just enough to ease the pain, but despite the meager offerings, Talen accepted them with humility and gratitude. As she did, her senses both expanded and drew in. Her awareness encompassed everything around her as well as the minute details of her own body. She could feel the wind softly blowing through the trees, pulling on the budding leaves. The smell of each tree, the damp earth, the nearby wetlands, even the wood and paint on the barn was clear and distinct to her.

Deep in the spell, she looked over her injury with pain-free detachment. Her upper arm was broken in two places, her shoulder was dislocated, and also had a fracture. Normally with so little to work with, she'd start by setting the shoulder straight and splinting the arm until she could get to more. In this case however, she had a reserve of power in her belly, one that in this spell sight, as she called it, burned like the noon-day sun itself. The problem was, she wasn't sure how to use it. Or rather, how to use it safely.

Healing magic, unlike using spell irons or any external charm, was a precise and delicate thing. Thankfully, the tattoos that been etched inside her markings—so they couldn't be seen—served as the charm to both her shadow cloak, and healing magic, but also served as a guide in how to shape the magic.

The extra power from the crystal, however, complicated things.

In a normal casting, the power available was usually small enough she didn't need to worry about the flow of it. She could just focus on the spell and the healing. While she'd practiced controlling the current from the crystal, she hadn't been weaving a spell at the time.

Anxiety nibbled at the edges of her mind, but in the midst of casting, it was easier to keep it at bay.

Push the doubts aside, and trust the magic, her mother said inside Talen's head.

Her heart filled with warmth. It had been so long since she'd prayed to her mother, and longer still since her mother had spoken back. Guilt tinged the joy and comfort.

"Mother, I'm sorry it's been so long—"

Hush, child, her mother said. *Not time, not distance, not even death can dampen my love for you.*

Amid the serenity of the healing prayer, she could just feel the weight of guilt and shame lift at her mother's words. Warm tears leaked from Talen's eyes and rolled down her cheeks.

Now remember what you've been taught, her mother said. *Magic serves life, and we serve magic. Trust in it, trust in yourself. Don't try to control it. You know that no one controls magic. We can work with it, but never truly control it.*

Talen's anxiety subsided and without any conscious thought, magic spread from the crystal, through her body. Not in a rushing flood, but a gentle, unhurried drifting, like a warm summer breeze. The power gathered at her shoulder and arm, suffusing it with light and heat. Talen wove and guided the magic around her broken bones and distantly felt the tinge of pain as they set themselves and started to knit back together.

A dark path lays ahead of you, her mother said once the healing magic was set and working on its own.

"I know," she said. "A town of stained, one of which has learned the detestable crafts. But these stained ain't like others. It's as if they're able to control the corruption."

Like pure magic, there is no controlling the corruption. These stained have simply learned to use it as we use pure magic. Such a thing has happened before, but not since the detestable crafts were first made.

Despite being bathed in warmth and peace, a shiver of cold ran through her.

The detestable crafts weren't forbidden simply because they're evil.

"It's because the evil intent behind them corrupts pure magic, and makes more corruption," Talen said, repeating the words she'd been taught since before she could even understand them.

We must only ever use magic to protect life.

"Never to satisfy rage or hatred," Talen said, but she thought back to Weaver, and how she'd not only used a geas stone, a detestable craft, but done it so the foul little man would feel it. At the time she had thought it human-made, not from the Elven texts, but that didn't matter.

You're right to question yourself, her mother said, not unkindly. *Like my mother's mother, you started down a dark path for noble reasons.*

"Does that mean I corrupted pure magic when I bound Weaver?"

You did.

Something cold and sharp twisted in Talen's heart. "Then I failed in my duties as a Shadow Warden. Wait, but then why did the elemental still call me a protector? Why did it help me?"

Because no one is damned by a single misstep or even a dozen. Our fore-mothers saw what they were doing and, far later than they should've, stopped. They saw it was wrong, and what it was doing to the pure magic. No one has ever lived without corrupting magic at some point, but the power of life isn't so weak and fragile that it can be so easily destroyed. We serve it when we destroy the irredeemably stained. The elementals act on life's behalf when they draw the corruption in and bind it until it can be purified. In time, the magic heals. Our purpose is to give it that time, to stop the source of the corruption from spreading.

Talen knew this, most of it anyway. Or at least she'd been taught it, even if she didn't recall all of it. Even so, things were very different on the other side of innocence—

"Wait, did you say *irredeemably* stained?" Even as she said the words, Talen remembered her teachers using the same qualifier, but she'd never thought about it at the time. "Can some stained be redeemed?"

Of course. Just as one has to invite corruption in, so too can it be driven out, but it's no small feat. That's why the Shadow Wardens only hunt those who are truly lost to the dark, consumed and rotted away, until the rot is all that remains.

Talen felt the fool for not putting it together before. She'd never encountered anyone who'd saved themselves or wasn't lost to corruption, because her role was to deal with those that were lost. Part of her wished her teachers had put it so succinctly, but they probably didn't feel they had to. Talen had never been the best student. Her gifts and interest were in the physical, not the mental.

"Can anything be done to help those who can be redeemed?" She thought back the bodies they'd taken from the falls. "I've come to see not all who turn to corruption do so for dark purposes. Some are just desperate."

Desperation is what drove our foremothers to make and use the detestable crafts, her mother said. *The sad truth is that it doesn't matter how you find your way to darkness. It isn't easy or fair, but neither is it when someone dies of an infection found too late. Those without evil intent are most likely to find a way back, like our foremothers. But if the circumstances that led them to darkness remain, what is there for them to return to?*

Talen thought of all the pain and misery in so many human nations, especially this one, so ironically proud to proclaim its origins in a desire for freedom. Equity given quite unequally.

"Is there any hope for them?" Talen asked. "For us? For anyone? It seems those bent on cruelty, and those willing to overlook it if they benefit, are legion. I feel like an ant trying to remove filth, a grain at a time, while some huge, foul beast spews it like a geyser."

There is always hope, if you hold to it.

There seemed to be sadness in her mother's voice, though Talen couldn't be sure.

But we don't serve hope. We serve the magic. Our duty, our promise, was never conditional on the assurance of victory. If you do good for any reason other than it being the right thing—

"You're not doing good," Talen finished. "You're doing what's convenient."

You were a better student than you think. And you were always stronger than you believed. Hold to hope, child. You've the strength to hold it when others let it slip away.

Talen closed her eyes and more tears rolled down her cheeks. "It's hard sometimes."

That's when it matters most. Not just for you, but those around you.

Talen had never thought of herself as inspiring, but isn't that what she'd done for Margaret, and Wilfred, and Draven? Isn't that what they'd done for her? Isn't that what friends and family did for each other?

Promise me.

The weight of those words settled over Talen. The last time her mother had asked for a promise, it'd been the end of her people. That promise had bound Talen to inaction as she watched it happen.

Promise me you won't lose hope, no matter how hard it might get.

Talen was sure of it now, there was something behind her mother's words. Was is it sadness or desperation? Despite the warmth and calm that suffused her, a shiver of disquiet ran through Talen.

"What have you seen?"

Her mother said nothing.

"I promise," Talen whispered.

I love you, and I'm so proud of you. Never forget that.

"Mother, what is it you're not telling me?"

There was only silence.

Her mother was gone, and Talen felt more alone than she had in years.

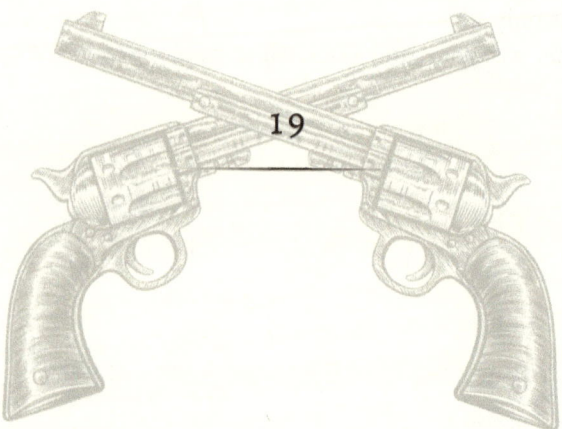

19

When the sun rose and the first rays hit her, Talen's body drank up the heat and energy. Added to the waning surplus in the crystal, her bones and muscles were healing faster than she'd even dared to hope. She might not be back to normal at the end of the day, but she'd be able to move and function without debilitating pain.

Through the serenity of the healing prayer, her mother's words hung in her heart. No one had ever gotten clear answers from mothers that had crossed to the next world. But Talen sorely wished her mother had been plainer about the promise. Were her people suffering hopelessness on their reservation? Talen had been the only one of her nation to survive, and she'd refused to join the other nations in the Washington Territory, opting instead to become a stalker. At the time, she'd convinced herself it would be the same as being a shadow warden. That the only way she could continue to hunt stained was swearing an oath to the US government and getting that brass star. She'd never had cause to question that decision, until now.

She remembered then a promise she'd made months ago to visit the Oglala people on their reservation. Yet another oath unkept. Hopefully, there was still time.

It took an effort of will not to wander too deep into the shadows. All the peoples pushed onto tightly controlled areas for simply having the temerity to not give up their lands, beliefs, or their culture.

One thing at a time, she reminded herself. No use getting twisted over a waterfall a day down the river when you're drowning right now.

She turned her entire focus on Aspen Hill, what little she knew at least. Not that she needed a lot of information to know the only way to take down an entire town was one person at a time. Even if all the newly re-enslaved joined, a straight up fight would end in far too many innocent dead. They'd have to bleed the city from the shadows. Just like her sisters and the *Oceti Sakowin* had done against the bluebacks. This time though, the dwarven machine would be on their side.

When the sun touched the western horizon, Talen ended her prayer and opened her eyes. To her surprise, Gaoth stood over her, keen eyes watching all around.

"You looking out for me, old friend?" Talen asked.

Gaoth chuffed and bobbed his head.

Talen's heart swelled and she, very cautiously, sat up. She was still sore, but the all-encompassing sharp pain had become a low, dull ache. She moved her arm, rotated it, and tested the limits of her motion. Not quite as good as new, but leagues better than it had been.

Gaoth bowed his head and whinnied.

"Thank you, kindly," Talen said and wrapped her good arm around his neck and pulled herself to her feet.

Once she was standing, the horse nudged her with his head.

"Don't know what I'd do without you." She leaned in, hugged him tight, and stroked his neck.

He snorted.

"I know," she said. "You were made to run, not stand around in the belly of an airship. I promise we'll get more trail time."

He whinnied and pressed against her, forcing her to take a couple steps to keep from falling over.

"I love you too," she said and kissed between his eyes. "Now I best get dressed and head inside to see where things stand." She went to the stone and pulled on her trousers, but paused when the foul stench of stained reached her, buried just beneath the equally unmistakable stink of burned flesh. It was a twisted sort of comfort to smell the rot again.

"Guess they burned the bodies," she said.

Gaoth huffed and pawed at the ground.

"No, I don't expect they have any more apples." Talen slipped on her shirt and realized the crystal in her belly wasn't lighting up the area. Hunching forward, she found it faded to an almost imperceptibly faint glow. Though still warm, it had cooled noticeably. To say she was conflicted would be a massive understatement. Part of her like the idea of having the extra magic available, but a larger part didn't feel right about it. Somehow it felt like a cheat.

Gaoth bumped her and snorted.

Talen resisted rolling her eyes. "Yes, I'll ask." She buttoned her shirt and tucked it in. "It's a good thing you're so handsome or I might find your pestering a nuisance."

He whinnied and shook his mane.

Talen laughed and finished getting dressed. Once she had the weight of her spell irons on her hips, she led Gaoth back to the barn and promised to return for a ride shortly. After his protests had settled down, she took a short walk, following the smell of rot, just to be certain. As expected, she found a good-sized hole dug some ways away from the house and barn, at the bottom of which were the charred remains of—she presumed—the Red Hand stalkers.

Wishing she'd been able to light the fires herself, Talen turned and headed for Harriet's house.

When she stepped inside, half a dozen humans were gathered together, conversing with Harriet, Delia, Wilfred, Draven, and Margaret. All of whom stopped talking and turned to stare at her. Reflexively, her left hand went to her back and took hold of her spell iron.

"Evening," she said and, reminding herself this was Harriet's home, released her iron as casually as she could. "Am I interrupting?"

"I was just about to go check on you," Margaret said. "I tried earlier but Gaoth seemed intent on keeping everyone away."

"He can get a mite protective," Talen said.

"Your arm," Delia said, her eyes a little wide. "It's healed already?"

"Not quite," Talen said. "Another few days or so and it should be. It's fair enough to serve though." She looked over the faces of the strangers, then to Harriet. "And my question still stands. Am I interrupting?"

"The conductor elf," one of the strangers, an older woman with graying hair said. "As I live and breathe!"

Talen bit the retort that tried to leap from her mouth.

"Her name is Talen," Harriet said. "And she ain't some oddity for you to gawk at, Odie Brown."

Odie's mouth came open, as if to argue, but Harriet pinned her in place with a hard look. "Yes, of course." Odie turned to Talen. "I apologize. I just only ever heard stories about you."

Some of Talen's anger faded, or rather it redirected back to Thompson and Aspen Hill. "I weren't no conductor." She nodded at Wilfred. "That was him. I reckon you could say I just kept the tracks clear."

There was a round of chuckles.

"And since we're talking Railroad business," Harriet said, "you ain't interrupting nothing." Harriet motioned to the collection of strangers. "All these folk were once passengers. When others thought the Railroad weren't needed no more, they all made sure the wheels didn't stop turning."

Harriet introduced the two men and four women.

"Support ain't entirely gone," Booker Steen, a rather polished man said. "Though it has waned quite a bit. The work ain't any less gratifying though."

"We got word an airship had come to see Moses," Frieda Thomas, a tall and broad woman of an age with Harriet said. "It was all the buzz in town."

"We'd planned on coming for a visit early in the morning," Cyrus Mack, a bald, slender, smooth-faced man said. "But when we heard gunshots, we gathered together as many people and guns as we could and came running."

"They showed up not long after I got you settled," Wilfred said.

"Your friends" Alice Adams, a young slip of a woman said and gestured to Wilfred, Margaret, Draven, and Delia, "told us about your plans. We've been figuring how we can help."

Talen arched an eyebrow. "How? Don't mean no offense, but short of joining us, I don't see what you can do."

"Actually, that's just what we're planning," Booker said.

"That a fact?" Talen asked, not unkindly. "You all got experience with fighting?"

"Yes, ma'am," Cyrus said. "Booker and I fought with Nelson in the Eighth."

"And I fought with the Thirty-First," Alice said, one side of her mouth pulling up into a lopsided smile. "Though in order to enlist, I went by Alan."

Talen couldn't help but smile back. It surprised her, pleasantly, to respect and admire a human so quickly.

An awkward silence settled over everyone, and the others seemed determined not to look directly at Alice.

She glared at them before turning to Talen. "The notion a woman posed as a man don't sit well with their sensibilities, but I ain't never seen the sense of just allowing the men to fight when we're just as capable of firing a rifle."

"Amen to that," Harriet said.

Harriet's approval apparently quashed the disapproval, or at least convinced the others to keep it to themselves.

Talen stifled a chuckle but couldn't hold back a grin.

Just when I thought I couldn't hold that woman in any higher esteem.

"Yes, and, um, Frieda, Odie, and I got experience tending wounds," Pearl Thomas, Frieda's twin sister said.

"Folks in this town have a small arsenal if you put all the arms together," Cyrus said. "Should any of those we free want to join the fight, we'll make sure they have the means."

"I'll be coming along too," Harriet said. "I got a bit of experience when it comes to fighting. The plantation owners along the Combahee River can attest to that." The faintest hint of a smile settled on her face. "Them that's still alive that is."

None of Talen's friends seemed especially pleased with the idea.

"I wasn't there for John Brown," Harriet said. "I ain't saying this is as grand a plan as his, but neither am I going to miss out again."

Nelson opened his mouth.

"Nelson Davis," Harriet said without looking at him, "I love you, but you will keep any thoughts you have on this to yourself."

Nelson, to his credit, had enough wisdom to keep quiet.

Talen eyed the rather unexpected group of volunteers, and though it did her heart good to see, she knew they didn't have any idea what they were agreeing to.

"If you'll permit me to speak up then?" Talen asked.

Harriet narrowed her eyes. "You going to tell me I shouldn't go?"

"I am," Talen said. "Though not without reason." She turned at the others. "Some of those reasons apply to you all as well."

"I ain't never taken to being told what I should or shouldn't do," Harriet said.

"I'm much the same, ma'am," Talen said. "Which is why I'm not telling, I'm asking. Fact is, this ain't like any sort of fight you ever taken part in. Won't be no uniforms. No armies. It'll be an entire town. Every one of them stained, if what we hear is right. Any of you gone toe to toe with a stained?"

Only Alice didn't avert her gaze, instead, she lifted her hand. "I did. He took out a dozen of us before we finally got him."

Talen nodded. "And that was just one. From what I saw from those Red Hands, these ain't no typical stained." She turned back to Harriet. "You've done some plain amazing things in your life. Fought fights few others was willing to, and did so in some horrendous circumstances. But, to be plain, you're an important figure, and I reckon you'd be a distraction."

"I beg your pardon?" Harriet asked.

Talen lifted her hands. "I mean to say, even if we don't mean to, all of us would be keeping one eye on you, making sure you're safe, but we'll need both eyes when the fighting starts."

No one said anything for a long moment, and Harriet just stared at Talen, her expression hard, and a little sad.

"You done enough," Talen said. "More than most anyone else. I know you got regrets, and there is still fire aplenty in you, especially seeing a fight that needs fighting." She shook her head. "But this one ain't for you. Let us do this so you can be there for the next one."

Everyone waited for Harriet to speak.

"I don't like it," she said.

Talen thought back to the day her people were slaughtered as she hid in the shadows, bound by a promise to her mother. She finally understood how her mother must've felt asking for that promise. Talen's heart ached, and she wiped at her eyes.

"No one said you should," Talen said. "I know what you're feeling. It's a bitter swill, but sometimes we got to sit out one fight so we can be there for another. I expect there are plenty more coming that'll need you, that maybe can't be won without you. This one? I reckon it could be."

One by one, the others nodded in agreement, if hesitantly.

"Don't none of you say a word," Harriet said. "I know she's right, but I don't need to hear nothing from you." She turned to Nelson. "Especially you."

159

Nelson bowed his head. "I ain't saying nothing."

"I'd find it mighty flattering if you're saying the same about us," Booker said. "But I think we'd all protest being grouped with the likes of Moses here."

"Not for me to say," Talen said. "I know you two was soldiers, but soldiering won't do us much good here. This is going to be mostly sneaking and striking from the darkness. We can't fight a beast this big head on, we got to bleed it out."

"You'll still need those that can tend to the sick and wounded," Frieda said and motioned to her sister and Odie. "Some of them we mean to get out might need help."

"They might at that," Talen said, "but if you come along, you're staying on the Cumulus. Won't be completely safe, but same as with Harriet, I don't want you getting into the fray and the rest of us having to watch you and ourselves too."

The three women exchanged a look and nodded.

"Reckon might be need for a couple of skilled shooters on the ship then," Cyrus said. "Booker and I weren't snipers, but we were good. We can stay on board and make sure no one gets too close."

"Notice you ain't said nothing about me," Alice said. "That mean you ain't got no arguments to make about me staying behind?"

"You know how to hide in plain sight," Talen said. "That's the sort of thing we'll need."

Alice smiled.

"What about me?" Delia asked.

Everyone, absolutely everyone, turned to the girl.

"You'll be staying here with me and Nelson," Harriet said. "You can help us make ready for them that'll be coming. They'll need places to stay, food to eat, probably clothes. It's a lot of work, and I'll need a hand."

"Harriet Tubman herself is asking for your help," Wilfred said to Delia. "I don't know many that can say that. You ain't going to say no to her, are you?"

Delia looked from him to Harriet. "No, ma'am." She furrowed her brow. "I mean yes, ma'am. I'll help you."

"Looks like we got the start of a plan," Wilfred said.

"Speaking of," Odie said to Harriet, "it's near on supper time and I expect you could use some help in that regard."

Harriet nodded and gave everyone a list of chores to help with dinner, to which no one argued. As they all went to their assigned tasks, Draven stepped over to Booker and Cyrus.

"How many and what sort of guns you got?" she asked.

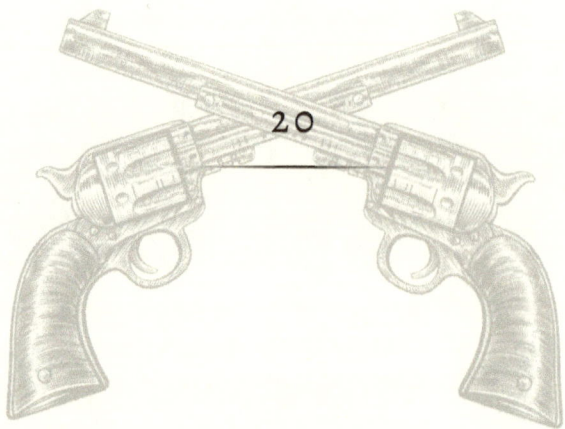

20

After the meal was finished and clean up was done, they set to collecting weapons from the town. It seemed while Talen was healing, word had spread to every house. The locals were eager to contribute their arms and prayers. As she had no need or interest in the latter, and no real knowledge of the former, Talen kept her mouth shut.

Draven gave each offered weapon a quick but careful review before either accepting it or politely refusing. It seemed not everyone took care of their firearms, and not all those in good condition were ones that Draven had ammunition for. It wasn't long before Talen had reached her limit of being a pointless add-on and excused herself. She and Gaoth were overdue for a nice long ride, and the night, though chill, was clear.

As a testament to his heart, despite wanting to run, Gaoth kept a gentle pace so as not to jostle Talen and her not-quite-fully-healed shoulder. Once they got outside Auburn, it was as if a heavy weight had been set down. It wasn't a big city—certainly nothing like Boston or Chicago—but Talen didn't find any human town, of any size, the least bit comfortable. Alone with Gaoth though. Well, that was home. Nothing seemed impossible or overwhelming while in the saddle.

After insisting, and promising to rein him in if it hurt too much, Gaoth finally broke into a full gallop. Talen didn't bother trying to guide him. Instead, she closed her eyes and savored the wind on her face, the smooth rocking motion, and the feel of his strong muscles under her.

They rode for hours and were both exhausted when they got back to Harriet's house, which was dark upon their return. No surprise there, the hour was late enough that everyone else had to be in bed.

Talen walked Gaoth to the trough and let him drink as she removed the saddle and bridle before wiping him down and brushing him.

The sound of Draven's heavy footsteps sounded on the Cumulus's gangway and approached the barn.

"Have a nice ride?" Draven asked as she stepped through the doors.

"I did," Talen said, her attention completely on Gaoth, caressing as much as brushing. "I'd apologize for leaving you all to collect the guns, but I ain't really sorry."

Draven chuckled. "You weren't exactly providing much help, so we didn't really notice you'd gone."

"How many extra guns did you get?"

"Twenty-six total," Draven said. "Four repeaters, a dozen shotguns, and ten rifles of various make. There were thirty or so muskets, but I didn't think they'd do us much good."

"Not much, no."

"Oh, we also had someone donate this to the cause."

Talen glanced over to find Draven holding out a spell iron. Her eyebrows went up, and she almost dropped the brush. Out of all the possible weapons that might get donated to the cause, Talen had never expected a spell iron to be among them, but she couldn't be happier to have been wrong. An extra spell iron could make all the difference in a fight.

She walked over to give the iron a closer look. "Can't believe anyone was willing to part with it."

"Former Cavalry officer," Draven said. "Name of George Wilkerson."

Anger, fear, and revulsion all mingled and danced together in Talen's chest. She drew her hand back as if the iron had suddenly burst into flames. "Cavalry?"

"He left the Army after the Confederates surrendered," Draven said. "I didn't figure you'd want nothing to do with one that had found its way out west."

Talen went back to Gaoth and resumed brushing him down. "Not much interested in any Army weapon, to be honest. Course, I ain't got but the two hands and two irons of my own."

"I understand," Draven said. "But you got to admit that having another could be useful. Ain't like it was used by the Red Hand."

Talen glanced over her shoulder. "Speaking of—"

"Margaret insisted on tossing the irons, including the rifle, in with the bodies to burn with them."

"Remind me to thank her."

"Think giving her this one would be a fine way of doing that?" Draven asked, stepping over to stand next to Talen. "Seems a child of the Railroad taking up an iron what was used to free her is fitting."

Talen nodded. "Well, she's gotten to be a decent shot with that repeater of hers." She thought back to how Margaret had used a spell iron on Tuller and likely saved Talen's life by doing so. "Though she proved herself a fair enough hand with a spell iron too, I reckon."

"So I heard," Draven said. "I'll see if she wants it or not."

Talen chuckled. "I expect if she doesn't, Alice would take it gladly. Don't know as she ever used one, but I pity whoever finds themself in her crosshairs."

Draven laughed. "That is a fact. They all seems like good folk though."

"They do at that." Talen pointed at nearby tools. "Hand me that pick."

Draven did.

Talen set to checking Gaoth's hooves to make sure he didn't pick up any stones or such on their ride. "You think we can pull this off?"

Draven took a long breath and seemed to genuinely consider it for a few heartbeats.

"Not sure if the hesitation is troubling or reassuring," Talen said.

"I didn't much think about it before," Draven said and shrugged. "But, yeah, I do. Don't know as we'll all come home from it, or what shape we'll be in, but that don't matter."

Talen arched an eyebrow. "Don't it?"

"I don't mean that I don't care," Draven said. "Obviously I'd prefer we finish in the same condition we started. I'm saying what matters is that it's the right thing to do, that it needs doing, and we can do it."

"Well, hells," Talen said, setting down Gaoth's leg, "I don't know as I could've said it any better myself."

"As to the figuring how we all come out in piece," Draven said and chuckled. "I leave that out to you."

Talen let out a breath. "Wish I had your confidence in me. I weren't lying inside. I don't reckon anyone has ever stepped into a fight like this. Me included."

"Don't change the circumstances though, does it? It still needs doing."

"True enough," Talen said and draped a blanket over Gaoth. "But it don't make the fact I'll be responsible for not just you, Margaret, and Wilfred, but Alice and the others, any easier to bear. Not to mention all them we're going to help."

"You know damned well you ain't responsible for none of us," Draven said. "Everyone that's going is doing so by their own free will, knowing exactly what it could mean."

"Sure, but—"

"If any of us gets hurt or killed," Draven said, her expression stoney, "it's because we chose to take the chance. And you know I think of you as kin, but no one, not even you, gets to take that from us."

Talen's eyebrows lifted, her face flushed hot with anger, and her defenses went up. Thankfully, she did have the sense to take a breath before saying anything. "That ain't what I meant."

"I know, but that's what you'd be doing." Draven's eyes got a little wet. "We got to trust you to not die, knowing full it might still happen. You got to trust us too."

Talen opened her mouth.

"I know it ain't easy, especially for someone who lost as much as you." Draven wiped at her eyes and shrugged. "But that's what family is. Whatever this costs, we'll all pay it. Whatever the burden, we'll all carry the weight of it. Together."

Talen took a moment to think about how full her heart felt—and regularly did for the last several months. Such a contrast from the years before. She still wasn't used to it, but she was getting there. Lacking any words to reply to what Draven said, Talen just stepped over and hugged her friend.

After a moment, Gaoth snorted and stomped a hoof.

Talen let out a sigh. "Fine, we'll go see if Harriet's got a root cellar with any apples."

Draven laughed and the pair of them went on a search for apples. As it happened, Harriet did have a cellar, and there were a couple of apples. They were a little soft and mealy but Gaoth, in his magnanimity, accepted them with only a slight snort of disapproval. Once he'd finished, Draven returned to the Cumulus.

"You mind if I stay the night here with you?" Talen asked Gaoth, stroking his forehead.

He nickered softly.

"Elise, Joseph?" Talen asked Wilfred's mare, and Margaret's huge draft horse. "You got any objections?"

Both just stared at her silently.

"I'll take that as a no," Talen said.

Gaoth found a clean spot and laid down on his side. Talen settled down next to him, rested her cheek to his neck, and closed her eyes. As she began to drift off, Gaoth gently draped a foreleg over her.

Talen woke before sunrise. Gaoth—who needed even less sleep—still lay on his side, foreleg still draped over her. He looked to her with one eye.

"Morning," she said and kissed his neck. "Let's get you and the others some breakfast, huh?"

He snorted and removed his leg.

Talen took a minute to stretch and test her shoulder. It was still stiff and sore, but didn't protest much as she moved it around, so long as she was slow and deliberate. As such, she was mindful, favoring that arm, as she set to getting the horses fed. Once they were all chomping away happily, she decided to clean the barn. It didn't really have stalls for the horses. It seemed not only the polite thing to do but also a good way to see how her shoulder held up to some exertion.

It wasn't even an hour before a dull ache had settled into the joint. Working a little more carefully, and taking regular breaks, she managed to get the job done not long after sunrise. Wilfred showed up a short while after that.

"Booker and the others are inside and ready," he said. "But Harriet is insisting on feeding us breakfast before we leave."

"I'm sure she had to twist your arm," Talen said. "I'm going to pass though. We're going to be in the air for the next few days at least, so I figured I'd take Gaoth for one more ride." She went to grab her saddle, but her shoulder protested when she tried to lift it.

"Let me help," Wilfred said, stepping over.

Talen took up the saddle blanket and draped it over Gaoth's back. "Didn't feel that heavy last night when I took it off." She stepped back so Wilfred could get the saddle into place. "Of course, it's always easier coming off than on."

"It doing alright?" Wilfred asked, making sure the saddle was set.

"Damn sight better than it was," she said and set to securing the saddle.

"The bone is set and pretty much back to normal, but that took most of the spell. The meat is still bruised and battered, but I should be good after a day or two on the deck healing."

"Reckon I'll explain to our new friends now," Wilfred said, chuckling. "Rather than letting them stumble upon you."

Talen climbed onto Gaoth's back. "I won't be gone but an hour or so, then we can head out if everyone else is ready."

"The guns are on board," Wilfred said. "Draven spent the evening looking them over and making any needed adjustments."

Talen chuckled. "I'm guessing they all needed something."

"Like as not," Wilfred said. "You want me to save you anything from the breakfast table?"

"Nah," Talen said and urged Gaoth out of the barn. "Plenty for me out and about."

"Know I don't need to say it, but—"

"I'll be mindful where I'm riding and who sees me," Talen said. "I ain't forgot I'm in violation of the Eldar Treaty. I know that just cause some folk have been welcoming don't mean everyone will be, and I ain't looking to get shot again."

"Like I said, I know I didn't need to say it."

"But you feel better having said it," Talen said. "I understand."

"Enjoy your ride," Wilfred said then looked to Gaoth. "And keep your eye on her, just in case."

Gaoth snorted and bobbed his head.

Talen urged him on and they rode off, turning south, away from town. It was a mild morning and for a while, she let Gaoth choose the path. She just enjoyed the cool air and warm sun on her face. When her stomach made it known she needed to eat, Talen broke a new growth branch from a black cherry tree. Gaoth keeping a leisurely pace as she ate the bark and wood, saving the few berries for last. She did make sure to spit the pits into soil suitable for them to take hold and grow.

By the time they returned, just under an hour later, Wilfred was leading Joseph and Elise onto the ship while Draven, Booker, and Cyrus carried the newcomers' gear onboard. Talen felt a brief stab of guilt for not helping, but reminded herself that several people would protest any attempt, at least until her shoulder was healed.

Harriet stood in front of her house with Nelson, Margaret, and Delia. As the girl made her goodbyes to Margaret, Harriet strode over to Talen.

"Still ain't keen on the idea of staying behind," she said, as Talen slid from the saddle.

"I understand," Talen said. "But we both know I'm right."

"I suppose."

Talen nodded at the house and smiled as Delia gave Margaret a hug. "Besides all I said last night, I can't think of no one better to watch over Delia. Hopefully it's just for a bit, 'til we get her family back here safe. But—"

Harriet patted her good arm. "I'll keep her safe. Don't you worry."

"I weren't," Talen said. "All the same, keep your eyes open. I don't expect more Red Hands to show up soonish, if at all, but best to be prepared all the same. Have a plan to run if they do. I assume you got folks in town who will back you up?"

"You know," Harriet said, narrowing her eyes, the barest hint of a smile on her face, "I got a bit of experience watching out for myself and others."

Talen winced. "I reckon you do at that. Apologies."

Harriet chuckled and waved it off. "I know you wasn't talking down to me. But if it makes you feel better, Draven left a spell iron someone in town had offered up, and some loads for it. I ain't got much familiarity, but I expect I'll make do."

"I expect you will," Talen said, more than a little grateful it wouldn't be joining them on the trip south. She offered Harried her hand. "Thank you for your kindness. It's been an honor and a pleasure."

Harriet eyed her for a moment, then took her hand. "Don't go talking like you ain't coming back. I expect to see you, and the others, before too long. Along with a boatload of free folk as well."

"That be my preference as well," Talen said. "But—"

Harriet leaned in, her expression hard. "Then make it happen." She put her other hand over Talen's.

Talen was taken aback how strong her grip was.

"One lesson I learned," Harriet said, her eyes holding Talen's, "if you're going to do something that looks impossible, you got to believe you can do it. I saw you when we was talking about God, and I understand why you feel the way you do. Plenty of them that beat me the worst were the same who talked up the Lord the most. I know it ain't what you believe, and I won't tell you to listen, but I'll pray for you." She cracked a slight smile. "And I don't care if you like it or not."

Despite herself, Talen chuckled. "I ain't fool enough to argue."

"I knew you was a smart one," Harriet said, winked, and shook Talen's hand again before letting go. "Now go on, you got good works to do."

"Yes, ma'am," Talen said and turned to the house. "Margaret, it's time to go."

Margaret glanced back, nodded, and then knelt down to give Delia another hug.

Talen led Gaoth into the Cumulus without looking back.

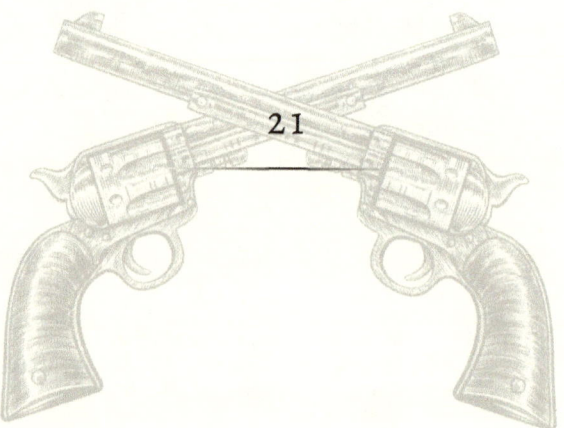

21

Gaoth stepped into his stall, clearly unhappy about it. Elise and Joseph greeted him, both of them far less concerned about the accommodations, but Gaoth barely spared them a nod.

Talen closed the door, stroked Gaoth's cheek, and rested her forehead against his. "I know you don't like it. I don't much fancy my quarters neither, which are smaller than yours, I might add."

Gaoth snorted.

"Yes, obviously you need more room because you're bigger, but my point was that you ain't alone in this. It's a hard thing, but we got a family here. We both need to run and feel the wind and I promise, we'll figure something out when this is done."

Gaoth chuffed.

"I don't know," Talen said. "Maybe you and me will start riding from one place to another and meet the others, but that's got complications too. We'll find something though."

He bobbed his head and pawed the floor.

"Thank you for being so understanding," she said. "I know you play it up, but I also know that you do a lot you don't like for me. I appreciate it." She kissed between his eyes. "And I love you."

He bumped her with his head, gently, and nuzzled his cheek to hers.

After a lingering moment, Talen wiped the tears from her eyes and kissed his brow again. "All right, I got to get topside and get some more healing in. I'll be back down later."

Gaoth snorted.

Talen went up the stairs and found Draven escorting the new passengers. A vague uneasiness soured her stomach, putting her on edge. She didn't mind them coming along—they would certainly need the help—but having strangers in what had become her home put her on edge.

"These here will be your rooms," Draven said, gesturing at the doors to the unused cabins. "Afraid space being as it is, you'll have to pair up."

Booker opened one of the doors, peeked inside, and laughed. "This is downright luxurious compared to some of the places we stayed."

"Sure beats sleeping on wet, muddy ground under a soaked tent," Cyrus said.

"That is a fact," Alice said, stepping past them and into the room. "I call the top bunk."

"Where will the others stay?" Frieda asked Draven.

"I got a mess of cots we'll put out in the hold," Draven said. "We can hold better than two-hundred folk if need be, though some will have to sleep on the floor."

"I expect they'll just be glad to be inside and heading north," Odie said.

"That sounds familiar," Frieda said. "I'd hoped when the war ended, we wouldn't need to run people no more."

"I expect that's the opinion of everyone on board," Talen said, eager to move past the crowd blocking the way.

"Oh, pardon me," Pearl said and stepped to one side.

The others followed suit, and Talen wove her way past them and started up the ladder. She paused after a step and looked back. "I'll be on the top deck saying my healing prayers, and if any of you got issue with seeing me naked, best to avoid it while the sun is up."

All of the newcomers went silent and appeared more than a bit taken aback.

Alice stuck her head out of her room, one eyebrow raised and a slight smile on her face.

Talen didn't quite know what to make of that, but it did settle some of the uneasiness.

"Get settled," Draven said, chuckling. "Once we're moving, I'll come back and show you to the galley."

Talen continued up the stairs, Draven following behind, still snickering.

When they reached the top deck, Draven went to the bridge, Talen to the front of the ship. As she kicked off her boots, the low buzz of the engines started up, and the Cumulus slowly lifted into the air, rising above the trees.

In short order, Talen had stripped down and laid out on the deck. She would've preferred to continue healing on the ground, where she could draw on more sources of energy, but seeing as she didn't have any other option, she closed her eyes and started her prayer.

Though obscured by scattered clouds, the sun answered her plea for assistance, and the warmth of it flowed into her. She set to work, guiding the magic to her shoulder and arm, knitting the bone, restoring the muscles, and repairing the tendons.

Her mother was silent.

When the prayer ended, the sun hung low on the western horizon, and the sky was painted shades of purple and orange. The air had a chill, but the lingering warmth of the sun kept it from bothering her. Much to her surprise, Talen noticed the crystal in her belly was once more shining bright. It wasn't blinding as it had been at the falls, more akin to a crafter's light. It wasn't likely anyone could see her just know, but she suspected it would be a damn sight easier once the sun set. As such, she got to her feet and dressed quickly.

That done, she tested her shoulder and arm again. The bone seemed to be healed, but the muscles and tendons still didn't feel quite right. If she'd been laying on the earth, she'd probably be done, but with just the sun to work with, she'd need another half a day to finish. She touched the crystal and wondered if maybe it was drawing power away from the healing magic.

Of course, it hadn't ever done that before.

A stab of fear crawled down her spine as she considered that maybe she'd done something to the crystal; changed how it worked. Could it be that it wouldn't trap stained no more? Maybe all it could do now was hold pure magic. Not that she was eager to fill it with corruption again. That had been an unpleasant experience and would've killed her, had the dwarves not intervened.

An instant later, the sheer arrogance of that thought dawned on her.

Who was she to imagine herself capable of changing something made by an elemental?

But hadn't humans done just that? Granted, there was a significant and willful effort put in, but it didn't change the fact it could be done.

This train of thought lead her back to the falls. Those crystals had been created without thought or concern for the elementals, but they were created all the same. Had Talen made a mistake leaving them behind because of how they were made?

It'd be useful to have a mess of bounty crystals when taking on a whole town of stained.

No, she decided. Using the results of terrible deeds, even for good, was an endorsement of the deeds themselves. Making exceptions was a short path to hell, morals and principles left by the roadside as you went.

The enormity of the task ahead settled over her like a slow-moving avalanche. She honestly didn't know if she could take down an entire town. Even if she did manage, what were the odds of not losing any of those she meant to help? Not to say she'd be doing it alone, but there was only so much the others could do.

Hell, even if the town weren't stained, even if they weren't armed, Talen and her companions were so massively outnumbered, they could easily lose to sheer numbers alone.

When her stomach grumbled its discontent, Talen decided to distract herself with something to eat.

Laughter and chatting reached Talen long before she got to the galley. She stopped on the stairs, listening. It sounded like everyone was there, and they were having quite a nice time of it. A twinge of envy stabbed at Talen's heart that they weren't overwhelmed by the task ahead. When she stepped inside, the smell of vegetable soup and whisky hung in the air. Everyone was indeed there, and they all turned to greet her with smiles.

"How are you feeling?" Margaret asked. "There's some soup saved for you."

"Much obliged." Talen went to get a bowl. "Another half a day, maybe a bit more, and I should be back to my full self."

"Broken arm healed in just a couple of days?" Booker said, shaking his head. "Best I ever saw was a week, and that was for an officer who paid dearly for the healing charms."

"The bone is healed," Talen said, filling her bowl. "It's the meat that needs more time."

Cyrus laughed. "Don't suppose you could share the secret?"

Wilfred and Margaret made a space between them, and Talen sat down.

"Ain't no secret." Talen ate a spoonful. She'd come to love Margaret's soup. "We pray to the earth, and all life around us for aid, and it answers with the magic to heal ourselves. I was always taught so long as you ask with humility and gratitude for the sacrifice of the gift, help will always be there."

"So, you're saying it's a healing spell that don't use no crafting?" Alice asked, an eyebrow raised.

"I didn't say there weren't no craftings involved," Talen said and took another mouthful. "But our craftings are our own."

Alice nodded but didn't say anything else.

Odie narrowed her eyes. "Are you suggesting we couldn't show humility and genuine gratitude?"

Talen looked to the others and furrowed her brow. "Did I say that?"

"You did not," Alice said and glared at Odie.

Odie stiffened a little. "I was just—"

"You were just insulting a new friend," Alice said. "Someone who, despite having no reason to, is putting herself in danger to help folks in need. Maybe you ought to try showing some of that humility and genuine gratitude for her assistance, instead of seeing a slight where there wasn't none."

Everyone went quiet as Odie glared back at Alice, who looked utterly unperturbed by it.

"You ain't entirely right," Talen said, holding her cup out. "Can I get some whisky?"

"Course," Draven said and gave the cup a good pour.

"I got reason to help." Talen took a sip. "It's the right thing to do. It's the same reason my people stood with the *Oceti Sakowin*."

Several brows drew together.

"Seven Council Fires," Talen said.

More blank expressions.

"Lakota, Dakota, and Nakota?" Alice asked. "Right?"

Talen nodded and smiled briefly before turning to Odie. "I could go on about how everyone in this room knows all too well how judging a whole group of people and being cautious around them ain't rude, it's survival. But I reckon that's unnecessary, and not a particularly pleasant conversation."

"It is not," Frieda said. "You'll have to forgive Odie. She don't always think before she speaks."

"You mean she was born with her foot in her mouth," Pearl said and laughed.

Everyone else chuckled. Odie looked put out, but after a moment she started laughing too.

"I'm sorry," she said to Talen. "I didn't mean to—"

Talen lifted a hand. "Already forgotten." It wasn't, not really, but she knew when to let things go and move on.

The conversation slipped back into lighter, more casual fair, including more than a few stories of Odie's lack of discretion. Talen finished her soup without saying another word.

"I hate to end the fun." Draven held up a rolled piece of paper, "but with all of us here, I reckon we should start talking about Aspen Hill." When everyone cleared a space, she unrolled the map she'd drawn. "Delia didn't know the whole town too well, so we either left it blank, or if she wasn't sure, it's drawn fainter." She pointed to a few spots in soft gray instead of stark black. "I'll fix it after I get a look over the town, but this should be enough to give us some idea."

Like all Draven's maps, this one was expertly drawn, and everyone gathered around.

"Town ain't small size-wise," Draven said. "Ten or so miles across." She pointed out the town center. "Ain't much here but a jail, courthouse, saloons, dry goods store, church, and the like. Mostly it's small farms of a hundred acres or so with two large plantations on either side of town."

Alice tapped the plantations. "I'd bet good money most of the people we're looking to free are going to be here."

Wilfred nodded. "Yeah, the small farms ain't like to have more than a few prisoners working them."

"We sure about that?" Talen asked. "This ain't the same as before the war. These folk are bound by dark charms, and from what Delia said, this preacher ain't doing it for money."

"Money wins out every time all the same," Wilfred said. "I guarantee the owners of those two plantations got more money each than the rest of the town put together. Even if they ain't buying people outright, they'll be paying them that decide who gets sent where. Or they buy off those getting working hands to 'lease' them."

"Well, I'll put down them that have two people enslaved as quick as them that have a hundred," Talen said. "I'm just trying to put a plan together here."

"According to Delia," Draven said and noted a section near the town center, "anyone not held on the farms themselves is going to be here."

"She have any notion where this preacher lives?" Talen asked.

Cyrus exchanged a look with the others and his brows furrowed. "Probably at the church," he said, and chuckled.

Though Talen didn't let the sudden flash of anger get the better of her, she couldn't keep it from her words. "You reckon I should know that? What with all the time I spend in human towns?"

His expression fell. "Right, of course. Apologies."

Talen waved it away. "What about this Forrest fella and his hooded knights? Any idea where they're going to be?"

"The plantations," Alice said. "Like Wilfred said, money wins over every time. They might work for, or with, the preacher, but the more folk you got in chains, the more gun hands you'll want to keep them getting any ideas."

Talen drew in a breath and looked over the map. The town being so spread out actually gave her some hope. It would mean the numbers they'd face at any given time would be much less than she feared.

"Alright," she said, "I figure we need to take out the guns first. Stained or not, a hundred farmers ain't going to be as much trouble as a dozen soldiers with battle experience, or Red Hand stalkers."

"Then get the folk on the plantation out," Booker said, nodding. "We keep it quiet and move quick enough, we can get most of the prisoners out before the rest of the town knows what's happening."

"The size will work to our advantage," Talen said. "Once we clear the big farms, we can take down the little ones with less trouble and work our way toward the center of town. Or, if we can't get to the plantations first, we bleed the town by clearing the small farms and working our way to the big ones. Either way, we'll have dozens, not hundreds to deal with at one time."

"Won't that leave anyone not held on the farms at risk?" Margaret asked. "What's to stop the townspeople from killing them before we get there?"

"Those are the folk we arm," Alice said.

Everyone looked to her.

She met Talen's gaze. "This ain't something we can do in a day," she said. "If we're going to do this, and do it right, we got to plan ahead. We sneak into town and get to them not on the farms. Let them know what our plan is, and give them arms enough to fight back. When we moved into the town itself, we'll have armed folk ready to catch the slavers by surprise, and from behind."

"That's assuming they want to fight," Frieda said. "Or can."

Odie nodded. "Not everyone will."

"And what if someone spills the beans before we're ready?" Booker asked.

That got him some dirty looks.

"I ain't saying anyone will, but all it would take is one," he said. "Y'all can't tell me you didn't never see someone get scared and think only of saving their own skin, even if it means throwing others to the wolves."

"This is where having Moses with us would come in a mite handy," Cyrus said. "I can't see no Black person turning on her."

"I don't know," Booker said. "I don't like to think that, but it could be. Also, we don't know these despicable crafts don't make someone ready to turn against their own."

"Detestable," Talen said.

"Apologies," Booker said.

Talen wasn't sure of his sincerity. Experience taught her that humans tended to offer insincere apologies for offenses they didn't personally find offending, but she kept these thoughts to herself.

"The only charms that would do that are the geas stones." She nodded at Wilfred. "He'll be able to tell if they're bound by one."

Wilfred nodded back, but didn't otherwise comment.

As she had no interest in explain to these—essentially—strangers their previous experience with geas stone, she was exceedingly grateful for Wilfred's silence.

"I suspect," Pearl said, "some of those we free along the way will be eager to take up arms and help."

"John Brown thought that too," Odie said. "Didn't work so well for him, did it?"

"That was for a slave revolt before the nation went to war over it," Alice said, pinning Odie with a glare. "If Captain Brown were here, I'd wager a hell of a lot more folk would rise up to fight by his side."

"Ain't no one arguing that," Frieda said. "But that ain't going to happen."

Talen saw the look on Wilfred's face. A thought had taken root in his brain, and it was sprouting fast. "What are you thinking?" she asked.

"Might be that ain't the case," he said.

Talen briefly worried Wilfred might be considering his hand at necromancy, seeing as Preacher Thompson had pulled it off, but she brushed the thought aside. However bad things might get, Wilfred would never sink to that sort of thing. Whatever he had in mind, he was still turning it over in his head, and she knew he didn't like sharing his thoughts until he had them in order.

"You got a way to raise the man from his grave?" Cyrus asked. "If you do, I expect he'd be up for the fight." He laughed, but no one else joined him.

"Nothing so dark and terrible," Wilfred said and met Talen's gaze. "But I need to think on it a bit more before I'll even know if it'll work."

"While he's thinking," Talen said, "we get back to planning."

"Can I ask a question?" Margaret said. "I know this isn't really my area of expertise, but—"

"Go on," Talen said. "If you got a question, we want to hear it."

"What do we do about the children?" Margaret asked.

Talen's brows drew together. "I don't follow. We ain't taking just the parents to freedom, we're taking everyone."

"I don't mean those children," Margaret said and swallowed. "I mean the children of the slavers. Surely many will have children, and some of them will be young. Maybe even babies."

The room went entirely silent, and Talen's blood turned to ice.

It hadn't even occurred to her. This situation was so unlike anything she'd dealt with before.

Margaret looked from Talen to Wilfred, and then to Draven. "Is the plan to, um, to kill them? Because I don't think I could. Or stand by while others do."

"No," Talen said. "We ain't killing children."

There was a long silence as everyone exchanged glances.

"And anyone who thinks otherwise is welcome to leave now," Talen said.

Another heavy silence settled over them all.

"I'll ask if no one else will," Alice said. "What if they're stained too? Or they decide they don't like that we put down their ma and pa?"

Everyone looked at Talen and the weight of it near on snapped her knees. "Wrong done in the name of right is still wrong."

"I don't disagree on the face of it," Alice said. "But do we need to decide what is and ain't a child? Some six-year-old holding his daddy's revolver ain't harmless but is more like to shoot himself in the foot." She shrugged. "But if that boy is twelve…"

"On the plains, I saw more than a few children dressed as soldiers," Talen said. "I expect you saw your share in the war."

Cyrus, Booker, and Alice nodded.

"Not all of them were the same," Talen said. "There ain't no magic age you reach and suddenly ain't a child no more. You do what you think is right, just know you got to live with it the rest of your lives."

No one was looking at her now.

"That said," Talen said, her tone cold and hard.

All eyes went back to her.

"I find out you put down a child," Talen said and turned to Alice, "and we all know damned well what I mean." She met each set of eyes, one by one. "Either by accident or otherwise, and you best not come back, cause I'll kill you myself."

She let the words hang in the air.

"You hear me?" she asked after a moment.

"Yes, ma'am," Alice said, seemingly mollified.

Margaret seemed uneasy still. "So, we're just going to make them orphans and leave them to fend for themselves?" She shrugged. "Is letting them die any better than killing them? Seems the same to me, just slower, and spares you from having to see it happen."

The complete and utter foulness of the few options available left Talen with a fetid knot in her guts she didn't know could ever be undone. It also fed her incandescent rage for Thompson, and every other stained that put her, her friends, and especially the children in question, in this situation.

"You saying we should take them slaver kids with us?" Alice asked.

"I'm not saying anything," Margaret said. "I'm asking because I genuinely don't know. I don't see any clean or easy way this can end." She let out a breath. "I just want to make sure we're really understanding what we're committing to."

"I might know someone who could help," Draven said.

Talen silently pleaded with her to have a solution.

"There's a fella named Dino Hicks in Tennessee," she said. "Know him from the Railroad. He was a station master, and there were a few times I found myself dealing with little ones that didn't have their slaver or catcher parents no more. He took them in and made sure they got someone to care for them."

"You think they're gonna go along nicely after we gun down their folks?" Alice asked. "They might be kids, but they were raised by slavers, in the ashes of the confederacy."

"Children can grow and change," Margaret said. "Eventually, they might come to see that what they were taught was wrong."

"I do admire what you're saying," Alice said. "It is certainly the Christian way of seeing it, but even if you're right, we won't have years to let them grow and learn."

Talen looked at Wilfred. "Those slumber loads you made up for the train job, would they hurt a child?"

Wilfred shook his head. "Nah. Worst might happen is they sleep longer."

Alice scoffed. "Oh, I'm sure they'd do much better waking up with—"

"Ain't no plan perfect," Talen said. "And I got more than a little experience saving folk I knew damned well were like to grow into someone who'd just as soon see me dead."

Alice's expression softened.

"Margaret brought up something I am ashamed to say I hadn't considered," Talen said. "It is surely a—" She turned to Margaret. "What's it called when there ain't no good answer?"

"Moral dilemma?" Margaret asked.

"Thank you," Talen said and turned back to Alice and the others. "It is a moral dilemma, but I think we got a solution. It ain't nice. It ain't easy, and it might not even be right, but it seems the least wrong."

Alice let out a sigh and nodded. "Wading through a river of shit, best you can hope for is that none gets in your mouth."

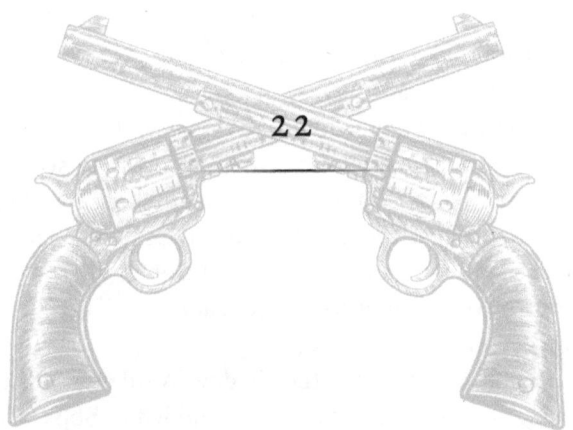

22

After a few more hours, they had a rough plan: what order things needed to happen, how to deal with the hired guns, and how to arm those in town. Booker, Cyrus, Alice, and even Odie had kept trying to get more detailed, but Talen kept shooting them down.

"I think it's time we all got some rest." Talen looked to Draven. "You got a way to get in touch with your friend?"

She nodded. "He should still have his wireless telegraph. I'll send word tonight and again tomorrow if I don't hear back."

"I don't think we're done yet," Cyrus said.

"If he can't," Talen said, ignoring Cyrus, "we should probably plan on dropping the kids off somewhere on our way north."

"I agree with Cyrus," Booker said.

"I was thinking the same," Draven said.

"Best the rest of us get some sleep then," Talen said.

"You ain't even going to acknowledge them?" Odie asked, putting herself right in front of Talen, who towered over her.

Talen bit back her anger and frustration. While she might have plenty of practice with people questioning her experience and knowledge, it never stopped feeling disrespectful. "I hadn't planned to, no," she said. "Cause there ain't nothing left to say. We got a good plan. Ain't no point in doing more until we know more."

"We have the start of a plan," Booker said.

Cyrus, Odie, Frieda, Pearl, and even Alice nodded.

"You ever made a battle plan?" Talen asked, perhaps more forcefully than she'd intended.

Booker furrowed his brow, clearly annoyed. "No, I wasn't an officer, but—"

"Have any of you?" Talen asked the others.

They all shook their heads.

"I have," Talen said. "When it comes to things you got experience with, I'll gladly defer to you. I am all ears when it comes to secreting people away, best routes and tactics for running, and anything else. I know fighting, and I got experience being outnumbered. As such, I'm telling you, doing any more planning is a waste of time and energy."

"With all due respect, I disagree," Cyrus said.

All due respect felt like none at all.

"There is an old saying among the Shadow Wardens," Talen said. "The first to die in battle is a detailed plan." She nodded at Booker, Cyrus, and Alice. "You all did some fighting. You ever, even once, have a plan that lasted when the shooting really started? I'm talking more than 'hold the line' or 'fix bayonets,' I mean."

The three veterans exchanged a look. Alice smirked.

"I ain't saying we're done," Talen said. "Not by damned sight. We'll go over it again after we get a better lay of the town. Might be we'll learn something, and if we do, we'll adjust the plan. But you can't account for everything in a fight. You got to keep enough options to react and then react to the other side reacting, and so on."

After a long moment, they nodded, if begrudgingly.

"I listened while we were figuring things, didn't I?" Talen asked.

"In fact, you did," Alice said.

"I ain't disrespecting no one here," Talen said, though she did feel more than a little disrespected herself. Not that she wasn't used to it.

"We all want the same thing," Draven said. "This is what she knows, and you best believe that she knows it well." She eyed everyone. "If you can't trust her skills or my opinion, well then, there ain't much point in you going the rest of the way. I'll gladly put down and you can make your way home."

There was a silent exchange of looks.

"I didn't mean no disrespect," Booker said.

"Me neither," Cyrus said.

"I ain't do nothing that needs apologizing for," Alice said.

"We're all tired," Talen said. "Get some sleep. Tomorrow I'll start showing you how take down stained."

As Draven led the others out, Talen gestured for Wilfred and Margaret to stay. Once the voices had faded down the hall, she looked to them both. "Was I out of line?"

"Nah," Wilfred said. "You got folk that are passionate about the cause is all."

"You can't tell me they would've pushed back like that if Talen was a human," Margaret said. "Or a man."

This caught Talen off guard. Not Margaret speaking up for her—they were sisters after all—but to word it so bluntly.

Wilfred lifted his hands. "I didn't say otherwise. But we're all weighed down by the baggage of our past, and it ain't easy seeing something you carried all your life ain't but a rock with no purpose. Makes you feel a bit of the fool for having carried it for so long."

"There's the philosopher coming out again," Talen said. "But I don't recall you having any problem listening to me when I talked. Even when we first met."

"Some of us know we're fools." Wilfred shrugged. "So, looking foolish is our day to day."

Talen laughed. "I can't argue the wisdom there."

"What did you mean earlier about John Brown?" Margaret asked as they started toward the door.

"That's right," Talen said, having forgotten. "I admit, I'm more than a little curious myself."

"Well, I don't know as it's even possible, but here's my thinking."

Talen leaned in.

"Back in Lawrence," Wilfred said, "fella came through with some new crafting contraption. Called it a Project-o-graph. It could cast photograph-like images into the open air, but in color and big as life."

Margaret nodded. "I think I saw that at the state fair a few years ago. The projections could move and some of them had sound too."

"That's the thing," Wilfred said. "It didn't look solid, mind. Sort of how you'd imagine a ghost would look. But that fella showed a train moving, half the folk in the tent near ran in fear they was about to be run down."

Talen thought she knew what Wilfred had in mind, but kept quiet.

"Spent many of my off hours trying to recreate the thing," Wilfred said. "Never quite managed, but I think maybe I know why. Up 'til now, never had reason to go back to it." His eyes sparkled, and he smiled wide.

"Reckon a ghost of John Brown himself might unsettle a number of these folk, and serve as a proper distraction should we need it."

"Lord preserve," Margaret said, eyes a little wide. "That would certainly unnerve me."

"You never shy away from audacious, do you?" Talen asked through a grin.

Wilfred chuckled. "Like I said, I don't know if it's possible. Even if it is, I don't know as I'll have the supplies to craft it."

"If anyone can do it, it's you," Talen said.

"That is a fact," Margaret said.

"I'm going to do some research and figuring before I go to sleep," Wilfred said, opening the door to his room. "Good night."

"Night," Margaret said as he closed the door. When they reached her room, she opened the door and turned to Talen. "I'm sorry for catching you off guard about the kids."

Talen turned to face her full on. "Don't never apologize for being who you are." She shrugged and let out a breath. "I'm a weapon. I destroy and kill. That's what I know, and who I am."

"I don't think that's a fair—"

"Not saying I don't care," Talen said. "I ain't some mindless killer like a stained, but when your job is killing, even for good reason, you don't always hear so well when your heart starts talking." She smiled. "You always hear your heart, and I count on that when I can't hear mine."

Margaret pulled her into a hug. "Thank you."

"No, thank you," Talen said, hugging back. "I'm going to need you on this job. We're going into some right murky places with what might need doing, and I'll need you to make sure I don't get lost in the darkness."

Margaret drew back a little and looked up at her. "I don't think you'll need me as much as you think you will." She tapped on Talen's chest, just over her heart. "And you hear more clearly than you give yourself credit for. But I'll always be there for you, just the same."

They made their good nights. Margaret went into her room and, after grabbing an apple, Talen headed below to the stables. Gaoth was lying down in the straw so Talen settled in next to him, her head on his neck and held up the apple for him.

Gaoth happily crunched it and draped one leg over her. Talen absently stroked it, stared at the ceiling, and turned over the whole situation in her head. It wasn't the morality of it that she doubted. That much at least was unambiguous. A single stained was a threat, a whole town was a nightmare. Add to that the detestable crafts, and people being held in bondage. Any single factor would be enough to drive Talen to act, all three just solidified her certainty.

The problem was in the doing and living with it after. Taking down a single stained was clean, if not always easy. Sure, sometimes innocents got caught in a crossfire, but not often. This though, this was different.

Even if everything went right, which it certainly would not, there would be children with their lives destroyed. It's easy for someone fully grown to see children were better off with no parents than one who was stained, but that sort of logic didn't hold for a child. Most of them would only know that their mother and father were taken from them.

It occurred to Talen then that some, maybe even most, of the kids in Aspen Hill were already dead. Either by direct murder from their parents, or neglect.

That terrible idea brought her more comfort than she liked.

Talen woke to an utterly quiet ship. She presumed that everyone else, like Gaoth, still slept. Carefully, she slipped from the horse's leg, kissed his cheek, and silently made her way toward the bridge. She wanted to check with Draven and start healing before dawn. If she did, she might finish up before the day was over.

The sky was shading from deep blue to pale, a line of orange on the horizon. The air was less chilled, but heavy with moisture. Talen could taste a storm building. Dark, heavy clouds to the south looked ready to burst. All that could work to her advantage. Talen didn't need to actually see the sun to benefit from its energy, and storms carried their own power. Might be she'd finish up sooner than she'd expected.

Draven waved from the bridge as Talen approached. "Morning." She took a drink from a mug of strong-smelling coffee.

Talen eyed the horizon. "Still an hour or so to go, I think."

"If I can see the sun's light, it's morning."

"Fair enough," Talen said, reaching for the mug and glancing at Draven.

The dwarf nodded.

Talen took a drink and felt it surge through her bones. "Did you reach your friend?"

"I did. He said he'd be glad to help."

"You tell him it could be a lot of kids?"

She nodded again. "He said he'll make sure everyone is seen to."

"And you trust him?"

"Entirely."

"Good enough for me," Talen said and patted Draven's shoulder. "How far away from Aspen Hill are we?"

"We could be there as soon as late tonight, early tomorrow," Draven said, then gestured at the storm to the south. "Looks like it's moving north, so it could slow us down. Based on what I see, shouldn't be more than a day though. Of course, could be there's worse farther south, in which case we might have to set down 'til it passes."

Talen eyed the dwarf. They'd flown through some pretty bad storms over the past months. One in particular had been rough enough to send everyone but Draven to the railing to retch up their guts. Never once had it been bad enough to set down.

"We got some on board ain't used to rougher sailing," Draven said. "They're green enough. Don't need to see them turn green literally."

"How uncharacteristically thoughtful of you."

"Don't say I don't never learn from past experience," Draven said and chuckled. "I am kind of hoping the storm lingers though. It'd give us some extra cover for our survey."

"It would be a nice change of pace for things to go our way," Talen said. "With that in mind, I'm going to finish my healing, so best warn the others to stay below if they don't want a show."

"Reckon Alice might see that as an invitation," Draven said, smirking.

"Another time and place, it might be just that," Talen said. It wasn't that Alice didn't pique her interest, but such a dalliance was like to ruffle things with Alice's companions. Talen didn't want that sort of trouble, especially before what was sure to be a trying time.

Draven, to her credit, didn't say anything more, so Talen went to the deck, stripped down, and started her healing incantation.

It wasn't long before the power of the storm flowed into her. She was distantly aware of the rain pelting her body and the rumble of thunder in the air. While she had drawn on what others would consider foul weather before, she didn't have the crystal in her belly then. It felt different, not just from other sources of energy—which she expected—but also different than any other time she'd drawn on a storm. Though powerful, storms tended to offer chaotic, inconsistent sources of power. This one however, while still frenetic, felt vast, while both eternal and fleeting. The humbling immensity reminded her of the lake elemental that had given her the crystal.

That's when a huge, ancient intelligence reached out to her. It wasn't as massive as the old one from the lake, but only in the sense that the ocean wasn't as big as the sky. It was, however, still impressive and just as alien.

Cleansing force. Inviolate protector, it said, more concepts than actual words.

As before, the elemental held the incantation together while also feeding power into it. Whereas the old one had been an overwhelming sensation, like being pulled under the surface of an infinitely deep lake, this power was raw and coursed through her like, well, like lightning.

The elemental of the Great Lake, and even of the falls, had been a singular being, solid and constant as a mountain. This one was more diffuse, somehow both temporal as the wind, but as everlasting as the sky itself. The others had also been beyond understanding because of their sheer presence. This one was just as incomprehensible because it was a literal contradiction.

Talen stopped trying to understand it, and simply accepted the gifts it offered, with humility and gratitude.

Typically, her healing prayers ended gently, as if waking from sleep. This time, however, it came abruptly. An instantaneous jolt, like the darkness following a flash of lightning. Talen sat up with a start and sucked in a deep breath. The rain blew in at an angle, drenching both her and the deck. All around, the storm roiled, and it took a moment to realize the Cumulus wasn't being tossed about in the tempest.

Talen couldn't help but wonder if the elemental was somehow keeping the worst of the gale winds from the airship. It seemed unlikely it would bother, or understand such short-term concerns, but then how could she know?

A chill ran through her soaked body, but it wasn't unpleasant. Talen leapt to her feet, not out of urgency or need, but simply because she could. Her body screamed to move. She gave it what it wanted, jumping, running, fighting invisible foes, and even swinging from rigging. If anyone were watching, she'd look a madwoman, but the simple act of moving was euphoric. In a brief instant, she understood the contradiction of the storm. It was the eternal present. No future, no past, just existing now and now and now. It had never been before, would not be in the future, but was forever here and now.

Even that sliver of understanding was impossible to hold, and it slipped away like the wind through her fingers. Inch by inch, she returned to herself, her body small, and confining after tasting the storm, but it was hers. Rather than be angry or resentful at what had been taken, she focused on being grateful for what had been given.

She closed her eyes, breathed slow and deep over and over, settling into her body, which was now fully healed. When the moment passed, she opened her eyes, smiled, and whispered, "Thank you."

Talen bent to pick up her, no doubt soaked, clothes, only to find them gone. Had they been carried off by the wind? It seemed unlikely because even her boots were missing, and if the wind had gotten enough to blow them overboard, Draven would've set down.

"I brought them into the cabin when the rain picked up," Draven shouted from just outside the bridge.

"What?"

"Your clothes," Draven said. "I'm guessing that's what you're looking for."

"Yeah, thanks," Talen said, coming back to herself and understanding what Draven was saying. She hurried to the bridge and followed Draven inside.

"I figured you'd appreciate them being dry when you finished," Draven said, after closing the door. She handed Talen a blanket. "Reckon you're probably cold after spending half a day laying out under a storm, getting water logged."

"Not really," Talen said, but accepted the blanket and used it to dry off. "To being cold, I mean. I do appreciate the dry clothes. Half a day, you say?"

"It's not much past noon," Draven said then glared at the storm. "Though you'd never know through these clouds. Luckily the wind ain't pushing us around too much."

"Yeah. Strange that," Talen said, getting dressed. She felt Draven staring at her with narrowed eyes, but Talen didn't look up.

"If I'm figuring it right, and the winds keep as mild as they are, we'll reach Aspen Hill sometime around dawn tomorrow."

"So not much delay then?"

"Not too much, no," Draven said, finally turning away. "What the hells were you doing out there anyway? Dancing about and such. Got worried you might jump over the railing for a moment there."

Talen buttoned her shirt, and realized for the first time her crystal hadn't grown much brighter, but she could feel significantly more power in it. "Can't really explain it. Least not in a way that would make a bit of sense. Just felt the need to move, so I did."

"Uh huh," Draven said, eyeing her again. "What ain't you saying?"

Talen let out a breath and shook her head. "You don't miss much, do you?"

"I do not."

"You ever hear tell of a storm elemental?"

Draven stared at her for a long, quiet moment, her expression blank, which was the dwarven equivalent to her jaw dropping to the floor.

"I think I might've just met one."

Draven's brows drew together. "You saying you had *another* elemental reach out to you?"

"I think so, yeah." Talen said. "So, it was an elemental? Not just me imagining?"

Draven shook her head. "Elementals exist anywhere enough life energy, and hence, enough magic, has gathered to allow them to come into being. There's a lot of lore on the different sort of elementals, but tempest elementals are the most mysterious. Some say they're all just a single being, manifesting in multiple places at the same time. Others say each is its own distinct entity, but it's all as much of a guess as it is educated."

"From what I felt, I understand why."

Draven held up two fingers. "Twice, twice you get an elemental to reach out to you, one of which was an old one. How the hell do you manage that?"

Talen shrugged and set down the wet blanket. "If I knew, you'd be the first I'd tell, but I reckon this time might have to do with the crystal in my belly."

"I suppose that makes some sense." Anyone else would've missed the almost imperceptible way the corners of Draven's mouth turned down, and her eyes softened.

Talen recognized the obvious disappointment in her friend's expression. Once again, she hadn't been touched by an elemental while Talen had been.

"If I could share the experience, you know I would."

"I do," Draven said. "I'm happy for you, and truly honored to know someone the elementals see as worthy." One side of her mouth pulled up into a slight smile. "But I'm also more than a bit jealous."

"Next time, I'll see about making an introduction."

"Don't you mock me! Just cause the elementals favor you, don't mean I won't put you on your ass." Draven's words were harsh, but the lingering smile belied any actual anger.

"I wouldn't dare," Talen said, tugging on her boots. "Truly though, if I could let it be you instead of me, I'd do it, gladly."

Draven's expression turned wistful. "And I appreciate that. If it's meant to be, it'll happen. Now you best head below and get something to eat. I expect you got some folks waiting to hear about how to kill a stained."

Talen got to her feet. "I'd almost forgotten." She bent and hugged Draven from behind. "Thank you, my friend, for everything."

Draven patted Talen's arm with her hand.

"And I'm sorry you're not special enough to—"

Draven playfully pushed her away and faux glared. "Get the hell off my bridge!"

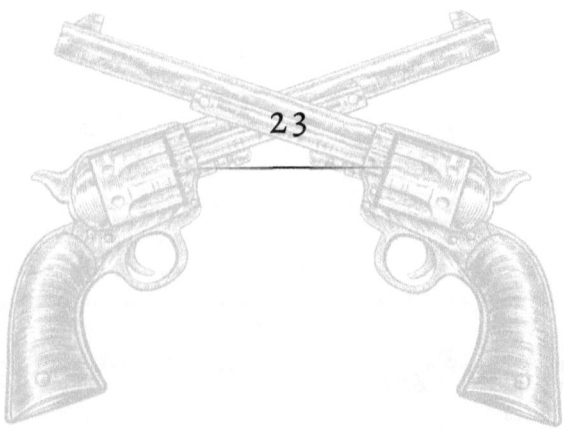

23

As Talen descended the stairs, she felt energized, but also lighter, as if she could float through the air. However, her mind had returned to normal; confined and limited. She found everyone in the galley finishing up lunch. The newcomers sat in front of plates in various states of uneaten, their pallor a little green around the edges.

"You finished healing?" Wilfred asked, from what was probably a second bowl of stew.

"I am." Talen went to get herself something to eat. She wasn't in the mood for something heavy, so she skipped the stew and gathered some branches and leaves that were on the edge of not good anymore.

"Well, you look refreshed and rested," Margaret said, as Talen sat down next to her.

"Thank you, I think," Talen said and grinned. She chewed on a sugar maple branch, took in the slightly queasy sextet, and turned back to Margaret. "They don't look so good."

"That's actually a mite improvement over how they looked a couple hours ago," Wilfred said. "Winds didn't ever get too bad, but you remember how the swaying, even gentle, got to us at first."

"We can hear you, you know," Booker said.

"And talking about it ain't helping none," Pearl said.

"Wasn't being dismissive," Talen said. "And I ain't trying to make you—"

"Don't say it," Frieda said. "The word might be enough."

"Sorry." Talen turned to Margaret and Wilfred. "You didn't give them none of Draven's tea?"

"We did," Wilfred said. "I suspect that's why they don't look worse."

"How about a distraction then," Talen said and chewed on some leaves. They were dry and didn't have much flavor, but they served.

"I'm willing to try anything," Cyrus said.

"I'll make some more tea," Margaret said and got up. "Just keep breathing deep. It eases the, um, the reflex."

Talen waited for Margaret to return with the tea. From the smell, she used extra ginger in it. Their green-gilled guests carefully drank it down. Sure enough, after a short while, their color returned to something closer to normal, and Talen didn't worry so much about anyone retching up on her.

"Feeling better?" Margaret asked.

They all nodded.

"A bit, yes, thank you," Odie said.

Once they'd finished, Margaret went and made another round.

"All right then," Talen said. "First question: any of you ever had run-ins with stained?"

"Not as such," Frieda said. "There were rumors some of the catchers were stained."

"And we did see a couple get taken down by stalkers," Pearl said. "But we never had to face a stained ourselves."

"I ain't but read about them in the papers or heard others tell," Odie said.

"What about you?" Talen said to Booker, Cyrus, and Alice. "Never had a soldier turn stained?" She'd heard it wasn't uncommon during the State's War for some soldiers to take to the dark.

"Not that I recall," Cyrus said and looked to Booker. "You ever hear tell of any?"

He shook his head. "Not that I ever saw. There was plenty of rumors about happenings in another company though."

"Yeah, always someone who knew someone who knew someone," Cyrus said. "Once found a couple of dead slavers I think might've been stained." He shuddered. "Hard to tell the difference in smells between a stained and a corpse that's been in the sun too long though."

Everyone took a deep drink of their tea.

"I damned near got ripped apart by one," Alice said.

Everyone turned to her.

"It was at Vicksburg." Alice's expression turned to stone. "We didn't have enough training or supplies, but we kept the slavers at bay. They didn't like it much, and there were three who charged ahead. We shot them dozens of times, but they didn't hardly slow. I saw some terrible things done during the war, but what those three did was unholy. We ended up having to literally club them to death with our rifles."

There was a long moment of silence.

"I won't soon forget the smell," Alice said. "Lord knows ain't no one smelling like fresh-picked flowers, but they were foul beyond words."

"You never told us about that," Pearl said.

"Not exactly something I think back on if I can help it," Alice said. "I'd just as soon forget it ever happened."

"The more rot, the worse the smell," Talen said, her own stomach turning at the memory of the fetid stench. "You don't never get used to it, and I expect the very earth itself will be tainted by rot. Even if you don't smell it, you'll feel it."

"Like at the falls?" Margaret asked.

"Though I reckon it'll be worse." Talen turned to the others. "But like Alice said, stained don't go down easy, especially with a mundane shooter."

"Then why don't we have spell irons?" Booker asked.

"Them Red Hands had some," Frieda said. "Why'd we leave them behind?"

Fresh indignation sparked in Talen, but she kept it from exploding. Instead, she pinned Frieda with a cold, hard stare. "Because I won't have them near me. Use of blood magic is profane."

Odie and Cyrus looked as if they wanted to protest, but they kept quiet.

"Draven has some special ammunition," Talen said, glad to move on. "Might not do as much as a spell iron, but you get a clean shot, and it'll bring them down. Stained are tough, and they heal fast. So, if you're going drop them, you need to do as much damage as possible, as fast as possible." Talen tapped her forehead, then her chest over her heart. "If you don't hit their head or heart, keep shooting 'til you do. Anything else, even if they get tore up inside, they will get back up eventually."

Alice shuddered and there was a nervous exchange of glances between the others.

"So, I hope you're a good shot," Talen said, looking from Booker, to

Cyrus, and then to Alice. "If they get close enough, follow Alice's example, and use the rifle butt to go at their skulls. Don't bother with nothing fancy. All that matters is getting the job done."

The three veterans nodded but wouldn't meet her eyes.

"You all came of your own free will," Talen said, as gently as she could manage. "That said, I won't judge you if you decide you want to stay on the Cumulus and—"

"As good as I imagine you are," Alice said, "I don't think even you could take them all on your own. I didn't volunteer to stay behind. I might not be a crack shot, but I'll get the job done." She shrugged, still not looking at Talen. "Or I won't, but I'll be damned if I'll go without a fight."

Cyrus and Booker nodded their agreement.

The sense of relief that washed over Talen could've lifted her above the clouds. She did her best not to let it show—she didn't want it to demoralize anyone—but if it did, no one seemed to notice.

She hadn't lied. They were heading to what was like to be the hardest fight any of them, including her, ever fought, and she couldn't begrudge a change of mind after realizing the fact. That said, every additional gun on their side of the coming fight increased the odds of success.

Not to mention, a part of her looked forward to fighting with Alice at her side.

"All right then," she said, glad to move on. "Based on the layout, most of the town is spread far and wide. I don't expect we'll run into more than a handful at a time at first. The plantations and them hooded boys will be a different matter, but we'll thin them out beforehand. The Cumulus has some guns, and hopefully some of the folk we're here to rescue will be backing us up..."

"But?" Cyrus said.

"But," Talen said, "it'll be a hard and bloody fight."

Pearl sat a little more upright and nodded to her sister. "We'll get to you if you get hurt. Yell for us, and we'll come running."

"Damn right we will," Frieda said.

"Draven said we should get there sometime before dawn," Talen said. "I suggest using what little daylight, such as it is, we got left to do some target practice."

"In the middle of the storm?" Cyrus asked.

"You won't be using muskets," Talen said. "Your cartridges won't get fouled by the rain."

"How long will we set down for?" Booker asked.

"Who said we'd set down?" Talen asked, genuinely perplexed.

"You mean for us to practice shooting on the deck of an airship, in the air, in the middle of a storm?" he asked.

Talen looked at him, brow furrowed. "Is that a problem? Ain't like the stained are going to hold still for you, so it'll be good to get used to shooting on shifting ground. Rain could work to our advantage if any of them have muskets instead of rifles, they won't be able to shoot back."

"You'll get used to it," Margaret said to Booker.

Talen smiled. "I also suggest everyone take part. Might be you'll all need to take up arms at some point, so best to get some practice shots in."

"One afternoon ain't much time," Alice said.

"It's better than none at all," Talen said. "I don't expect miracles, but any bit will help."

No one looked terribly happy about the idea, but no one protested.

"If you feel the need," Talen said, shoving the last of the leaves in her mouth, "change into something you don't mind getting soaked, then grab a rifle from the armory and meet me on deck."

Wilfred was grinning into his stew.

Talen almost regretted spoiling Wilfred's belief he had avoided being out in foul weather. Almost. "Wilfred, come help me with the targets."

His smile faded, but he stood and followed her out.

"You are not a nice person," he whispered as they headed to the cargo bay.

"It'll build camaraderie," Talen said, flashing him a slight grin.

"Uh huh."

They gathered the metal painted targets Draven had made, and hauled them upstairs. The rain was still coming down, though the wind had eased so the gas bladder blocked most of the downpour. The two of them set the targets in place. Once they were secure, Wilfred went to the control mechanism and tested how it moved them. The targets began to shift and turn, moving back and forth smoothly.

Booker, Cyrus, and Alice arrived first. They hadn't changed, just put on coats. Frieda, Pearl, and Odie arrive a few minutes later. They'd changed into pants, which surprised Talen, but also impressed her. She was glad to see the women could be practical when needed.

Everyone eyed the turning and twisting targets.

"You can thank Draven for that," Talen said. "Not always easy to find places to shoot."

"You suggesting white folk get nervous seeing Black folk, and an elf, honing their skill with arms?" Cyrus asked.

"Oh, heaven's no," Alice said.

Everyone laughed.

"First rule," Talen said. "Your finger stays off the trigger 'til you've taken aim and are ready to shoot." She motioned to the targets. "I don't want no bullets going any direction but that one, understand?"

Everyone nodded.

Talen gestured at a collection of X's drawn on the deck. "Those are your firing points. You don't shoot unless you're on one of them. When you shoot, hit or miss, move to the next."

"If the targets are moving, why do we need to move too?" Pearl asked.

"Cause it won't just be what you're shooting at that'll be moving," Talen said. "Best way to get shot is to stand in one place. Aim, shoot, move, aim, shoot, move. When you run dry, step back, reload, then get back into the rotation."

They all nodded again.

"Have at it," Talen said and stepped away.

Unsurprising, the vets had the most confident stance and the best aim, though even they only hit one in five shots at first. Alice was the best, and once she found her air legs, she was hitting three or four out of five. Booker and Cyrus eventually found the rifle's sweet spot and were matching Alice shot for shot. Talen imagined that they were likely sent to fight undersupplied and were used to making every shot count.

Pearl and Frieda, who weren't doing so well and were getting frustrated, needed extra guidance and encouragement. Talen let them stay in place until they started getting some hits and built their confidence. They weren't doing much better than one in four or five, but Talen made it a point to praise every hit. It wouldn't do to have anyone questioning themselves now. It'd only get worse when there were bullets coming back their way.

The biggest surprise was Odie. She handled the repeater with ease, and while she didn't get a lot of center hits, at first at least, almost every shot at least nicked the target. Talen couldn't help but admire the steady consistency with which she fired and moved, almost like a dance.

Wilfred brought more ammunition as needed, and Margaret came up after a bit and offered some suggestions from her own experience of learning to shoot. Talen could tell Margaret enjoyed showing off her customized repeater and her skill with it.

Once Frieda, Pearl, and Odie were confident and comfortable with the weapons—though Odie never really lacked the latter—and Booker, Cyrus, and Alice's muscle memory returned, Talen had them focus more on their accuracy.

The storm never faded, but neither did it worsen. The rain only occasionally blew in from the side, but it was enough to soak them all eventually. It also seemed focusing on shooting worked well to push back the lingering motion sickness. By the time it started to grow dark—well, darker—they called it a day. Everyone was tired, but smiling, and went to change into dry clothes.

Even though the storm wasn't bad, Draven set the Cumulus down in a clearing and joined everyone in the galley for supper. As Margaret and Wilfred set to making beans with bacon and some biscuits, Draven instructed the others on cleaning and caring for the rifles. Talen knew the basics of caring for a mundane shooter, but Draven was the expert.

There was some grumbles and glares at Draven's meticulous instructions, but everyone complied. Talen took the time to care for her spell irons, even though she hadn't used them. It was calming and provided a sense of community.

Of course, she finished long before the others. As such, she took the opportunity to go outside and forage. She wasn't sure which state they were in, but there was less chill in the air, and some of the trees were already flowering. She collected some new growth branches—which would keep longer—as well as a large collection of leaves and even some of the flowers to enjoy immediately.

When Talen returned to the galley, Draven had apparently been appeased with the cleaning and had returned the rifles to the armory. Everyone sat at the tables with steaming bowls and biscuits. All eyes went to Talen when she came into the galley and then to Margaret.

She gave them a stern look. "You can wait another minute or two for her to sit down."

Talen's mouth pulled up at one corner. Leave it to Margaret to enforced decorum, allowing no one to eat a bite until everyone was there and seated with their food. Talen went to stow the branches and some of the leaves. Not wanting to draw Margaret's ire at failing to follow proper table manners, she put the remaining leaves and all the flowers into a bowl.

Wilfred tried to surreptitiously steal a spoonful of food, but Margaret lightly slapped the back of his head without even looking at him.

That eased the mild tension and impatience. Everyone, including Wilfred, shared a laugh. Talen held back a grin and made a point of very slowly going to her seat, seven sets of hungry eyes following her every move.

"Okay, now you can eat," Margaret said in her schoolmarm voice, though she was smiling and clearly proud of herself for ensuring proper manners.

Everyone set to eating.

Talen had never understood the human fascination with what was and wasn't permitted while eating at a table, but she respected and loved Margaret, so she never griped or pushed back. If these little rituals made her sister happy, Talen was glad to oblige, especially when it didn't really take any effort to do so.

The leaves and flowers were sweet and a kind she hadn't tasted in a very long time. It took her a moment to recall when she'd had them last, and with that, the memories of running with the Railroad, with Wilfred, came flooding back. That was before the elves had joined the *Oceti Sakowin* in their fight against the US, and before her people had been slaughtered.

It was also before the Eldar Treaty pushed the surviving elves onto reservations and made it legal to kill any elf that crossed the Mississippi river. It seemed so long ago. Despite the work she and Wilfred had been doing—helping people escape to freedom—it'd been a happy time for her.

In the end, they'd each gone their own way, grown and changed over the years. While Talen did think back on the time fondly, she also knew those days were in the past and no one could live there.

"We had to have fired off a few hundred shots," Cyrus said.

Talen snapped out of her nostalgic reverie.

"How many bullets you got on this boat?" Cyrus asked.

"We stock up when the opportunity arises," Draven said, between mouthfuls of beans and biscuit. "But I also make my own."

"Including the powder?" Alice asked.

Draven nodded. "What I make is cleaner and makes less smoke than human powder."

"I just thought it was the wind blowing the smoke away," Booker said.

Draven shook her head. "Dwarven powder is basically smokeless. We use it underground, and it ain't a good idea to use something that creates a lot of smoke when ventilation is limited."

Talen listened absently to the discussion, not really interested. At some point, she met Wilfred's gaze, and they shared a knowing glance. At least it seemed to be knowing. Wilfred, despite often playing himself off as oblivious, rarely missed a thing. Did he notice what she was eating and knew it was taking her back? Or was it doing Railroad business together again? Or was she wrong on both counts and he just noticed her wrestling with something? Whichever it was, he didn't say anything, or move closer to her, but he did give her a warm, knowing smile. Which was exactly what she needed at the moment.

With full bellies and dry clothes, spirits were high and the conversation turned light and jovial. Talen even laughed from time to time. It had been a long day for everyone though, and soon the call for sleep was too much to ignore. Draven returned to the bridge and set the Cumulus back on its path to Aspen Hill. Frieda, her sister, Odie, and Margaret were the first to excuse themselves and head for their bunks. Booker and Cyrus stayed to help Wilfred and Talen clean up, much to Talen's surprise. They headed off to bed once everything was dried and stowed.

Wilfred and Talen stood alone in the galley, a comfortable silence between them.

"You okay?" he asked after a bit.

"I am," Talen said. "Damnedest things can stir up memories, you know?"

He nodded, stepped to her, and wrapped his big arm around her. "I do, indeed."

"I said I was fine," Talen said in mock protest but hugged him back.

"I never said I was." He gave her another squeeze. "Maybe I'm the one needed a hug."

Talen smiled and squeezed back, enough to make him wince.

"Easy now. Don't break me," he said and leaned his head against hers.

"You nervous?"

"Be a fool if I weren't."

"Well, you said you played the fool daily, so does that mean you ain't?"

He chuckled. "I'm nervous, but not scared. This ain't like what we've gotten into before. Odds ain't anywhere near in our favor. The plan's got a lot of moving parts, which is a lot of spots something can go wrong."

Talen nodded. "That is a fact." Typically, when Wilfred was serious like this, it tended to unnerve her, but she found it a comfort just now.

"But ain't nothing else to be done. This is something that needs doing, and there ain't no one else to do it." He pulled back, met her eyes, and smiled. "And I don't know of anyone else I'd trust to do it and come out the other side."

Talen took his face in her hands, kissed his forehead, and then rested hers against his.

To his credit, he didn't say anything, just stayed with her in that silence.

Yes, there were times Talen missed what she and Wilfred had, but this wasn't one of them. Their relationship might be different, certainly not as physically intimate, but it wasn't any less. Hell, she'd argue they were even closer now, and their bond even stronger. That filled her heart with warmth and comfort. However, it also fed the fear that tried to crawl up her spine. The cold dread served as a hard reminder that to be afraid meant having something to lose. Before meeting Margaret, Talen had rarely been scared. But now, she had a family again. Worse, she knew firsthand what it was like to lose one.

Even so, she wouldn't go back. Life, especially one as long as hers, was rife with change. Sometimes it was devastating and sometimes it was like an entire new world being born.

If you spent too much time longing for what had been, or fretting about what would be, you won't never appreciate the moment.

Talen closed her eyes and savored every passing second.

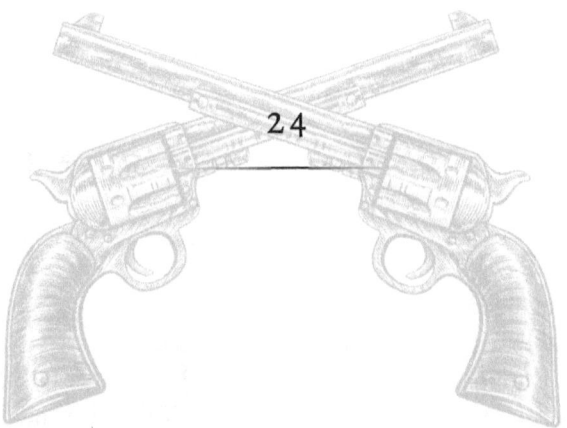

24

As was usual of late, Talen woke in the stables, her head on Gaoth's shoulder. That was at least one good thing about him having a stable. He could lay down and sleep more freely. When they were riding in the wild, Gaoth would only lay down to sleep for very short periods. Talen didn't like him being cooped up so much, but she couldn't deny how rested he seemed.

"Don't worry, old friend," she said, stroking his flank. "We'll find a good balance. Giving you a safe, warm place to sleep, and plenty of time to run free."

Gaoth twitched in his sleep but didn't otherwise stir.

Talen carefully got up, kissed his cheek, and went to her cabin to change. The stables were remarkably clean, thanks to Draven's spindles and her own diligence, but there was no escaping the musky scent from sleeping with a horse. Talen herself didn't mind, but even Wilfred and Margaret had commented on it before.

Peering through the port hole in her cabin, Talen noted the sun was still an hour or so from clearing the horizon, which meant, unless something had happened, they'd be arriving at their destination shortly. She made sure to don her holsters and coat. After a moment of consideration, she retrieved the pouch from a small drawer and tucked it into a pocket. It held the last two glamour stones she'd been given before going to join the *Oceti Sakowin* in their fight. She'd used the other four last year to disguise herself as human in Chicago and Boston, and though she still hated the idea of using them, there was no denying they might be needed.

Letting out a sigh, she left her cabin and made her way up to the cabin to see Draven and where things stood.

Topside, she found the storm had mostly passed. The clouds were still heavy and gray, hiding the fading stars from view, but the rain had stopped. She took a moment to breathe in the fresh, predawn air, savoring the taste of dew, pollen, and damp earth, and then went to the bridge. Instead of Draven, Wilfred sat behind the large wheel.

"Morning," he said. "Or near morning, I suppose."

One side of Talen's mouth pulled up into a half grin and she arched an eyebrow. "Draven, you've grown."

Wilfred chuckled. "She decided to get some sleep so as to be rested when we get to where we're going, so she asked me to mind the shop."

"You got any notion as to how close we are?"

"Well," he said and took a drink of coffee, "Draven went down about three or four hours ago and said we were five or six hours out still. Our stop-off for dinner costs us some time. Figuring she's right, and she always seems to be, I'd say we've an hour or two to go."

Talen felt a twinge of regret that she hadn't taken the opportunity to let Gaoth, as well as the other horses, out to walk and run a bit when they'd stopped. She'd have to make it up to him, and Joseph and Elise.

"It seems you take to being an airship captain," Talen said, trying to distract herself from the guilt.

"Well, the ship damn near pilots itself. Ain't much to it really. The hard part is the map-reading and navigation. I ain't got anywhere near Draven's skill, but I reckon I'm learning."

"You're one of the sharpest people I ever met, so I suspect you'll have it down before long."

Wilfred smiled. "Kind of you to say."

Neither of them said anything for a long while, just watched the sky lighten as the sun crept closer to the horizon. The clouds still blocked most of the sky, but the colors painted across them were plenty pretty enough.

An hour or so later, Draven came onto the deck. She carried three mugs, so Talen opened the door for her. Talen couldn't say she looked refreshed or well-rested, but mostly because the dwarf never really looked tired either.

"Morning," she said and handed a cup of coffee to Wilfred and Talen each.

"Morning." Talen accepted the cup and took a sip. "How'd you know I'd be here?"

Draven shrugged. "You're usually up well before everyone else, and you weren't in the galley so I took a gamble. Figured worst case, I'd have an extra mug to drink."

"Well, much obliged."

Draven turned to Wilfred. "Anything I need to know?"

"We didn't budge more than a hair or two," Wilfred said, "and I made sure to ease her back on track when it happened."

Draven checked some of the gauges and instruments and smiled. "Well done. We're right on course. Also, much obliged for letting me get some shut-eye without having to stop."

"Happy to help," Wilfred said. "I rather enjoy it. It's quite a feeling, steering something so big and complicated."

Draven practically beamed. "Isn't it just? Glad you're comfortable with it. How would you feel handling the controls while we do our survey of the town?"

Wilfred's eyes went wide, and he froze, mug halfway to his mouth. "Pardon?"

Talen hid her own smile with another drink of coffee and concentrated on resisting the urge to tell Wilfred, I told you she was sweet on you.

"We need to make sure our map is as accurate as possible," Draven said. "No offense to any of you, but I'm the one with the experience and knowledge about such things, so I'd like to be the one observing and noting. Can't do that from the bridge, and I can't pilot while I'm on the deck."

Wilfred's ever-present smile faltered. "Well, I don't know. It's one thing to just keep us on track and bring it back into line if we drift, but actually piloting—"

"I got every confidence in you," Draven said.

"As do I," Talen said. "I don't expect Draven would ask if she didn't think you capable."

"I damn sure ain't asking *you* to do it," Draven said to Talen. "I love you as a sister, but I expect you'd find some way to turn us upside down or crash into a damned cloud."

Wilfred let out a belly laugh, but stifled it to a chuckle when Talen shot him a, mostly, faux glare.

She opened her mouth to protest, but couldn't. "I confess I'm not at all mechanically inclined, and this entire contraption is a total mystery to me." She grinned. "Though I do take it as a compliment you think I'd be capable of such a monumental screwup."

Draven arched an eyebrow and then looked back to Wilfred. "I'll be just out on deck if anything happens, and I'll give you signals on when and how much to change direction."

Wilfred shrugged. "You're the expert, so I ain't in no place to argue. If you think I can manage, I reckon I can."

"All right then. I'll have the others"—Draven nodded at Talen—"including you, Miss Monumental Screwup, making notes as well. I'll take it all and put it together with my own observations. That should get us a useful map."

"What about the masking charms?" Talen asked. "Margaret managed, but it seemed a heavy lift so maybe I—"

"You still got that crystal shining in your belly?"

"I do." Talen didn't mention how it seemed to be holding even more magic than it did before. "But I think I got a good handle on keeping the flow under control."

"I don't doubt you do," Draven said, not unkindly. "But we got to weigh the chance of something going wrong with how bad it would be if things did. If Margaret can't manage to power all the charms up, you can go and help her, in which case there ain't nothing lost but a few moments. If you do it and pour too much power in, you could overload and completely burn out the charms."

Talen disliked the idea of foisting work onto to Margaret, especially since it would be so much harder for her. However, she also hated the idea of being the reason this endeavor failed entirely. "So best to go the route where that ain't like to happen then?"

"I know you feel the need to carry three times the load as anyone else," Wilfred said, "in no small part because you can. But it's okay to let others help a little from time to time."

Talen wanted to argue, but neither of them had said anything she disagreed with. In fact, her desire to argue just proved Wilfred's point.

"Also, I know for a fact Margaret, at times, feels like she ain't pulling her own weight," he said.

"That's not true at all!"

"Of course it ain't," he said. "We all know that, but it don't change the fact she feels that way. You let her do this and apart from not risking the charms, Margaret gets to feel her true importance. Reckon that makes a nice little extra bit."

Talen sighed in resignation. "Well, if I could've fooled myself into arguing before, I sure as hell can't now. I suppose it won't do no harm for me to feel like I ain't doing as much as I should for a change."

"Yeah, that'll be a refreshing twist," Draven said, stone-faced.

Wilfred didn't even bother holding back his laughter.

"You can both kiss my ass," Talen said through a glare, but couldn't keep the hint of a smile from her lips. "I reckon I'll head below and make sure everyone's got a pencil and paper."

"Much obliged," Draven said, her expression still stoic, as she gathered up her own papers.

An hour later, everyone had gathered on the deck, save Wilfred who was in the bridge.

Draven handed out pencils and paper. "Don't worry about being exact. I'll take care of that. You note anything of interest. Number of buildings, best guess of distance between them and the like. If you see anyone out and about, how many? If you can see a weapon, note it, and obviously, if you see anyone chained or charmed."

A round of nods.

"We dropped to one thousand feet to let you see better, but we should still be high enough that most won't notice us," Draven said. "Now it's possible some might hear the engine noise. As such, I got Wilfred running them slower to keep them quiet as possible. If anyone does look up and the masking charms don't fool them, they might take a shot at us."

"Will we be in range?" Alice asked.

"We'll be too far for most rifles to have any sort of accuracy," Draven said. "Especially shooting straight up. Even a Sharps ain't like to hit nothing but the ship itself, which can take it. But that don't mean someone won't get lucky, so you see them take aim, get out of sight and let the rest of us know."

"And if what we heard is true," Talen said, "these are stained, and they can be a mite unpredictable. Could be some have a spell iron, so don't be stupid."

"Do we need to worry about them hitting that?" Odie asked, motioning at the gas bladder.

"The outside is a weave of dwarven steel," Draven said. "A cannon shot might get through it at close enough range, but short of that, ain't nothing —mundane or spell—going to so much as scratch it." Draven looked from one face to another. "Any other questions? Ain't no bad ones, so if you got them, ask them."

No one said anything.

"Let's get to it then." Draven to Margaret. "If you'd be so kind."

Talen went to stand next to her. "You did this before. You can do it again."

Margaret nodded. "It is a bit of heavy lifting."

"Good thing you're strong as an ox then." Talen winked.

Margaret smiled and bent down, putting both hands on the wooden disk connecting all the masking charms. She drew a few slow breaths and closed her eyes.

Talen could actually feel the flow of magic from Margaret and into the disk. It was a new sensation, and more than a little odd. Not unlike pouring power into a charm herself, but from the outside, like someone else touching fire and she feeling the heat. More bizarrely, which was saying something, she could almost smell and taste the power—the purity and light of it. It was indescribable, but it reminded Talen of drinking clear cold water from a stream on a hot day.

Margaret's brows drew together, and her breathing grew more labored.

Curiosity got the best of Talen, and she bent, hovering her hand over some of the threads that ran from the central disk to the charms on the underside of the ship. The magic, buzzing like bees, flowed just beyond her fingertips.

Like with Margaret, it hit on multiple senses. Her brain struggled to define something she had no context for. It was akin to being in the midst of a healing prayer, awash in the pure energy of life itself. This however came without the sense of being outside herself. Even having lived as long as she had, she'd never experienced this before. It wasn't hard to imagine it was the result of the crystal or the power she'd drawn from the storm. Or both. What she didn't know was if it was simply a novelty or had some deeper significance.

When she noticed Margaret visibly struggling, Talen put a hand on her shoulder. "You're doing good. Don't force it. Let it flow on its own. There ain't no rush."

After a bit, the thrumming drone of the magical flow stopped and what she assumed was the charms activating. Margaret let out a breath, opened her eyes, and sat on the deck.

"It's done," she said, between breaths.

"Proud of you, little sister. You okay?"

Margaret smiled and nodded. "I am. Just need a minute to catch my breath."

Talen gave Draven a thumbs up and turned back to Margaret. "You want some water?"

"I think I do."

Talen fetched a waterskin from the railing and sat with Margaret.

Draven signaled Wilfred, who got the Cumulus moving, though at a noticeably slower pace than usual. They'd purposely stopped a few miles from the border of town, so it would take a bit to reach anything worth noting.

"You good?" Talen asked.

"Yes. You can stop dotting now," Margaret said. "I think I'll go sit with Wilfred in the bridge though."

Talen helped her to her feet and handed her cane over. Once Margaret was inside and seated, Talen went to her spot at the railing, took up her paper, and waited to see something of note.

Five or ten minutes later they came upon the first homestead. The trees gave way to a swath of cleared land, a modest house at the far end. A thin trail of smoke came from the chimney.

Talen made some notes about the house, but focused more on looking for anyone outside it. There wasn't, but she did notice a small, ramshackle cabin a short way off, almost entirely concealed by the trees. It seemed a reasonable assumption to call it slave quarters.

The next several hours were much the same. As luck would have it, no one seemed to notice the Cumulus. The storm had passed, but there was still heavy enough cloud cover to let the air ship blend in. It also hid the sun such that no shadow was cast to the ground. To be safe though, when they neared the two plantations, Draven had Wilfred climb to five thousand feet, which had the lower clouds brushing the gas bladder. At that distance though, Talen and Draven were the only ones with eyesight good enough to make out any details.

Well, only Talen, but Draven had some goggles with lenses and some sort of contraption attached to it that apparently let her see at a distance. Neither spotted any of the hooded knights, but they did see a couple dozen men spread between the two plantations who were armed up like former soldiers. Could be they only wore the hoods when trying to scare and intimidate. Assuming they didn't ride all together all the time, Talen figured a kill box would work nicely to corral the bastards and to take them down—

Talen spotted a bizarre contraption in a wagon, and it took a moment for her to recognize the collection of barrels. Her stomach dropped, and her blood ran cold. "Well, shit."

"Yeah. I see it, too," Draven said.

"What?" Alice leaned over the railing and squinting.

"Unless I'm much mistaken," Talen said, "they got themselves a Gatling gun."

"I'm sorry. What did you say?" Booker asked.

"It's on a wagon near the main house," Draven said, "but it's a Gatling gun all right."

"That'll require a change of plans," Talen said.

"Really?" Cyrus asked in a flat tone. "Do you think?"

"Gatling wasn't a half-bad engineer," Draven said, "but he was only human. Those things like to jam if the crew don't know what they're doing. Also, they're easy to wreck if you can get close enough."

"I can," Talen said.

"Wouldn't some sort of bomb work better?" Alice asked. "Assuming you can set it off from a distance, it'd take out the gun and anyone nearby. Seems more likely to do the job than just shooting it with your spell iron."

Talen smiled and found Alice had somehow gotten even more attractive. "That's a good plan. But I think we should hold off on discussing particulars until we're done mapping the place. That way we can figure it into the larger plan. The good news is, they ain't like to take it far from the house."

"Wonder if they got a second one at the other plantation," Booker said.

"Wouldn't be surprised," Draven said. "We'll see soon enough."

As it happened, there was a second one there. It took a couple more hours for Draven and Talen to get a lay of the two large estates and the town center. As Delia had said, there wasn't much to it, but it looked as though the courthouse, which also held the jail, was one of the largest buildings in town, second only to the church. A few townspeople milled about as the day went on. All the stained Talen had ever come across were, at best, eager to use violence to get whatever they wanted, as soon as they wanted it. At worst, they were just bloodthirsty monsters who delighted in the pain and suffering of others. Neither had much patience or self-control.

It was a damn peculiar sight to see people, likely stained, still going about their normal lives. It left Talen more than a little unsettled.

They also got a clear view of the walled-in section where the "free" Black folk resided. It was empty, though dozens of people worked the fields, tilling the ground, and getting it ready for planting. Most were in chains, watched over by armed men on horseback. A dozen or so shuffled about or worked almost mechanically. It wasn't hard to figure they were the ones the detestable crafts had been used on.

Talen couldn't sense the taint of dark magic. Even without the crystal, at this distance, it wouldn't reach her, but something churned her guts and send ripples of cold down her spine. A soul-deep unease, a wrongness to everything. Not just the people, but the buildings, and even the land itself. Once they'd given the town a good once-over, Draven went to the bridge and set to work compiling all the notes and updating the map. While Wilfred piloted them away from town and higher into the sky, everyone else retreated below and had something to eat.

The reality of it all hung in the air like a wet, wool blanket on a summer day. There wasn't much small talk. Not much had to be said, though. Talen figured they all felt the same anger and indignation at what they saw. The fear was still there too, but the burning anger did a good job quashing it.

Shortly after the sun crept down to the western horizon, Draven and Wilfred came into the galley. She laid out the updated map, and everyone gathered around it. Not only had she filled in the blank spots, there'd been a few changes made to the areas that had been drawn in darker lines as well.

Talen went over the general plan again, fleshing out more details based on the new information. Booker, Cyrus, Alice, and even Odie, Pearl, and Frieda offered some good suggestions, but otherwise nodded in agreement or just asked clarifying questions.

"I'm going to need a day or so to put together some bombs for the Gatling guns," Wilfred said.

"Too bad there ain't no way to set them off from a distance," Talen said as the idea blossomed in her head. She didn't have any notion how such a thing could be done, but she knew two people who likely could figure it out. "Sure would make a fine distraction."

Wilfred and Draven looked at each other, eyes narrowed.

Talen smiled.

"Think something could be rigged up?" Wilfred asked her.

"Not if you're making a spell bomb like you did in Boston," Draven said. "Now, a conventional bomb, it'd be easy enough to make something that works like the wireless telegraph."

"Did you say 'spell bomb?'" Frieda asked.

"Used it to blow up a factory," Talen said.

"You blew up a factory?" Alice said.

Margaret shrugged and grinned. "Just the one."

Alice leaned back, eyebrows up, and chuckled.

"You got what you need to build it?" Talen asked Draven, smiling from Margaret's comment. "It'd need to be small enough to carry and not be noticeable. Figure I could sneak in, stick it on the underside of the wagon."

"Just needs to be big enough to make the gun unusable." She held her hands out at about the size of a cannonball. "This size ought to do the job and take out anyone within twenty feet. Do a number to the hearing of anyone within fifty. I got some resin glue that works quick, and should hold the bomb in place."

"What about your special project?" Talen asked Wilfred.

His eyes sparkled as he smiled. "I think I figured out how to make it work, and I don't reckon it'll be as difficult as I thought. Shouldn't take more than a couple of days to put it together."

"That enough time to make your bombs?" Talen asked Draven.

"More than."

"Sounds like we got ourselves a plan then," Talen said. "Best we keep up high and out of sight. The masking charms going to hold for a while?"

Wilfred shrugged. "Honestly, I got no idea. I wouldn't be surprised if some were burning out even now."

"I'll take us west toward the Blue Ridge mountains," Draven said. "There's more than a few dwarven outposts. There and back should be enough time to finish what we need."

"Let's do it then," Talen said.

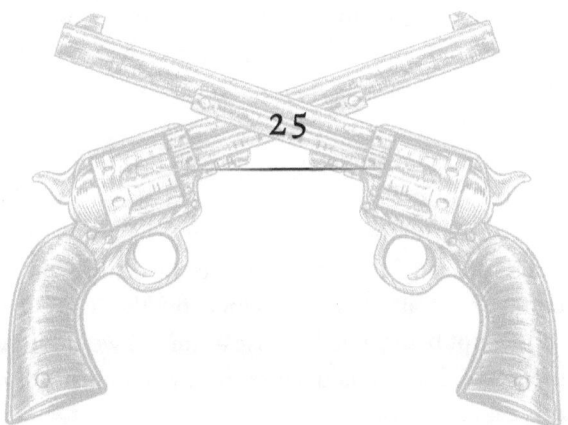

25

They reached the Blue Ridge Mountains in less than a day, and Talen had to admit, they were quite a sight to see. Lush rolling hills with a misty haze hanging over them. Talen suggested they set down so Draven could work on her bombs; since Wilfred was still working on his invention, best not to worry who was piloting the ship.

Draven, Wilfred, and Margaret all could tell Talen needed some time with Gaoth off the ship, so they set down in a small valley. The gangway had barely touched earth when she rode Gaoth out of the ship and into the densely-wooded twilight. The terrain was rough and uneven, rolling hills and mountains with narrow trails. Gaoth couldn't run as fast, but he still got to work his muscles. The air smelled fresh and clean, a welcome change from human settlements.

The serenity of the moment shattered when Talen remembered the worker at Niagara Falls, and how he'd said there was a similar crystal harvesting facility in this very mountain range. The notion another elemental being profaned turned her stomach and stoked her already well-fed, if currently slumbering, anger back to life. She considered telling the others about the facility, and suggest destroying it before returning to Aspen Hill. That thought, much to her shame, set her to wondering if they might find enough bounty crystals to deal with the stained town.

With a slow, deep breath, she pushed that, and all other thoughts, aside. Instead, she just savored each moment with Gaoth, fresh air blowing over them, and for a time at least, no demands or responsibilities.

After a couple of hours, they came to a stream and stopped to drink. The water was clean, cool, and tasted like—Talen froze. She glanced at Gaoth who was drinking his fill happily, seemingly unaware of the taste. Talen cupped her hands and drank again. There was no denying it this time; she tasted magic in the water. Or at least it tasted the way Margaret's magic had.

It wasn't surprising to find magic in the water. It was everywhere after all—every leaf, blade of grass, and creature, but she'd never been able to sense it so directly. During her healing prayers she could feel it, but that was in the loosest sense of the word. Before she'd filled the crystal with power, she could smell and taste a stained on the air, but never pure magic itself. While not being able to sense a stained would make her life a bit more bothersome, if she could sense pure magic instead, it seemed a much more agreeable tradeoff.

Her curiosity piqued, Talen went to some nearby trees and carefully pulled some newly budded leaves from a maple and ate them. They had the usual sweetness of that kind of tree, but sure enough, beneath that, was the same taste as the water. She took a branch from a birch and chewed on it. Same thing. In fact, the more she chewed, the more prominent the power seemed to be.

"Could I be standing on top of an elemental, and that power is soaking into everything around it?" Talen asked.

Gaoth didn't answer. He just chewed some ground growth that he clearly found much more interesting.

Talen knelt, pushed her fingertips into the earth, and opened herself up the same way she did with her healing prayer, except she didn't actually begin the incantation. As she wasn't in need of help, it would've been incredibly rude to ask for it.

A massive flow of power washed over her, filling every inch of her body with light, heat, and, well, life. The impact nearly knocked her over, not from the force of it, though it was colossal, but rather the suddenness of it.

Once she'd recovered, she could sense the presence of an elemental, much more like the one from Lake Michigan. No big shock that the elemental here would be an old one. The mountains were probably ancient when the lake had come into being.

She recalled how the sheer presence of the Lake Michigan old one had merely been overpowering, while its direct attention had mind crushingly immense. This elemental didn't seem to be reaching out to her, which was both a relief, and a bit disappointing. When she made to draw back her senses, it didn't seem to work, but then she realized it was actually a rivulet of power flowing into her. Or more accurately, it flowed through her and into the crystal. The contrast between the initial wave and this current trickle was so immense, it made noticing this thread of power at all a miracle. It was as if she'd been in a dark room, instantly found herself staring right at the sun, and then, after returning to the dark, noticing a firefly.

Out of curiosity, Talen lifted her shirt. The crystal burned with a soft, warm light. Not blinding. In fact, it wasn't even noticeably brighter than it had been. Yet, somehow, it illuminated everything Talen could see, even beyond where the light should be able to reach. The longer she looked around, the more the light seemed off somehow. Not bad. Just not normal.

After a few minutes, she figured it out. It wasn't the crystal, or any external source at all. Rather the trees, and terrain, and everything else, shone with their own light, and it seemed to be coming from the inside.

Talen tucked her shirt back into her pants, but nothing around her dimmed in the slightest.

"Gaoth, you seeing this?" she asked, paying extra attention to every detail.

Gaoth walked over and joined her, scanning all around. After a moment, he eyed her quizzically.

"You don't see the glow everything has?"

He looked again, and apparently not seeing it, chuffed.

She stroked his forehead. "I'm okay. Least, I hope I am. I'm getting the feeling the elementals are tinkering with the crystal, and it's tinkering with me. Ain't quite sure how I feel about that."

Gaoth's eyes narrowed, and he surveyed their surroundings yet again. After a moment, he snorted, whinnied, and stomped at the ground.

Talen couldn't help but smile and leaned forward to kiss between his forehead. "Thank you, old friend, but I don't reckon even you could intimidate an elemental." She let out a breath and ran a hand through her hair. "Timing of this ain't exactly helpful," she said to the empty woods. "I ain't got time to figure out what you all want from me. I know it's beneath you, but there's a whole mess of people that need help."

The darkening woods only answered with the buzz of insects and the chirping of birds.

She sighed again and walked to the stream to have another drink of water. When she bent to fill her cupped hands, her mouth fell open. The flowing water had the same soft glow as everything else, but it seemed to made of countless, shimmering threads. Thousands, maybe millions of them, swaying and shifting with the flow of the river.

Talen scooped up some water, and when she lifted it, the tendrils passed right through her. The water she held quickly lost its glow. She drank it, and though it still tasted of magic, it was less than it had been.

Could she actually be seeing the flow of pure magic? Was that even possible?

She filled her hands again and drank it quickly.

The magic was stronger, like the first time.

"Mother's mercy," she said, glancing around. "That's it." She turned and studied Gaoth, but he didn't have the same radiance as everything else. The idea he didn't have any magic was more than a little disconcerting. When she looked herself over, she didn't have it either, save for around her belly where the crystal was.

"No," she said. "I'm not seeing all magic. I'm see the elemental's."

She took several minutes to take everything around her, marveling at what she saw, and the simple fact she could. Eventually though, she couldn't put it off any longer. It was time to return to the Cumulus.

She climbed onto Gaoth and together they made their way back. As they rode, Talen kept glancing about, noticing the shifting flow of power, seemingly stronger at some points, and weaker in others.

They reached an overlook with a broad view of the mountains and valleys. The radiance, or rather the elemental's power, stretched as far as she could see, at least several miles. However, one hill shone noticeably dimmer than the surrounding area. Not less intense, she realized after a moment, but incomplete. The magic shone with a consistent brightness, but a large section apparently had little or no power.

"I'd bet my left-hand iron that's the bounty crystal farm."

Gaoth snorted and bobbed his head.

"You seeing it now, or just trying to make me feel better?"

Gaoth looked away.

Talen stroked his neck. "Well, I appreciate the sentiment." She noted the direction of the mountain, as well as her position based on the moon and stars. Might be Draven could mark it on a map. They needed to get to

Aspen Hill, but she reckoned the dwarves in the outpost would find the information a mite handy.

Using her height in the saddle, Talen collected some choice branches and leaves and urged Gaoth on. When they finally returned to the airship, Margaret was just nudging Jospeh and Elise back on board where Alice and Cyrus waited. The only light came from inside the cargo bay. Talen smiled, glad to know the other horses had gotten a respite as well.

"I was beginning to worry," Margaret said, as Talen came into the light of the ship. "Sun went down more than an hour ago. I feared maybe Gaoth or you slipped in the dark."

Talen slid off Gaoth and removed his saddle. "I could still see just fine, and Gaoth can handle himself in the dark pretty well."

Margaret frowned.

Talen chastised herself for dismissing her sister's concern. "But I appreciate your concern, and I apologize for making you worry."

Margaret's glower gave way to a smile. "Come on. Frieda, Odie, and Pearl are fixing dinner. The others got some rabbits, which I think are going into a stew, but I told them to make something for you, too."

"You know there ain't no need," Talen said, walking with her friend. "But again, I appreciate the thought."

"You're a member of this family," Margaret said. "You certainly compromise enough for us. It won't do anyone any harm to give something back the other way once in a while."

Heart swelling near to bursting, Talen wrapped her arm around Margaret and gave her a long, but gentle squeeze.

"Did you have a nice ride?" Margaret asked, as they slowly climbed the gangway. "Looks like beautiful country here."

"I did, and had something interesting happen."

"Oh?"

As Talen led a reluctant Gaoth back to his stall, she recounted what had happened, including the possible location of the crystal farm.

"I'd almost forgotten about the crystal farms," she said, shaking her head. "Niagara wasn't even two weeks ago, but so much has happened since then it completely fell from my mind."

"Mine too."

"I think you're right, though. Draven will be interested in hearing that, and I think the other beardless will as well."

Talen secured and checked the gates to the stalls, turned to follow

Margaret to the galley, but stopped and glanced back. She stared at Gaoth, then went and looked at Elise, and then at Joseph.

All three glowed.

"What is it?" Margaret asked.

"I'll be damned," Talen said.

"Yes, clearly." Margaret was using her patiently impatient tone.

"Sorry. I told you I couldn't see no magic on myself or Gaoth, like I could everything else."

"Right."

"Well, I think I can now," she said. "In fact, I think I see it on all of them." It wasn't that the radiance surrounding the horses was faint. Now that she noticed, it was strange to think she'd ever missed it, but it seemed to shine from deep inside the animals, whereas the woods seemed to be entirely radiant.

Talen looked down at herself, and while the glow from around the crystal was more noticeable, she also shone from within. She turned, mouth open, to tell Margaret, and the words vanished. Her sister had it too, and there seemed to be a focal point of radiance behind her eyes.

Margaret grinned, her cheeks flushing. "Why are you looking at me like that? Am I glowing too?"

"In fact, you are."

Margaret straightened and stood a little taller. "Well, I'd argue I always have." She chuckled.

"And I'd agree."

Margaret waved the words away. "It's impolite to tease. I was making a joke."

"I wasn't," Talen said. "And I mean that figuratively and literally."

Margaret narrowed her eyes. "Okay, now I'm not sure what you mean."

"You're a beautiful woman, inside and out," Talen said plainly.

Margaret's cheeks flushed again. "Oh, um, well, thank you."

"But I also suspect you always had what I'm seeing now, too," Talen turned over the lessons she'd had on the nature of magic and the world. Unfortunately, centuries had passed since then, and she'd never been the most attentive student.

"I see your brain is working." Margaret stepped closer. "What are you thinking?"

Talen pursed her lips, narrowed her eyes, and dug deeper through her memories. "I don't recall ever hearing about anyone seeing magic. Not literally. Most could feel it when it was flowing strong, but only then. Idea was, because you were always floating in magic, so to speak, you wouldn't notice more around you."

"Like being in a river?" Margaret said. "You wouldn't notice someone dumping a bucket in because you're already submerged."

Talen nodded. "Now what if when I could only see the elemental's power, it was because it shone so bright, I couldn't see nothing else?"

"Like how you can't see the stars when the sun it out," Margaret said. "But now you can since the proverbial sun has set."

"Exactly."

"That doesn't really explain why you can see it at all, does it?"

"It does not."

They started their way to Draven's workshop, Margaret taking the lead, Talen following.

"Could it perhaps be a kind of opposite effect as the stained?" Margaret asked.

"What do you mean?"

"Everyone can smell a stained, and when we first met, you said elves were even more sensitive to it."

Talen grimaced. "I was more sensitive, yes."

Margaret paused to rub at her bad leg. "And I don't think that's a coincidence."

"I don't understand."

Margaret's brows drew together, and she looked at Talen hesitantly.

"What is it?"

"Most people"—Margaret shrugged— "most humans I mean to say, wouldn't take what I'm about to say very well."

Talen smiled. "Is that a clever way of ensuring I do?"

Margaret didn't smile back.

Talen's faded and her heart twinged in sympathetic pain. She kicked herself, again, for misreading the situation. Again. "I hope you know well enough that I ain't like to take offense at anything you say to me. You ain't got a cruel or unkind bone in your body, and I don't believe you even got the capacity for cruelty. So go on and say what you want to say."

Margaret leaned against the railing and shifted her weight back and forth from her good leg to her bad one. "In a very real sense, you're a cripple now."

Talen thought about it for a moment. For the entirety of her life, she'd taken for granted being able to sense a stained and corrupt magic. Now,

217

the crystal allowed her to see the pure magic, but in so doing, essentially blinded her to any stained. Even the memory of the fetid taste the wafted of a stained, sometimes for half a mile or more, seemed less vivid.

"I reckon I am. I honestly hadn't thought about it that way. It's a sort of blindness, I suppose."

Margaret nodded. "Exactly. Well, not exactly. More like losing an aspect of your sense of smell, which I confess I don't know the term for. However, my point is that it could be your other senses are trying to take up where one is lacking." She rubbed at her bad leg. "I've got this, which means I'm not winning any races. But my other leg is probably twice as strong as most people's because it's had to carry my weight most of my life. Likewise, years of using a cane have made my right arm and shoulder stronger."

"I get your thinking, but I ain't seeing stained. I'm seeing everything else."

"I think you're hung up on the specific senses," Margaret said. "Since we've been traveling together, I've learned a thing or two from you and from Wilfred about magic. It seems to me we sense the stain of dark magic, but I don't think it's an actual scent. That would require particles of dark magic to reach us, and I don't think it works that way. I could be wrong, but it doesn't make sense to me. What if, however, the simplest way for our minds to convey that sense of dark magic was to create a smell in our heads?"

Talen didn't say anything. Margaret was as smart as they came, picked up on things so fast it sometimes made Talen's head spin. She wasn't entirely following Margaret's thinking, but she suspected it was worth listening to.

"All our senses are just in our brains anyway," Margaret said. "What if our brain gets some kind input, but can't figure out any way to put it into terms it can understand. The brain knows this input is bad, but has no other context and limited options. So, the sense of corrupt magic becomes a bad smell. Something we associate with rot and foulness."

Talen still didn't understand everything, but enough to get the general idea. "All right. I reckon that makes sense."

"But now, you can't sense that anymore," Margaret said and pointed to Talen's belly. "The power in that crystal has effectively blocked it from reaching you. However, the part of your brain could sense the presence of dark magic is still there and still trying to work. Now, instead of showing you what is there, it's showing you what isn't."

Talen furrowed her brow. "Now you lost me again."

"Like you said, you didn't sense pure magic before, because you're surrounded by it. You're in the river, so you never notice the rain soaking your clothes."

"Okay."

"But maybe you're noticing the difference in temperature between the rain and the river now." She shook her head and let out a breath. "I'm not sure I'm explaining this well."

"No, I think I see where you're going," Talen said as pieces came together. "Before, I could sense the presence of corruption, but can't no more. So, the parts of me that could, are now seeing the difference in true magic instead, and I'm seeing it instead of smelling it."

"Yes!" Margaret thumped the railing. "Exactly! Obviously, this is all just conjecture. We won't know for sure until you come near a stained."

"Maybe not." Talen thought back to the overlook and the gaps in the elemental glow where she suspected the crystal farm was located. She recounted it all to Margaret.

Margaret's eyes went wide and lit with an excitement as infectious as her smile. Though she still struggled to fully comprehend everything Margaret had said, the relief of even partial understanding was exquisite. With the grim and staggering tasks still ahead, this moment provided a welcome, if brief, respite and ray of hope.

"As you say," Talen said, reining in her enthusiasm, "we won't know for sure until we confirm that's where the crystals are being made, or I see a stained, but I think you might've figured this out. Little sister, I genuinely don't know what I'd do without you."

Margaret stood a little taller but then shrugged and looked away. "Well, I just got a lucky guess. I don't know as I'm indispensable, but—"

"You absolutely are," Talen said, stepping up to stand in front of her and meet her eyes. "Don't you never think otherwise, or for one moment discount what you offer to the world, to this family, or to me."

Margaret's expression went a little slack, and her mouth came open.

"You are speaking of my sister, whom I love dearly. I do not take to anyone, and I mean anyone, speaking ill of those I love. You hear me?"

Margaret swallowed, and she wiped her eyes. "I do."

"Good."

"And I love you too." Margaret smiled, put her arms around Talen, and hugged tight.

Talen replied in kind. "Don't think this'll make me go easy on you if I catch you bad-mouthing yourself again."

Margaret laughed and stepped back. "Understood. Now let's go tell Draven what you found."

When they reached the armory, which also served as Draven's workshop, she was just finishing the last of the half dozen bombs she'd made. They were small, barely the size of an apple, but she swore they'd get the job done and then some.

Each bomb had a flat base covered with paper and underneath was the glue. Draven explained how, when ready, to just remove the paper and press the base against damn near anything, and it would stick. That done, it could either go off by a timer, or from the wireless telegraph sending a certain message.

"You say dwarves don't do magic," Talen said, looking over the devices. "But these sure seem like magic to me."

Draven grinned and chuckled. "Maybe we'll just say we got a different sort of magic."

"How dangerous are these to handle?" Margaret asked, keeping her distance.

"Not at all," Draven said. "It's made of two components that are completely inert on their own. When they get mixed together, it's a different matter."

Margaret nodded but didn't get any closer.

"I don't know about you two," Draven said, standing and stretching, "but I could eat half a herd, and whatever Odie and the Thomas sisters are making smells good."

Talen had no idea what about the odor was good, it smelled like most other human food to her. "First, I found something that might interest you, along with the Granite Lord, and the other beardless."

Draven arched an eyebrow.

Talen recounted what she'd seen and what she suspected it meant. When the story was done, Draven gave her a level look, brows furrowed.

"For those keeping count," Draven said, "and I am, that would make three elementals, two of which were old ones, reaching out to you."

"Three?" Margaret asked.

"We think the storm was an elemental as well," Talen said to Margaret and looked to Draven. "And this one didn't communicate nothing to me. It just fed power into the crystal, which, if I'm being honest, seemed a mite impolite to do without asking."

Draven's expression didn't change. "You reckon an old one—a being so old 'ancient' don't even begin to cover it—should've had a little chat with you?"

Talen grinned and chuckled. "Being old don't excuse bad manners."

Draven gritted her teeth and narrowed her eyes. "You trying to get me to toss you out this porthole? Don't think I won't make you fit through it."

"I'm pretty sure she's teasing," Margaret said.

"I know," Talen and Draven said at the same time.

Now it was Margaret's turn to laugh.

"I'll get word to the Granite Halls," Draven said. "I expect there will be a visit to the facility in short order. Bad enough what they're doing, but doing it in our backyard, so to speak, well, that will not stand."

Margaret's brow furrowed. "They won't just kill everyone, will they?"

"Nah," Draven said. "I mean, there'll be some that will want to, and call for it, but the Granite Lord knows that won't serve no one. Though I expect he'll make it clear continued operation won't be tolerated."

Draven's stomach rumbled loud enough for everyone to hear.

"But that message can wait 'til I get some food in me," Draven said. "Come on."

They all made their way to the galley where Odie, Frieda, and Pearl were finishing up their cooking. Cyrus, Booker, and Alice sat—mostly—patiently at a table, chatting. Wilfred was nowhere to be seen. Talen knew that when he got into a project, any sense of time fell to the wayside. She'd make sure to bring him a plate or two.

"Whatever it is, it smells good," Draven said.

"Rabbit stew," Odie said.

"Hope you don't mind, Miss Talen," Frieda said. "We didn't have much by way of seasoning so we used some of your leaves."

Talen did mind a little but not enough to raise a fuss. "It's fine."

"We didn't forget about you, though," Pearl said. "Margaret reminded us you don't eat meat, but we found some fine-looking mushrooms, and they appear to have roasted up quite nicely."

Talen couldn't quite hide her surprise at the extra effort on her behalf. More than a little shame followed right with it. Though born from experience, her quickness to anger and frustration wasn't fair. She promised herself to at least try to do better. "Much obliged. I do enjoy mushrooms."

"Well, get a plate," Odie said. "It's done."

Draven conjured a bowl from seemingly nowhere and stood ready. Alice, Cyrus, and Booker were right behind her. They all got their food, along with some sort of bread or biscuit, and were eating almost before their backsides touched the chairs.

Talen picked up a large bowl and spoon. "Mind loading this for Wilfred first? I'll bring it to him and have those mushrooms when I get back."

"Of course!" Odie said and filled the bowl. "Don't take too long, though. Don't want them to get cold."

"We'll keep them warm for you," Frieda said and set two pieces of bread in the bowl. "Don't worry none."

"Thank you kindly," Talen said and looked to Margaret. "I'll be back shortly." As everyone else started eating, Talen carried the food to Wilfred's cabin.

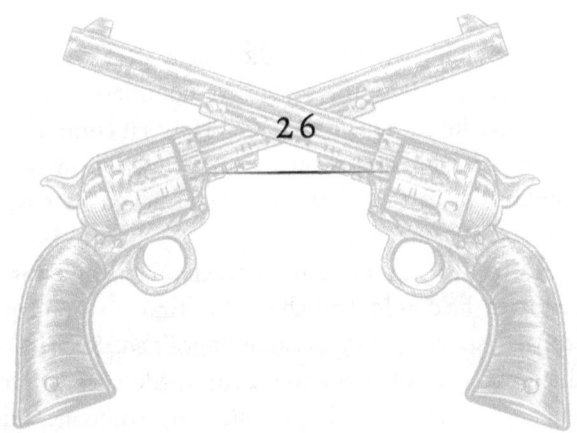

26

It's open," Wilfred said, after Talen knocked on his door.

She opened it to find him hunched over his work table. Like everyone else's cabin, his was small, but Draven had added drawers along every wall. Crafting materials littered his work table, but Talen knew that despite the apparent chaos, he could reach for anything without looking. Unless something got moved, even an inch, in which case it could take him weeks to find it.

"Brought you dinner," Talen said.

"What time is it?" he asked, still focused on his work.

"An hour or so past sunset." Talen stepped into the room.

"Already?" he asked.

"Time does fly, don't it?"

"It surely does."

Talen stood, bowl in hand, waiting patiently. She knew better than to interrupt when he was working. Not because he'd be angry, but he'd lose his place in what he was doing, and it could take him hours to get back to it.

After a few minutes, he let out a breath, leaned back in his chair, and stretched. When he turned to face her, he sniffed the air and smiled. "Smells good."

Talen shrugged and offered the bowl. "I reckon it's the maple leaves they used."

Wilfred chuckled and accepted the bowl and spoon. "Much obliged." He dug in, taking another mouthful almost before he'd swallowed the last.

Talen leaned against the wall, smiling and marveling how little some things change. "Ain't no one gonna take it from you. You can take your time."

He glanced over and began eating ridiculously slow.

Despite the fact he'd done the same joke countless times before, she still could only shake her head and chuckle. "How's it coming?"

He chewed, swallowed, and turned to set the bowl in the only clear spot on his table. "I'm getting there. Got sidetracked part way through with another idea that came to me."

When he shifted to put himself between Talen and his food, she recalled the stories he'd told her about his time in bondage and the lessons he learned so well, they became engrained. Such as when you needed to take your eyes off your food, you made sure to put it out of sight and reach of others, lest it get taken by someone hungrier, or knocked away by a cruel overseer.

It pained her to see those instincts hadn't faded, but she supposed they never would, and he likely didn't even notice anymore. She certainly wouldn't point it out to him, so she just smiled and nodded. "Of course you did."

He passed her a pouch and then took up his bowl again.

Talen opened the miniature sack and found half a dozen spell iron loads. She took one out and examined it. She recognized a few of the components, but the loads were new to her. "What are they?"

"I call them Gaia loads."

"Gaia?"

"An ancient Greek word for the Earth personified as a goddess," he said, scraping the bowl clean and spooning the last of the stew into his mouth.

Talen arched an eyebrow. "Ancient Greek? You never fail to surprise."

He took a swallow of water from a canteen and smiled. "For a long time, I wasn't allowed to read nothing. Once I learned how, I set to reading as much as I could. Had my fill of asking others for information, especially when they, like as not, told it as best suited their wants."

"Fair enough."

Wilfred arched an eyebrow. "I always meant to ask you what was it like?"

Talen furrowed her. She knew a setup when she saw it, but she couldn't stop herself. "What are you talking about?"

"Ancient Greece, of course."

Talen wanted to be angry, but she'd done it to herself, so she did what she always did, and played along. "First, you know damned well I ain't that old. Second, my family had been in Tara, Ireland, for several centuries before that."

"I keep forgetting you're Irish."

"I ain't Irish," Talen said, faux exasperation in her tone. "The Irish are Taran. We was there first." Her thoughts turned to the task ahead, and the countless atrocities left in the wake of human progress. The playfulness melted away from her words. "Not that humans ever much cared who was already there when they wanted something. Why do you think we feel a kinship with the Seven Council Fires people and other tribes?"

"I honestly didn't never think about it, and for that I apologize."

"No need," she said. "We should've taken a stand when we saw what they was doing to your people."

"There's plenty of regrets to go around," Wilfred said. "I'd say we're both doing our best to not make more."

"You seem especially philosophical lately."

He shrugged and smiled. "Reckon I'm just getting more thoughtful in my old age."

Talen didn't return the smile. She purposely never spent time thinking about his age, not that she knew how old he was. Like many born into bondage, he didn't know for certain himself. But all the same, the shortness of human lifespans didn't usually bother her none. However, there were some humans she'd like to have around a lot longer than she could ever hope for.

"So, what do these Gaia loads do?" she asked by way of changing the topic.

"They return the target to the earth," he said. "Like what happens after we're dead and buried, this is just a mite faster. Or should do. I ain't exactly tested them."

Talen nodded. She might not know exactly what that meant, but she didn't need to. She trusted Wilfred and knew his crafts always delivered. Also, the idea of renewal appealed to her Elven sensibilities. It was a tenant of her people to live with as small a footprint as possible. In fact, the goal of every Elven community was, should it vanish, within a month or two, there'd be no sign anyone had been there at all. She still believed in that with all her heart and understood the importance of it. That belief did, however, make her return home last year a little bittersweet. Until she'd stood in the seemingly untouched redwood forest where she'd been born and raised, she hadn't ever understood the human saying "you can never go home again."

"I got no notion how they'll do against a stained," he said. "Might treat them the same. Might leave a mess of rotted plants."

"So, you're saying I shouldn't count on them to end a fight?"

"That's a fair way of putting it."

Talen pocketed the loads. "Wish you'd make some more of those basilisk loads. Save for Tuller, turning folk to stone was mighty handy."

Wilfred laughed. "You find me enough palladium, and I'll make as many as you like. It's about as rare a material as you'll find."

"What about your other, actually magic, magic lantern?" she asked. "You know, the whole reason we came out this way."

He scowled but it had no anger behind it. "I told you it's coming along. Reckon I should be done tomorrow sometime."

"I'll tell Draven, who is finished by the way, to fly slow."

Wilfred stood and offered Talen the chair. "You are welcome to take over and show me how it's done."

Talen lifted her hands in mock surrender. "Even if I were a crafter, we ain't got years to waste on my attempts."

Wilfred nodded once and sat back down. "Thank you, I appreciate that you recognize—"

As Margaret once described it, the devil on Talen's shoulder whispered into her ear, and she couldn't resist. "I could see if Draven wants to take a crack at it though."

He scowled, almost. "You think you're funny, but that don't make it so."

She put a hand on his shoulder. "You know I ain't got nothing but awe and amazement at what you do, right?" she said, seriously. "Even the master crafters of my people would be impressed."

Wilfred's cheeks flushed a little, his smile broadened, and he sat a little taller in his chair. "Well then, you are forgiven."

She pointed at the empty bowl on his desk. "You want another?"

He picked it up and handed it to her with a sheepish grin. "If it ain't too much trouble."

Talen took the bowl, bent down, and kissed the top of his head. "Lucky for you I'm a kind and generous sort."

"I am, indeed. Thank you."

Talen stepped to the door. "No thanks needed, but you're welcome."

"I don't just mean for the supper."

She turned back to him. "I know, and I still say ain't no thanks needed. We're family."

Wilfred didn't say anything. He just gave his signature smile and nodded.

Talen loved that smile. Maybe as much as she loved the man behind it.

"I'll be back," she said and headed back to the galley.

She refilled the bowl, delivered it, and left Wilfred to finish his work. She would've told him not to work all night, but she'd have more luck telling the Cumulus to swim like a duck. When she came back to the galley the second time, she found Frieda, Odie, and Pearl had, true to their word, kept the mushrooms warm, though Talen wouldn't have cared if they hadn't.

They sat her down and put a bowl in front of her. It looked to be three or four different kinds, none of which Talen was familiar with, but the smell was enough to set her stomach to rumbling in anticipation.

"Don't worry," Odie said. "We got a charm to check if they're safe to eat."

Such diligence surprised Talen, though she knew it shouldn't. It only made sense that humans would come up with a charm to ensure whatever they ate wouldn't kill them. Elves, however, could eat just about any plant without worry. Bringing that up felt a bit like bragging, so Talen kept it to herself.

"I appreciate knowing you ain't trying to poison me." Talen winked and smiled.

All three women watched intently. Talen found it a bit disconcerting to have an audience, but she understood it came from a place of pride in their craft.

She skewered a few pieces with her fork and took a bite. The exquisite, earthy taste was only topped with the buttery texture that near melted on her tongue. Her eyes closed and she sighed without even realizing as she chewed. "Oh my."

"Good?" Frieda asked, the cautious hope evident in her tone.

"No ma'am, not good," Talen said. "Amazing."

They all beamed and stood up straight.

"You ain't just being polite, are you?" Pearl asked.

"I am not," Talen said. "I ain't never had nothing like them. These are delicious. Thank you."

"You're welcome," they all said near at once.

"Now would you sit down?" Talen said around a mouthful. "Having you hover over me has me uneasy."

"Fine, but first..." Odie brought over the pan and emptied the last of the mushrooms into Talen's bowl, filling it near to overflowing. "So you don't need to get up for seconds."

Talen couldn't help but chuckle, though she still found it strange to have those she hardly knew doting on her. Though she had to admit, it was something she could get accustomed to. "Much obliged," Talen said and took another mouthful.

At last, they all sat, and everyone sank back into the easy chatter they'd been sharing most of the day. Talen didn't say much, mostly because she was busy enjoying her dinner, but also because she understood the conversation wasn't for her. Draven was similarly silent, and they shared a nod. Talen figured she felt the same. Alice and the others were good people, but Talen couldn't deny she did miss the quiet when it was just her, Margaret, Wilfred, and Draven.

After a while, Odie, Pearl, Frieda, and Margaret headed off to their respective cabins Talen stayed to clean up, which was only fair since she hadn't done nothing by eat.

Alice joined her but eyed Cyrus and Booker, sitting fat and happy. "You two plan on getting off your butts and pulling your weight?"

They gave her a questioning look, and Booker opened his mouth.

"If the words 'woman's work' leave your mouth, your teeth will be following close behind," Alice said, as she gathered up the bowls. "You helped a few days ago. You can again now."

Talen chuckled.

Draven leaned back in her chair and watched with obvious interest.

The two men grinned and laughed too.

Alice did neither.

They both went quiet, their smiles vanished, and an instant later, got to their feet and set to work.

Alice watched them for a moment, still not smiling, before returning to her tasks.

Talen watched Alice for a heartbeat and noted that the room seemed to get warmer all of a sudden

Draven got to her feet and started to help as well.

"You sit back down," Talen said, as she cleaned the cookware. "You worked all day on those bombs, and you'll be piloting all night. You earned the right to sit."

"Might be," she said, "but I don't much like seeing others work when I'm able."

"Then get up to the bridge and get us underway," Talen said.

Draven set down her bowl and gave a small nod. "Yes, ma'am." She made her goodnights to Booker, Cyrus, and Alice, and left the galley.

When they were done, Talen looked from Booker and Cyrus to Alice.

"Go on," she said to them.

"Ain't you going to thank us for our help?" Cyrus asked.

Booker winced. "He does not speak for me."

Talen took a step back and leaned against the wall, out of range, but still close enough to enjoy the forthcoming fireworks display.

"Thank you for pulling your weight?" Alice asked. "Did you thank Odie, Frieda, or Pearl for cooking?"

Cyrus's brows lifted, and his mouth opened.

"No, you did not," she said, stepping close. "Neither did you last night or the night before."

"True, but—"

"I am not finished speaking," Alice said.

Cyrus wisely went silent.

"If you'd like a thank you for doing what needs doing, might be you should offer some yourself, don't you think?"

"You are correct, and I do apologize," Cyrus said after a couple of heartbeats. "Thank you."

"You're welcome," Alice said. "Thank you for helping." She motioned to the door. "You may go now."

"Night," Booker and Cyrus both said and quickly departed.

"Just us then, it seems," Alice said, turning and putting the last of the dishes away, as if nothing had just happened.

Though she couldn't help herself from smiling, Talen decided it best not to comment on it either. Instead, she put up and secured the stew pot. "Seems to be."

Along silence passed between them. When they'd finished their work, Alice stepped close, very close, and met Talen's eyes.

The heat from Alice's body paradoxically sent a shiver through Talen, and she sucked in a breath. The air smelled of cotton, sweat, and mutual desire.

"Am I reading this wrong?" Alice asked, almost whispering. "I got the feeling you fancied me, but if I'm wrong, just tell me."

Talen didn't back away, but, through no small effort of will, neither did she move to get any closer. "You ain't wrong. I find you a mite appealing."

Alice smiled and leaned in a little closer.

Though Talen very much would've liked to learn how Alice's lips tasted, and memorize every curve of her body, she wrestled that want aside. Wilfred, Margaret, and Draven might not raise a fuss, but Talen knew most humans didn't look upon this sort of thing kindly. Normally, she happily tell them where to stick their judgement. But any divide, however inane Talen might find it, could jeopardize the outcome. People, innocent people, were counting on them all.

She took a steadying breath, but still didn't back away. "And were we not about to take part in what will surely be some terrible tasks, I would take you to my bunk and show you a time like you never imagined."

Alice shuddered and while her smile waned a bit, her eyes narrowed and twinkled. "Damn, if that ain't the most enticing, thought-provoking rebuke I ever heard." She looked away for a moment, and her expression softened. "You know I ain't of a mind to tie you down, or get tangled up in anyway but the physical, right?"

"I suspected as much," Talen said and drew in another slow, steadying breath. She had to admit, Alice smelled good. In the back of her mind, she let herself imagine how their night could go, and found it more than a little pleasant.

"And we don't know if we'll see the other side of this," Alice said. "To my mind, it's the best time to live a little and indulge." She reached out to caress Talen's cheek.

Talen let her, closing her eyes briefly and leaning in to the touch. It'd been a good while since she'd shared her bed with anyone, and while she had never opposed the idea of purely physical enjoyment, this wasn't the right time. She opened her eyes, took Alice's hand, and pulled it away.

"I appreciate that," Talen said.

Alice's face fell. "But."

"But, I ain't like that. Were I to share myself with you, it'll be when there's no dark clouds hanging over head. It'll be for the sheer joy and pleasure of having each other's company." She shrugged. "I ain't saying

230

there's no sense in finding refuge with another, a moment of sweetness in a world that too often ain't. I'm saying I want it to be because we want it, not because we think we might not get another chance."

Alice grinned, chuckled, and shook her head. "I don't know if you're trying to make me want you more, but you're doing a damn fine job of it." She let out a breath. "But I understand what you're saying, and I can respect that. Maybe we can resume this discussion when the job is done?"

Talen smiled. "I look forward to it."

Alice narrowed her eyes, her cheeks flushed, and looked away as she stepped back. She opened her mouth to say something, but closed it again, laughed to herself, and ran a hand over her face. "Good night," was all she said as she left the galley.

"Night."

In the now-empty room, Talen retrieved a bottle of whiskey and took a couple of pulls from it. She leaned against the wall, closed her eyes, and savored the silence. When she'd first come on board, it hadn't taken long for her to miss the silence of the outside world, which of course wasn't silent at all. There was always wind blowing, birds or insects chirping, or animals calling to each other. The Cumulus had its own ambient music: the low hum of the engines, the gentle creek of the wood, wind blowing over the hull, and even the sound of her own beating heart.

The same, but different.

When the moment passed, Talen stowed the bottle and made her way below. She didn't go to Gaoth this time, but opted instead to sleep in her own bed. Alice's desire to not be alone before a coming storm was understandable, and very human. Talen, however, wanted to be alone, well, mostly alone. Once she'd settled into bed, she closed her eyes, and spoke a prayer.

Mother, help me see the way. Guide my hand so my aim is true. Let the darkness fall, and spare the innocent. I know what must be done and I'm ready, but I fear others may burn in the fire I bring. Keep them safe, and open the eyes of those who have only known darkness.

Her mother didn't say anything back, but as Talen drifted off to sleep, she did softly sing.

Talen woke before dawn. It wasn't a slow emergence from sleep, rather that she opened her eyes and was awake.

231

No lingering drowsiness, no anxiety or worry.

They'd come all this way to see people freed and put down the stained, and the time had come to set to it. Wouldn't be no quick or easy task though, and it'd likely take days, if not weeks, to finish. Aspen Hill spread out across nearly a hundred square miles. Even if they managed to clear ten houses a day, it'd take nearly two weeks. The trouble, of course, was they didn't have that kind of time.

Talen sat up and set to cleaning and caring for her spell irons. They didn't need it. They hadn't been used, but the motion was meditative. As she set to work, she ran through the plan in her head, over and over.

On paper, as Margaret would say, it seemed simple enough. The first night, Talen would slip into town under a shadow cloak, carrying as many arms as she could, and get them to any who wanted to fight. The next day, she, Alice, Booker, and Cyrus would start at the very edge of town, as far from the big plantations as possible. Move in fast, drop any stained, clear any children, ride to the next house, and do it all again. There were maybe thirty farms they could deal with that weren't close enough to either the center of town or a plantation to bring anyone running at the sound of gunfire.

Once the free locals, or at least those not in literal chains, were armed, it'd be time to see to the plantations. This would almost certainly bring the "knights" Delia had mentioned. There was a plan to round them up and take out as many as possible as fast as possible. This would be after Talen, again hidden in shadows, planted Draven's bombs to take out the Gatlin guns.

With both the plantations burning, and those in bondage freed, it'd be time to move into town, and hopefully Wilfred's ghost crafting would be ready and work as well as Talen hoped. Stained weren't often given to fear, but these seemed to have more of their mind working, so maybe they would. If not, it was like to piss them off something fierce, and that could serve too. Angry shooters didn't take time to aim, or pay attention to their ammunition.

If things went well, in a couple weeks, Preacher Thompson would be swinging from a rope while his town and church burned behind him, and the Cumulus would be sailing away with a hold of free folk bound for a new life.

Talen finished with her irons and mentally chewing on the plan. Nothing left but to actually do it. She rose and dressed. It was almost a ritual for her, each motion purposeful. She cinched her gun belt, slipped into her coat, and loaded her spell irons, heavy on force loads. Spares slid into the slots on her belt. Then she filled her coat pockets with more, including Wilfred's Gaia loads.

Girded for war, she took a long, slow breath, left her room, and made for the bridge.

Draven, Wilfred, and Margaret were already there, silently looking off to the horizon Talen joined them, watching the sun rise, and paint the sky —as well as a fresh gathering of storm clouds—blood red.

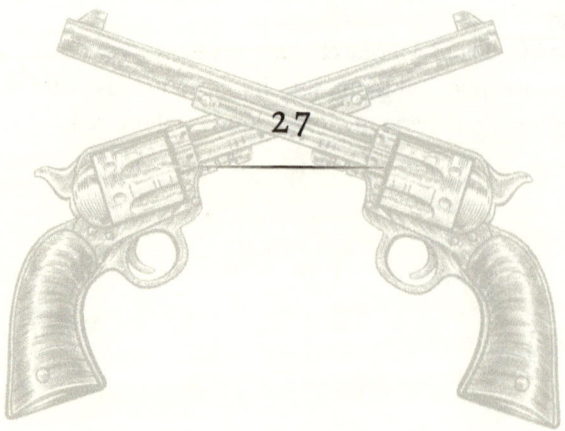

27

It wasn't long before the sky filled with dark, heavy clouds, and a gentle rain started to fall. The world appeared to be trying to wash the stain from itself. In the distance, clouds lit with lightning, and the air rumbled with thunder.

No one was much in the mood to eat breakfast, so they gathered in the armory. Wilfred had confirmed that enough of the masking charms had burned out to make them useless, but he'd planned for that. As everyone loaded and checked their shooters, Talen went over the plan one last time, making sure everyone understood it. Since they'd arrive in the morning, they all agreed to start with clearing the more remote farms instead of Talen hauling arms into town.

"Since we ain't got enough horses," she said, "the Cumulus will be close. If it turns bad, hightail it out of there. Those on board will cover you. Don't look back. Leave any trouble to me."

Everyone nodded.

"Last chance to change your mind," Talen said to Booker, Cyrus, and Alice. "You step off, you fight. So, if you want to stay, now is the time to speak up. No judgement."

None of them said anything. Alice just smiled and levered a round into her repeater.

By this point, Talen hadn't expected anyone to take her up on the offer, but she wanted to make it all the same. "All right then. Let's get to work."

Thirty minutes later, she rode Gaoth along the edge of a field waiting to be plowed and planted for the coming season. The Cumulus hung well above the trees ahead of her, having dropped off Booker, Cyrus, and Alice. When she neared the farmhouse, Talen slid from the saddle, and drew both spell irons.

The sun hung to her left, burning through the sliver of cloudless sky on the horizon, but it hadn't quite cleared the trees. A heavy silence hung over the world, save for the rain pattering against her coat and soaking the ground. A whisp of smoke rose from the chimney of the farmhouse, carrying the smell of cooking meat with it. As she walked, slow and purposeful, not making a sound, Talen kept her eyes and ears open. In the woods, behind cover, Alice and the others neared the slave quarters, ready to free whomever might be there.

Talen gave the barn a quick check but found it empty. An old mare stood in a dirty stall, obviously hungry and mistreated. Ire rose in Talen's stomach at the sight of lash scars along the horse's flank.

"Don't worry. We'll get you out of here and someplace safe," she said to the poor animal.

After leaving the barn, Talen approached the house, watching the windows, but no one inside seemed to be any the wiser to her presence. She wrapped herself in shadow and ran up to the house, ducking low just to be safe. At each window, she paused long enough to give a good listen and get an idea of who was inside and where. She didn't know if anyone in town would have an eyepiece that could see through her glamour, but neither did she see any reason to take unnecessary risks. Focusing on the sounds inside, she painted a mental picture.

Two adults, a man and a woman, snapped at each other over the clink of plates and utensils. Aside from the stench of mundane filth, a familiar fetid scent seeped from the windows.

She didn't smell stained, not that she expected to. What she smelled was death. There was a corpse inside, more than one from the punch of the odor. Talen clenched her jaw, barely containing the rising fury.

Not that it was needed, but when they'd touched down, Margaret and Wilfred had confirmed they felt much like they had at Niagara.

This was indeed a foul place.

Despite the pyre of burning indignation in her chest, Talen's heart beat slow and steady.

She went to the front door and kicked it hard enough to send it into the house.

The stink of death hit her like a herd of stampeding horses, but she pushed past it. Before anyone could react, she moved inside, and away from the door in case anyone got a lucky shot off.

Time froze for a lingering instant.

The foul odor made Talen's eyes water, but she clearly saw four children, ranging in age from five to maybe twelve, at a table in the middle of the room. From the look of them, they youngest had been dead for several weeks, the oldest just a few days.

A haggard man and woman, somehow even grubbier and filthier than the dead children, sat at either end of the table. There wasn't even a hint of radiance shining from them. In fact, the lack of it seemed to swallow the natural light around them. Both stared at the open doorway with wide eyes, oily black threads tracing across the whites.

Time restarted, and several things happened at once.

The woman stood and grabbed one of the corpses, pulling him or her —Talen couldn't be sure—in front of her as a human shield. The man grabbed a mundane shooter that had been sitting on the table, stood, and leveled it at the doorway.

Still wrapped in shadow, Talen crossed the room. She cracked the man across the skull with one unlit spell iron.

A shot went off as he crumpled and fell to the floor.

Before his head hit wood, Talen stepped from the shadows and lit up both irons. She aimed one at the woman's face. Blue spellfire filled the runes and reflected in the stunned woman's wide, black eyes.

Talen pulled the trigger. A blast of pure force pulverized the upper half of the woman's head.

A spray of gore pained the far wall.

The headless body and the corpse she'd been holding both thumped wetly to the floor.

The man got his wits back, turned, and fired at Talen.

She pivoted away, and the mundane shots slammed into her magic-laden coat. Rage drowned any pain from the impact, though she knew they'd leave bruises. But the bullets fell to the floor at her feet instead of punching through her, so it seemed a fair trade.

When his revolver clicked on empty, Talen planted a boot on his chest, eliciting a satisfying crack from his ribs, and put him down with a force blast from her right-hand iron.

The floorboards cracked and broke amid a cloud of bone, brain, and blood.

Talen rolled both irons to fresh cylinders, watching the bodies for any sign they might get back up. After almost a full minute, she felt confident they were dead. She hurried from the house and sucked in fresh air. The smell of rotting dead and human viscera followed her, but thankfully, the wind blew at her face. The cool, damp, and—comparatively—clean air served as a balm to the soul wrenching horrors inside the house.

The sound of approaching footsteps ended the brief reverie, and Talen drew her right-hand iron but didn't light it.

Alice came around the house, her rifle raised and ready, but quickly pointed it away when she saw Talen. "You okay?" she asked and apparently caught a whiff of the stench from the house. "Oh, sweet Jesus!"

"No," Talen said, "but it's done. Kids are long dead, and now the stained parents are too."

"You'll understand if I take your word for it and don't go see for myself."

"I will, indeed."

Alice turned away and gagged a bit. "We found two boys, the youngest just barely ready to shave for the first time. They're hungry and scared out of their minds, but alive. Booker and Cyrus are taking them to the Cumulus. I heard the shots and thought I'd see if you needed any help."

"Much obliged." Talen started back to the barn, her already ragged heart twisting further at the thought of the abused mare.

Alice followed behind. "Sure would be nice if they're all like this."

"I could do with fewer dead children," Talen said flatly.

"No, I didn't mean—"

"I know you didn't."

When they reached the barn, she stopped and turned to Alice. Even the smell of manure and urine-soaked hay was a delight compared to the house.

They stood there for a long moment, not saying anything.

"Anything I can do?" Alice asked.

"Just need me a moment is all," Talen said.

She'd known it not just possible, but likely, they'd find dead kids, but it didn't make the seeing any easier. She deliberately hadn't let herself look close enough to see how they'd died. Terrible as it was, she hoped they'd gone quick, gunshot or the like. Seeing how the mother treated the corpse though, that seemed unlikely.

"Wish like hell we could burn the place," Talen said, "but that would let everyone know we was coming."

"No reason we can't see to it when we're done," Alice said. "I, for one, would take great pleasure in lighting the torch for you."

Talen couldn't bring herself to even force a smile, so she just nodded.

"You ready to head back?" Alice asked, after another minute.

"Got one more to free," Talen said and opened the barn door.

They led the horse from the barn back to the Cumulus. She shied away from the other horses, but stepped into an empty stall without complaint. Talen made sure to put her next to Gaoth, who showed her kindness and concern. Once some feed was put in front of her, the mare began eating as if she hadn't been fed in a week or more.

By the time she let Talen stroke his forehead and seemed to relax a little, word came down they were nearing the next farm, and it was time to do it all over again.

The next farm thankfully didn't have any kids, dead or otherwise. Five adults, two of which were in the barn when Talen kicked in the front door of the house. They were unsuspecting, but faster than the others. One went down fast, but her second shot only winged the other, leaving Talen two stained to deal with at once.

Adding to the difficulty, she heard a barrage of gunshots from outside as Alice, Cyrus, and Booker found the two in the barn. When a second and third barrage of fire sounded from the outbuilding, Talen knew the others weren't having any better luck than her.

Facing down two stained required her full attention though, so she trusted her compatriots to take care of themselves.

"Fucking leafer!" one of the stained, a youngish woman with oddly well coifed blonde hair, said. Her left arm, pulverized by the force blast, resolidified.

"We're gonna have some fun with you!" the other stained, a man a few years older, said from the opposite side of the room, as he waved a large carving knife.

They exchanged a look Talen had seen before. The soldiers and Red Hands had looked the same when they'd tortured, violated, and burned her people.

Talen's blood ran cold but also burned with hatred.

The woman glanced to her left where several rifles sat on racks. A couple of holstered pistols hung on either side, and a single spell iron sat on its own shelf. She smiled when she saw Talen notice the spell iron.

All three moved at once, lunging for the weapons.

Well, Talen pretended to.

It'd have been stupid to put herself in striking distance of the two frothing stained. Instead, just as they snatched up the shooters, she sent a blast of artic air at them.

Everything in a ten-foot circle turned to frost and ice. The temperature dropped to near freezing, and a dense fog filled the room.

Both stained gaped at their icy limbs and howled in pain.

As Talen fired her left-hand iron at the woman, she rolled her right-hand iron to another cylinder and shot at the man.

The twin blasts of pure, kinetic force struck, one an instant behind the other. Frozen limbs, the guns they held, and the frost-covered wall behind them shattered.

A spray of icy shards pelted the intact portion of the wall and the ground outside the newly made doorway.

"Let's see you put that back together, rot," Talen said, rolling both cylinders to fresh loads.

The woman screamed and made to leap at Talen with her remaining hand.

Before the stained even finished pivoting, Talen fired another force blast.

The woman's head became a spray of liquified brains.

The man, seemingly unbothered, juked to one side, lunged, and slashed out.

Talen caught the blade on her spell-covered coat sleeve. Seizing his intact arm, she spun, and drove the butt of her iron into his head.

He stumbled back, dazed for a half a second.

Talen aimed at the center of his chest, and fired.

A pulsing green ball of light streaked from the barrel, and hit home.

For an instant, Talen panicked at the unrecognizable spell, realizing she'd lost track of what loads were in which cylinder.

The man fell back against the table as the green orb vanished inside him. He looked down at his undamaged chest, touching it briefly to make sure. Once he'd confirmed the lack of injury, he gave Talen a vulpine smile, and made to take a step forward, but didn't move.

What had been his foot, and shoe, had turned to wood. A tangle of roots grew from it, boring down through the floorboards, and into the earth.

His confidence melted into confusion, and then panic.

Talen stepped back and could only watch in shock and wonder.

The man stretched and swelled, transforming into a tree two or three times his own size. A pitiful scream of pain and terror died as his face became a gnarled knot. Twisting branches erupted from his head and shoulders.

In just a few heartbeats, an oak tree stood in the man's place. Not some majestic, beautiful oak though. Rather, a bent and twisted mockery of one, dark and foul as the soul inside it.

The knot bore the stained man's contorted expression of anger and fear. However, the farther Talen looked from that nightmarish depiction, the less profane the tree seemed. Leaves, lush and green, sprouted from at the tips of the farthest branches, the wood almost normal.

Talen stared at the oddity for a moment, trying to decide if it was fascinating or horrifying. Ultimately, she decided to put the consideration off until a later time, and hurried outside to see if Alice and the others needed help.

As it happened, they didn't. Not anymore.

Cyrus had caught a grazing shot across his arm, but no one else was hurt. Two stained lay dead on the ground. A trickle of blood leaked from the small entry wounds. Filthy viscera spilled from the massive exit wounds at the backs of their heads. Though not as gut-wrenchingly foul as the first house, the smell was far from pleasant.

"Any sign of prisoners?" Talen asked.

"Not out here," Alice said.

"Maybe they didn't have none," Booker said, as he tied a cloth around Cyrus's arm, eliciting a grunt as he knotted it.

"These ain't poor farmers," Talen said. "They wasn't dressed fancy, but their clothes were new and in good repair, and they had a spell iron." She shook her head. "I don't believe if they had the cash for all that, that they wouldn't make sure to have a shackled hand or two to work their land at least."

"We didn't see no quarters," Alice said.

"Check the house," Cyrus said. "Might be a cellar or such."

Talen thought back to the twisted smiles and the man's blood-chilling threat to 'have some fun' with her. "Yeah, that would fit." She turned to Booker and nodded at Cyrus. "Get him back to the Cumulus so Frieda and the others look him over." She turned to Alice. "You and me will check the house."

The men reluctantly agreed and made for the airship.

Alice hefted her rifle. "Lead on."

They returned to the house and stepped inside.

Alice stopped and gaped at the tree in the main room. "What in the name of everything holy is that?"

It had grown another couple of feet, and was now well-covered with healthy-looking leaves. In fact, it looked almost entirely normal, which made the screaming face knot stand out all the more.

"A field test," Talen said.

Alice arched an eyebrow but didn't ask any more questions.

Talen didn't blame her.

Stepping over and around the two bodies, and the putrid mess spilling from them, they searched the house.

"Shit. This can't be good," Alice said, as they looked through the largest bedroom.

Talen glanced over.

Alice stood, pulled up rug in her hand, staring at a trapdoor.

Talen thought back to a similarly hidden entrance in the factory in Boston, where Tuller had kept her stained crafters. She swallowed back the rising bile. "No, I'm gonna bet it ain't."

Alice bent as Talen drew her spell irons and took aim.

"Do it," Talen said.

Alice lifted the hatch, revealing a set of wooden stairs that vanished into darkness.

Talen shifted to get a better look but didn't see anyone. She couldn't be sure, but she thought there was the faintest hint of a magical glow coming from the shadowy depths.

"I'll go first," Talen said. "You watch my back and follow my lead."

"Yes, ma'am," Alice said, getting to her feet and leveling her repeater.

They descended the stairs, slow and careful. Both kept their footsteps to the far sides to keep the wood from creaking.

Very little light reached the bottom. Talen took a moment to let her eyes adjust and spotted some oil lamps. Choosing to err on the side of caution, she poured magic into her irons, lighting them with blue spell-fire, and casting away the gloom.

They stood in a small, empty chamber, ten feet across. A heavy wooden door, bolted from this side, stood opposite them.

"You got any matches?" Talen asked in a whisper, nodding at a collection of lamps.

Alice lit each until the small antechamber filled with orange, flickering light.

She put the matches away, met Talen's gaze, and gave a wry smile. "Might be I was hopeful we'd get to play General Sherman."

Talen drew her eyebrows together. "Who?"

"Sherman's march to the sea?" Alice asked.

Talen shrugged.

"Another time." Alice took up a lamp and held it across her body, letting her rest the rifle barrel on the wrist of that arm. "Need you to get the door."

Talen slid the bolt to one side, careful not to make much noise. She took the handle of the door and glanced back at Alice.

She nodded.

Talen pulled the door open, making sure to put herself between Alice and any potential incoming fire, but she needn't have bothered.

Another room, three times the size of the antechamber, opened before them. Several bedrolls had been laid out together, making one large sleeping surface that took up half the room. The stale air stank of sweat and sex, leading Talen to believe sleeping wasn't the primary interest here.

A young man, probably all of thirteen, one who might've been twenty, and a woman somewhere between them, lay on their backs, wearing nothing but raggedy britches.

None of them moved. At first glance, Talen thought them dead, but she saw their chests rise and fall in slow, steady breathing.

"Hey, can you hear me?" Alice said. "We're here to get you out."

None of them moved, or even acknowledged Talen and Alice's presence.

It took a moment to realize what Talen was seeing, and it was even worse than her first thought.

"*Anamara gani shanzi fetsuian,*" Talen spit.

"Are they dead?" Alice asked.

"No."

"What's wrong with them then?"

Talen didn't answer. Instead, she holstered her irons and bent down to check the bodies, hoping she was wrong.

She wasn't.

Each of them had a small cut just above their collarbones that had started to heal. A bulge under each wound, twice the size of a pea, confirmed Talen's suspicions.

Talen's head fell and fresh disgust warred with rage inside her. "Hobble stones."

"What?"

"They're *Malihane Carid*," Talen said. "Detestable crafts. They're called that because they trap you inside your body. You can see, hear, and feel, but you can't move or speak."

"Who the hell would make such a thing?" Alice asked.

"The mothers who made them convinced themselves at first it was a mercy," Talen said, shame washing away the anger and revulsion. "They was used on prisoners and seen as kinder than killing them. They could live, but wouldn't be able to hurt anyone."

Alice didn't say anything, but Talen felt the—well deserved—judgement in her eyes.

"Ain't none been used in going on fifteen hundred years," Talen said. "It didn't take us long to see how twisted the thinking had been, but any time at all is too much."

"Can anything be done for them?" Alice asked, her tone flat and cold.

"Might be," Talen said and drew her knife. "The stones ain't been completely absorbed. If I remove them, they might recover, though it could take some time."

"Then get those things out of them."

Talen set to work, carefully reopening the wound, removing each hobble stone. When it was done, she crushed the stones under boot, and wrapped each of the poor souls in a blanket.

"Let's get them back to the Cumulus," Talen said. "I don't know how big the stones started as, but I think we got them out before the magic was permanent."

Alice set the lamp and rifle down and helped Talen hoist each of the boys onto a shoulder. Alice herself took the woman over her own shoulder, picked up her rifle, and the pair of them slowly left the terrible chamber and house.

The walk back to the airship was slow, and neither of them said a word. The rain still fell, but they were all well past soaked by that point. Talen motioned for Alice to place the hobbled woman on Gaoth's back, but she refused.

Talen instantly understood and felt a bit of shame for not having realized sooner. The poor hobbled woman had enough of her humanity stripped away. No reason to compound that by draping her over Gaoth like a sack of flour.

Frieda and Odie met them at the bottom of the gangplank. Talen gave them a short explanation of events and that there was nothing to be done but watch and wait. She and Alice gently laid the limp forms on cots set up in the cargo bay.

The younger boy and the woman had tears running down their cheeks.

An icy fist of shame twisted Talen's heart. "I'm so sorry," she whispered. "I promise I'll make them pay for what they done to you."

There was no outward sign of recognition, for which Talen both regretted and was grateful. She said a silent prayer to her mother to purge the detestable magic and give these innocents back their lives.

A short while later, the gangway retracted, the Cumulus lifted into the air, and they were heading for the next target.

Talen stood by herself in one corner of the cargo bay wrapped in self-recrimination, guilt, shame, and disgust.

Alice walked over, stopping a few feet behind her. "I don't even want to imagine what terrible things were done to them."

"I can't stop myself from it," Talen said and wiped at her eyes.

"Didn't say I wasn't imagining," Alice said. "I said I didn't want to. Sadly, I know personally what some of those things were." She stepped up beside Talen. "I suspect you do as well."

"Saw more than enough," Talen said. "Never had to live through it myself."

Alice drew in several slow breaths. "It ain't your fault, you know."

"Maybe not me personally, but I carry the responsibility of my people. If we hadn't made those—"

"Humans damned sure would have," Alice said. "Honestly, I'm surprised we ain't come up with them already. Suppose it's a blessing we ain't as skilled with magic as you. We'd have come up with works that would make your detestable crafts look mildly unpleasant."

Talen couldn't argue the truth of that, but it didn't ease her guilt or responsibility.

"You all did some terrible things in your past," Alice said. "I confess I don't know the whole of it. Just what you've explained. Meanwhile, we're doing terrible things now. At least you saw the awfulness of it and not only did you recognize it and own it, you wore that shame as a reminder to never let it happen again. I'm not sure we'll be ready to own our wretchedness even a hundred years from now."

"Your people didn't do the terrible things. You suffered from them."

Alice laughed, but there was no humor in it. "We ain't a monolith, nor are we innocent of cruelty and evil. No mistake, we suffered, and I fear will for some time. But our hands aren't free of blood neither. My brother was in one of the all-Black regiments fighting the Cheyenne, Commanche, and such on the Great Plains."

Talen looked over and fought back a rising ire. She'd never encountered the so-called Buffalo Soldiers herself, but she'd heard plenty about what they'd done.

Alice grimaced. "He was genuinely proud of some of the horrible things he and his fellow soldiers did. At first, anyway. Eventually, he realized that justifying cruelty by calling them savages and such wasn't any different than what white folk had been doing to us."

Talen stayed silent.

"I ain't saying it's the same." Alice shrugged. "But seems to me just because someone else tortured hundreds of thousands, it doesn't make it okay for you to torture dozens. Neither does our cruelty excuse the cruelty we suffer. Wrong is wrong." She chuckled. "I don't know what I'm trying to say except that everyone is capable of evil. It's what you do about it that matters."

"Humans like you give me hope for the rest," Talen said.

Alice laughed. "Shit. I ain't got no use for that kind of pressure. Don't put that on me. I'm just trying to do the best I can."

Despite herself, Talen laughed too, just a little.

"Now, if you're done wallowing in guilt and self-pity, we got more work to do. There's still people out there counting on us."

Talen shook her head. "Damn, you don't sugar coat, do you?"

"Nah, I figure you're sweet enough." Alice grinned and winked.

Talen wished, again, that she and Alice had met under better circumstances. However, she also remained grateful to have met her at all. "You are one of a kind, that's for damned sure. I don't recall ever being called sweet, but I'll take it. And you're right, there's work to be done. Best get back to it."

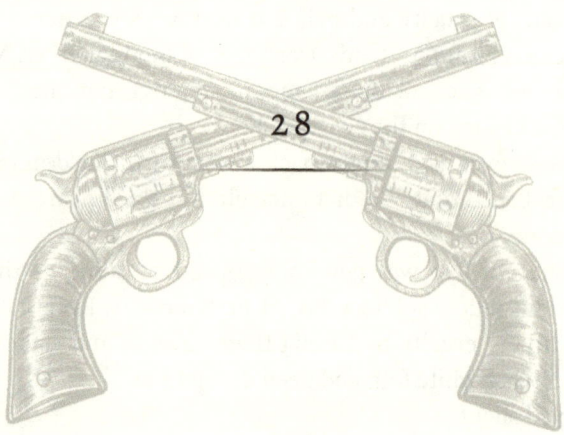

28

The next two farmsteads were cleared in short order. The first was a solitary stained who had two enslaved men working the fields. Thankfully, neither were under the effect of any detestable crafts. The second was a family of five, husband and wife, and three boys in their teens. All of them were stained, and all of them were put down. It wasn't something Talen enjoyed, but there hadn't been any other choice. Booker had killed the youngest, he was fourteen or fifteen. It clearly weighed on him after the fact, though freeing the woman tending the house and her two sons in the field seemed to ease his guilt some. Thank the mother, they weren't enchanted in anyway either. They bore scars and wounds of cruel treatment, but would live and hopefully find a new life well away from this place.

Cyrus appeared less bothered, but only Alice seemed to manage to leave the fight without carrying any emotional burden.

"Wasn't any choice," she said to Booker. "All else aside, they were shooting at us. If we hadn't killed them, they would've killed us." She motioned to the growing collection of people in the cargo bay. "These folk are free now because of us."

Booker nodded. "I know that. It's just…" He shook his head.

"He had to die because of what his parents done to him," Talen said.

"Something like that, yeah," he said.

Talen tried not to think of the stained she'd seen at Niagara, who probably turned to the dark because there'd been no light for them.

"Then it's on them, not us," Alice said. "They took their children to a place where there was no coming back from. Even if you want to excuse him from his part in being a slaver, he was also stained." She looked to Talen. "He had to choose that, right?"

"That's true," Talen said. She would've added that sometimes, some people didn't have a glut of choices, and sometimes none of them were good, but it didn't seem the time. Also, even she had to admit it sounded too much like making excuses.

"So, you did what you had to do," Alice said. "Remember all the people he and his family would've hurt and killed if we hadn't stopped them."

"That's what I hold to," Cyrus said.

"If you want to sit the next one out, I understand," Talen said.

Booker stood. "No. There's still work to do, and I know what I signed up for. Plenty of people before me walked a darkened path to help lead others to the light. Now it's my turn."

"That's God's truth there," Alice said.

The three of them bent their heads and began to pray together. Talen didn't feel like bringing up how that god was used to slaughter her people and keep theirs in chains, but again, it wasn't the time or place for that. Instead, she went to tend to Gaoth and the other new horses they'd collected.

The stables were almost full up now, and Gaoth seemed less than thrilled, but he bore his unhappiness with grace and dignity. Mostly.

They'd only brought the sick or weak back to the ship—those animals that needed care. The healthy ones were turned loose, after having their shoes removed. Talen made sure to let them know of the others in hopes they'd form their own herd and run free and wild. She knew it likely they'd get spotted and taken in, but there was a chance they wouldn't. Or if they did, those who found them might treat them well. That was the hope she held to.

They did keep two young mares and a stallion for Alice, Booker, and Cyrus. Having them on horseback would make the work easier and save time. When this foul work was done, Talen would make sure the horses were set free with the others, once they were well enough to make it on their own.

"Dark and bloody business, old friend," she said to Gaoth, as she stroked his forehead. "I'd have thought soldiers wouldn't be weighed down by it as much, but I reckon it's different when the other side ain't wearing uniforms."

Gaoth chuffed and leaned in to her touch.

"No surprise, Alice has the broadest shoulders for carrying the weight." Talen kissed Gaoth's cheek. "I love Wilfred and Margaret, but humans still confound me. They put all the burden on women to carry the emotional load, but refuse to give them credit for being the stronger."

"It's because our men are cast iron," Alice said, from the far side of the stables.

"How's that?" Talen asked, without looking over.

"They have their uses." Alice walked to a column and leaning against it. "In the right time and place, they're strong and quite useful. But they do require a lot of upkeep, and they crack real easy."

Granted, Talen's experience with human men was limited, except for Wilfred, but she couldn't, and didn't much feel the need to, argue. She glanced over. "Is that why you favor women?"

Alice shook her head. "Wasn't never a choice. As far back as I can remember I always knew I liked women and had no use for men in that way." She shrugged. "Not that I could tell much of anyone. Or that it would matter if I did." She narrowed her eyes and furrowed her brow. "You elves get to choose?"

Talen shrugged. "I know some that never desired a man, others that didn't take to women, but it ain't something we spend much time fretting over. To us, you love who you love, however much and however long your heart calls for it."

"I envy you that," Alice said. "It is quite a thing for humans to fret over. It's funny. The folks who rail about their own freedom, liberty, and right to live their life as they please, they're the first to shout at you for living yours wrong."

"I do have some familiarity with that," Talen said.

"I expect you do."

They didn't say anything for a long while. Then, Alice set to helping Talen care for the horses.

When Alice turned her back, Talen slipped Gaoth an apple, and he crunched it happily.

Alice pretended not to notice, but Talen saw her smile.

It wasn't long before word came that they were approaching the next farmhouse.

Even just the thought of doing this, over and over, for a week or more, seemed to drain Talen's physical and emotional strength. Instead of letting it weigh her down and overwhelm her, she drew in a breath and just focused on the next task.

Cyrus and Booker showed up shortly after, and they all led their horses to the gangplank.

The rain had stopped, or at least wasn't falling here. Though the wind blew harder and the thunder was closer.

"It's well past noon," Alice said. "Like as not, the stained will be inside for dinner. If they ever left in the first place."

"If there's anyone working the fields, we'll get them clear first," Talen said. "After that, we'll check the barn. If we find a stained, and there's only one, I'll slip into shadows and take them down. More than that, or no one at all, we'll take care of the house."

The others nodded.

"I'll go in first," Talen said and looked to Alice. "You follow when I say." She turned to Booker and Cyrus. "You two make sure we don't have any surprises from behind."

"I'm fine," Booker said, more than a little defensively. "I can still shoot and—"

"I know you can," Talen said, despite him feeling the need to reassure a concern no one raised. "I want you two watching our backs because they likely won't be expecting two women. Might be they'll hesitate and give us an advantage."

Booker and Cyrus exchanged a look and seemed to accept that logic.

Alice arched an eyebrow and gave Talen a small, half smile.

This farmhouse was larger than the others and had quarters for a half dozen enslaved at least, so they set down a couple miles out. Quarter mile or so away, they tied the horses in the cover of the woods. Gaoth could undo the slip knots and get them loose if need be.

No one was working the fields, so they moved to the barn, slow and cautious, Talen a couple dozen paces ahead.

Alice and Booker took up on either side of the closed barn door. Cyrus watched their back for any surprise visitors.

Talen put her ear to the door.

Floorboards creaked, someone grumbled and, unless she was much mistaken, turned straw or the like. So good news was, they'd have their hands full. Bad news was, they'd be full of pitchfork or the like.

She held up one finger, looking from Booker to Alice, each of whom nodded and readied their rifles. Talen wrapped herself in shadow and gently pushed the door open just enough to slip in.

A grimy man in his early twenties was pitching hay to a couple of old, weary—but well-fed—plow horses. His clothes were worn and ragged, covered in stains and filth Talen didn't want to imagine the source of. He stank of sweat and shit and had the telltale lack of light around him. It was especially evident close to the horses who shined, soft and warm.

The man mumbled and cursed under his breath, entirely oblivious.

Talen drew a knife, crouched low, and waited for an opening.

When he let go of the pitchfork to wipe his brow, she struck.

Taking him from behind, she drove her knee into the back of his.

He went down, hard and fast.

Her left hand covered his mouth, and she opened his throat.

That wasn't enough to end him, and she hadn't expected it to, but since he couldn't scream, she had her left hand free. When he dropped the pitchfork and reached for his throat, gasping out a silent cry of panic and rage, she pivoted and drove him face first to the ground.

He wriggled and tried to pull his arms out from under himself.

Talen planted a knee on his neck, the other on the small of his back. She didn't weigh much and wouldn't hold him long, but it was enough for her to drive her blade between his ribs and into his heart.

The tip of her blade hit bone as the hilt pressed into his back. Using all of her considerable strength, she twisted the knife and dragged it back and forth, shredding his heart beyond repair.

She hoped.

To be sure, when he stopped moving, she withdrew the blade, pushed his head forward, and drove the point into the base of his skull, punching through the thin layer of bone. Again, she twisted the knife handle, this time scrambling his brains.

Deed done, she made to clean the knife on his clothes, but thought it might actually come away dirtier. In the process of looking for a clean spot, she noted five gunshot wounds that had healed over. With him being stained, she had no idea how old they were. Could be years or days. The placement, though, seemed deliberate, right at his shoulders.

A morbid sense of curiosity got the better of her so she checked his back and saw another five scars closely grouped around his lower back, right on the spine. They didn't look to have happened at the same time. It didn't take a genius to figure the other stained, likely his parents, had done this as punishment.

She didn't indulge in the many complex thoughts and feelings she had about this situation. Instead, she found the least filthy rag and cleaned her blade. After sheathing it, she left the corpse and moral deliberation behind, and went to the horses. She whispered to them of open fields and wind in their manes as they ran with a herd under the sun.

Both chuffed happily, and she set to work removing their shoes using the tools in a satchel she brought for just this occasion. When they were free of iron, she removed their bits and bridles—it rankled her that they'd been left in—and led them to the door.

Careful not to make too much noise, she swung the barndoor open, walked the horses out, then whispered that they were free and where they might find a herd.

Cyrus, Alice, and Booker just stood to one side, not saying a word.

The huge, powerful animals trotted off, probably the best pace they could manage at their size and age, vanishing into the woods. The sight gave Talen a moment of untainted joy and pleasure, which she savored for an entire five seconds.

When the moment passed, she drew both spell irons and motioned to the others. Together they moved quick and quiet to the farmhouse, keeping low and well clear of the windows. Booker and Cyrus took up at the corners of the house, eyes open, and repeaters ready.

Talen slipped into shadows again and made a full circuit of the place, listening under each window to get a clearer picture of what and who was inside. She counted five, two adults and three kids on the smaller side, all near the front of the house. If anyone was upstairs, they were either light-footed enough to not make a sound, or simply weren't moving.

Talen briefly debated climbing up to a second-floor window, but decided against it. No chance she could do that without being heard. Best to act now and get the jump on anyone inside.

Returning to Alice, Talen leaned in close and very, very gently, touched the other woman's shoulder.

Alice flinched, but not too much, and swore silently.

"Two adults, three kids," Talen whispered into Alice's ear, barely audible. "All together. Don't hear no one upstairs, but watch for anyone just in case."

Alice nodded.

Talen tapped Alice's shoulder three times, then stood and went to the door.

"Stop that sniffling or I'll give ya something to cry about," a man shouted from inside.

"Yes, sir," a soft, young voice replied.

"I put a bullet in you, you won't heal like Jacob does," the man said and chuckled.

"There's plenty of space for another hole in the ground," a woman said and laughed. "Toss you in with them worthless, lazy slaves. After all, I ain't too old to make more of you."

"No, mama, you ain't," the man said.

Both of them cackled and made kissing sounds.

Talen kept herself from puking up her guts, drew in a breath, and kicked down the door.

Time slowed, as she stepped inside and moved clear of incoming fire.

Two kids, maybe eight and ten, stood frozen next to a table, plates of food in their small hands. A third, a few years older, was at the cookstove. All of them were as filthy and ragged as the man in the barn, but unlike him, they all had a faint glow to them.

Thank you, Mother.

When the door struck the far wall, the kids jumped and dropped their plates.

A haggard man and woman, stinking and foul, sat at the table. The darkness around them seemed to swallow light from the children. Both adults stared at the open doorway with wide eyes, black threads criss-crossing the whites.

Outside, as if on cue, a crack of thunder boomed, and a gust of wind blew into the house.

"I told you to fix that damned door." The woman smacked the man.

He cracked her across the face with the barrel of his revolver, sending her to the floor.

She got to her feet and smacked the nearest kid. "Pick this mess up! And don't think I won't take the cost of that plate out of your hide!"

Talen used the ruckus to position herself and take aim, ensuring the kids were out of the line of fire. When the woman sat back down, Talen stepped from shadows and lit both spell irons. Blue spellfire filled the runes and sigils.

Their stained-filled eyes went wide, and their mouths fell open.

Talen fired.

A blast of kinetic energy shot from each barrel, striking both adults square in the face.

Because of how close her targets were, the magic didn't quite get to full power. As Talen had hoped, it didn't pulverize the skulls and paint the room with brains and blood. It did, however, crush in the faces, snapping their necks. Both tumbled back and fell to the floor.

The heads looked like sacks of wet mud, and blood ran from the eyes, mouths, and ears. While not pretty, it wasn't nearly as grotesque as it could've been.

In the silence that followed, Talen rolled both irons to fresh cylinders and watched the stunned kids, silently praying to her mother that they wouldn't make her do something terrible.

Well, more terrible.

None of them moved. They just stared, eyes moving from Talen, to their dead parents and back.

"I'm sorry I had to do that," Talen said, as gently as she could and holstered her irons. "But I ain't going to hurt you."

Alice appeared around the doorway; rifle leveled.

Talen motioned for her to lower it.

She did.

No one moved or spoke for a long while.

Talen looked to the oldest, just into their teens maybe. The child stared at the ruined body on the floor and then up at Talen with rage-filled eyes.

Talen swallowed and slid her hand to her knife but didn't draw it. *Please. Don't.*

"You son of a bitch!" the child shouted and tears began streaming down their cheeks.

Alice made to lift her rifle.

Talen waved her off again. "I know you—"

The child turned back to the dead man, spit at him, then went to the corpse and started kicking it. "Rot in hell you son of a bitch! I told you I'd see you dead!"

Talen glanced over at Alice, but she seemed just as surprised.

"I hope you burn forever!" the kid shouted, stilling kicking.

The other two then joined in, the youngest kicking the mother's body.

Talen looked to Alice for help, but found none. Talen had spent more than a little time imagining how kids might react to their parents being killed, and how to manage it, but this wasn't anywhere on that list.

Eventually, after a much longer span than Talen expected, the oldest tired or just had their fill and stopped their assault on the corpse. The two younger ones followed suit.

"You all right?" Talen asked, her tone gentle and cautious.

The kid nodded and motioned for their siblings. The other kids rushed over and the older one nudged them behind them.

"You mean to kill us too?" the oldest asked.

"No," Talen said. "I'm Talen. This here is Alice." She motioned to the bodies. "We came for them and to free anyone here against their will."

"I'm Maggie." She gestured to the others. "This here is Joshua and Mary. Jacob, my older brother is out in the barn." Her eyes narrowed. "You kill him already?"

"I did," Talen said. "Like your parents, he was stained."

"I know." She eyed Talen and Alice in turn. "Jacob wasn't so bad when I was little, but he turned into a right bastard after the war. Ma and Pa always were."

"They hurt you," Talen said.

"Pa thought me being his daughter meant he was entitled to me."

Talen didn't ask her to elaborate.

"Ma didn't never argue about it," Maggie said. "I'd planned on killing them myself, but when Preacher turned everyone stained, I wasn't sure I could no more. Thank you for doing it for me."

"Uh, you're welcome," Talen said, again taken aback. She hadn't been prepared to be thanked by anyone white.

"You aim to do the same to the rest of the town?" Maggie asked, in a tone that belied her age. "If so, I hope there's more of you, cause there's folk meaner and tougher than Ma and Pa."

"We got a good idea what's in store," Talen said. "You got somewhere you and your brother and sister can go?"

Maggie shook her head. "This is all the family we got."

"It's all the family we need," Mary said.

"I took care of everyone before. I reckon I can keep doing it." Maggie's face drew in a little. "Course I don't know shit about farming or the like. Jacob took care of that."

Alice gave Talen a hard look.

"There anyone else here?" Talen asked. "Any—"

"Slaves?" Maggie asked, looking from Talen to Alice and back. "Nah. Ma and Pa weren't liked enough to get any that weren't already taken by Bennfield or Perkins."

"Who are they?" Alice asked.

"Rich folk," Maggie said. "Their plantations take up most of the town. They screamed the loudest about the Yankees taking their slaves, but none of them could be bothered to fight in the war."

"We got someone who can help you," Talen said. "We can't get you there until we're done here, but until then, you'll each have a bed and food."

Maggie narrowed her eyes, as if sizing up Talen and Alice. "I never did give much care for the slave talk." She looked to Alice. "All the white folk kept talking how you and yours weren't as smart or were dangerous and such."

Alice stiffened. "And what do you think?"

"Seems like a load of horse shit to me," she said. "For all the talk, I ain't ever heard of any Black folk doing nothing near as terrible as my own did to me." She turned back to Talen. "I ain't all that smart, but I know Mary and Joshua here need more than I can do for them. I'd be grateful for taking them in, but I earn my keep. You give me a rifle, and I'll help with the killing."

Talen and Alice exchanged a look. She obviously wasn't any fonder of the idea than Talen.

"Appreciate your passion," Talen said. "And I understand, but I can't let you do that."

"I'm a keen shot," Maggie said. "Better than anyone I ever went up against. I can hit a rabbit at a full run at eighty yards."

"Can you now?" Alice asked, her eyebrows lifted.

Maggie stood a little straighter. "Yes, ma'am. If we're eating meat, odds are I'm the one who bagged it."

"I don't doubt your skill," Talen said. "But you've seen and survived enough, more than someone twice your age should've. I'm not—"

"Ain't I entitled to get some justice for what was done to me?" Maggie asked. "Everyone in this town knew what Pa was doing and that he was putting eyes on Mary next. None of them did a damned thing, even before they was stained. So long as Ma and Pa were at church on Sunday, raising their hands and saying 'praise the Lord,' no one asked about my bruises."

Talen shook her head and opened her mouth.

"You don't trust me with a gun?" Maggie said and looked at Alice. "I understand. I'm one of them that kept your people in chains, even went to war over it. Most of my life, I just figured that was how it was supposed to be. But if you let me, I can help you."

"Might be you can," Talen said. "We know you ain't the only kids in town, and I don't reckon most will be as agreeable as you. Might be you could help us with them."

"Some you'll have to drag away," Maggie said. "And they'll bite and kick the whole way."

"We got a means of making them sleep until we can get them somewhere," Talen said.

Maggie shrugged. "Ask me, there's plenty ain't worth bothering with, but if you want the trouble, I suppose that makes you better than me."

"Why don't you, Mary, and Joshua go collect your things?" Talen said. "Then we'll take you back to our airship."

All three kid's eyes widened.

"You got an airship?" Maggie asked.

"Well, it ain't mine, as such," Talen said. "Belongs to a friend of mine. She's a dwarf."

"Ain't never seen a dwarf," Maggie said. "Course before today, I ain't never seen an elf neither."

"Go get your things," Talen said. "Then we'll get you all out of here."

"Yes, ma'am," Maggie said and turned to her siblings. "You heard the lady. Go on and gather up whatever you don't want left behind cause we ain't never coming back here."

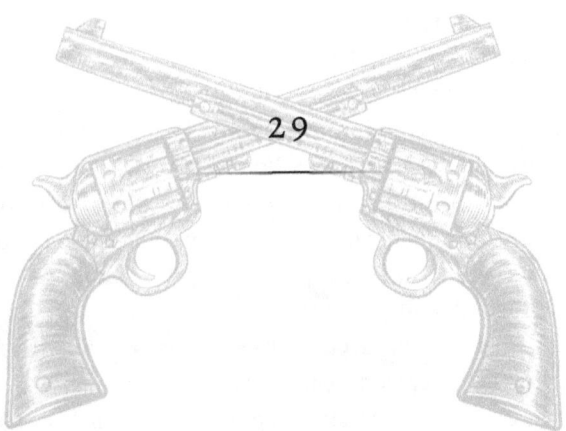

29

Maggie's arrival drew a lot of attention, from the recently freed as well as the Alice's compatriots. As such, Margaret took charge, setting Maggie and her siblings up with some cots in a section of the cargo bay away from those who'd been freed, at Maggie's request.

The distrust rankled Talen, even if she understood it. It took some effort to keep quiet, but she did. She knew firsthand how hard it could be to work past judgement, especially when born from true horrors.

The annoyance turned to outright heartbreak when Margaret brought them some food. The poor, starving kids ate like they hadn't been fed in weeks. From the look of them, Talen figured that couldn't be far from the actual truth. Jacob literally licked his dish clean.

That sad display seemed to soften the harsh judgement of the others in the hold, a bit at least. For her part, Talen wished she could kill the parents a second time. And a third.

The girl hadn't been lying either. She jumped at every opportunity to help, no matter how small. When not doing chores, or asking what needed doing, she eagerly shared all she knew about who and how many people lived in the nearby farms. What she knew beyond that was admittedly less, but still helpful.

Any debate about whether she could be trusted ended when Talen and Alice recounted how things had gone down.

It soon became obvious Maggie truly didn't much care for the others in her town, even some of the kids. She held a special disdain for the children of the wealthier families, whom she deemed as cruel and worthless as their parents. Despite her judgements, she did agree to help with any kids Talen and the others managed to rescue., Though she did suggest putting them all to sleep until the job was done.

Based on her information, Talen, Alice, Booker, and Cyrus made short work of four more farms before the sun had set. They freed nine more prisoners, unfortunately, geas stones bound two of them. A wave of guilt threatened to drown Talen, remembering how she'd used one herself. Granted, it'd been a human-made version, and she'd used it on the filth who'd crafted it, along with various slaver wares. None of those details made it right, or eased a bit of her shame.

They also found six children in the homes, ranging from three to eleven. None of them reacted near as well as Maggie. Talen had to use slumber rounds on them. Even knowing it wouldn't kill them didn't make it any easier to light her irons and shoot children. Each time she fired on confused, terrified, or furious child, her irons seemed to get heavier and heavier. If Alice or the others had noticed her shaking hands or wet eyes, none of them said anything.

Talen insisted on carrying the small, sleeping bodies back to the Cumulus, laying them gently on cots near Maggie's brother and sister.

Then she went out and did it all again.

When the day finally came to an end, Talen stood on her own in the cargo bay. The crushing weight of her actions pressed down on her, and it seemed beyond belief the Cumulus could still fly. She knew when it came to dealing with the children, the options available ranged from horrible to horrific, but that didn't stop it from chewing up her insides.

"Might be you could turn your guilt to anger," Margaret said softly and put a hand on Talen's shoulder.

Talen flinched a bit, taken aback that she hadn't heard Margaret approach. She hadn't realized how all-consuming her self-loathing had gotten. "Oh, there's plenty of anger too."

"For their parents, I mean," Margaret said. "They're the ones who chose to turn stained. They chose the side of slavery, and even after losing, chose to keep fighting for it. All those choices stripped you of any good ones. I know it probably doesn't help, but you truly are doing the best you can with the terrible options left to you. I'm sorry it falls on you to be the one who finally does the right thing."

"Thank you." Talen put her arms around her sister and kissed the top of her head. "And I know you're right, but you're also right that it don't help none."

"Wilfred is working on some new charms for them," Margaret said, leaning into Talen. "The slumber rounds won't last long, but he said these new ones will keep the kids asleep, sort of like a hibernation. He also said it'll give them nice dreams."

Talen clung to that ridiculously small bit of decency like a drowning woman in a storm held to a bit of debris. "Leave it to him to find a way to give some peace and show mercy to children of them that would see him chained or swinging from a tree."

"I think that's what makes us the good guys in this," Margaret said.

"I don't know if I find that word a fit to how I feel just now."

"I'm the heart, remember?" Margaret said. "So, you need to listen and trust me."

Despite herself, Talen smiled a bit and nodded. "Yes, ma'am."

They shared a companionable silence for a while before Wilfred came down with his new charms. Margaret took them and activated them, for which Talen was grateful. As she did, Wilfred went to Talen, and put a dozen small stones into her hand.

"I reckon using these will be less of a burden on you than shooting a child," Wilfred said as he watched Margaret tenderly set a stone on each child and push magic into it.

Moments after she did, the expression on each child's face softened and they looked genuinely peaceful.

"I confess," Talen said, pocketing the stones, "I didn't think this through when I offered up the option."

"I didn't neither," Wilfred said. "It weren't until I was wondering what we'd do when the slumber magic wore off. They won't work so well on an adult, but on a child, they'll sleep and dream until the stone is removed."

"You're a good man," Talen said. "A good person, and I'm damned glad to have you here. No way I could've done this without you and Margaret."

He smiled his usual smile. "I always figured that was how a family was supposed to work."

The weight on Talen's heart eased a bit more, and a spark of hope flared to life where there'd only been despair. As a crafter, Wilfred could only create magical devices; he couldn't cast. However, that never stopped him from performing miracles.

When Margaret had all the slavers' kids sleeping and dreaming, she came to stand with Wilfred and Talen.

"You sure they'll be okay?" Margaret asked. "Without any food or water, or use of the necessities?"

"They might look to world to just be sleeping," he said, his tone unusually serious, "but it ain't no ordinary sleep. So long as the magic is active, time as such ain't passing for them."

No one said anything for a handful of heartbeats.

Talen drew in a slow breath and let it out as long sigh. "I reckon I ought to see to packing up the rifles."

"It's being taken care of," Wilfred said. "Alice pulled the others into helping her check and load them into a sack for you, along with plenty of ammunition. Should have everything ready for you before too long."

"Wait, you're going tonight?" Margaret asked. "Is that a good idea? You're soaked to the bone, and you must be exhausted."

"I am," Talen said, "but I'll be fine. Besides, it needs to get done tonight. Every day brings a better chance someone finds the corpses we left behind, and they start expecting us. I need to get those arms to free folk in town as soon as I can. We wait, and I might not get the chance."

Margaret looked as if she wanted to argue but knew there wouldn't be a point.

"I promise I'll be careful," Talen said.

"Wish you didn't have to go alone," Wilfred said.

"What's that you used to say?" Talen asked. "Wish in one hand and—"

"I remember that aphorism," Wilfred said. "No need to repeat it."

Margaret picked up on his discomfort and smiled. "I don't know that one." Her smile gave the lie to her words. "What's the rest? I'd really like to know."

Talen bit back a chuckle.

Wilfred narrowed his eyes. "Dig a hole with the other."

"I don't remember it like that," Talen said.

"Then you are mistaken," Wilfred said. "Now I have work to do."

Talen nodded, gave him a long hug, and kissed his cheek. There were no words for how much she appreciated even this little reprieve from the grim tasks both behind and before her. Even if she felt guilty for getting the break, and worse for enjoying it.

He hugged back.

Margaret wrapped her arms around them both and gave them a long squeeze.

When the embrace ended, Wilfred returned to his work, Margaret went to check on Maggie, Mary, and Jacob, and Talen headed for the armory.

Before she even reached it, Talen heard a discussion from inside.

"I'm telling you, they're too heavy," Booker said.

"And I'm telling you she is plenty strong enough," Alice said.

There was a grunt and something heavy thumping down. "I can hardly lift it!" Cyrus said.

Talen stepped through the doorway to find Booker and Cyrus facing Alice. Three large bundles of rifles rolled up in blankets, belted with leather straps, sat between them. Frieda, Odie, and Pearl stood off to one side, staying out of it.

"We need to pack as many guns as we can," Alice said. "Ain't like she can make a dozen trips back here for more."

"She's right," Talen said.

Everyone turned to look at her.

"I don't mean no disrespect," Booker said.

"I sense a 'but' coming," Talen said.

"But," he said, lifting his hands then gesturing at the bundles, "each of these must weigh near on two-hundred—"

Talen sighed, walked over, lifted a bundle with a single hand, and moved it to her shoulder, testing the balance and weight. "Yeah, that sounds about right." She hefted another bundle onto her other shoulder and got it settled. The weight wasn't as troublesome as the size. She could just barely hold on to them, but it'd do. "Reckon I'll only be able to carry two at a time then."

Cyrus and Booker stared at her, their brows crawling toward their hairlines. Alice and the other women chuckled.

Talen had been underestimated by humans—especially men—so many times, proving them wrong had gone from satisfying to a chore. "How many rifles in each bundle?" she asked and set them down.

"Twenty-five," Alice said. "All of them are loaded and ready to shoot." She gestured to a nearby satchel. "That's got six hundred rounds in it, boxed in sets of fifty."

Talen lifted the satchel. It wasn't more than thirty pounds. "Guess they'll have to make their shots count."

"I made sure to reinforce the straps," Odie said. "Wouldn't do for one to break on you."

"Much obliged. Six hundred don't seem like enough. We got enough spare rounds to fill another bag?"

Everyone laughed.

"Is that all there is for this sort of rifle?" Talen asked, confused as to what was funny.

"Are you joking?" Pearl asked and gestured around.

"I don't fire mundane shooters," Talen said. "I know Draven has bullets to spare, but I don't know how much or of what size." Yet another reason Talen preferred spell irons, a load for one iron would fit any other.

"Best I could figure," Frieda said, "is she's got several hundred thousand rounds in here, probably fifty-thousand to fit a Winchester repeater."

"So, it weren't exaggeration when she says she could supply a small army?" Talen asked.

"It was not," Alice said.

"Plenty of battles I'd have given my left hand for a third of this supply," Booker said.

"That's God's truth," Cyrus said.

"Give me a bit to get you another satchel full," Alice said.

"I'll get these down to Gaoth then," Talen said and took a single bundle. The confined space on the airship would make carrying more than one at a time impractical, so she'd have to make a few trips.

When she reached the stables, Gaoth saw the bundle, gave her a side-eye and chuffed.

"There's two more just like this."

The horse shook his head and snorted.

Gaoth wasn't near as large as Joseph, and even the large draft horse would struggle carrying that much weight on his back. Carrying and pulling, though, were two very different things. They didn't have a cart or carriage, but even if they did, Talen wouldn't want to use one. Apart from the wet ground, it'd take too long to free Gaoth if they needed to make a run for it. They did, however, have a simple sled. Not only would it slide nicely across the mud, it could be secured quick, and cut loose just as fast.

When Talen fetched it and set the first bundle on it, Gaoth seemed less concerned, but was still eying it dubiously.

"We both know you can pull this just fine. You just won't be running when you do," Talen said as she secured the bundle.

Half an hour and two trips later, Talen had all three bundles and two satchels fixed to the sled.

"Is this really a good plan?" Margaret asked, as Talen dragged it to the gangway and hooked it to a makeshift harness she'd rigged up for Gaoth.

"It is not," Talen said.

From the look he gave her, Gaoth was not fond of any of this either, but he'd get over it.

"What it is," Talen said, checking everything, "is the best of the bad options we got."

In point of fact, it was the only option if they were going to get these arms to the folk in town. With near a thousand pounds of gear, pulling was the only way it would work. Worse, they'd need to avoid roads, which meant uneven terrain, and Talen would have to walk Gaoth so she could make sure the sled didn't get hung up on anything. And worse, she'd still have to haul the gear a mile or more into town. Her shadow cloak would barely conceal her and the bundles, much less Gaoth and a sled.

Ideally, she'd cut the sled loose once they reached a good staging point, and she'd send Gaoth back to the ship, but she knew he'd never leave her behind. It'd be nice not to walk all the way back though. She was strong, but even she'd be taxed hauling the gear that far while holding her shadow cloak. Even thinking about it started to tire her out. But exhaustion wouldn't make the long night ahead, or longer days after, any shorter. If she wanted even a chance at a bit of sleep before sunup, she needed to get started.

"Just about there," Draven's voice said, through a nearby speaking tube.

"Right," Talen said and turned to Margaret. "If I ain't back by sunrise, make sure everyone follows the changes to the plan I gave you."

Margaret frowned. "You think Wilfred and Draven will just go on and not come looking for you?"

"Not if they don't want me to put my boot up their asses," Talen said. "We've been over this. If I don't come back, it means either I'm dead, or holed up somewhere waiting for a chance to make a break for it. I don't plan on dying tonight, so it'll be the latter. If you follow the plan, I'll know where to find you, and I will."

Margaret sucked in a breath and met Talen's eyes. "You promise you're not going to get killed out there alone?"

"If I do, you'll know because I'll be taking a whole mess of stained, and their town, with me."

"That isn't what I asked."

"No, it ain't." Talen hugged her. "You know I can't promise that, but I can promise I will do all I can to make sure I don't."

"I suppose that's all I can ask," Margaret said, hugging her back, tight.

They broke the hug when the gangway lowered and found everyone else, including Draven, had come down to see Talen off.

"*Terisan ut marrin,*" Talen said and glared at them. "I don't much like how you all are treating this like I'm marching off to certain death. I'll be back well before sunrise."

Wilfred, Margaret, and Draven gave nods.

"Good luck," Alice said.

"Thank you." Talen turned to the others, gesturing to Alice. "That is the proper way to send me off."

Wilfred and Margaret smiled, only a bit, but it was enough.

Talen turned around and led Gaoth down the gangway and into the night.

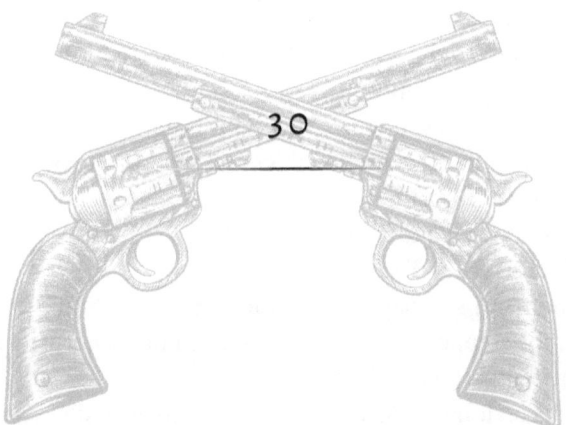

30

Neither Talen nor Gaoth were happy with the slow progress through the dark woods, but they didn't have any other options. Thankfully, the trees and undergrowth kept the wet ground from becoming a quagmire. The time also gave Talen a chance to go over the map in her head and where the people who'd be receptive to receiving the arms lived. Of course, if the people she chose had been taken to a farm, or worse, it'd make a long night even longer.

She immediately winced and shame draped over her like a cold, soaked blanket. The inconvenience of having to find new allies because the first choice had been dragged off or murdered sure seemed the better end of the bargain.

Deserved as it may be, she knew self-recrimination could wait, so she tucked it away for later and refocused on the matter at hand.

She took a path longer than necessary, but it did keep them away from the roads and farms, and hopefully, anyone out. Most had probably bedded down by now, but she knew damn well that slave catchers worked at night because that's when people tended to run. Luckily for her, humans didn't see as well at night, even in good weather. That meant they'd have torches or lanterns, and she'd spot them coming long before they got close enough to see her or Gaoth.

Unless, of course, they had some charm to let them see in the dark, or

265

the corruption somehow gave them that ability. She'd never heard of that happening before, but nothing about this town could be called typical.

Thankfully, if anyone was out, they never got close enough to even be heard. A mile or so from town, Talen unloaded the sled, broke it down, and lashed the pieces to Gaoth.

"I suspect I know your answer," she whispered to him, "but would you please head back to the ship?"

Gaoth didn't make a sound but shook his head.

"Figured as much. All right, I ain't gonna fight with you, but you need to stay here at least. I can't hide us both."

He bobbed his head and nudged her with his cheek.

She stroked his face. "Yeah, I'll be careful."

After a moment, she hefted a bundle onto each shoulder. Once they were settled, she stepped into the shadows, and made her way to the first, and hopefully only, stop that night.

It didn't take long to get close enough to actually see the town. Though small, it didn't feel as cramped or closed in as the towns out west and north. The huge church stood in the center, its three stories and bell tower loomed over the one- and two-floor buildings making up the rest of the town.

Out front, a lone, huge, dark and bent ash tree stood. Unlike every other tree Talen had seen since developing her new ability, this one had no light shining from it. Darkness surrounded and radiated from it.

Even more disturbing than the notion of a stained tree were the eight bound bodies swinging from nooses on the lowest branches. Another dozen ropes hung empty, but looked almost eager to be filled. Dark filaments, like threads of darkness, ran from the bodies and into the tree.

A cold, rancid ball hung in Talen's chest, and every breath tasted foul.

Turning away from the abomination, Talen refocused on the task at hand and moved between the buildings, keeping to the shadows. When she spotted the bank, saloons, and general store, she was able to get her bearings. The free Black population had been relegated to one section of the town, next to the jail and surrounded by a wall a little taller than her.

The squelching sound of hoofbeats drew her up short, and she ducked behind the corner of a nearby building, hoping the rough, weatherworn wood offered enough cover.

A few minutes later, two men on horseback rode by at a languid pace, each carrying a torch. Both wore white robes and bizarrely pointed hoods. The pale, but dingy, rain-soaked cloth accentuated the lack of radiance coming for either of them. These two weren't just stained, they were wholly corrupted. If she'd been able to smell them, Talen suspected she'd be hard-pressed not to vomit.

Seeing humans stained to the very soul, laughing, joking, and, apparently, following another's orders somehow disturbed her more than the extent of their stain.

Fear tried to wriggle its way up her spine, but she beat it back with pure, undiluted anger. It took all her willpower to not drop her burden, pull them from their horses, and see how much cutting it would take to kill them.

However, that wouldn't accomplish as much as the plan, and the very people she meant to help would suffer for any bodies found.

Grudgingly, she let them ride by.

Once they were well away, Talen hurried to the wall and followed it, looking for a way in. Eventually she found a heavy iron gate, locked.

Of course.

Given time, she could force the lock open, but that would mean someone would find it, and again, those trapped inside the wall would suffer. Horrid as the wall was, it probably meant that no one felt the need to patrol inside. That was something at least.

Unfortunately, the road seemed to follow the wall all the way around, and there were long burning torches in regular intervals. Best she could do was find a section farthest from the main part of the town.

She checked all around, looking and listening. Hoofbeats sounded from somewhere on the other side of the makeshift prison. Despite being wrapped in wool blankets, just tossing the rifles over the wall could make too much noise. Carefully, she set each bundle on the top of the wall and made sure it wouldn't tumble one way or the other. Satisfied, she clambered up between them, dropped to the other side and took the rolls down.

When she turned, anger sparked anew in her heart. The houses—and that term could only be used in the loosest sense—were little more than shacks of loose, ill-fitting boards. She'd seen jails more spacious and well-maintained. A stiff breeze could probably bring them down.

Fury seethed at the sight of people confined to such conditions, but she couldn't manage any surprise.

There were no markings on the outsides of the "houses" to denote who lived there, so she had to think back to the map and Delia's notes on who lived where. Talen started toward what she hoped was Delia's house.

No telling if the girl's mother or brother were still there, but it seemed the best place. Hopefully, she'd find someone who didn't panic at a strange elf showing up at their door in the middle of the night.

Only if my luck changes.

When she found it, she set the bundles out of sight, and still wrapped in shadow, tapped on the door.

Silence.

She knocked again, a bit louder, and this time, she tapped out the tune of "Go Down Moses," a tune she'd heard used by Railroad workers and escaping slaves.

Someone inside moved, trying to be silent but Talen heard them clear enough. Soft footsteps approached the door.

"Go down Moses," a woman whispered from the other side of the door.

"Way down in Egypt's land," Talen sang back softly.

The woman didn't say anything, but her breathing grew ragged and her heart pounded.

"Delia got to Moses," Talen whispered. "We came to get you and everyone else out too."

The door opened and a short human woman of middling years stuck her head out and looked around. "Where are you?"

"Right here," Talen said and stepped from the shadows, hands up.

The woman, flinched back, eyes wide, but kept from making a sound.

"I reckon you ain't seen many of my kind," Talen whispered, glancing about to make sure no one was watching. "But you can see who I ain't, and I think we'd best talk inside."

The woman hesitated, looked Talen up and down, her gaze lingering on Talen's right-hand iron.

Talen drew both, slowly, and offered them to the woman, handles first. "A show of trust."

The woman stared at Talen in wide-eyed, open-mouthed shock for a couple of heartbeats. When the moment passed, she didn't take the irons, but stepped back and opened the door just enough for Talen to step inside.

Talen holstered her irons and slipped in. "Much obliged."

"Did my Delia really make it all the way to Moses?" the woman asked, as soon as the door closed, her voice breaking a little, and tears rolled down her cheeks. "I heard word Preacher Thompson sent men after her."

"He did," Talen said. "And ain't a one that'll be coming back. We saw to that."

The woman straightened. "She's really safe?"

Talen nodded. "I swear on my mother. I was there when she arrived, and my friends and I helped Harriet put down the men sent to bring her back."

The woman started crying and almost fell to her knees, but Talen caught her.

"Thank you," she said, over and over.

Talen gave the woman a moment to get it all out, it was the least she could do.

"I'm sorry," the woman said, wiping her eyes a moment later.

"No need to be," Talen said and offered her hand. "I'm Talen."

"Yes, of course." She took Talen's hand. "Henrietta Mason. Call me Etty."

"Etty," she said and nodded again. "Like I said, me and others come to get you, and anyone else we can, out."

"You best have brought an army with you," Etty said. "Preacher Thompson got the whole town turned stained, including them knights of General Forrest, most of who is Red Hand."

"We ain't got an army," Talen said. "But we got a plan, and I got arms for you and anyone else ready to take them up."

Etty looked hesitant.

"I've been killing stained since before your great-grandma spoke her first word," Talen said. "We got an airship to carry you all north, and we've already started clearing farms on the edge of town. But it'll go a lot easier if there's any here that are willing to fight."

Etty fretted her upper lip. "I ain't no soldier. None of us are."

"You don't need to be," Talen said. "And truth to tell, we ain't got enough for everyone anyhow, so if you ain't going to fight, pass the rifle along to someone who is."

"They got folk on the farms and the plantations," Etty said. "And they did things to them, dark and terrible magics worked on them."

"We know," Talen said. "And ain't no one asking you to stand up and fight on your own. We'll see to the knights and Red Hands, and free them working the plantations. But we need to end that preacher too. That means coming into town. We ain't got the numbers for that, but when that fight comes, you all pitching in would make a hell of a difference."

Etty listened and considered Talen's words. "My baby is safe? You swear it?"

"I do," Talen said. "Can't think of no place safer than with Harriet Tubman herself."

"Then you give me a gun, and I'll use it," Etty said, her jaw tight.

"We need you to get them to others too."

"I can do that," Etty said, nodding. "I know plenty that will jump at the chance. But they keep that gate locked from the outside."

"When the time comes, I'll make sure it's open."

"All right then," Etty said.

Talen retrieved the bundles and brought them inside. She purposely made a show of her strength in hopes it would give Etty some confidence.

She watched Talen in obvious surprise, but didn't comment.

"There's one more of these I'll fetch back here when I'm done," Talen said. "But first, let me talk you through our plan."

Talen explained how things would progress, ideally, and what would happen if anything went wrong. She also gave Etty a primer on how to put down a stained.

Etty listened and nodded, and though she was clearly nervous, agreed to arm as many as were willing. While she couldn't promise specific numbers, she didn't have any concerns with finding someone for every rifle.

After answering a few questions, Talen hurried back for the last bundle. Unsurprising, Gaoth was still there waiting. Knowing where to go, Talen made better time heading back to Etty's house.

"Best get these to folk as quick as you can," Talen said. "And make sure they keep them hidden. If anyone finds the farms we've cleared out, I don't reckon they'll think you or yours are responsible, but they'll be on edge and might come looking to make sure you all don't get any thoughts on rising up."

"I might've been just a child before the war," Etty said, "but we all know how it was, and what needed to be done to keep safe."

"It's important that no one does nothing until it's time," Talen said. "If anyone gets ideas and tries something too soon, it'll make things a mite more troublesome."

"Don't worry none," Etty said. "We'll be waiting and ready, and won't no one make a move until your signal."

Talen looked at the small woman with admiration and more than a little awe. Etty reminded her more than a little of Harriet. Small in stature but a towering will and strength to spare. "I wish it didn't have to be this way."

"If wishing made it so, there wouldn't have need to be no war."

"I'll leave you to your work then," Talen said. "Good luck."

"You too," Etty said.

Talen made to leave, but Etty grabbed her shoulder. "If I don't make it—"

"Delia will be well cared for, but that ain't a worry you need to carry. I've seen fewer do more."

There was nothing more to say, so Talen gave a final nod and left.

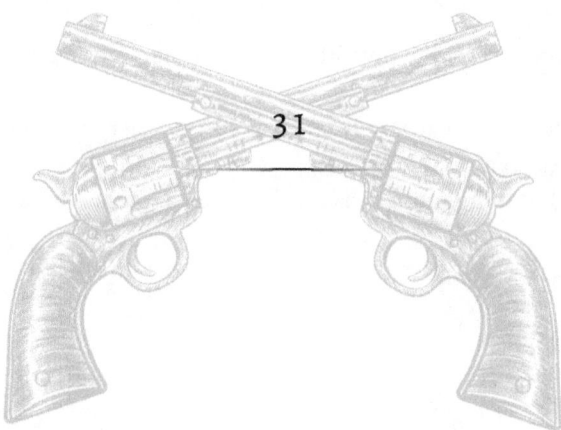

31

Talen returned to the Cumulus several hours before sunrise. Though all her friends had attempted to wait up for her, only Draven managed to stay awake. The dwarf stood sentinel, leaning against the open cargo bay doorway. Just inside the airship, Margaret, Wilfred, and Alice slept in chairs. Though she did her best not to rouse anyone, Gaoth's hoofbeats on the gangplank rendered her efforts moot. The heavy thumps woke them all before he'd gotten even halfway up.

Talen wanted to feel bad about it, but sheer exhaustion wouldn't let her. As she unsaddled, dried, and brushed Gaoth down, Talen recounted the events of the evening.

Maragret's brows furrowed. "They locked them in?"

Alice shook her head. "Can't say as I'm surprised."

"You look ready to collapse," Wilfred said.

She did, but Talen wasn't so tired that she could let that comment go unanswered. She forced a grin. "Thanks for that. It's been a long night, and we got more ahead of us. Best if we all get some sleep."

"More sleep, you mean," Draven said, eyeing the others.

Wilfred opened his mouth, presumably to protest, but he ended up yawning instead.

Talen motioned to the stairs with her head. "Go on. Tomorrow we're back to it."

Alice, Margaret, and Wilfred did a good job feigning reluctance and made their way upstairs to their cabins.

"You going to sleep down here?" Draven asked.

"Gaoth gets all sorts of temperamental when he has to sleep alone. Besides, the straw will help dry out my clothes."

Gaoth snorted and settled down onto a fresh pile.

It took Talen's addled brain a second to realize the stall hadn't been that way when she'd left. "Who cleaned the stables?"

"I did," Maggie said, poking her head from around a column.

Talen was too tired to be surprised. Besides, the kid had a talent for going unnoticed. "Well, thank you for that."

Maggie shrugged. "Feeling a bit useless around here, and it needed doing." She scowled a little. "Not like I ain't got time, since you won't let me help you with anything off the ship."

Talen was too tired to argue about this again. Even so, she opened her mouth.

"This where you tell me I'm too young, or it's too dangerous for a girl?" Maggie asked.

Draven chuckled.

Talen really just wanted to get some sleep, but it seemed her wants had to wait. She glanced at Draven, and then back to Maggie. "We're like to be the last two folk who'll say being a girl should stop you from anything."

Maggie's brows drew together. An instant later her eyes went wide in understanding and she turned to Draven. "No shit? Do all dwarves got moustaches?"

"Facial hair ain't just for the men, if that's what you mean," Draven said.

"I kind wish I could grow one," Maggie said. "But only if it was nice as yours."

Draven stroked her long whiskers and smiled.

Talen chuckled. "You certainly know which hive has the honey." She bent down to be on a level with Maggie. "I know you got a burning need to help us, to do right against them that did you and others so wrong. That's a desire I am well acquainted, but we ain't going to let you."

Maggie scowled again.

Talen held up her hand. "It ain't just about being young. Yeah, it does play a part, but you done already seen more than anyone should. I, for one, ain't inclined to add killing to that. Neither am I eager on risking your life when it ain't necessary." She put her hand on Maggie's shoulder and leaned in a little. "This is what it's like to have someone give a damn about you."

Maggie's expression softened and, after a moment, she nodded. "Reckon I can't argue when you say it like that." She glanced back toward the hold where the freed passengers slept. "They probably wouldn't be keen on me having a gun neither, huh?"

Talen sighed. "Much as I'd like to argue, there is some truth to that."

"It's okay," Maggie said. "I understand. If I were them, I likely wouldn't trust me neither. I can help though, and I want to. So do Mary and Jacob. You saved us, and we mean to show our thanks."

"I expect we can find some chores for you all," Draven said.

This emotional exchange had officially sapped the last of Talen's reserve. In short order, her body would be on the floor. If she wanted some say on where that happened, she needed to act now. "Tomorrow," she said to Draven and looked to Maggie. "I'm about to drop, and you need some sleep too."

"Yes, ma'am," Maggie said. "Night." She turned and headed down the ramp back to the cargo bay.

"I'll see to it," Draven said. "You get some rest."

"Ain't got to tell me twice."

Draven patted her shoulder, turned, and left.

Talen settled down with Gaoth and slipped into sleep almost before her eyes closed.

The next few days were like the first. They'd ride up to a farm, put down the stained, rescue anyone there against their will, and wrangle any kids they found. Some fights were tougher than others, but thankfully the worst they suffered was Cyrus getting grazed. Talen's coat took more than its share of bullets, and twice they encountered a stained with a spell iron.

Sadly, they found more people bound with detestable crafts, geas, and hobble stones. Talen managed to remove most, but in a couple of instances, she couldn't do anything for them. The worst was a ragged, starving man in his thirties. The geas stone binding him had been entirely absorbed. Nothing they did could pull the man from working the fields. From the look of him, he'd been at it nearly a week nonstop. Despite his dry, cracked lips, he couldn't be convinced to drink any water.

In the end, they freed him the only way they could. Talen had offered to do it, but Alice argued that Talen shouldn't be the only one to carry a burden like that. At least he got a proper burial and some words spoken over his grave.

Most of the kids didn't put much of a fuss, either out of fear or having no other option. A few kicked and screamed, and tried to fight back. One took up his father's shooter and fired at Talen, but none of his shots got close.

She had to use a slumber load on him.

Maggie became a surrogate big sister to most. Almost all of them knew her, or of her, and went along with her guidance, some more hesitant than others.

Talen had been concerned about babies, or those too young to walk or speak. In the most cursed blessing that ever was, they didn't find any that young still alive. Their parents had either killed them, presumably in a fit of rage, or neglect had taken them. She'd known it'd be a hard and heavy task, but even Talen and her callous-covered heart wasn't prepared for the abject brutality and utter indifference she found.

Of course, she knew all too well that humans, stained or otherwise, were capable of unimaginable cruelty. And yet, somehow, she'd managed to hope at the least, these monsters would spare their own children, especially the babies.

Thinking on it, she realized how ridiculous that notion had been. These people didn't think twice about tearing crying babies from their mothers. They slept peacefully after brutalizing a child, or having their way with a screaming, crying victim. The sort of people they'd been before wasn't too far off from who they'd become. It was just a matter of restraint. What little empathy any of them had was the first thing to rot away.

As one day went into another, the notion of a town turning stained seemed less and less strange a feat. In fact, Talen was surprised it didn't happen more.

By the fifth day, the rain had stopped, though low gray clouds still filled the sky. Talen had lost count of how many she'd killed, and how many corpses had been found. At least she could easily see how many they'd freed—seventy-two—and how many kids had been rescued—thirty-six.

Talen sat by herself on the gangplank, a bowl of branches and leave uneaten at her side, watching the night sky. For a brief moment, she managed not to feel or think about anything.

"You going after the plantations tomorrow?" Maggie asked, having appeared out of nowhere.

"We still got plenty to clear outside of town first," Talen said. She'd stopped trying to spare the child with gentle words. This girl had seen plenty, and she didn't need to be coddled no more.

"But tomorrow is Saturday."

Talen turned and looked at her, confusion and the hint of anxiety slipping through her moment of detachment. "I suppose. What's that got to do with anything?"

"Day after is Sunday?" Maggie said, brows knitted together.

"Usually how it goes." Her brain spun, trying to understand, but it couldn't get a hold of nothing. "I still ain't seeing where you're trying to lead me. Help me out."

"Do your folk not do church on Sundays?" Maggie asked. "Around here anyway, everyone goes. Whole town packs in to hear Preacher Thompson go on about the truth of magic and God, and all that bullshit."

It took another moment for Talen to understand. Her stomach dropped, and she chided herself for not seeing it before. "Mother's mercy." She gave Maggie a hug and kissed the top of her head. "You got no idea how big a mistake you may have kept us from making."

Maggie smiled and blushed a little. "You're welcome."

Talen got to her feet and hurried upstairs. She found everyone gathered in the galley for their evening meal. Frieda, Odie, and Pearl cooked practically full time at this point, and took turns bringing food down to the freed men and women in the cargo bay. Talen almost bowled right over Odie in her rush.

"Sorry," Talen said and slipped into the galley. "We got a big change of plans."

Everyone turned and looked at her. None of them had been eating much, save for Draven. "What happened?" she asked around a mouthful of food.

"Day after tomorrow is Sunday," Talen said.

It took a bit for realization to dawn, though not as long as it did for Talen.

"Going to be a lot of empty pews," Booker said.

"Even their rotted brains will figure out something ain't right," Alice said.

Talen nodded. "Which means we got one more day at most to thin down the number. We need to take out them knights while it'll just be them, and not them and two-hundred others."

Margaret put a hand to her face. "I can't believe it never occurred to me."

"Didn't occur to any of us," Cyrus said. "And we'd just been talking about holding a little service Sunday morning since we couldn't get to a church."

"We all missed it," Talen said, eager to get started. "But thanks to Maggie, we still got time, a little anyway."

"Maggie?" Alice asked.

Looks of suspicion, disbelief, and doubt cycled through the room.

Margaret's expression hardened. "She's a smart girl."

Talen nodded again and gave everyone a mild glare. "She is that, and she potentially saved our skin. Now, we need to make use of what she gave us and plan for tomorrow."

Draven got out the map, and everyone seemed to liven up as they decided on timing, tactics, and fallback options. Talen could appreciate the distraction, but as time passed, memories of similar discussions with various war bands of the Seven Council Fires came to the forefront of her mind. The latter ones were almost jubilant, as their victories piled up. For a time, it looked as if they might win, and the US Government would decide to make, and keep, a peace treaty with the Lakota, Nakota, and Dakota.

Then Whitestone Hill happened, and everything changed.

Despite her best efforts, she could hear the metal creaking and scraping of the leviathans as they rolled and crawled closer, seemingly unstoppable. The roar of their cannons drowned out all other sounds, the explosions sending bodies, and pieces of them, flying. The brief silences between the relentless barrages were filled with the screams and crying of the dead and dying.

"Talen!" Margaret shook her.

Talen sucked in a breath and came back to herself.

Everyone stared at her.

"Are you okay?" Booker asked.

"Of course she ain't," Alice said. "Look at her."

"Sit down," Margaret guided Talen to a chair.

"I'm fine." Talen made to rub her eyes, but her hands were shaking something awful. Her heart pounded in her chest, and she couldn't draw in a decent breath. "When did it get so cold in here?"

"You are not fine," Wilfred said.

Suddenly, the room had shrunk to the size of a coffin, and the light started to dim. Everyone crowded around her, talking at once, and beneath it all, people screamed as they burned.

Talen collapsed to the floor, drew herself into a tight ball, tried like hell to stop shaking, and to quiet everyone, but they wouldn't stop screaming.

The maelstrom of chaos and horror pulled her down into darkness, and though she clawed at the walls to get out, it was too strong.

"Talen," Margaret said.

Her voice was calm and cut through the din of insanity around Talen.

"Talen, listen to me, to my voice," Margaret said. "It's okay, you're safe. This isn't Whitestone Hill. You're on the Cumulus. You're safe."

Talen clung to the words like a lifeline, and a distant warmth spread through her.

"You're safe," Margaret said softly, over and over.

Inch by inch, Talen fought back against the darkness, and eventually, her body stopped shaking, the darkness gave way to light, and the cold surrendered to warmth. When she opened her eyes, she found herself on the floor of the galley. Margaret sat next to her, holding her tight, cheek against Talen's head. Wilfred stood to one side next to Draven. Alice and the others were nowhere to be seen.

Talen let out a deep breath and leaned against Margaret's shoulder.

"You back with us?" Wilfred asked.

"I am," Talen said. "Help me up."

"You sure?" Margaret asked, pulling back enough to look at her. "There's no hurry."

"I'm sure."

Wilfred offered a hand and easily hauled Talen to her feet. The room spun for an instant but settled back quickly.

"Here," Draven said, offering a cup whiskey.

Talen accepted the drink with some concerted effort to ease her shaking, downed it in one, and handed the cup back. The slow burn down her throat that settled into a pool of warmth in her belly served as something viscerally real she could cling to amid the maelstrom in her head.

She rubbed at her eyes and focused on breathing. "Where are the others?"

"Cargo bay, I reckon," Wilfred said. "Margaret told them, and I quote, to get the hell out before she threw them out."

Talen looked to Margaret.

She smiled a little and shrugged. "It wasn't any of their business."

Talen chuckled, then pulled her sister into a tight hug, and kissed her forehead.

Margaret hugged back. "That was a bad one," she said, still holding tight.

Talen clung to her, something real and solid, and true. A physical manifestation of hope and reassurance that things could get better.

"Yeah." Talen swallowed. "Don't know where it came from."

Draven and Wilfred stood by silently and a little awkwardly.

"Get over here," Margaret said.

They stepped over and joined the hug.

Talen didn't resist, rather she took the strength of her family and used it to piece herself back together. When it ended, she felt almost normal again, and accepted another shot of whiskey. "I don't know what happened. Usually, I can fight it back."

"Well, you're exhausted, for one," Draven said.

"And if I had to guess, something feels like then," Margaret said.

"Reckon so." Talen shook her head. "Shouldn't have let it get to me—"

"We've been over this," Margaret said. "It doesn't have anything to do with weakness. You might've gotten away without any physical injuries, but you can't see what you've seen and not carry some scars on your heart and soul. The human psyche isn't made to deal with horror on that level."

Talen sipped at the whiskey. "I ain't human," she said and immediately knew she shouldn't have.

Margaret glared.

"I apologize for making fun," Talen said. "And I understand what you're saying, but it was four years ago now. You'd think I'd be over it."

Wilfred chuckled but it lacked any humor. "I have nightmares most nights. The bad ones, I can still feel a lash at my back, or hear my mama's crying stop when that overseer split her skull with his rifle butt. I close my eyes, and I can see her lifeless eyes staring at nothing as she lay there, blood soaking the ground."

Talen knew he had nightmares. There'd been more than one time together when she'd just held him crying through the night.

It hadn't been easy for Talen, sharing with her new family about these episodes she'd have, but it'd been worth it. Not so long ago, she might've been concerned what Alice and the others might think, but now, she couldn't be bothered to care.

"Like we keep telling you," Wilfred said, "we all got ghosts that haunt us. Ain't no shame in that."

"Even you can't always carry everything yourself," Margaret said. "That's why we're here, to help you when the burden is too heavy."

Talen nodded. While she could accept—still—being a poor student, she did wish she might finally pick up the important lessons. "I love you, all of you."

"We love you, too," Margaret said.

"You going to be okay for tomorrow?" Draven asked. "I wish it were otherwise, but ain't no way we can do it without you."

"That's not true," Margaret said, putting a hand on Talen's shoulder. "We'll figure something else out if we have to. You don't—"

"It's all right, little sister." Talen put her hand over Margaret's. "Draven is right. I can't do it alone, but neither can you all do it without me. Work needs doing, and I'm the one needs to do it. I got you all, so, I know I'll be fine."

"Are you sure?" Margaret asked. "Because if not—"

"I love you to death, but it's really all right," Talen said. "I do think I'm going to get some air and spend some time with Gaoth though." She looked to Draven. "You know the plan as well as me, can you—"

"I'll make sure the others have it down, don't you worry," she said.

"We'll be here if you need us," Margaret said.

"I know," Talen said. "Now come here one more time."

They all stepped into another hug. When it ended, Talen headed below, and after a brief detour to collect what she'd need tomorrow, went to get Gaoth. He knew immediately what was wrong and almost broke his gate trying to get to her. She calmed him, saddled him, and led him out of the ship. Though she didn't look back, Talen could feel eyes watching her as she left. Outside, she drew in a breath of cool night air and let Gaoth decide where they would go.

The rain started to fall again, and it felt a comfort. Like shared tears. In time, the screams settled to whispers, and were soon lost to the sound of the wind and rain on the trees. Talen and Gaoth slept under the sky that night, and together, found a measure of peace.

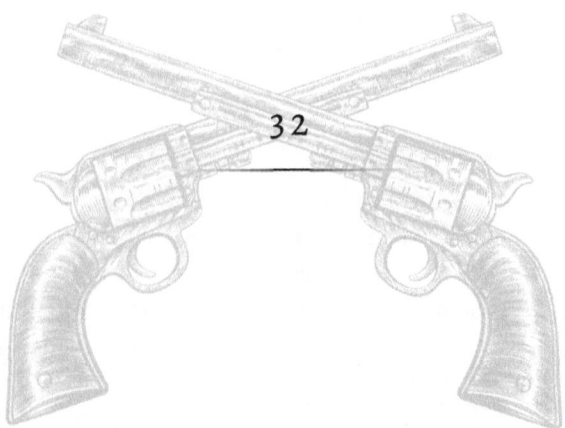

32

Well before dawn, Talen woke and rode Gaoth as close to the Bennfield plantation as she dared. Once there, she wrapped herself in shadow, and slipped onto the grounds. The only lights were from crafter lanterns on the massive porch of the huge main house. Two men sat on rocking chairs, rifles across their laps, clearly bored and fighting to stay awake. Both of them were shrouded in a darkness that roiled at the edges. Thank the mothers, neither of them had an eye piece.

Even so, Talen moved slowly and silently to the far side of the house where they'd seen the Gatling gun. If she hadn't experience firsthand how profound human arrogance could be, she'd have been surprised to find the gun unwatched. It sat just out of view of the men on the porch. To their credit, they weren't but fifty feet from it. Which gave her more than enough room to set a couple of bombs and be gone without them being any the wiser.

Ducking around the corner, she pulled two of Draven's bombs from a satchel and bent down to set them. With almost excessive care, she peeled the paper off, and pressed each to the underside of the wagon, careful not to make a sound. True to her word, Draven's glue stuck fast and true. A quick peek around the corner of the house confirmed the two sentries hadn't budged.

A prickle of fear ran down Talen's back. It almost felt too easy. To ease the doubt, she checked her surroundings. Nothing and no one stirred anyway nearby. She rechecked the bombs, but they were ready and hadn't moved from where she'd stuck them.

As she turned to leave, Talen glanced back at the gun. She'd never really seen one up close. It was smaller than she'd expected, at least compared to the carnage it could unleash. In that regard, it wasn't unlike Draven's bombs. Considering what magic Draven could work on rifles and mundane shooters, Talen couldn't help but wonder what the dwarf could do with a weapon like this.

Talen smiled at the idea of turning their own weapon against them. The best part would be when they found it missing, they likely wouldn't ever consider someone from outside of town took it. Folk like this were self-centered, and jealously guarded their power, even when they weren't stained. With their brains rotted, they'd likely set to killing each other before they knew the truth.

But what if they didn't learn the truth? Or even better, had their suspicions confirmed?

Why bother fighting multiple opponents when you can get them to fight each other instead? Even if the two plantations didn't entirely wipe each other out, there'd still be a hell of a lot less stained when the fighting ended. It'd also be deeply satisfying.

Her mind spun, forming together a plan. It wouldn't be without risk though, and judging by the sky, she didn't have but a couple hours at most to enact it.

She took a moment to consider the options.

The first and safest choice would be to blow the gun as planned. That would render it useless and maybe take out some of Bennfield's men at the same time. The resulting explosion could serve to stir panic and suspicion, but Talen didn't imagine anyone in town could make anything close to Draven's bomb. That meant they'd be looking to outsiders, and nothing unified humans like an "other" coming for them.

If, instead, she took the gun back to Draven, they'd deprive one group of a fearsome weapon and have it to use themselves. This choice had a better chance of turning Bennfield against Perkins, but without proof, who could say how long the rivalry would last? If either side did manage to convince the other of the truth, once again, the collective suspicion turned to the outsider.

However, if she could set it up to look like Perkins had actually stolen the gun, then Bennfield might go to war thinking Perkins meant to take over the town. Or at the least wanted sole control of the town's business. Hell, Perkins might even assume Bennfield was setting them up, and faking a pretense to kill them off.

Unfortunately, all this ended with Talen holding a whole mess of assumptions about how they'd react. If they somehow figured out the truth, this plan led right back to both plantations unified against outside attack.

True, these stained didn't act like any other she'd ever come across. They had more control and still had some sense. However, from what she'd seen anyway, that only seemed to be the case until some darker emotion or desire came into play. Could be, if she got them angry, or jealous, the rot wouldn't be so easy to ignore. After all, even without being stained, would rich, powerful, arrogant slavers, who'd coveted power all their lives, imagine anyone would, much less could, set them up? Or would their first thought be someone meant to take what rightfully belonged to them?

Talen wished she could talk to the others. They'd have a better understanding of human behavior.

Then again, Wilfred often said, *"You rarely go wrong assuming the worst of those with power."*

The weight of each passing second pressed down on her, piling up. She needed to decide now. There might be things she hadn't considered, but time didn't allow for any more thinking.

"Hell with it," she whispered to herself and drew both spell irons. She rolled both to a slumber round. As she crept back toward the porch, she said a silent prayer to her mother that Wilfred's crafts would put down these stained.

Thinking about it that way actually filled her with confidence. Wilfred's crafting skill had never once let her down. She trusted they wouldn't this time either.

The two men sat twenty or so feet apart, angled slightly away from each other. As she got closer, she noticed they both sported spell irons on their hips, a sizeable "CSA" stamped on the butt of each. A significant part of her screamed to put these confederate bastards in the ground here and now. However, she managed to calm the bloodlust with the thought of them using those irons on other slavers first.

Rage mollified, for now, she turned her attention to the porch and stairs leading up to it, with the intention of deciding where to step so the wood planks didn't creak. After all, being in shadow didn't do anything for sound, and any sound might alert the guards. Even if she managed to drop them fast, they might shout or otherwise alert others.

She smiled when she saw both stairs and porch were made of polished marble, and savored the poetry of their opulence working against them too.

Even so, she climbed the stairs as light-footed as she could, keeping a careful aim at both men, ready to drop her shadow cloak, and fire in an instant. It was just like on the plains, where she and her sisters would step from shadows only long enough to fire their spell irons before stepping back out of sight.

The two men reeked of sweat and booze, their eyelids heavy. Every sound or movement from them brought Talen up short, and she froze until they settled back in. It felt like it took a couple of days, but she eventually stood on the porch between them.

With as much care as she'd ever summoned, she took aim with both irons, double and then triple checking each.

Heart beating slow and hands steady, a familiar peace settled over her, and she closed her eyes. In the space between heartbeats, she dropped her cloak, poured magic into her irons, fired both, doused them, and slipped back into shadow.

The burst of bright light from the spellfire filling her irons was so brief it could've been lightning. But even with her eyes closed, her night vision would be hindered for a second or two.

She stood frozen, cloaked in magical darkness, and opened her eyes.

Both men were slumped to one side in their chairs.

She waited a couple of heartbeats to make sure the slumber load took.

Neither man moved.

Talen smiled and, just to add more trouble, carefully laid their rifles on the ground. She made sure to position them to look as if they'd fallen when the men fell asleep on sentry duty.

The guards dealt with, Talen hurried back to the Gatling gun. The sentries might have been sleeping, but that didn't mean someone else might not hear her at work. No reason to be stupid. Gingerly, she climbed into the wagon and, as it happened, the cart was well maintained. The freshly oiled springs didn't make a sound.

Talen had never been inclined toward mechanical contraptions, but even she had picked up a thing or two just from being around a genius of Draven's level.

Next to the gun was a wooden crate, inside of which were a couple dozen long metal boxes that Talen knew held the bullets. With exceeding care, she transferred the ammo boxes to her satchel. Only half of them fit, but she figured that would be enough.

After that, she looked over the gun and the swivel mount it sat on, hoping she wouldn't need to figure out how to get the whole damn wagon out of here. The gun itself didn't seem to be even five feet long. She didn't have Draven's head for engineering, but she didn't imagine it could weigh more than a couple hundred pounds at most.

At the back of the mount, she found a large screw that appeared to be for adjusting the angle of the gun. Otherwise, it seemed to be held in place by nothing more than a pair of metal pins, one on either side. Each pin sat between two metal brackets, which themselves were held together by a pair of screws.

All four screws were large and loose enough for her to remove. Gatling, or whomever designed it, probably did so to allow for easy care and maintenance in the field without tools. Talen didn't know who was responsible, but she gave them a silent thanks.

As she removed the screws, she glanced around and gave a listen just to make sure there weren't others about.

That done, she eyeballed the center of gravity of the thing, and gave it a test lift. She half expected to find the gun held in place by other, unseen, mounts, or even that it was too heavy to carry.

Neither fear proved out.

The thing wasn't light by any means, but it didn't even weigh two-hundred pounds, and it came free with nary a sound.

Inching her way around, she set the gun down on the wagon's floor-boards near the open back. The wagon shifted as the weight moved, but still didn't make a sound.

She stepped out and back to the ground.

Still silence.

The angle to lift the gun meant she had almost no leverage, making it seem even heavier. However, with jaw clenched, she managed to lift it without scraping the wood, causing the springs to squeak, or grunt with the effort.

After a bit of consideration, she set the gun on the barrel end and hefted it onto her right shoulder. She briefly considered collecting the bombs she'd just set. It did seem unlikely they'd be found; the missing gun would almost certainly be the focus. She decided to leave them. It might work out they'd bring the wagon with them to confront Perkins and deliver explosives into the middle of a firefight.

That settled, she made for a large willow, putting it between her and the main house. As she glanced around, ready to go to the next tree, movement caught her attention.

Pressing her back to the tree, her left hand went to her spell iron, and she prepared to dump the gun and run. The idea of leaving it, especially intact, left a bitter taste in her mouth. However, even in the worst case, they'd remount the gun, and Talen could come back and blow it up later.

Turned out, it wasn't a sentry or guard she spotted. Rather, it was a collection of men and women working the fields in total darkness. They themselves shone with a faint radiance, but dark tendrils writhed and wrapped around them.

Her heart twisted.

It had to be geas stones, again.

As she tamped down her rage and the desire to set the house ablaze, two other figures toiling away stood out from the others. No light of any kind shone from them, but neither were they the swallowing darkness she'd come to associate with stained. There was a darkness there, but at its center was just, well, nothing.

That didn't seem possible, as every living thing had a magic in it, true or corrupted. Her blood ran cold as she remembered what Haddox had said: *They even found a way to animate the dead as mindless servants.*

A shudder ran through her, like icy fingers dragging down her spine, and she wanted nothing more than to be away from that place.

It took an effort of will, but she managed not to run. Instead, she crept from tree to tree, casting glances back to the porch to ensure the guards still slept. The sense of dread eased when she left the plantation property, and before long, she'd returned to Gaoth. There was no way he could carry both Talen and the gun, but after some jury rigging, she managed to secure the weapon on his back in a way that wasn't uncomfortable for him.

When she led him, quickly as she could, away from the Cumulus, he eyed her.

"New plan," she said, trying to shed the unease that still clung to her. "Just crazy enough to work."

Gaoth bobbed his head but kept looking at her.

"Just when I think I'm done being surprised by humans," she said. "They decide the *Malihane Carid* ain't a warning but a challenge. Foul enough to think up something fouler than the detestable crafts, but then to actually do it."

Gaoth snorted.

"Yeah, I know Margaret and Wilfred are different."

He chuffed.

"And, Alice and the others."

He snorted again.

"Yes, and Maggie," Talen said. "There's plenty of folk who are decent, but it don't make what these done any less awful. I never said it was all of them, though it sure does feel like a large percentage are determined to win the contest of who is the vilest."

That seemed to sate Gaoth's indignation, and they walked the rest of the way in silence.

When they neared the Perkins plantation, Talen led Gaoth behind a tree, stepped into the shadows and did a quick scouting of the property. Like Bennfield's, darkness-tinged forms worked the fields, which she pointedly ignored. Nothing she could do for them just now anyway.

Unlike the other slave nest, this one had half a dozen men out walking the property. Thankfully, none of them had any eye pieces either, but she did catch the whiff of blood-soaked leather on the air. Of course, she'd known there'd be Red Hands here somewhere, but that didn't put her any more at ease.

She watched them for a bit, learning their paths and timing, keenly aware of the sky getting lighter and lighter. Time was running out, and not only did she need to stash the gun, she still had to make it back to the Cumulus, all without being spotted.

It took longer than she liked, but eventually Talen managed to figure out the pattern, or at least something like a pattern. With that, she hurried back to Gaoth, retrieved the Gatling gun, and moved as quickly as possible toward the nearest outbuilding, which looked to be a barn.

The trees were sparser than at Bennfield's. That combined with more —and seemingly more attentive—guards, slowed her progress. The shadows should be hiding both her and the gun, but despite the time pressure, she decided not push her luck.

Her patience frayed, and nearly snapped at the slow progress, but Talen managed to keep her anxiety and eagerness in check. After what seemed a week, she made it to the barn and slipped inside. It was filled with all sorts of machinery, none of which she knew the purpose of, and a full up hay loft. There weren't any animals, which she figured meant there were separate stables. All the better not to have to worry about horses or mules making a fuss and drawing attention.

It didn't take long to find a spot to stash the gun and ammo boxes where they'd be hidden, but easy enough to spot from even a casual search. As she pulled the last ammo box out, she spotted the other bombs and cursed silently. Finding the other Gatling gun would take time she might not have, and she'd risk being spotted. However, the idea of leaving it intact was risky as hell. The notion of facing it later wasn't a pleasant one, even with her a magicked coat, which the others didn't have.

"No choice," she said to herself.

Before leaving the barn, she did place two bombs; one near the pilfered weapon, and the other farther in. Neither explosive would be easy to spot without a determined search. Hell, even if they were spotted, odds were, no one would know what they were.

Without the heavy load, she felt light enough to take flight. This combined with having to obscure only herself meant she could move quicker and easier.

After taking a breath and thinking back to the map and where the other gun might be, Talen peeked out and made sure no one was about. Once clear, she slipped from the barn and hurried to where she hoped and prayed, the other gun sat.

Thank the mothers, it was. Even better, it wasn't guarded.

Not wasting a moment, she set the last two bombs and hurried back to Gaoth. More than once she ducked behind a tree or bush, but if anyone spotted her, no one reacted.

When she reached Gaoth, despite her desire to bolt, she walked him deeper into the woods, putting distance between her and the road, before saddling up and letting him choose the pace.

After a bit, Talen decided they were far enough from anyone to chance the road to make better time. Hopefully, at this distance, being spotted would only feed suspicion and paranoia when the gun was found.

By the time they returned to the Cumulus, the eastern sky was a pale blue and a hint of orange touched the horizon. For the sake of those still sleeping, Talen pulled the saddle off and left Gaoth outside the airship to wander and graze free. She set the saddle down just inside the cargo bay. Might be she'd need it again soon. She hurried up the stairs to find Draven and whoever else might be awake.

Odie, Frieda, and Pearl were all at work in the galley making breakfast. They looked over as Talen poked her head in. They shot each other quick glances, over and over, not saying a word. It seemed apparent to Talen they struggled over whether or not to mention her episode.

"Draven?" Talen asked, not bothering with decorum. Their issues were their own.

"Uh," Pearl said, looking to the others then back to Talen. "On the bridge. I just brought her some coffee."

"Much obliged." Talen didn't wait for a response, just hurried up the stairs. She reached the top deck and burst into the bridge.

"Morning," Draven said, over her mug of steaming coffee and arched an eyebrow. "You appear a mite troubled."

Talen recounted the events on the plantations.

Draven's eyes narrowed, and her brows drew together as the telling went on. At the end, she just took a sip from her mug, sighed, and shook her head. "And here I was worried things might be progressing too smoothly."

"You think I made a mistake?" Talen asked, concern tightening her chest.

"Nah. Actually, seems like a solid plan for letting the troublesome thin themselves out for us. Assuming it works. If it don't..."

"I just made things infinitely more complicated," Talen said, nodding. "I know."

"Reckon we better tell the others," Draven said. "I'm sure they'll be fine with completely changing the plan at the literal last moment."

Talen bit back a flash of anger. She'd made the call, which she still believed to be the right one, and she was prepared to defend that choice. If it turned out she got it wrong, it wouldn't be the first time. A sliver of doubt slid through her insides, and she tried not to think about anyone else suffering for her mistakes. Again. "You done?"

"Suppose so," Draven said, her tone flat and even, and then gestured to the door. "After you."

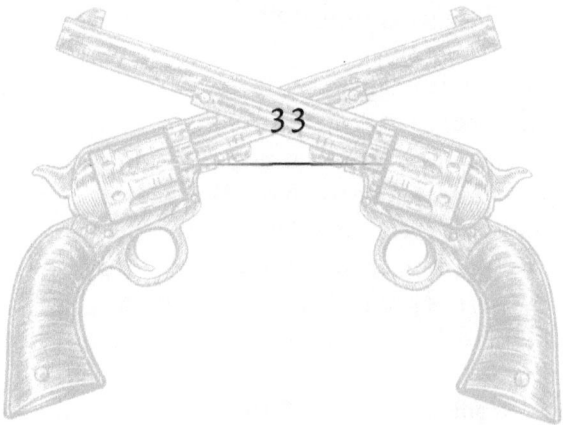

33

I'm sorry, you did what?" Booker asked, when Talen had finished.

Wilfred started laughing.

"I know it isn't what we planned," Talen said, "but I think this was the best option. Worst that happens is we blow Perkins's gun and have to deal with Bennfield's. Might be the explosion gets both. Best outcome, the two biggest threats in town go at each other, and we got fewer to deal with. All without firing a shot of our own, or risking our own hides."

"We all agreed to let you take the lead," Cyrus said, "but this isn't some small change."

Talen used every bit of willpower she could muster to keep hold of her patience. "It ain't a change, it's a reordering. We always knew we'd have to take on the plantations. All I did was change the when."

"I ain't seen cannonballs like that since I was in the Army," Alice said, grinning and chuckling. "How you carry them without tearing your pants?"

Everyone but Wilfred turned to her. Wilfred laughed harder.

"I fail to see the humor in this," Booker said.

"I do apologize," Wilfred said, composing himself, but still smiling. "You ain't run with us long enough to know crazy notions like this always seem to pay off. What I did find humor in though is that an elf, who ain't had much to do with humans that weren't Sioux, working for the Railroad, or bent on killing her, understands humans so well."

"You think this plan of hers will work?" Cyrus asked.

"I do." Wilfred looked over to Cyrus and the others. "I'm guessing ain't a one of you born free. Like me, you all was born to chains."

They nodded.

"Was you on small farms or plantations?"

"What difference does that make?" Booker asked. "You saying one was worse than the other?"

"Oh, I ain't said no such thing," Wilfred said. "And I don't much appreciate you suggesting I did."

"He's asking because plantations ain't like nothing else," Odie said. "I was born and raised on the Stewart plantation in Mississippi, one of eighty-three in chains. Old man Stewart weren't just rich, he was a dozen generations of folk with fancy titles back in England rich. When I was twelve, my mama and I was sold to a man and taken to North Carolina. Mind, he was rich too, especially by our standards, but he wasn't fancy English title, plantation owner rich."

No one said anything, and Talen started to regret some of her harsher opinions of Odie.

"She's got the right of it," Odie said, calm and matter-of-factly. "When folk get that rich, they're convinced everyone is after what's theirs, and they see everything as theirs. If it ain't already, it should be. I worked parties as a child, and I saw them talk so sweet to each other that you'd think honey dripped from their lips. But soon as they was out of earshot, it was a different matter. They don't much like each other, and they sure don't trust one another."

"You ever met a white person, especially a confederate, that wasn't paranoid?" Alice asked. "Hell, they lived every moment terrified we was going to rise up. It's why they didn't want us learning how to read or even touching a weapon."

Booker furrowed his brow. "I can't say as I can argue with that."

Talen tried not to show it, but she felt a huge sense of relief. Truth was, up until that moment, she wasn't entirely sure she'd made the right choice.

Margaret remained silent, but reached over, took Talen's hand, and squeezed it.

Talen squeezed back.

"It could still go bad," Cyrus said.

"Might be we could help make sure it goes the way we want," Alice said, eyes narrowed.

"What are you thinking?" Draven asked.

Alice turned to Talen. "Can you shoot when you're"—she waved her hand—"can't remember what you call it, but you're invisible?"

"In the shadows," Talen said. "No, I can't split my magic between the shadow cloak and my irons."

"But a mundane shooter?"

"Never have, but don't see why I couldn't. Why?"

"I expect when Bennfield, or his men, come and confront Perkins, it's like to be tense," Alice said. "Slavers loved playing at honor and all that. Being called a thief will insult their delicate sensibilities. Being called a liar back ain't no better."

Talen looked to Margaret, but she didn't seem to be following either.

Frieda nodded. "I see what you're saying. They're all on edge, waiting for something to happen. We just need to set the first stone to rolling down the hill."

"It quickly becomes a landslide," Pearl said.

"You're saying we fire the first shot," Talen said, finally understanding.

"Exactly," Alice said. "Once the shooting starts, it ain't like to stop easy, and if you do it from your shadows, they won't know it wasn't one of their own."

"Might I suggest you fire from a place with good cover?" Wilfred said.

Talen didn't have Wilfred's wit, but she couldn't resist firing back. "Thanks for that well-considered wisdom," she said, giving him a level look, and then turned to Draven. "I did plant the bombs, so once the shooting starts you can set them off, and it'll just add to the turmoil."

"What about those knights?" Margaret asked. "Do we know if they have loyalty to one side or the other?"

Talen's smile faded and her stomach dropped. She hadn't considered that.

"Sorry," Margaret said.

"She's got a point," Booker said.

"Only ones I saw was in town," Talen said. "They was patrolling the Black folk in that section of town they made into a prison."

"Perkins and Bennfield will have their own people," Odie said. "Overseers and such. Unless any of them knights got hired on, I wouldn't expect them to be involved."

"They're outsiders," Wilfred said. "This would be a personal matter between the two big men."

"Delia said Forrest came to support the preacher," Talen said. "I expect that's who his knights are working for, but ain't no way to know for sure. Even if they do get involved though, any chance they can talk anyone down once that first shot goes off?"

"Not before there's a whole lot of dead and dying," Pearl said.

Talen let out a long sigh and rubbed at her eyes. "Reckon I'll be heading back to Perkins's place."

"For me to set off those bombs," Draven said, "I need to get the Cumulus close enough that we'd sure be visible to anyone who looked up."

"Of course," Talen said, pinching the bridge of her nose. "Reckon you'll need to show me how to work your contraption."

"It's easy enough," Draven said. "But I expect we best get to it cause you're going to need to head out soonish."

Everyone stood and went to return to whatever they were doing before.

"We should go along too," Alice said to Booker and Cyrus. "Ain't right that she should go alone."

"Are you out of your mind?" Booker asked. "We ain't elves that make ourselves disappear. Three of us show up, not in rags, and not ready to pick or plant, they ain't going to hesitate to shoot us down."

"Or use one of them detestable crafts on us," Cyrus said.

Alice scowled.

"They're right," Talen said, putting a hand Alice's shoulder. "I can't hide anyone but myself. I appreciate the notion, but you wouldn't do me no good there."

"I don't like that you won't have no one there backing you up."

Talen chuckled. "I don't much care for it neither, but there ain't any other options. Besides, I'm the one who chose to take this gamble. Only right I'm the one there when the cards are dealt."

"Good luck then." Alice started to move forward, but stopped herself.

Cyrus and Booker nodded.

"Thanks," Talen said, to Booker and Cyrus and then gave Alice a look. She could only hope it made clear she knew there was meant to be some gesture, but it couldn't be given.

"Let's go to my shop, and I'll show you the transmitter," Draven said.

Talen turned, followed her out, and saw Wilfred and Margaret following along. "You two don't need to come."

"We do," Wilfred said.

Margaret didn't say anything, but obviously would not be moved.

"Let's go then."

It didn't take long for Draven to show Talen how to work it. Just a switch, a button, and then a series of loud booms. The device was bigger than the bombs themselves, but would fit into Talen's satchel. When the three-minute tutorial was over, Draven handed Talen a repeating rifle.

"Fully loaded," she said. "Reckon you know how to work it?"

"Seen it done enough," Talen said. "Though truth is, I ain't never fired one."

Margaret swallowed and forced a smile, though the corners of her mouth trembled. "You'll do fine." Her wide eyes grew wet.

Talen pulled her into a hug. "Yes, I will. I ain't stupid. Plan is to shoot one of them bastards, take cover, and if the chance comes, blow the bombs. After that, I'm high-tailing it out of there. I've been in worse places with more guns, and they was actually aimed at me."

"Promise you'll be careful," Margaret said.

"I promise." Talen looked to Wilfred. "Pick some leaves for me for dinner, would you?"

Wilfred chuckled and gave her a hug, shorter than Margaret's but significantly tighter.

"Damn, you all are making me feel like you know something I don't," Talen said. "This ain't no crazier than jumping from an airship onto a moving train."

"It is a bit," Draven said.

Everyone laughed. Shaking her head, Talen left. Gaoth waited not far from the ship, grazing away. When he saw her holding the saddle, he trotted over.

"Ready to head back into the fray?"

He straightened, snorted, and stomped at the ground.

"Damn right we will." Talen secured the saddle, mounted up, and they rode off.

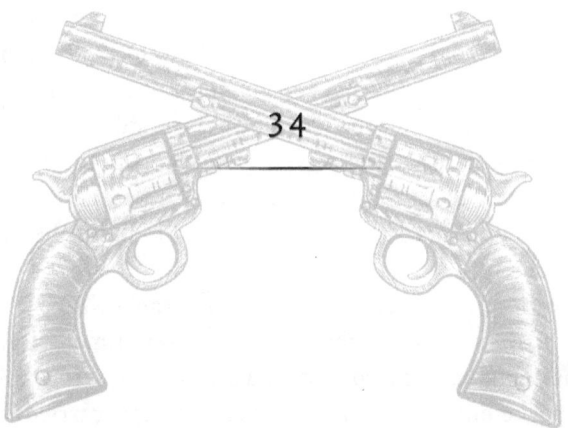

34

The sun edged over the horizon, painting the sky the colors of fire, which Talen found more than a little fitting. Gaoth ate up the distance, the uneven terrain and trees hardly slowing him. Talen ducked low branches and savored the feel of the cool morning wind on her face. Deep inside, she girded herself for the coming fight.

The plan might only be for her to start the shooting, but she knew damn well there'd be survivors. With them wounded and confused, she wouldn't have a better chance to easily bleed the town's numbers. Every stained that died now would be one less in the final fight. Unbidden, she caught the phantom scent of *Oceti Sakowin* war paint, but this time, the dark memories couldn't push past the good ones: fighting side-by-side with her sisters and a proud people just trying to keep their homes and way of life.

The similarity of this fight and those wasn't lost on her.

There was nothing she could do to change the past. She couldn't save her people or any of the Seven Council Fires, but she could do something for those held in bondage by souls that had been foul and rotten long before they turned stained.

Reluctantly, Gaoth agreed to wait for Talen a safe distance from the Perkins plantation. In fact, it was farther away than where he'd waited just an hour or so ago. Talen didn't feel the need to take any chances of him being discovered, or catching stray fire, if the fighting spilled beyond the plantation. She kissed her friend between his eyes, wrapped herself in shadow, and sprinted to her destination.

She found a spot behind some trees with a clear line of sight of the barn, and within the repeater's range. The quiet belied the tightness in her stomach and the bloodbath she hoped would come. Before long, the smell of wood smoke, coffee, and cooking food wafted through the air as people woke in the house. Half a dozen armed men led at least forty slaves to the fields, where those that had been working before, still toiled mindlessly.

It tore at her heart to see the ragged, gaunt faces of the enslaved bound by geas stones—not that seeing the "unbound" filled her with joy either. Despite her best attempts, she couldn't help but look for the human voids she'd seen earlier.

When she finally spotted one, her blood ran cold, and her breath caught. The man, or at least what had once been a man, shambled into view. His dark skin had turned gray and sallow. Even from this distance, Talen could make out the brutal wounds he must've carried to his death and now would never heal. All of those not under the magic of a stone kept their eyes down as they worked. When they did glance up, as soon as the walking dead man crossed their line of sight, their gaze went quickly back to their work.

The overseers laughed and jeered as they paced and patrolled.

Talen's blood screamed to spill theirs, to gut them, and leave them dying amid spilled entrails. There was no cruelty or malice that wouldn't be justified for that sort, stained or not. It took her a few moments to calm her mind and, again, remember that acting now wouldn't help in the long run. However much it might disturb her to see it, it was nothing compared to those people who were, and had been, living it. With that thought anchoring her calm, Talen settled in and waited for Bennfield to show, rifle at the ready.

Time dragged, and without the sun crawling up the cloudy sky, Talen wouldn't have known only an hour had passed, not a week. As the minutes crept by with no sign of Bennfield or any of his men coming, a wriggling unease started in her stomach.

Her patience eroded away like sandstone cliffs to the ocean, and panic replaced the disquiet as the voice of doubt grew louder and louder.

Terisan ut marrin, I got it wrong, didn't I? Bennfield ain't coming at all.

Her brain churned through options. At the least, she could set off the bombs here—those at the Bennfield plantation were likely too far away—and take out the Gatling guns. Maybe some stained as well.

Could be the bombs would still spur some paranoia. Might Perkins and his men think Bennfield had done it? It didn't seem likely. Not just because that would require a massive shift in Talen's luck, but it felt too brazen a move. From what she'd gleaned, this sort preferred more subtle machinations.

Nothing for it though. At least the explosions would cause confusion and buy her time to get back to the Cumulus. Hopefully they could move on Bennfield's while—again hopefully—all attention was focused on Perkins's.

The really hard part would be resisting the urge to butcher the overseers.

Talen cursed silently, drew out Draven's contraption, and studied the area around the shed. All the innocents working the fields looked to be well out of range. Unfortunately, only a couple of gun hands had wandered close enough to maybe catch the very edge of the blast.

Relying on the last of her frayed patience, Talen watched, one finger on the switch and another on the button. She waited for someone, maybe even multiple someones, to get closer to the shed.

A gruff, scowling man and a younger slack-jawed one came out of the house and started toward the barn.

"Two is better than none," Talen whispered to herself.

She watched them meander and tried willing them to just walk to the damn barn or wagon. As they drew near, she sucked in a breath, flipped the switch and—

The sound of hoofbeats in the distance, men urging horses on, and the rumbling of an empty wagon came from the distance.

Despite the relief and elation, Talen still cursed her impatience. After a steadying breath, she set the switch back and turned to get a better view.

At least two dozen men on horseback, led by a well-dressed man in his thirties, came up the wide path from the plantation's entrance. She recognized the wagon at the rear as the one she'd pilfered the gun from, the empty mounting point clearly visible.

After a silent thanks to her mother, Talen set the detonator aside and took up the rifle again.

A couple of Perkins's hired guns spotted the approaching group, and while one ran into the house, another whistled. Twenty or so men appeared and gathered in front of the house. All but one of the overseers left their duties to join their compatriots. Including three that wheeled a wagon mounted gun, a twin to Bennfield's, into view from around the shed. None of them climbed into the wagon, instead joining the mass of others.

Damn, is this really going to work?

A dapper, rotund, balding man easily pushing sixty emerged from the house, wiping at his mouth with a napkin. He passed it to a man on his left and walked to the front of the large porch.

The Bennfield posse came to a stop a dozen paces from the Perkins crew. Every hand but the two leaders' rested on the butt of a gun or spell iron.

"Jackson Bennfield," the man on the porch said, his tone hard but genial. "To what do I owe the pleasure?"

Bennfield motioned, and his men parted to let the wagon come to the fore. "Seems someone decided to take our Gatling gun. You wouldn't know anything about that, would you, Robert?"

Perkins's eyes narrowed. "Your daddy should've taught you to respect your elders. Mr. Perkins is the proper way to address me, boy. Bad enough to be so familiar, worse to be so while accusing me of thievery."

Bennfield smirked. "I do apologize, Mr. Perkins, but I laid no accusations. However, I understand how hearing can fade in the latter years." He cupped his hands over his mouth and pitched his voice louder. "I merely asked if you might know anything about the theft of my property."

Bennfield's men chuckled.

Perkins's expression remained mostly unchanged. The corners of his mouth pulled into an almost imperceptible sneer and his eyes hardened. The heat from his building rage even reached Talen.

Her muscles hummed in anticipation of the coming bloodshed, but she kept her breathing slow and even. A single finger lightly tapped the repeater's trigger guard.

"If you'd shown half as much interest in your schooling as you did chasing your cousins," Perkins said, "you'd understand the concept of implication. And how your question forces me to infer that you believe I'd know something because I was involved." He looked to the man on his left and nodded.

That man gestured to another. Two of those who brought the wagon out went to it, clambered into it, and took up position behind the gun, though they didn't turn it to bear.

"Why would I take your gun when I have one of my own?" Perkins asked.

Bennfield drew a spell iron and leveled it at the men on the wagon.

In the same instant, both groups of men drew their shooters, mundane and magical, and took aim at each other.

"You best tell your boys to step out of that wagon," Bennfield said. "I came here as a gentleman."

"You haven't the faintest notion what that word means," Perkins said. "And I have every right to defend my property and my honor from libelous accusations. Now you and yours can get the hell off my land."

"For a man with nothing to hide, you see awful eager for us to be gone," Bennfield said, spell iron still pointed at the wagon.

"You might while away your days drinking the cellar your parents left to you dry," Perkins said. "But I have a business to run. So, unless you've got evidence, I'll say again, for the last time: get off my land."

The two closest to Perkins turned their shooters on Bennfield.

Talen couldn't help but smile and took aim with her rifle at the man right next to Perkins.

Bennfield holstered his spell iron and showed his palms. "Seems we got to a bad start here, sir. I apologize for my insinuations. I didn't mean to suggest you were responsible." He looked to his men, and they reluctantly holstered their weapons.

After a moment, Perkins nodded, and his did the same.

Talen swore silently. Her terrible luck didn't seem to be changing after all. *How the hells could it be that two stained are going to come to an amicable agreement?*

"Sad truth is," Bennfield said, "hired hands don't always do what they're told. Sometimes they even do things without you knowing. I'm sure, if one of yours did this, you'd want to know." He eyed the barn, and the partially open door. "Weapon like that ain't exactly easy to hide. I propose you let one of my boys have a quick look around, and when we find nothing, I will apologize and we'll be gone."

Perkins glanced from Bennfield to the barn and back, and then to a man closest to the barn. "Tommy, open the barn and show him there ain't nothing there so we can be done with this."

Tommy hurried to the barn and pulled the door open.

Talen sighed in relief and took up her aim once more.

Perkins turned back to Bennfield. "Go on then, see there ain't nothing—"

"Uh, Mr. Perkins, sir," Tommy said and stepped into the barn.

Perkins's head snapped around, anger flashing in his eyes. "What is it?"

Tommy called for some help, and two men hurried into the barn. A moment later, the three of them carefully heaved the previously hidden, albeit poorly, Gatling gun into view.

"Well looky what we have here," Bennfield said.

Perkins looked over each his men, all of whom wore the same surprised expression as him. After measuring them up, he narrowed his eyes and furrowed his brow. After a moment, his confusion shifted to anger. He turned back to Bennfield. "You sniveling little shit! You put that there!"

Every man present drew their weapons again.

"Now who is partaking in libelous accusations?" Bennfield said. "You, sir, are clearly in possession of my property, and I demand satisfaction."

"I ain't as dull-witted as you boy," Perkins said. "Awful convenient your 'pilfered' property just happened to be in my barn and easily spotted the moment someone stepped in." He scoffed. "I shouldn't be surprised you don't have the sense to make this even the slightest bit believable. As I'm in a generous mood, I might just let you go with the whooping your daddy never gave you!"

Talen sighted down the barrel, took a breath, and held it.

"Sir, you steal from me," Bennfield said and drew his spell iron again. "And when caught red-handed, have the gall to insult and then threaten me?" His iron lit with spellfire. "No, sir! I will not—"

Talen pulled the trigger.

The crack of the shot split the air.

An instant later, the head of the man standing next to Perkins snapped back, and a spray of blood painted the front of the house behind him.

His body hadn't even hit the porch before the shooting started.

Talen ducked as a deafening barrage of gunfire erupted, punctuated only by the occasional roar of a spell iron's fire blast or crack of a lightning strike.

Men screamed, and horses whinnied in fear.

The rhythmic chatter of the Gatling gun started, eliciting more screams and shouts of angry defiance.

Talen crouched lower, grabbed the detonator, flipped the switch, and hit the button.

The bombs exploded in quick succession. The concussive blasts shook the trees and washed away all sound, save for a dull ringing in Talen's ears.

For several moments, only Talen's heartbeat sounded over the droning whine. Bit by bit, pitiful whinnies from dying horses mixed with the screams, sobbing, shouts, and desperate pleas of the men, and replaced the monotone buzz. The all too familiar sickly-sweet scent of burning flesh saturated the air. It tasted of blood, burnt leather, and the sharp tang of Draven's explosive material.

Only the righteous indignation burning in her heart kept Talen from being dragged down by the memories of Whitestone Hill.

After a moment, she chanced a look and surveyed the carnage. Chunks of meat, that moments ago had been men and horses, littered the ground. Most of which she couldn't identify one way or the other.

Amid the pieces, some stained still lived, writhing in pain, more than a few missing limbs. A handful had somehow managed to avoid the worst of it, and even now continued fighting, shooting at each other from behind cover. Fewer still fired from where they lay, some under dead horses, others simply too broken to stand.

It wouldn't be long before those surviving stained had recovered enough to rejoin the fight. As she thought that, some had already started getting back to their feet.

Talen stood, drew both spell irons, and with a belly full of steel, waded into the fight.

Only a few of the men wore the remnants of gray uniforms, but as Talen looked around, ghost-like images of calvary soldiers from her past floated among them.

The fire burning in her heart flared.

Moving like a shadowy angel of death, Talen stepped from the shadows just long enough to light a spell iron and pulverize a stained head, before slipping back under her cloak.

Few seemed to notice as she set to finishing off those already down.

If there was a blessing in this, a dozen or more horses had escaped and were vanishing into the distance. Though it chewed at her soul, she had to leave the suffering horses until the stained were done.

Shots whizzed by, none of them aimed at her, just stray shots. She only noticed a few smack against her coat.

A huge bear of a man stood and fired both revolvers at another stained taking cover behind a ruined section of overturned wagon. Bullets struck the bear over and over, but he only twitched and jerked.

Talen emerged from darkness right behind him and fired her left-hand iron, loosing a blast of frozen air at his head.

He managed to get off a last shot, though it went wild, as Talen vanished again.

BISHOP O'CONNELL

He fell, and his frost-covered head struck the ground. A chunk of frozen brain and gore broke away and slid across the ground.

In a deathly dance, Talen crossed the wasteland, appearing just long enough to kill before slipping back into shadows.

As the number of survivors dwindled, they began to notice something amiss. None of them seemed to know what, much less where, she was. They fired at her, or where she'd last appeared, but nothing got close.

The last few ran. She had no idea whose side they'd been on, nor did she care. She'd never admit to anyone how much pleasure she took in shooting them in their backs.

Silence eventually fell on the battlefield, and though the fight seemed to last hours, Talen knew it had likely been closer to five or ten minutes.

Not taking any chances, she made her way through the dead. Anyone even only mostly intact, she ended with blasts of force or ice.

Bennfield lay on the ground, next to his dead horse. From the look of it, he'd caught most of the opening fire. In fact, it was only because of what remained of his clothing that Talen recognized him. His head and chest had been chewed up, the former beyond recognition.

She looked, but couldn't find Perkins anywhere, and that just wouldn't serve.

Calmly and still in shadow, she reloaded both irons, all force save for one fire load, and climbed the porch stairs. Stepping over the dead, she walked into the house through the hole that had been the front door.

Either side of the—former—doorway was pocked with bullet holes. The wall to her right, the side closest to the barn, had all its windows blown in. The rest of the house remained an offensive show of wealth and opulence.

After checking the first floor for anyone else, and finding no one, Talen made her way upstairs, irons out and ready, but still dark. Somewhere on the second floor, a woman sobbed, and someone barked something at her in reply.

"Yes, Mother, I heard you," a man said. "And for the hundredth time, I'm waiting for Father!"

Talen followed the voices down a hall to a room at the back of the house with the door closed.

"The shooting has stopped, you coward!" the woman snapped. "Your father is probably laying out there dying because you're too much a coward to—"

A gun went off.

"You shot me!" the woman shouted. "You foul, wretched boy! How dare you shoot your own mother!"

"I shot your leg. You'll be fine," the man said, almost sounding bored. "Now do be quiet, Mother, or I'll shoot you someplace less able to be suffered."

"You ungrateful child," the woman said, though in a quieter tone.

Talen debating leaving those two to tend to each other, but that felt too much like mercy. Listening at the door, she got an idea of where they were, holstered her left-hand iron, and then looked around for something heavy.

As further evidence of the ego that resided here, she found a sizeable marble bust of Perkins. She picked it up, testing the weight, and found it satisfactory.

Positioning herself to one side, she hurled the bust at the door. The polished maple door broke apart.

As expected, gunshots answered, the bullets striking the wall several feet away. When the shooter ran dry, Talen drew her left-hand iron and stepped into the room, moving well away from the door.

A human man, in his early twenties and dressed in clothing finer than even Perkins, stood in front of a large, finely-carved, wooden desk, desperately fumbling to reload his revolver.

Behind him, a woman twice his age, with a cruel face, sat in a chair. Her intricate, pale blue dress was marred by a bloody hole over one leg. Both of them roiled with darkness.

Talen took aim, let her cloak fall, and lit her irons.

Both humans gaped in open-mouth shock, their wide eyes filled with hate, fear, confusion, and tendrils of stained magic.

"Wait," the man said. "Don't! We're very rich, we can give you whatever—"

Talen pulled the trigger.

What had once been his head spattered both the wall behind him and his mother.

She shrieked in fury and made to lunge.

Talen fired her left-hand iron.

The woman's roar ended abruptly, replaced by a wet squelch. Only the drip of blood and gore falling to the floor broke the silence.

Talen spit on the corpses, doused her irons, and wrapped herself in shadow again.

It took her a bit to check every room on each of the three floors, but she found no one else inside.

Perkins must've run for it. Safe to say he'd make for the preacher. As all the horses had either run off or been killed, he'd be on foot. If she hurried, she might catch up to him.

She sprinted down the stairs, out of the house, and down the porch stairs. No sign of Perkins in any direction. Around back, she found all the enslaved on the ground, terrified, and offering comforting whispers to each other.

Well, almost all. The geas bound still toiled, the "others" just stood there, unmoving.

Talen scanned all around, but still didn't see Perkins anywhere.

"*Terisan ut marrin juarchian!*" she said, jaw clenched.

A Black woman of middling years looked her way, eyes wide and filled with terror. It didn't take much imagination to figure what would happen to these people if they were still here when the preacher's men arrived.

Talen stepped from the shadows, holstered her irons, and showed her hands.

"It's okay," she said. "My name is Talen. I'm here with the Railroad."

The woman's brows rose. "But you're a, um…"

"An elf, yes. Moses herself sent me and some others, thanks to Delia Mason."

"Delia?" the woman asked. "Little Delia made it out? And got to Moses?"

"She did. She's with her right now, in fact. Now I know you're scared, but we need to get all of you out of here. Looks like Perkins got away, and if he fetches people—"

The woman got to her feet. "Yes, ma'am, we need to go. I'm called Natty."

That's when Talen noticed the others watching intently.

"Little Delia got to Moses!" Natty shouted. "Freedom train has come for us!"

The others slowly got to their feet. It was more than a little disturbing how they didn't seem to acknowledge the bound or standing dead, but then Talen couldn't blame them. Couldn't be easy having them right there every day.

They looked from Talen to each other, unsure.

"I'm sorry we ain't got time to be more gentle," Talen said. "But we need to go now. We got an airship a few miles from here. I ain't forcing none of you to go, but if you're here when Perkins comes back, I don't need to tell you how it'll go."

More people rose into view, and they all made their way toward Talen, near on fifty people in total.

"Any of you know how to work a shooter?" Talen asked.

More than a few nodded.

"Then I want you collecting whatever guns and bullets you can pick off the dead," she said. "You do that while I see to putting these horses out of their misery."

More nods and yes ma'am's.

Talen led them to the front of the house. While they starting picking the corpses clean of weapons and ammunition, Talen fetched her repeater rifle and put down the few horses still alive. To soothe her own anxiety, she checked the Gatling guns and found both had been severely damaged. Part of her wished one had survived, but the regret didn't last long.

"Let's go," Talen said. "Keep together. If anyone falls behind, you call out. We ain't leaving no one, hear me?"

Everyone nodded.

Talen led the way, and she was reminded how even the beaten and exhausted could keep a quick pace if it meant freedom waited. As they crossed the road, Talen and a few of those who'd taken up arms watched in either direction.

Before long, they'd returned to Gaoth. Talen found those most struggling and got them onto Gaoth's back. They were all children, ranging from six to ten. All five of them fit in the saddle, though they held tight to each other.

Less than an hour later, they'd reached the Cumulus and had everyone safely on board. Then and only then, Talen allowed herself draw in a full breath and let it out. Alice, Booker, Cyrus, Odie, Frieda, and Pearl took the lead, helping to get people settled, fed, and looked over.

Margaret, Wilfred, and Draven came over to Talen as she pulled her saddle from Gaoth.

"I reckon your plan worked," Wilfred said.

"And then some," Talen said. "I got plenty to fill you in on."

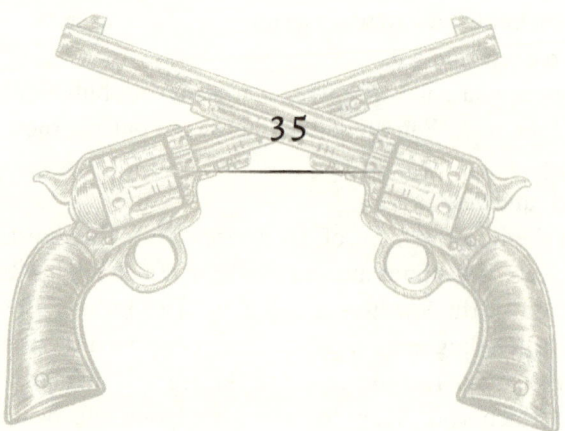

35

Talen told them what had gone down at the Perkins plantation, leaving out the more gruesome details. Just didn't see any need for them. As she filled them in, they all helped with settling the new passengers in. Talen made sure to halt the retelling when near the passengers.

"Sounds like the plan worked better than we'd hoped," Draven said.

"For a time, I admit I had my doubt, but that does seem to be the case," Talen said. "Could be some rabbited and got away that I didn't see, but it couldn't have been more than one or two aside from Perkins."

"I'd say I can't believe he left his wife and son," Margaret said, "but I know all too well how selfish men like Perkins are."

Talen and Wilfred had learned about Margaret's parentage last year. Her father had owned her mother, and the slaver's wife wasn't too happy to find a slave pregnant with her husband's baby. Margaret's mother had escape via the Railroad and settled in Boston with a white family. They'd taken Margaret in as their own when her mother died of consumption a few years later. Draven hadn't been told until some months later, but not out shame. Margaret had moved past the fear of her parentage being discovered, but rather because she just didn't much talk about it.

"I wouldn't be opposed to swinging by and settling accounts with the man that impregnated your mama," Talen said. "After we drop these folks off of course."

Margaret gave the hint of smile. "He isn't worth the time. He took everything from my mother, and I'm not about to give him anything else." She looked around the cargo bay, a third full with people. "This is a much better vengeance, if you ask me."

"Margaret Jameson," Wilfred said, "you are a rare sort. Be a damned fine world if more people was like you."

She smiled again, and this time it didn't seem forced. "I'm just trying to do the right thing."

"You seem to see it clearer than most," Talen said. "Damn proud to call you sister, and even more grateful."

"I feel the same," Margaret said. "So, what's the next move?"

"Time is an issue now," Talen said. "Like as not, Perkins will be back to his place before long and like to have some of them knights with him."

"I don't think he will," Wilfred said. "Least I don't expect he'll have the support you imagine."

Talen didn't bother hiding her surprise, though she figured Wilfred would know better than her. "How do you reckon?"

"One thing about being a slave," Wilfred said, "white folk never much watched what they said around you. I heard plenty of squabbling and plotting, even among preachers. I remember hearing tell of a failed slave revolt a few towns over. Them that tried to rise up were mostly killed, or worse, but the farm and house was burned down too."

Talen smiled, imagining how lovely a sight that must've been, and wondering what colors the flames were. "Oh, ain't that a damn shame?" she said flatly.

Wilfred nodded. "Ain't it just. But the owners went asking for help to rebuild, having lost everything. Plenty of offered prayers, but no one gave one penny or minute of labor to help. Even the local preacher said they did it to themselves for not having better control of their slaves. God's righteous punishment for their leniency or such."

"Evil has no friends or family, and even in victory, will eventually devour itself," Talen said.

"What's that?" Draven asked.

"Elven saying," Talen said. "Evil don't love, ain't loved, and is always hungry. It'll turn on anyone soon as there is a chance."

"That is a fact," Wilfred said. "Which is what I'm saying. Pro-slavery preachers ain't never preached about the love and caring for each other parts of the Bible. They focus on the sins, and how everyone but them is doing them."

"Well, even if Perkins don't return with any knights, I do expect he'll return all the same," Talen said. "And I didn't get a chance to see to them bound by geas stones and"—she swallowed and her chest tightened—"we got to do something about the, um, the others."

"We call them the quiet ones," Natty said. "Or the troubled."

Talen turned to find the woman standing just off to one side.

"Beg pardon," Natty said, "I didn't mean to snoop, just meant to come and thank you."

"None needed," Talen said. "Thanks or apology. I weren't trying to keep nothing from you all. I just figured you'd prefer not to think about them any more than you had to."

"We had to work the same fields as them," Natty said. "Ain't none of us gonna be forgetting them anytime soon. Especially not those of us what had family torn from their peace to keep working."

Talen winced, her heart breaking, but those cracks nearly closed up from the heat of her anger and such a vile torment.

"Sacred stones," Draven said.

"Merciful God," Margaret said.

Talen and Wilfred were less polite.

"Robert, my husband," Natty said. "They worked him right to death, but weren't happy with that."

"I'm so sorry," Talen said, knowing those words were woefully insufficient, to say the least, but she needed to say something.

"Ain't your doing. We all knew them the troubled used to be." Natty shook her head. "Making slaves of folk, whipping them, helping yourself to them, tearing children from mothers. We'd thought we seen the very edge of cruelty. Then Preacher Thompson found a whole new land of malice."

"Do you know of anything we can do for them?" Talen asked.

"Find some way to give them peace," Natty said. "True and lasting peace."

Talen looked to the others and then back to Natty. "I—"

"Don't matter what you need to do," Natty said. "We seen what they can endure and keep going." Her face hardened. "As the wife of one, I'm telling you, whatever got to be done, know it'll be a mercy in the end."

The thought of having to end more innocent lives turned her stomach and filled her with barely containable fury. She pushed the anger down, saving it for those who deserved it, and swallowed back the knot in her throat. "Yes ma'am. I'll see to it."

"Might be these will help," Natty said and held out a dozen black stones, each carved with the same symbol.

The surface of the stained charms—they could be nothing else—seemed to move, as if coated in a putrid ooze. Around them, a fetid miasma roiled. Despite only being able to see the foulness, a putrid taste settled in the back of Talen's throat. She couldn't bear to look at them longer than a second or two before having to turn away.

"What are those?" Wilfred asked, leaning in. He produced gloves from a pocket and slipped them on.

"Overseers used them to direct the troubled," Natty said. "When the others were collecting the guns and such from the dead, I went looking for these. Thought maybe I could use them to give Robert some peace, but I couldn't do it."

Talen noticed a nearly invisible thread running from each stone and stretching back in the direction of the plantation as far as she could see. That's when she thought back to how the troubled had just stood there earlier. Puppets without a master to pull their strings.

"May I?" Wilfred asked.

Natty nodded.

He took up one of the stones and examined it. Talen couldn't bear to watch him handling the foul thing.

"I ain't never seen nothing so, well, wrong," Wilfred said. "I don't reckon anyone but a stained can use them."

"Can we destroy them?" Talen asked. "Would that break the hold on them?"

Wilfred shrugged. "Might, but I can't say for sure."

"I vote for destroying them anyway," Margaret said.

"If I get a vote, it's the same," Natty said.

"Damned right you get a vote," Talen said.

"I ain't about to argue," Wilfred said, his expression dour. "Fire should work if it burns hot and long enough. Bodies ought to be burned too. Ain't no bringing back ash."

The dead eyes of the young stained girl broke through Talen's mental wall. A cold fist of hate and rage gripped her heart and squeezed. It took a moment to push the memory back, and unclench the fist, but she managed. However, she held onto a piece of the lingering pain to use as fuel for the task ahead.

"I'll see to it," she said and glanced at Natty.

Natty's expression softened, and she put a hand on Talen's arm. "I done told you. Whatever you got to do is a mercy. Ain't a one of us won't be grateful for you doing it."

"Yes, ma'am," Talen said and swallowed back the conflicting emotions warring inside. "Like I was saying before, we can also get to them bound by geas stones."

"You mean the obliged?" Natty said. "Them that work without rest or food? Most of the troubled were obliged first."

Talen clenched her jaw and drew in a breath to calm her fury and heartache.

"You all right, miss?" Natty asked, genuinely concerned.

The care and kindness just twisted Talen's heart all the more, but this woman didn't need any more burdens, so Talen wrestled her shame and guilt down. "I'll be fine. If they ain't too far gone, the stone can be cut out, and they'll eventually recover."

"If they are?" Natty asked. "Ain't nothing can be done?"

"Only show them a final mercy," Talen said.

Natty met Talen's eyes. Iron wove through every inch of the woman's soul, and Talen couldn't look away.

"I ain't never met no elf before," Natty said. "So I don't know as you carry or feel guilt like we do. But from what I see in your eyes, looks like you do, and you got a heap of it already." She put a calloused hand on Talen's cheek. "I do know, with these, you got no reason nor right to feel guilty. You're doing what any of us would want in their place. You hear me?"

While Talen appreciated the words, Natty had no idea this was all Talen's fault, or rather, her people's. But Natty didn't need to know that either, so she just nodded. "Yes ma'am."

After a moment, Talen turned to Draven. "When the business is done at Perkins's place, we need to hurry over to Bennfield's and see those folk freed. I got no idea how many guns might be there still, but it can't be many."

"Reckon the Cumulus landing in the fields ought to provide a distraction," Draven said.

"Alice and the others can position themselves on deck," Talen said. "Pick off anyone they can without risking hitting an innocent. I'll see to the house and whoever might be inside." She sucked in a steadying breath. "Then I'll tend to the obliged and quiet ones."

"What about us?" Margaret asked, nodding toward Wilfred.

Talen met her eyes. "If you're willing, you can join the others on deck."

"These are stained," Margaret said, her expression hardening. "As if that wasn't enough of a reason, they're also slavers. There isn't any helping or redeeming them."

"Then it sounds like we have a plan," Talen said. "Once that's done, all that'll be left is the preacher, the knights, and them in town."

"That's all," Wilfred said.

No one laughed, but Talen still appreciated the attempt, as it seemed did everyone else.

"I'll get to the bridge and get us underway," Draven said and hurried off.

"You go sit and rest," Talen said to Natty. "We've got this."

Natty looked as if she wanted to argue but didn't. She turned to Wilfred and offered him the rest of the wretched black stones.

He took them in his gloved hand and dumped them into a pouch. The foul tendrils passed through the cloth as if it wasn't there.

"Thank you," Natty said, looking from Wilfred to Talen. "From all of us."

Talen lifted a hand. "I told you it weren't—"

"Yes, it is," Natty said, her eyes hard. "It is necessary."

"In that case," Talen said. "You're welcome."

Natty turned and went back to her cot.

"Best get ready," Talen said to Margaret and Wilfred. "Won't take long by air."

"Remember what Natty said about it being a mercy," Margaret said.

"Wouldn't be a need for that mercy if it weren't for—"

"This isn't on you or your people," Margaret said, softly but there was an edge to the words. "Neither of you made anyone steal that book, or force them to make those horrible crafts., And you most certainly didn't compel anyone to use them."

"I hear you, but—"

"No," Margaret said with finality. "No but. Listen to me. Every iota of blame or responsibility for these horrific deeds you try to foist on yourself is one less on the shoulders of the twisted, evil, repugnant sons of bitches that actually did it. Don't you dare take any of that off them."

The words hit Talen like a falling tree, and it knocked the guilt and shame right out of her. "I admit, I ain't never thought of it that way, and I sure can't make no argument against it."

"Good," Margaret said.

Talen sighed. "I won't lie to you though. It does help, but we both know guilt don't wash away clean."

"Neither is it often swayed by logic," Margaret said and nodded. "I know. But if it means you'll go easier on yourself, that's what matters."

"Have I mentioned that I'm damn proud to call you sister?"

Margaret smiled. "I said my piece. Let's get to work."

"Yes ma'am."

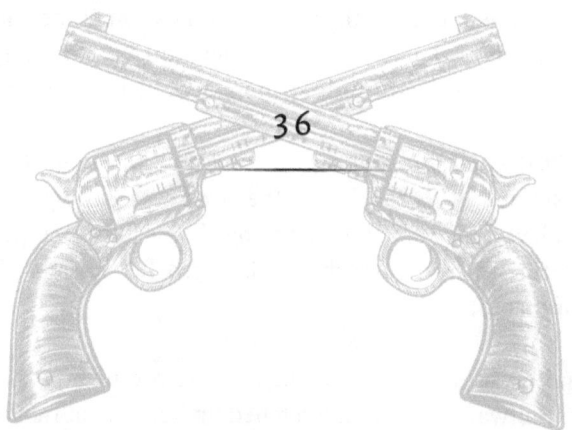

36

The Cumulus reached the Perkins plantation significantly faster than Talen and Gaoth had. The place was just as Talen had left it, but Booker and Cyrus kept watch on deck for anyone approaching. Draven set the ship down between the house and the field. It took some convincing, but eventually Alice agreed to go with some of the freed folk to collect food and other supplies from the house.

As they did, Talen tended to the obliged and quiet ones. It was gruesome work, but she steeled herself with Natty's words, that it was ultimately a mercy, even if it didn't feel like it.

Of the nearly twenty obliged, less than half had any remnant of a geas stone left. Three of those were so small Talen suspected they'd never recover. That didn't stop the freed people from taking them in and promising to care for them as long as needed, even if that meant forever.

That simple display of kindness restored more than a little of Talen's waning faith in humanity. When lost in the deepest, darkest part of the night, even the light from a single firefly can be enough to find your way.

The only upside to dealing with the obliged, if you could even call it that, was that they didn't resist in any way, or even react to Talen cutting on them to get the stones out.

The quiet ones, of which there were nine, offered no resistance either, but with them, it felt so much worse. They just stood there, staring off into the distance with empty eyes. All of them were in various stages of decay, though the magic that bound them apparently slowed that.

It did nothing for the smell though.

Natty and some others had asked to go along and see their loved ones put to rest, but Talen assured them they didn't want to be there. Seeing the rotting puppets that had once been their kin up close and personal would nightmarish enough. Ending them would be neither clean nor pretty.

Thankfully, they all agreed to stay on board or help collect supplies.

Like the stained, a force load to the head was enough to end their misery. Talen had done some terrible things in her life, seen people killed in ways that turned her stomach and haunted her dreams. She'd even done some of that killing.

This was worse.

The sound, sight, and smell of their heads rupturing was too much even for her. Halfway through, she retched up her guts in the field. By the time she put down the last, she could hardly see through the tears in her eyes.

Grief and revulsion gave way to anger and indignation as she piled one body onto another. At least their destroyed heads meant none of them could stare back at her. Even so, she made sure to turn what remained of their faces away from her.

Not wanting to touch the vile stones that had controlled these poor souls, Talen dropped the sack holding them onto the stack of corpses, and set it ablaze with three fire loads from each spell iron.

Despite the unholy stench, Talen stood witness to the pyre long enough to ensure it would be enough.

Thank the mothers, it was.

The pouch burned away quickly, and as the flesh and bone turned to ash, the stones cracked and broke. The oily corrupted magic covering them sizzled away, and the wispy tendrils evaporated.

Only when she couldn't see any hint of stained magic did Talen holster her irons and return to the Cumulus.

The freed folk wept, but thanked her, which only twisted Talen's heart near to tearing. She wanted to tell them how wrong it was that anyone should be thanked for such a task. That it was loathsome that such a thing was even needed, but she wouldn't be telling them anything they didn't know.

Besides, actually speaking was beyond her capabilities at that moment, so she just nodded at them and went to find a spot to sit by herself. The desecration of it all had soaked into every pore, saturating her. As such, she couldn't even bring herself to be near Gaoth.

Thankfully, Wilfred and Margaret knew her well enough to leave her be.

The airship took off, and there was a bit of relief to leaving that profane place behind. Only a little though, because Talen knew more of the same lay ahead.

As they neared the Bennfield plantation, Talen clad herself in the only armor she had available, anger and hatred for those who made all this necessary.

Draven circled the property first, giving Alice, Booker, Cyrus, Wilfred, and Margaret a chance to survey it and get an idea of what lay in store. Talen could've joined them, but she just stood sentinel at the cargo bay doors, spell irons drawn but dark, ready to cut down anything that might come for those under her protection.

"Looks to be half a dozen overseers in the field," Draven said, through the speaking tube. "They all got mundane shooters, but could be one or two with a spell iron on their hip. No one could see well enough to know for sure. I'll be setting us far enough away that there won't be no immediate risk."

An anger as cold and vast as the Pacific settled over Talen as a focused numbness. "Got it," she said into the tube and went back to where she'd been standing.

A short while after they began to descend, Margaret and the others came down. They made sure the passengers stayed as far back into the cargo hold as possible, and then took up position behind the cover of the thick wooden columns, shooters ready.

"I won't bother asking if you're okay," Margaret said.

"Appreciate that," Talen said.

"Do what you need to in order to get through this," Margaret said. "We'll be here to help you back when it's done."

Talen almost said "much obliged" but that word carried more weight than it once had, so she only nodded.

As the Cumulus touched down, Talen stepped into the shadows, opened the bay doors, and lowered the gangway.

Three burly, cruel-looking men with rifles leveled were approaching the airship. The other overseers kept back, watching. All had the now-familiar darkness to them.

Talen walked, unhurried, picking a spot between two of them.

"You can't set down here!" one of the men shouted to the ship. "This here is private land! It belongs to Jackson Bennfield, so you best get!"

No one from the Cumulus replied or came into view.

The three men made for the open cargo bay doors.

"Hey, anyone in there?" the one in the middle shouted.

"Yup," Talen said right before slipping from her shadow cloak, pouring magic into her irons, and obliterating his head, as well the head of the man to his left. She made sure to position herself so the one left standing would catch a face full of gore.

The shower of blood, bone, and brain left him stunned for the short remainder of his life.

She didn't have enough in her to feel ashamed at enjoying his revulsion.

As the bodies fell and he just started to comprehend what happened, Talen rolled her right-hand iron to a fresh load and fired.

Her aim wasn't as precise. The flesh on the left side of his face tore away an instant before the magic pulverized bone and meat. The resulting gory mist rained down behind him.

He had just enough time to look shocked and confused before his corpse fell to the ground.

The workers reacted before the remaining overseers, dropping down and getting what little cover they could.

Talen stepped back into shadow and sprinted toward the remaining men.

"Did you see that?" one of the other overseers said, leveling his rifle and taking aim at nothing.

"What the fuck was it?" another asked, doing the same.

The last, apparently just a bit smarter and crueler than the others, took aim at a young, cowering Black woman nearby. "Show yourself or she dies!"

His companions took his lead and did the same, one of them going so far as to grab up a man to use as a human shield.

Unfortunately for them all, Talen had already reached them. Standing behind them, she dropped her shadow cloak, and shot the stained with the hostage, as well as the one to his right.

"Here I am," she said.

The hostage slipped from his dead captor's grasp, and the terrified man dropped to his knees.

The last overseer spun toward Talen and fired.

She pivoted and twisted, catching the shot on her left shoulder. Her spell-covered coat stopped the round, but the impact staggered her back half a step.

He levered a fresh round into his rifle.

She'd already rolled her cylinders and rather than wasting the half second it'd take to raise her iron and shoot him in the face, she fired at his leg.

At the same moment, he pulled his trigger.

The shot whizzed by like an angry hornet, missing her by inches.

Pure force struck his leg, snapping it back, and transformed it instantly into a fleshy bag of obliterated bone. The useless limb twisted but didn't tear away. Instead, it slapped into his back and tried to wrap around his body. The impact sent him reeling to the ground, howling in pain.

The moment his body hit dirt, she fired her right-hand iron at his face.

A blast of flame swallowed his agonized cry, leaving only a blackened skull, cracked open like an overcooked egg.

After ensuring the corpses stayed corpses, Talen turned to the cowering former hostage.

"How many more are there?" she asked him.

He looked up at her, terrified and shaking, unable to speak.

She wanted to feel for him, but at the moment, nothing could make it across the icy wasteland of indignation inside her.

"Two more," a girl no older than twelve said from Talen's left. "They're inside with Missus and the children. Master took the rest of the guns with him to Mr. Perkins's."

"Ain't none of them coming back. You get everyone who ain't quiet or obliged onto the airship. There's folk there waiting to help."

"We're free?" she asked. "For real, this time? Some said we was free before, after word came that General Lee surrendered, but folk around here didn't seem to care."

"They should've surrendered too," Talen said. "Go on, get on the ship. Leave the rest to me."

The girl looked around, clearly unsure.

There was nothing more Talen could do, so she turned toward the house.

A crack split the air and a bullet smacked into her left side, where her chest and shoulder met.

Again, her jacket stopped the bullet.

Before she could react, a second shot struck the same area.

The impact turned her, nearly knocking her to one knee. A sharp, biting throb radiated from her ribs.

Fortunately, hate and fury made for excellent pain killers. Two things which she had in ample supply.

Straightening, she spotted a man on the porch of the house, near a half mile off, taking cover behind a column and reloading what had to be a Sharps rifle to get her at that range.

Bennfield should've brought you along with him.

"Stay down," Talen said to the girl, holstered her irons, slipped into shadows, and bolted for the house.

Even from this distance, she could see the surprise and panic on the soon-to-be-dead man's face. Despite the wrath fueling her, her shoulder and side ached with every stride. Likely she'd cracked or broken something. However, at the moment, she could only add it to the long list of wrongs the bastard was going to answer for.

The distance didn't allow for a short, easy sprint. In fact, it took her a few of minutes to get there. As she ran, the shooter recovered from his shock, and seemed to pick up on signs of her approach. He fired a few times, once getting within a foot or so of her. Luckily, while a Sharps might have range, it didn't reload as fast as a Winchester repeater.

Common sense eventually soaked into his stained brain. He cleared out from the porch and went into the house, shouting for help.

This let Talen slow her pace so she didn't reach the house out of breath. As she approached, she drew her right-hand iron and considered her options. It didn't take long to settle on just setting the damn house ablaze. When the stained ran out, she could put him down and leave the place burn.

She made a circuit of the house, keeping close and below the windows, listening carefully.

"Hell if I know!" someone said, in the house. "But I'm telling you he just vanished right before my fucking eyes."

"You sure you ain't seeing things?" another man asked.

"I ain't seeing things, dipshit," the first one said. "That's what I'm telling you! And I ain't imagining it. I could see footprints in the dirt, and some dust kick up where he ran."

"I suppose that ain't the strangest thing we seen."

"You think? Go watch the back door. I'll watch the front," the sniper said.

As she rounded a corner, the sounds of a crying baby sounded from the third floor. A twinge of compassion broke through her armor of indignation.

Well, shit.

"Damn it, Sadie, would you do something about that screaming child?" a woman shouted, from a different spot on the third floor. "Bad enough those fools are shooting just outside the house. My headache don't need a howling child, too!"

Someone replied, but Talen couldn't make it out. Regardless, the exchange meant Talen needed to be mindful where she shot. She didn't want to risk hurting those she'd come to help. As she finished her trip around the house, she replaced her spent loads and got an idea of where the two shooters might be.

The height of the windows meant she couldn't jump through them. If she kicked down a door, there'd likely be a spray of bullets in answer. Her coat might stop them, but her face, hands, and legs could catch a lucky shot. Even if they didn't, her aching shoulder spoke to the limits of her jacket.

As it happened though, the porch sported a few rocking chairs, a low bench, and several large windows.

Creeping up the steps, careful not to make a sound, Talen glanced into the windows. She spotted the stained that had shot her ducked behind a corner.

He crouched low, aiming a spell iron burning with spellfire at the door.

Cursing her luck, she made the only move available to her. She grabbed a chair, hurled it through a window, and dashed to snatch up another.

The chair shattered the glass and crashed into the room. Before it had even hit the floor, a blast of force splintered it and did a number on the wall next to the window.

She chucked another chair, then another, and finally heaved a bench through. Before it landed, she leapt off the porch and ducked down.

As she'd hoped, this stained just kept shooting, not paying any mind to what loads he fired off. A crack of thunder shook the house as a bolt of lightning leapt from the second window before arcing down to the earth.

A gout of flame belched from the last window, setting the curtains and section of the wall on fire.

"Shit!" the shooter shouted. "Look what you made me do, you son of a bitch!"

Talen crept to a side window and pulled herself up just enough to peek through.

The stained looked from to the front door and windows, to the fire, and back over and over again in obvious uncertainty.

Talen watched the filth work his rot-soaked brain, trying desperately to decide what to do, with more than a little twisted pleasure.

Take your time, filth.

"Damn it! Marcus, get in here and help me!" he shouted over his shoulder.

"You told me to watch—"

"I know what I told you! Now I'm telling you to get your ass in here!"

The utter stupidity of the scene might've almost made Talen suspect they were trying to lure her in. But then a second man—presumably Marcus—came round the corner, saw the flames, and gaped like an idiot for a full three count.

"Jesus, Jimmy, what the hell happened?" Marcus asked.

"Don't matter, you got a cold load?" Jimmy asked.

Despite being genuinely curious how this all might play out, Talen turned and ran for the back of the house. As she reached the now unguarded door, ready to kick it open, she paused and checked it instead.

It was unlocked.

Two things that humans never seemed to lack, and often went hand in hand: cruelty and stupidity.

Talen opened the door, careful it didn't squeak or catch, and stepped inside. The room was some sort of food preparation area, the kitchen being in a separate building. Drawing her left-hand iron, she checked the room. Two middle-aged women and a girl in her early teens hid behind a counter. The older women tried to comfort the younger one.

"Whatever happens," one said, "keep your head down. We ain't need to be dying for no white man's feud."

"Freedom train sent an airship," Talen whispered. "It's waiting for you in the field."

All three women looked around, eyes wide.

"Who said that?" the second woman asked.

"A friend of Moses," Talen said. "You all best get out now. It's going to get a mite bloody in here."

The second woman seemed ready to ask a question, but the first woman urged her and the girl up and out the back door.

Talen moved through the house, leveling her iron around each corner, as she made her way to the idiots and the fire. The place was ridiculously huge, with several rooms Talen couldn't even guess the purpose of. Luckily, the sounds of cursing and the smell of smoke served to guide her through the labyrinthian home.

"Found one," Marcus said, pulling a spell load from a pocket and holding it up.

"Well use it before the whole house catches!" Jimmy said.

Talen poked her head around yet another corner.

Jimmy, apparently not a complete moron, watched the back way while Marcus put the cold load into his own spell iron. Of course, he'd forgotten about Talen vanishing before his eyes only a few minutes prior. So, still mostly a moron.

Marcus took aim and fired a blast of frigid air toward the front of the house, almost all of which now burned. The flames snuffed out and a thick fog filled the room before settling to the floor.

"Got it!" Marcus turned to Jimmy, chuckled and smiled, showing as many gaps as teeth. "Boss is going to be pissed though."

Talen stepped from the shadows, poured magic into her iron, and gave the grinning idiot a force load to the face.

His skull caved in, his head snapped back, and he fell to the floor with a wet slap.

She doused her iron, slipped back into shadow, and ducked away.

A responding force blast tore a hole in the wall where she'd just been standing.

The fog had started, slowly, to dissipate, but had also spread to where she took cover. If she moved, even in shadow, the stirring of the vapor would give her away.

She decided to use it to her advantage. Hopefully, Jimmy wouldn't see it coming.

She dove low, both irons leveled, and slid across the damp wood floor.

The vanishing fog parted in her wake and Jimmy fired another force load right where Talen came to a stop. Except, thankfully, he'd aimed for a standing opponent.

Talen let her cloak fall, lit up her irons, and gave Jimmy both barrels.

His eyes went wide, and he started to lower his spell iron to take another shot.

Talen's force blasts crushed his head and chest, and sent him tumbling back like a rag doll. His body smashed into a table and began soaking the floor with blood.

Not taking any chances, Talen made sure he and Marcus wouldn't be getting back up. Confirming that, she turned to the large staircase that ran along the far wall and listened intently.

The baby had resumed crying somewhere on the third floor. Based on the creaking of footsteps, someone paced back and forth, presumably trying to comfort the child. Aside from that, nothing moved or made a sound.

That didn't make a lick of sense though. The fight had caused quite a ruckus, and no one upstairs—aside from the baby—seemed at all bothered by it.

While it didn't feel like a trap, Talen climbed the stairs slow and silent, spell irons at the ready. As a precaution, she checked the second floor before proceeding to the third. There she found an obnoxious number of rooms, but at least most seemed to have a recognizable function. An office, several bedrooms, and three separate toilets, but not soul in any of them.

Talen returned to the staircase and made her way up.

Unlike the lower two floors, this one looked be composed entirely of a single hallway and closed doors. Starting where she'd heard the shouting, Talen went to the door and pressed her ear to it.

A woman mumbled to herself, her words indecipherable, but no one else spoke or moved.

Talen decided to try a more subtle approach, slowly turning the knob, opening the door, and peeking inside.

The massive bedroom took up a full third of the top floor. Various pieces of furniture filled the room, including a huge canopy bed partially hidden behind the door. No people though.

Talen flung it open, hurried inside, and moved well away from the entryway. Her spell irons followed her gaze and she scanned the room.

An obviously drunk white woman in her late twenties lay in the bed. The telltale roiling darkness made her pallor even more ashen than it probably was on its own. Her head lolled toward the door, and she peered at it for a long moment with narrowed eyes.

"Sadie, you didn't close the door all the way!" she shouted, her words slurred. "You know I'm unwell and need my rest!" The woman groped for a bottle at the bedside, nearly knocking it over before getting a hold of it.

Talen stepped closer and saw 'Laudanum' written on the label.

The woman took some large sips from the bottle and tucked it against her side.

Talen slipped from the shadows and if the woman noticed, she made no sign of it. Neither did she seem to notice the runes lighting with spellfire.

Barely able to even manage contempt, Talen pulled the trigger and crushed the woman's head with a force blast. A spray of feathers exploded out from the bed and drifted around the room.

The pristine white sheets, and what remained of the once stuffed pillows and featherbed, soaked up most of the blood and gore. Talen ignored it all and left to check the last of the rooms.

Following the sound of the baby, now happily cooing and gurgling, led Talen to the opposite side of the house. She leaned in and listened at the door. Inside a woman whispered, presumably to the child, on the far side of the room.

"Go down Moses," Talen said through the door.

The whispers stopped.

"Way down in Egypt's land," Talen sang.

The reply was soft, wavering, but unmistakable. "Tell old Pharaoh."

"Let my people go," Talen said.

The door opened, and a middle-aged woman appeared. She gaped at Talen with wide eyes. In the crook of one arm was a white baby, no more than a few months old, swaddled in cloth likely finer than the woman's best.

"Yes, I'm an elf," Talen said. "Name is Talen. Me and mine are here to get you and yours up north. Look out the window, and you'll see an airship in the fields."

The woman cautiously stepped past Talen and glanced out a window at the back of the house. Her eyes went even wider, and she looked from it to Talen and back a few times.

"You come to set us free?" she asked, tears running down her cheeks.

"You was always free. I'm here to put an end to those who disagreed with that notion."

"That shooting I heard and smoke I smelled?"

"They opposed my argument. Ain't no one left alive in this house but you and that child." Talen spotted a second baby, of an age with the one in the woman's arms, laying in a cot. "Or rather children."

"What about Maddie, Sally, and Thea?" the woman asked, panic in her tone.

"If them the ones downstairs, two women and a younger girl, they got out the back."

The woman closed her eyes and let out a sigh. "Thank you, Jesus."

Talen bristled but didn't think it would be the best time to point out Jesus had sat this one out. "What's your name?" she asked instead.

"Hany," she said.

"Well Hany, my intention is to burn this house to the ground, so we best be on our way. Can you manage the babies on your own?"

"We're taking them with us?" she asked, clearly of a mixed mind on the idea.

Talen couldn't much blame her. If Hany was a wet nurse, it meant she had her own young child or children. That sort of thing could eat at the heart of the kindest sort.

"They didn't choose their parents," Talen said. "We got someone we're taking the children to, but the parents are all going into the ground."

"Suffer unto me the children," Hany said and nodded. "Let me gather some necessaries."

Talen waited, not entirely patiently, as Hany packed a bag with the aforementioned necessaries. While Hany collected the babies, one on each arm, Talen grabbed the bag, grunting against the pain in her shoulder, and they left the house.

Hany only paused long enough to spit at the two corpses on the ground floor.

Those in the field had apparently taken Talen's advice and boarded the Cumulus. Wilfred, clearly less than thrilled to see two babies, simply said he had to adjust his sleeping charms for them.

Meanwhile, the newly freed were tended to, and more than one family was reunited with tears and shouts of joy. Alice, Booker, and Cyrus led a small group to collect anything useful from the house. Talen hardened her heart, reloaded her irons, and then went to see to the obliged and quiet ones still in the field.

Some of the obliged looked savable, but not all. The quiet ones went down, well, quietly. Talen found the stones that controlled them on the overseers. Rather than touching the wretched charms, she dragged those bodies to burn with the others. The quiet ones didn't deserve to be burned with those that'd kept them in bondage, but the world was full of unfairness.

Once the stones and bodies were burning, Talen returned to the Cumulus, climbed onto the top deck, and sat by herself. Not long after, the foraging party returned. As the airship lifted off and headed away, she put a few of fire loads into the house. She watched it catch and the flames slowly swallow it as they sailed away.

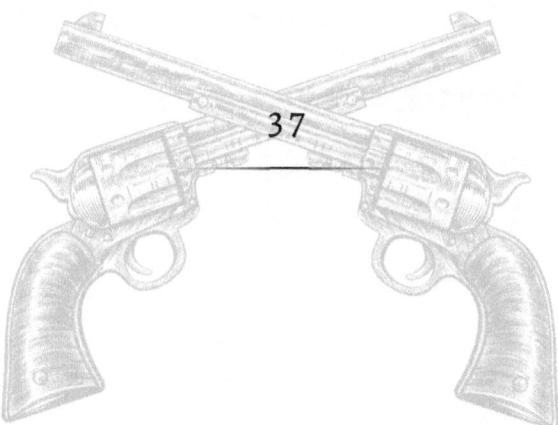

37

Talen tried to convince Draven to pass back over the Perkins house, along with the others they'd cleared out, so she could set them to burning too. Since Perkins had escaped, she didn't see any point in staying secret anymore. Besides, seeing signs of dozens of homes burning could give the impression that an army had come, not just a single airship and handful of fighters.

Draven insisted on bringing Margaret and Wilfred into the conversation. Margaret suggested that Alice, Booker, and Cyrus be included as well. They came up to the bridge once the newly freed had been seen to and settled. It was a tight fit, but they all made do.

Talen made her argument again, and though she dearly wanted to see the place burn, she kept her mind open.

"Just cause Perkins got away don't mean they know we're coming," Alice said. "Could be he'll think Bennfield set the place to burning."

"I don't disagree," said Booker, "but I think there is some merit to making them think there's a regiment of Union soldiers come calling." He chuckled. "Hell, they might just think Sherman himself is leading them, come to do to them what he did to Georgia."

The discussion continued, everyone noting the advantages and limits to each argument. Talen listened, not saying much, just taking in what everyone else had to offer. However, with the fighting done, the pain in her shoulder grew more insistent. She could still use her left arm, but it hurt every time she moved too fast or too much. Not that she could do much about it. Like as not, she wouldn't get a chance to heal until this was done.

"What if we play both cards?" Margaret asked.

Talen came back to herself. "What do you mean?"

"I don't have any military experience, so please correct me if I'm seeing this wrong."

"Go on," Alice said.

"If they're expecting soldiers," Margaret said, "they'll be expecting soldier tactics. Marching forward in ranks, I mean." She pointed to the two plantations on the map. "They're both north of town, so if we burn the cleared farms on the north side of town as well—"

"They'll think that's where the attack is coming from," Alice said. "That's a good idea. They set themselves to receive a charge, and we come in from behind and outflank them."

"Any commander worth the name would at least partially surround the town," Booker said. "Attacking a single point would leave them open to being outflanked themselves. Who'd be fool enough to do that?"

Cyrus laughed. "They'd figure it was just dumb Yankees being dumb. I ain't never met a reb that didn't think they had the best generals, the best strategy, and that they only lost because they didn't have enough guns or supplies."

Alice and Booker both grinned and nodded.

"They surely didn't expect us to fight like we did," Alice said.

"Forrest might be a bastard, but he ain't stupid," Booker said. "If he has any say, they won't just leave their backsides exposed."

"But even then, they'll be expected soldiers marching in formation," Talen said. "We'll be spread out, coming at them from multiple sides. I saw soldiers break and run when they thought they was surrounded, especially when they couldn't see who was shooting."

"We got enough guns to make it seem that way?" Wilfred asked.

"Your specter will cause some anger, confusion, and terror," Talen said. "The folks we got arms to are here." She pointed to a spot on the map on the southwest edge of town. "I can clear a way out for them, which'll give us more guns. Can't say as to how many, but more than we got now."

Alice, Booker, and Cyrus exchanged a knowing look.

"Yeah, about that..." Booker said.

"What?" Talen asked.

"More than a few of those from Bennfield's and Perkins's place want to fight too," Alice said.

"How many is more than a few?" Talen asked.

"Fourteen," Booker said.

"You explain they won't be fighting regular human slavers?" Talen asked. "They understand these are stained and might not go down easy?"

"You think maybe they didn't notice the whole town going stained?" Booker asked.

Talen opened her mouth to explain, but she didn't get the chance.

"Not to mention they were forced to work alongside friends and family bound by not just chains, but magic," Alice said. "In some cases, even brought back from the dead to work. I suspect they understand better than us what we're up against."

Talen winced, and it had nothing to do with the pain in her shoulder. Knowing she'd made a mistake, and that if no one pointed it out, she'd make it again, didn't mean she enjoyed it. "You're right. That was a stupid question. I'm sorry. I weren't thinking."

Alice eyed her, particularly Talen's shoulder. "All that's going on, it's easy to forget the obvious."

Talen didn't want anyone spending worry on her instead of focusing on the task at hand, so she turned her bad shoulder from Alice and faced Draven. "We got enough arms for them?"

"Aye, should have," she said. "We pulled from my stores to supply those in town, but if some don't mind using dwarven rail guns, I expect we can make do. Course, they'll need some instruction on the operation of them."

Alice appeared absolutely giddy. "Sign me up! I'll gladly offer my rifle to someone for a chance to use one of your weapons."

Draven's normally stony expression split into a broad grin.

"If they want to in, I ain't going to say no," Talen said. "This is their fight after all."

"So, we agreed then?" Draven asked.

Everyone looked to each other and nodded.

"Seems so," Talen said and turned to Alice, Booker, and Cyrus. "I'll see to the fires. You see to the volunteers."

"I'll send Frieda up to look at your shoulder," Alice said.

Talen bristled, but winced with the sudden movement. "I'm—"

"You are not fine," Alice said. "A blind man could see you're favoring your right side. I'm guessing you ain't got time to heal."

"Not at the moment, no," Talen said. "But—"

"Then you need to let Frieda see what she can do."

"She's right," Margaret said. "You know how important you are to all this."

Talen looked to Wilfred and Draven for support but found none. As much as she hated feeling like a distraction, or burden, she couldn't offer any legitimate arguments. Instead, she sighed in resignation. "All right, then."

Everyone filed out of the bridge as Draven set her course. Talen went to the front of the ship and loaded her right-hand iron with fire loads. A short while later, Frieda came up with a little bag and started poking and prodding at Talen's shoulder.

Talen winced and tried to pull away, but Frieda pinned her in place with a stare.

"Stop your complaining and let me work," Frieda said.

"Ain't caring for people supposed to include some actual care?"

Frieda arched an eyebrow but continued her exam. "Don't look to be nothing broken," she said, after a few agonizing minutes. "But I suspect you fractured your collarbone and cracked a rib or two. Unfortunately, ain't nothing I can do for that."

"If you'll explain that to the others, I'd see it as a kindness," Talen said, emphasizing the last word.

Frieda narrowed her eyes. "However, the pain you're feeling is probably cause your shoulder ain't seated right. It ain't fully dislocated, but it's out of position."

Talen opened her mouth and then closed it. Hearing it said aloud did seem to describe how it felt. *Damnit.*

"You want something to bite down on?" Frieda asked.

Talen offered her left arm. "Just get it done."

Frieda took hold of Talen's wrist with one hand and used the other to massage at the shoulder joint.

What had been a sharp, but—mostly—manageable, pain grew until Talen had to close her eyes and clench her jaw.

"On three," Frieda said.

Talen nodded.

"One. Two." Frieda pulled on Talen's arm and pushed at the shoulder joint.

"*Terisan ut marrin!*" Talen shouted in pain, surprise, and anger. She glared at Frieda. "That was not very nice."

"I ain't here to be nice."

"Job well done then."

"How's it feel?"

Talen kept glaring with narrowed eyes as she tested her shoulder. The pain had almost entirely vanished, just a lingering soreness, but it didn't seem to hinder her movement. Part of her almost wished it hadn't worked just to spite Frieda.

She gave a half smile. "It's better. Thank you.

Frieda returned exactly the same amount of a smile. "You're welcome." Without another word, she collected her things and turned to leave.

"Harder than dwarven iron," Talen muttered under her breath.

Frieda turned back. "You're damn right I am." She gave Talen a full smile, winked, and left.

Talen shook her head and, despite herself, chuckled.

It didn't take long to get back to the Bennfield place, and Draven brought the Cumulus low enough for Talen to get a couple good shots through the windows. In just a few minutes, flames had swallowed the entire house.

It took most of the rest of the day to travel to the selected farmsteads and set them ablaze. Few burned for more than an hour, so there weren't the columns of smoke reaching into the sky Talen had hoped for, but that didn't diminish her satisfaction.

Draven took the time between torchings to show Alice, Booker, and Cyrus—as well as a few volunteers—how to work the rail guns, but Talen was too lost in her own thoughts to pay much attention to them.

Despite the obliged and quiet ones being ash, they still haunted her. As much as the putrid smell of the corpse rot, and filth of the unwashed living turned her stomach even now, that wasn't the worst of it. Try as she might, she couldn't push away the empty eyes and utterly passive expressions on their faces as she ended them. She'd seen folks beaten so entirely into submission that the fight had all but left them, but even in those cases, a spark remained. Not hope, but, well, "life" was the only word she could think of.

Had seeing that utter emptiness, the complete destruction of the person within, been when her ancestors realized just how far over the line they'd gone? The horrific weight of a such a realization must've been unimaginable.

At the least, it hardened her resolve that whatever the cost, these people needed to be freed, any and all *Malihane Carid* had to be destroyed, and everyone behind it needed to die.

When the last of the houses had been set alight, Draven turned the ship away from town to circle around, well out of sight. As they left, Talen watched the dancing flames, entranced by them. They almost looked, well, alive.

She narrowed her eyes.

More than almost, in fact.

Twilight settled over everything as the sun dipped below the western horizon. The broken clouds turned a color to match the flames, which might be the only reason Talen noticed that the flames had a radiance emanating from them.

Well, obviously. It's fire, and fire gives off light.

But even before she'd finished that thought, Talen knew she had it wrong. This wasn't regular firelight; it was the glow of magic. She looked closer, just in case she might be imagining it.

She wasn't.

It had to be some lingering effect from the spell loads she'd used to start the fires.

Right?

As a warmth started spreading through Talen's belly, focused around the crystal, she noticed the radiance spreading to the land surrounding the house, well beyond where the firelight should be able to reach. She couldn't help but imagine the two had to be connected in some way beyond both being magic.

Could the fire be alive? Like an elemental, but cleansing the corruption rather than trapping it? After all, she'd used fire to destroy the stained charms and other foulness but... She touched the crystal in her belly, and couldn't help but wonder what she wasn't seeing, or understanding, or both.

"Hell, that's a list long enough to take the rest of my life to get through half of," she said to herself and tucked the questions away as something to ask her mother next time she prayed. There were more important things to focus on just now.

Having well over a hundred new passengers—not counting the sleeping children—had the Cumulus stretched to its comfortable limit, but the recently-freed folk insisted on helping out and lightening the load.

When Talen went below to find Wilfred, Margaret, Alice, and the

331

others, the obvious sense of community that had manifested in the hold renewed her hope. Even Maggie helped out, running food to people. Talen wouldn't go so far as to say the Black passengers had welcomed her, but neither did they seem to be shunning her. Cautious was probably a better term, which Talen understood, and she reckoned Maggie did too.

Talen found Alice and the others and gathered them to meet in the galley. Draven joined after settling the ship well away from town.

"I'm guessing we're going to hit the town at first light?" Booker asked.

"Can't wait that long," Talen said. "We got to do it tonight."

"You know we can't see in the dark like you, right?" Booker asked.

"And I suppose when you ran, you did it at noon?" Alice asked him.

"I knew the terrain when I ran. And avoiding catchers isn't quite the same as having a shoot-out."

"They'll be expecting us in the morning," Talen said. "That's when an army would attack. If we're going to win this, we can't make it a stand-up fight, and we damned sure ain't going to let it be anywhere near a fair fight. That means catching them when they ain't ready."

"Didn't you say they had patrols when you went to see Delia's mama?" Cyrus asked.

"I did," Talen said. "But most of the town was, and hopefully will be, sleeping. Even if they expect us to come during the night, it'll take time to gather together and react. That chaos will give us the edge."

"Won't there also be torches set up so as to see anyone coming?" Cyrus asked.

"Just like them, you're thinking like a soldier," Talen said. "Soldiers would be marching into town down the main road. We'll be coming at them from the woods and the shadows."

"Which means they'll be the ones those torches are making visible, not us," Wilfred said.

"So I understand," Booker said. "They'll be expecting us to come up the main road, so they'll likely have it covered with torches. And since they need to see where they're going, they'll be carrying some as well. But we won't be coming in from the main road, we'll be coming in from the woods, where's it dark and we can't be seen. But we'll be able to see them, from behind the cover of the trees."

"Exactly," Talen said. "And if they do come after you, they'll need time for their eyes to adjust from torchlight to moonlight. We can't do nothing they'll expect. This is already like to be a hard and brutal fight. We need to use anything and everything we can against them."

Alice chuckled. "Well, we got experience running through the woods and wilds under cover of night. It'll be a nice change to be shooting back." She nodded. "I think it could work."

"Don't look as if there'll be much cloud cover," Draven said. "Three-quarter-moon ain't as good as full, but it'll help."

"And white faces do shine brighter in moonlight," Alice said, grinning.

"It ain't a perfect plan," Talen said, "but I think it's the best option. If any of you got a better one, I'm open to hear it."

No one said anything.

"All right then, let's get into the details," Talen said. "I'll go in first and make sure Etty's folk got a way out. When that's done I'll set to bleeding the town's numbers down best I can. While I'm doing that, you all get yourselves into good firing positions behind cover. When I loose Wilfred's specter, that'll be the signal to open up. That'll let Etty know it's time to rise up and strike from the inside."

"It's like to be a bloody night," Booker said.

"We knew that when we stepped on board," Alice said. "There ain't no one taking up a rifle who don't know how it might end. Like Moses used to say. There was one of two things I had a right to: liberty or death. If I could not have one, I would have the other."

"What if something goes wrong, and we don't see the specter?" Cyrus asked.

"Then things went terrible bad," Talen said. "Get back to the Cumulus, and get out with everyone you can."

The weight of their stares nearly buckled Talen's knees.

"I'll see to myself," she said. "I ain't going down quiet or alone. There's a whole mess of folk on board counting on you to get them north."

No one seemed pleased with that, but they knew there was no way to argue against it.

"Um," Margaret said, "what about the passengers? Will they be safe through all this?"

"You, Draven, and the Cumulus will be outside the fray," Talen said. "No need to risk innocents by getting them into the line of fire."

"Are you trying to get me to slap you?" Draven asked.

Talen turned, unsure she'd heard correctly. At first, she thought Draven must be joking to lighten the mood, but her expression made it clear that wasn't the case.

"Beg pardon?" Talen said. "I didn't mean no—"

"The hull of this ship is twenty-four inches," Draven said. "It's made of old oak, with layers of dwarven steel between. I've run through blockades, faced down cannon fire, and entire regiments worth of rifles. I damn sure wouldn't have done none of it with people in the hold if I weren't absolutely sure they'd be safe."

Talen had rarely seen Draven this riled, and she did not enjoy being on the receiving end. She lifted her hands. "I apologize. I didn't mean to suggest—"

"You know your business. I know mine," Draven said. "I always have and will defer to you in matters you know best. I'd hoped you'd show me the same. No one knows this ship like I do, so kindly don't presume."

A very long, heavy silence filled the room. At least it felt long. Only Wilfred would meet Talen's eyes, and he was grinning.

"You're right," Talen said. "You know I didn't mean no offense. I was just thinking it best to keep those below well clear of danger. Sorry for my presumption and overstepping. You know I got nothing but love and respect for you."

Draven's expression softened. "I do, and I didn't mean to turn so gruff, but I get mighty protective of my Cumulus."

"Rightly so," Talen said.

"And you know I love and respect you too," Draven said.

"I do—"

"So, respectfully," Draven said, "you need to pull your head from your ass."

Wilfred laughed, but quickly stifled it and covered his mouth.

Alice looked ready to join him.

Booker and Cyrus didn't seem to know how to react.

Margaret's eyes were the size of dinner plates as she stared at Draven.

"I, um," Talen said, trying like hell to figure out how to reply to that. "Beg pardon?"

"You're damned good at what you do," Draven said. "But you don't know nothing about fighting from the air."

That's when Talen finally understood, and she wanted to kick herself for taking so long to get there. She'd gotten so used to taking charge, to her friends deferring to her, that she'd stopped discussing and just fallen to giving orders.

"You're right," Talen said. "What do you think will be the best use of the Cumulus?"

A small smile settled on the very edges of Draven's mouth. "Unless they got a twenty-four pounder or better, anything they fire at us will bounce away. My girl won't even get more than a little singed from explosive shells." Her smile grew. "Guns like that weren't common for the slavers during the war. I don't suspect even General Forrest could get one for this little town now."

Talen had seen artillery splinter trees well over twenty-four inches, and though it didn't sound right to her, she trusted Draven. When it came to airships, she'd forgotten more than Talen would ever know.

"You saying you want to lend some support from above?" Talen asked.

Draven nodded. "This ain't a gunship, but we get a dozen rifles on deck, I think we can add to the disarray." She looked to Alice, Booker, and Cyrus. "If one or two of you would join them with my rail guns, it would count for double."

Talen didn't like the idea of fewer guns on the ground, but if she trusted Draven. If her friend thought it could make that much a difference, Talen wouldn't argue. "I'll leave it to you."

"For my part," Alice said, "I prefer my feet on the ground when I'm fighting."

"I'll do it," Cyrus said.

All attention went to Booker.

"Feels a bit like a coward's path to stay on board," he said.

"You saying I'm a coward?" Cyrus asked.

"I know all too well that you aren't," Booker said. "I'm not even saying my feelings on it are correct, just how it sits."

"Those on board will be the volunteers," Talen said. "Reckon most of them ain't been in a battle before. Hell, most probably ain't even fired a weapon. Might do some good to have you both here to encourage and help when needed."

Booker seemed unsure but after a moment, nodded. "Suppose there's wisdom to that."

"I could do it," Margaret said.

Booker turned to her, brows drawn together.

"I certainly won't do any good on the ground," Margaret said. "But I've had some practice with the rail gun. If I'll be on board anyway, might as well be of the most use I can be."

Talen gave Booker and Cyrus a hard look, daring them to argue.

"I got no problem with that," Cyrus said.

"Me neither," Booker said.

"All right. that's the plan then," Talen said. She almost told Draven that if things went badly, or it turned out there was artillery, to get the innocent people on board to safety, but she resisted. Draven wouldn't do anything to put those in her charge at risk, and suggesting otherwise would be insulting. Instead, she said to Alice, Cyrus, and Booker, "would you three go below and let the volunteers know the plan? I'll meet with everyone before we head out."

They nodded.

"Guess we should get some food and sleep while we can," Cyrus said. He and his companions got up and left the galley.

Once they were gone, Talen went to Draven. "I'm truly sorry—"

"I didn't mean to snap—" Draven said at the same time.

They both smiled.

"Let's just admit we both got a lot on our minds," Talen said.

"That is a fact. Even so, I shouldn't have taken that tone with you."

Talen laughed. "Oh, I had it coming. I was an ass, and you were right not to stand for it."

"I don't know if I'd say you were an ass," Margaret said.

"I would," Wilfred said.

Margaret gave his shoulder a playful slap.

"I'm a bit surprised you weren't the one to speak up," Talen said, smiling a little herself.

"Don't seem right to never let anyone else have some fun," he said.

Despite his best attempts to keep the mood light, a heavy silence settled on them and stayed for a long moment.

"We can do this," Talen said, finally. "It ain't going to be easy, and fact is, not everyone will see the other side of this fight. But when the dust settles, this town will be no more, the man behind it'll be dead, and a whole lot of people will be free."

No one else said anything, but Wilfred pulled everyone into a hug, and really, Talen couldn't think of any words better than that.

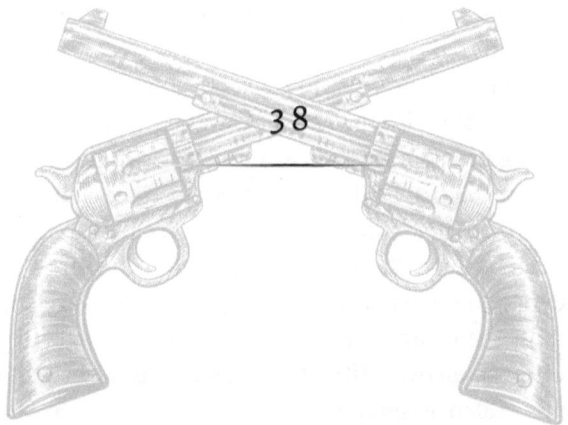

38

Talen stayed with Gaoth and, ironically, slept soundly. It'd always been that way. Knowing a fight, especially a big one, was coming seemed to lift the regrets, shame, and weight of her past. Or maybe it was just the only time she could put things in a larger context and her concerns seemed so small. Whichever the case, she slept hard.

A few hours later, she woke on her own, ready for whatever may come. The living with the aftermath was always a different matter.

Gaoth sensed what was coming, and he rose with her, ready to carry her into the very depths of hell if need be. She caressed his cheek, kissed between his eyes, and hugged him.

He pressed his head against her.

She took a moment to glance out the porthole and watch the darkened landscape drift by. In the pale moon light, the foulness soaked into the land roiled almost imperceptibly slow, like a filthy, slumbering nightmare. A false sense of peace that would soon be shattered, hopefully for good.

After giving Gaoth another caress between his eyes, Talen turned and left the stables. Much of the ship still slept, so she moved quietly through the wan light cast by Draven's flameless lamps. A few restless souls sat on the cots, or stood near loved ones. Those who looked up exchanged a silent nod with Talen.

When she returned to her cabin, she set to cleaning and then loading her spell irons. A single starburst load amid force in the left-hand iron, all force and a lone fire load in the right. It was like a ritual for her, each movement deliberate, meditative: pulling on her belt, cinching it, fastening it, holstering her irons, and slipping on her coat. She filled her pockets, each with a different load. Lastly, she sharpened her knives, and sheathed them. The familiar, numb sort of calm before just about every battle settled over her.

Armed and armored, she went to rouse the others.

Draven was, no surprise, awake and waiting. With the exception of Alice, everyone else looked tired. It was a surprise to see that none of the freed men and women who'd volunteered to fight had changed their minds. It wasn't that she doubted their courage; they faced daily horrors most would run from. Rather, with freedom finally achieved, she would've understood not wanting to risk it now, at the very end.

Instead, nine men and five women, ranging in age from perhaps twenty to probably well over fifty, stood as ready as they could be.

"You scared?" Talen asked them.

They hesitated at first but all nodded.

"Me too," she said.

Just about every set of eyes narrowed.

"Only a fool ain't scared when going into a fight," she said. "So long as you don't let it weigh you down, fear will keep you alive. It'll stop you from doing something stupid. Courage ain't about having no fear. It's doing the thing in spite of fear."

They all looked a bit more at ease.

"That's about as inspiring as this'll get," Talen said. "Don't matter if you'll be on deck or on the ground, you'll have good, smart folk with you. Listen to them. They won't steer you wrong." She took a slow breath. "I ain't got to tell you these are stained. They'll brush off a hit than would drop a normal human, but that don't mean they can't be killed." She tapped her forehead and then her heart. "Hit 'em here or here, and they'll go down, but don't hesitate to shoot them a few more times to make sure."

"What if we run out of bullets?" a younger man asked.

"That's up to you," Talen said. "Hopefully, by then, there'll be plenty of dead with guns you can take up if you're so inclined. If you can't get to one, a rifle butt does make a mighty fine club and will split a skull." She looked from one of them to another. "You all volunteered to be here, and I'm a mite grateful. But, if you step out there, you got to be ready to stay 'til the end." She gave them a moment. "Won't no one call you coward if you decide to walk away now. But you step off this ship, ain't no walking away. You hear me?"

A few nods.

"I need you to say it," Talen said. "And so do you."

They all straightened and said, "I hear you."

"Those of you on the ship," Talen said, "you take your lead from Margaret and Draven. They know better than me what you need to do, so mind what they say."

More nods and "yes ma'am's."

"How far out?" Talen asked Draven.

"Twenty minutes," she said.

"All right," Talen said before turning back to the group. "Say what you need to those you need to say it to."

The group broke up and hurried off.

Talen stepped closer to Margaret and Draven. The former looked more than a little unsure. "You're ready for this," she said. "I trust you." She turned to Draven. "Both of you."

They exchanged hugs and went their separate ways.

Alice and Wilfred waited for Talen at the gangway.

"You ready?" she asked them.

"You know I ain't the sort to not say what's on my mind," Wilfred said. "I already done said what needed saying."

Alice nodded. "Despite appearing the delicate flower, tied to propriety, I'm actually much the same."

Talen openly laughed. Wilfred and Alice joined her.

"After you then, madame." Talen, still chuckling, motioned forward.

"I believe she was speaking to you," Alice said to Wilfred.

"She was indeed," Wilfred said and led the way.

———

The Cumulus set down in a clearing a couple miles from town. Talen and Gaoth set out first, winding through the woods as Wilfred and Alice led the volunteers. The moon and stars shone bright and clear in the cool night sky. A mile outside of town, Talen slid from the saddle and walked Gaoth, mindful of every step. Thankfully, the soft earth swallowed his hoof beats, and they proceeded in relative silence.

At a point about half a mile out, she found a spot for him to wait. He'd be close enough to come running if need be, but not so close that anyone might spot him either from town or the road.

"Wish me luck, old friend," Talen whispered.

Gaoth didn't make a sound, just pressed his head to her shoulder.

She stroked his face, kissed between his eyes, wrapped herself in shadow, and set out.

The stench of the town—shit and human sweat rather than stained—steadily grew. Before long, the light of torches could be seen in the distance. All was still and silent, just the buzzing of insects. Talen moved slow and cautious, keeping an ear open for hoofbeats or humans talking.

Nothing.

She'd been expecting it to be relatively quiet, but also that there'd be some out and about making readying for an impending attack. But this level of stillness unsettled her. It wouldn't be the first time she'd come across humans so confident and arrogant they didn't keep a proper defense. All the same, she didn't feel the need to make any dangerous assumptions.

As she crept along the edge of the town, something about the torches chewed on a corner of her brain. The flickering orange glow looked normal enough, but at the edges, it seemed to swallow the pale moonlight around it. A closer inspection revealed them to be magical. She'd come across ensorcelled torches, crafted to burn through the night, plenty of times before. However, these carried a tinge of corruption. They didn't feel stained, as such, but they damn sure weren't pure magic.

Talen might be a caster, but she did know that a stained crafter could taint their wares so even simple magics carried some corruption. These didn't feel like that though. More like something between being made of filth, and just carrying the grimy prints of being handled by soiled hands.

The how or why of it eluded here. But, as she had neither the time nor inclination to think about it further, she just continued on to her first destination.

All the buildings, mostly the businesses you'd find in any town, sat empty as the streets, and—like the few homes around them—entirely dark.

As she approached the walled section where Etty and the other "free" Black folk lived, Talen finally heard hoofbeats. Two horses walking slow and easy, heading away from her.

The presence of sentries should've put her more on edge, and it did a bit, but it also eased her mind. The utter quiet and emptiness had started to feel like a trap. As if the town lay in wait for her and the others to arrive, but that didn't seem to be the case.

Still in shadows, Talen glanced around and made for the locked gate.

Talen never had much need for lockpicking before the Cumulus. If a lock needed opening, she'd just bash it. Draven and Wilfred had since convinced her that, sometimes, a more subtle approach served better.

Thankfully, she wouldn't have to tell either of them that they'd been right. A ring with a single key hung from metal peg set in the wall. Talen almost felt insulted but knew best not to curse good luck, especially in the form of an enemy's idiocy.

Thanks to regular use, the lock worked smooth and, mostly, silent. Exposure to the elements rusted the iron just enough that it didn't fall open. Talen left it open and in place so, to a casual glance, it would still appear locked tight.

Hopefully Etty would get close enough to see the truth.

That done, Talen set out to find the sentries. They seemed to keep the wall on their left, counter-clockwise Margaret would call it, so Talen did the same to ensure she'd come up from behind.

It didn't take long. After rounding the second corner, she spotted two men on horseback halfway down. They wore all in white, even the horses, which seemed an odd choice. The matching, tall, pointed, white hoods only made them look more ridiculous. As they rode, the miasma of corruption around them licked at the air, as if drinking in light.

She drew both spell irons and followed, keeping far enough back so as not to upset the horses, but close enough to be in range.

They rounded another corner and made their way along the front, taking them right past the now-unlocked gate. Talen readied herself to strike if either of them noticed. She'd prefer to take them out on the opposite side, farthest from town, but she might not get the option.

Neither so much as glanced over. They just kept yammering and riding.

Minutes dragged by, and Talen had to fight her impatience. If she didn't know better, she'd say the bastards had slowed their pace.

When, at long last, they rounded to the back of the walled area, Talen readied herself to strike.

"Hold up, I got to piss," one of the men said, bringing his horse to a stop.

"Yeah, me too," the other said.

They slid from their saddles and headed into the woods.

Talen holstered her irons, drew one of her knives, and closed in.

The two dead men found a tree a dozen or so paces from each other, and seemed to actually check to make sure they couldn't see each other.

Human stupidity.

As soon as the sigh of relief passed the first man's lips, Talen stepped up behind him. She covered his mouth with her right hand, pulled his head hard to the left, and drove her blade up into the base of his skull.

He convulsed a little as she twisted and turned the knife, scrambling his addled brains. An instant later, he went silent and limp as a rag doll.

"You all right?" the soon-to-be-dead-man-number-two asked, but pointedly didn't look over.

His seeming need to avoid seeing his friend's penis at any cost just made it easier for Talen. She didn't waste any time and took him down the same way as his friend.

To keep the bodies out of sight, she hefted them one at a time—dragging could cause too much noise—and hauled them deeper into the woods.

As she set down the second body, his eyes twitched and darted around. While it wasn't unheard of for corpses to move some, Talen didn't want to risk having to kill these two again. To be sure, she drove her knife between their ribs and shredded their hearts. Satisfied they'd stay dead, she set to the horses, unsaddling and them sending them off on their own, suggesting they might find others to run with to the east.

They galloped off happily, and Talen tossed the saddles into the trees. As she turned to leave, the nagging worry that these two might just get up again returned and ate at the edges of her brain. To relieve it, she went back to the corpses and spent a few minutes removing the heads. She could've put a force load into them. She had planned on shooting them to begin with, but while the shot wouldn't be as loud as a mundane shooter, neither would it be as quiet as blades.

With that grisly work done, Talen hurried back to town, keeping to the shadows the whole way. The town still slept, and the streets remained quiet which made Talen wonder if maybe they'd overestimated the number of stained they'd have to fight.

Like I ever been that lucky.

The town might be small, but it had more than its share of businesses: bank, blacksmith, miller, dry goods, stables, and the like. Safe to assume, except for the bank, those who operated the businesses lived above them. However, the biggest threat remained the knights and the general. Of course, she couldn't know for sure, but Talen figured it unlikely Forrest would stay at a saloon. Like as not, he'd be invited to stay at one of the bigger houses near town. His men, however, would be a different matter.

Before checking the saloons, Talen made for the stables to stop any calvary charges or quick escapes before they happened. Inside she found a couple dozen horses in open stalls. All horses happily and eagerly ran off almost before she'd finished telling them they'd find a herd to run with not far from town.

The recent rain had the ground softened, and muffled the hoofbeats quite a bit, but not entirely. Talen crouched low and watched for anyone to come running.

A man in a nightshirt emerged from the small house attached to the stables, lantern in one hand, a mundane revolver in the other. When he saw the horses gone, he hurried out to the street after them. As he opened his mouth to shout, Talen attacked.

Like she did with the others, Talen took him from behind, driving her knee into the back of his and covering his mouth with her hand. He went down, dropping the lantern, which shattered and made a puddle of burning oil, the acrid smell burning her nose. Talen drove the man to the ground, smothering the fire with his body, and made to drive her knife into his skull.

He kicked and twisted, trying to get her off his back, his screams and shouts muffled against her hand.

The bastard managed to pivot at the last minute, and Talen only succeeded in stabbing at his neck.

He bit down on her hand, his teeth tearing into the meat.

She snatched it away, hissing through a clenched jaw. A rush of unbridled fury burned away the last of her patience. She punched the back of his head, several times.

His face slammed into the ground with a satisfying crunch.

She shifted her weight and drove one knee into his neck, the other at the small of his back, robbing him of any leverage.

He tried to get his hands under himself to push off, but all he could do was wriggle and shift like a landed fish.

Though his furious but impotent squirming delighted Talen, she knew enough time had been wasted on this filth. She drove her knife into his back.

The man gasped and twitched as she buried the knife in him over and over, giving a pull and twist with each thrust.

Finally, after what felt like several minutes, he went quiet and still.

Talen glanced around to see if anyone had heard anything, but the night was quiet as before, the hoofbeats of the fleeing horses now too distant to hear.

Furious at the time wasted putting down a single stained, Talen cursed him under her breath. She drove the knife into his skull, scrambled his brains, and then wiped the blade clean on his night shirt. Unfortunately, it offered little satisfaction, and didn't get any of the squandered minutes back. Refocusing on the larger plans, she dragged the body inside the stables.

Any other time, scrambled brains would be enough to believe a dead man stayed dead. However, this being Aspen Hill, she didn't feel like taking chances. She grabbed a multi-pronged pitchfork and plunged it through his neck and into the ground. Not as certain as taking his head, but less messy and time consuming. Even if he did somehow come back, he wouldn't be getting up without help.

Another glance outside told her no one else had come running, so she spared a precious few seconds to consider her options. She'd planned on taking down any sentries or defenders that happened to be out and about, but there weren't none. Likewise, she'd intended to clear a path for Etty and her folk, but empty streets didn't need clearing.

The church seemed the next obvious choice. According to Margaret and them, preachers typically lived in their churches, and the size of this one looked to offer more living space than most of the homes. Even if Thompson could be found there though, Talen didn't think that the best way to go just yet.

Normally, killing the leader would cause at least some of their followers to turn and run. But these followers were stained. There weren't no reason to expect this snake to die if she cut off the head. Add to that, she didn't expect he'd go down easy. So far, they'd been lucky. No one had proved any tougher than any other stained. But her tussle with Elizabeth Tuller had taught Talen that some stained went down a hell of a lot harder than other. If anyone is this town proved to be that sort, Talen's figured it'd be the preacher.

The answer seemed simple enough then. Best to take out the underlings first. Cut off as many claws as possible, then go after the head. Fewer guns on their side meant more on hers could be brought to bear.

Likewise, as much as she'd enjoy killing Forrest, the stable hand showed how much effort could be required to take out a just one man.

Add to that, she had no idea where to find him, and no time to search him out.

Though possible, Talen didn't think it likely Forrest, if stained at all, would be like Tuller. Her gut told her that if there wouldn't be more than one dark caster in town. She couldn't imagine that sort sharing power. Stained didn't have allies, they had underlings or potential threats.

As such, Talen turned her attention to the two saloons. Both had three floors, though one was half again as big as the other. Any whores on staff would likely be set up on the second floor, the third being exclusive for boarders. A quick once-over told her neither place would be big enough to put up all of Forrest's knights, which meant she'd need to clear both.

Neither had any lights burning, not even in any of the upper floor windows, so she decided to start with the larger of the two.

The front door was unlocked, but Talen decided to peer in the windows first. It appeared much like any other saloon she'd ever seen, though dark and empty. However, she dismissed the idea of going in that way straight off. The old boards that made up the floor would almost certainly creak and groan with every step. Even if they didn't make enough noise to rouse anyone, the stairs looked even worse. Thankfully, both saloons had a sizeable wooden awning running the length of the building.

By standing on the hitching posts outside, Talen managed to pull herself up. She crept to the nearest window and peered inside. To her surprise, a man slept in the bed. The window didn't open as easy as she'd hoped, so she went to another, and then another.

On the fourth try she found one that would screech like a stuck pig when forced open. It didn't open silently, but neither did it beat the snores of the stained man sleeping on the other side of the room.

A gray uniform jacket and leather holster embossed with "CSA" were tossed on a nearby chair. A white robe and pointed hood hanging up on one wall further confirmed him as one of Forrest's boys. Her fingers itched with anticipation as she drew her knife.

She approached the sleeping filth, keeping close to the wall to lower the chance of a creaking floorboard. As if inviting her to end him, the stained slept on his stomach, head turned away from the window.

In one swift movement, Talen pressed his face into the pillow with one hand, both to quash any sound he might make and also hold him still, and used her blade to mince his brains.

He gasped and jerked, and then went still. As a precaution, she stabbed him through the heart too. Unfortunately, she wouldn't have the time to be this thorough with everyone. The idea of leaving anyone not less than entirely, undoubtedly, dead filled her with more than a little unease. Unfortunately, she didn't have any other options.

Or did she?

Bet these building sure would burn pretty.

She smiled at the mental image. She just needed to check for innocents before setting the places ablaze.

Creeping from one room to another, never slipping from her shadow cloak, Talen butchered every stained in their sleep. A dozen men—ten of which carried confederate regalia—and four women, died quick and quiet. A cleaner death than any of them deserved.

After clearing the saloon, she checked out back, just be safe. She found a rickety shack, and two young Black men sleeping in it. No chains held them, so Talen just let them be. She did, however, leave a couple of pilfered revolvers nearby. It'd be up to them if they wanted to run or fight. Either way, a shooter would come in mighty handy.

Based on the night sky, Talen had burned near an hour so far. That meant, hopefully, Wilfred, Alice, and the volunteers sat ready to attack, just waiting for the signal. She debated going and finding them before moving to the second saloon, but decided it best to keep bleeding the town for as long as possible. She trusted Wilfred and Alice to keep everyone calm and patient.

Getting into the second saloon proved easier than the first. Apparently, those staying there preferred to sleep with their windows open. Hopefully, the fact they slept through the fleeing horses and the stable hand's death meant they'd just keep sleeping.

The first two stained—both men, but only one had the white robe—went quiet and easy. Talen started to wonder if she might be able to just kill off the whole town on her own.

Careful now, over-confidence will just make you sloppy, she said to herself.

The open windows seemed a safer option than walking the halls, so Talen slipped out the way she'd come, went to the next room, and slid inside. Knife at the ready, she crept toward the stained. This one slept on his back, so Talen couldn't just ragdoll him like the others. It'd take a lot of force, and accuracy, to puncture a skull from the front with a knife. She could go through an eye, but even that might not kill him right away. Hell, her blade could just easily deflect and do nothing more than cut open his face.

She eyeballed where his heart would be and stepped to the bed.

The floor creaked, barely audible.

The would-be corpse opened his eyes, one of which was a carefully carved and polished blue stone.

Talen's blood ran cold and her heart skipped a couple of beats. She drove the knife down.

He shifted at the last second.

The blade sank into his shoulder, all the way to the hilt.

"Ah! You leafer bitch!" He slid back from her, drew a spell iron from under his pillow, and lit it up with red spellfire.

Talen pivoted, grabbed his right wrist, drove it down against the bed, and slammed an elbow into his face.

His head snapped back, and a blast of force spat from his iron.

A sizeable section of the wall, including the window Talen had come through, became a cloud of splinters and glass that rained down on the street below.

Shit. Ain't likely anyone is sleeping through that.

He punched at her with his left hand.

The knife in his shoulder reduced it to little more than a love tap, and Talen shook it off. Driven by a renewed sense of urgency, she shifted her hips, straightened her left arm, and put all her weight on his wrist.

It snapped with a deeply gratifying, wet crack.

He let out a shriek as the now dark spell iron clattered to the floor.

Shouts of surprise sounded through the door as the rest of the saloon, and maybe the entire damn town, woke.

The quiet part of her endeavor having come to an end, Talen stood and yanked the stained from his bed by the broken wrist, eliciting another scream. At the same time, she drew her right-hand iron and fired a force load into his face.

He went still and silent as the magic transformed his head to a wet, pulpy mess, and cracked several floorboards.

As she rolled her iron to a fresh cylinder, Talen noticed the blood-soaked, red, leather glove on a chair. She took half a heartbeat to delight in one less Red Hand in the world, drew her knife from the corpse, and took aim at the door.

At least half a dozen voices shouted over each other from the other side. The moment the knob turned, she turned away, covered her face with her arm, and pulled the trigger.

Men screamed and wood snapped.

347

Half a heartbeat later, she looked back. The wall around the now-empty doorway, the floor outside, and the wall across the hall, all burned. Smoke began to fill the building as the fire spread quickly.

Talen doused her iron, stepped into shadow, and leapt through the hole where the window had been.

Mundane bullets and a force blast followed her but missed.

She rolled down the overhang and fell to the ground below, landing on her hands and feet. Not waiting on ceremony, she sheathed her knife, drew her left-hand iron, and stepped from shadows. Both irons lit with blue spellfire, and she loosed the last fire load from her right-hand iron into the second saloon. The two from her left-hand iron went into the first.

The magical flames latched onto the wood and spread quickly.

She doused her irons, slipped back into the shadows, and ran just as two stained came onto the overhang and opened fire. Ducking around the side of the bank, she replaced her spent loads, made sure Wilfred's charm was still in her pocket, and readied herself for a fight.

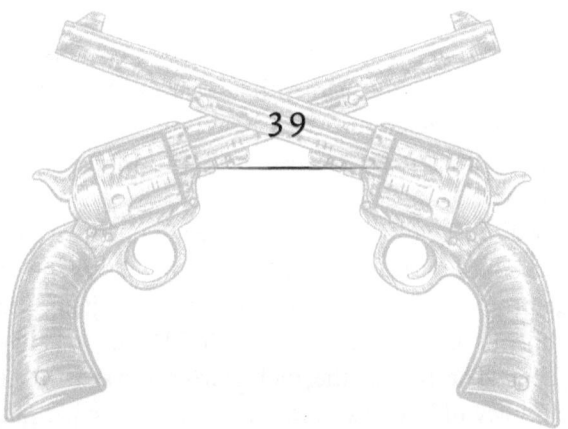

39

Thankfully no one came running out of the larger saloon, though she hoped the two young men had made it to the woods. However, a dozen men and a few women came out the smaller saloon in various stages of undress, all of them armed. Most burst from the front doors, some tumbled from windows onto the street, and a few emerged with clothes or body parts on fire.

Talen stepped from the shadows and took aim. Only when she knew the shot would count did she pour magic into her irons and fire.

One stained reeled as his head snapped back and a spray of red spattered those nearby. Another took a force blast to the chest and tumbled backward. He flopped on the ground, but Talen knew he wouldn't stay down for long.

She doused her iron and ducked behind cover as a hail of bullets peppered the building. Thankfully, the banker had built it from stone instead of wood. Chips and chunks flew, none hitting her.

As staying in one place would be a sure-fire way to get killed, Talen stepped back into the shadows and sprinted behind the building to find a new firing position. She'd missed the smell of the blood-soaked leather glove in that last room and stumbled on a Red Hand with an eyepiece. No telling how many others did too. As such, despite being wrapped in shadow, she kept away from the main street.

Before long, shouts and calls of alarm sounded from the surrounding buildings. It quickly became obvious she needed to get to, literal, higher ground. She jumped, grabbed hold of the roof of the dry goods store, and hauled herself up. Crouching low, she crept toward the front of the building, glanced over the street, and pulled Wilfred's charm from her coat pocket.

People came from seemingly every direction in response to the shouts and shots, filling the square. More than one opened fire on a fellow stained before being chided and shot in return. When the exchange of gunfire quieted, neither party seemed to have suffered anything worse than a mosquito bite.

Soon a crowd of fifty or sixty had gathered in the town square. It took a bit, and more gunfire, before word of the night's events had spread. Though some proclaimed the burning saloons God's justice for allowing such establishments in town, a handful—Red Hands mostly—did set to fighting the fires. The rest of the mob started toward the church. The moral inconsistency of humans never ceased to amaze her. Slavery, rape, murder, all perfectly acceptable, but alcohol...

Talen focused on breathing slow and steady. Fear tried to addle her brain, but she stayed focused on Etty, and all those who needed help. It might be she wouldn't live to the morning, but she'd make damn sure scores of stained dropped before she did.

Gunfire erupted from the darkness, and Talen flinched back a bit.

Dozens of stained jerked, spun, and fell as bullets tore through them. More than a few heads snapped to one side and exploded out, spraying gore on everyone nearby. Unfortunately, most of the others stumbled and staggered for a moment before running to find cover.

An almost silent *whoomp* sounded, and the head of the lead Red Hand stained vanished in a cloud of crimson mist.

That sent the other Red Hands diving for cover, and the stained started returning fire into the darkened woods.

Talen's stomach twisted, and she cursed under her breath as more and more stained got back to their feet and joined the fight. For every one that fell headless, three got back up.

She'd hoped to save Wilfred's charm until the preacher, or Forrest, had made an appearance, but she couldn't wait that long. Even with cover, Alice, Wilfred, and those with them, couldn't hold out against a prolonged barrage.

Admitting the plan had breathed its last, she ducked, slipped from the shadows, and inserted spell loads into the holes of Wilfred's specter charm. Tapping into the crystal in her belly, Talen poured magic into the crafting. After a slow three count, she popped up, hurled the stone into the middle of the square, turned away, and closed her eyes.

A couple seconds later, the street filled with the sound of a disembodied chorus. Barely audible under the gunfire at first, but the singing grew in volume until it drowned out the shooting.

Glory, Glory, Hallelujah
Glory, Glory, Hallelujah
His soul goes marching on
John Brown's body lies a-moldering in the grave
John Brown's body lies a-moldering in the grave
John Brown's body lies a-moldering in the grave
But his soul goes marching on

The gunfire ceased and, as Talen hoped, all eyes turned to the center of the square.

All but her allies in the woods, that is.

A flash of pure white light erupted, burning away the night like a dozen lightning strikes. Even with closed eyes, Talen winced.

Cries of anger and surprise sounded from the square, and a few stray shots went off.

When the light faded, Talen opened her eyes and peeked over the edge of the roof. Her jaw dropped, and she could only stare in complete awe.

The ghostly visage of a tall, lanky human man manifested, at first as if made of mist, but quickly solidifying. He held a spell iron in his right hand, a pike in his left, and scowled as he looked around. His mane of gray-streaked hair was only outdone by his long gray beard, his eyes burning with blue fire, and the massive feathered wings at his back.

"My name," this visage shouted above the continued singing, "is John Brown!"

Finally regaining her senses, Talen couldn't keep from chucking. "Damn, Wilfred. You don't do by half."

"I am returned as the righteous hand of God!" Brown took aim with his ghostly spell iron. "I will strike down all the wretched, slaver filth, and send your souls to Perdition!"

"It's a trick!" someone shouted.

Gunfire erupted, and Brown bared his teeth.

Talen didn't know for sure if the ghost reacted to the gunfire, or the timing just worked out, but it didn't matter. It sent shivers down her spine and despite just being a crafted apparition, her own righteous indignation rose to meet Brown's.

The runes on his spell iron lit up, and three blue spheres of power shot from it.

Actually, they came from the ground at his feet, but it happened so fast it would've been hard to see the truth of it.

They hit a building and exploded in a shower of sparks. The detonation sent stained reeling through the air. They screamed as the burning stars seared through clothing and flesh.

Brown turned and fired again and again, sending blasts of force, fire, ice, and lightning in all directions.

Talen had no idea how Wilfred had worked it, but none of the shots went into the woods. Every single one hit a building or house.

Including, unfortunately, the dry goods shop.

Talen barely managed to reach the far side of the building before a gout of flame washed over it. She jumped and hit the ground in a roll.

"I condemn your rotting souls to hell is his holy name!" Brown said.

A fresh barrage erupted from the woods, as the stained cowered and ran for sturdier cover.

Some just flat out bolted, deciding they wanted no part of this fight.

"Repent and accept his holy judgement!" Brown shouted.

Talen took full advantage of the chaos. Wrapped in shadow, she drew her left-hand iron and made for a cluster of half a dozen Red Hands near the bank.

Fear kept trying to make its way up her spine, but it didn't stand a chance against her burning fury. Add to that, plenty fought without the protection of an ensorcelled coat or even a single spell iron.

You, above all others, got no business playing it safe, she told herself.

The Red Hand's attention never wavered from the incoming fire and the avenging angel, John Brown.

Her heartbeat slowed, her hands steady as a mountain, as she took aim. She slipped from the shadows just long enough to light her irons and pull the trigger.

One Red Hand saw the spellfire and turned just in time to take a force blast square in the face.

The other never knew what hit him.

In an instant, one painted the stone with his brains, the other, the ground.

A heartbeat later, the others seemed to recognize they were being flanked. They turned and opened fire. By then, Talen had already doused her irons, stepped back into shadows, and leapt one side.

A few stray shots hit her coat and jostled her, but she kept moving.

The Red Hands fired at the open air, but thank the mothers, none had an eye piece.

Talen drove her boot into the face of one crouching Red Hand, breaking his jaw and sending him tumbling. As she turned and twisted, she stepped from shadows and fired before vanishing again.

Try as they might, the Red Hands couldn't keep up with her shadow dance. She led and they tried to follow, but always stayed a step or two behind.

"For my sisters," she said, as she obliterated one.

"For Delia and her mother," she said, pulverizing the chest of another. Once more in shadow, she drove a boot heel down onto the mangled remains of his heart, and twisted, grinding it into the earth. Each death fed the furious satisfaction but somehow still kept it hungry for more.

All the while, John Brown roared his invectives, turning and firing the last of the spell loads as the phantom chorus sang on.

Glory, Glory, Hallelujah

His soul goes marching on

When the last Red Hand lay dead at her feet, Talen fired a starburst load of her own into the air. The three blue comets soared high into the sky before exploding and raining stars down on the town square.

As Talen reloaded, more gunfire erupted, this time from well to the south. She ducked behind a corner and readied her irons.

The stained who'd fled John Brown's arrival now ran back toward the center of town. Fear creased their faces as they ran as fast as their legs would carry them.

A balding, middle-aged man chanced a look back.

Someone put a shot between his eyes. The back of his head exploded, and his twitching corpse fell to the ground.

A moment later, Etty stepped into view, followed by a couple dozen others. They levered their repeaters and shot down the fleeing stained.

A lightness filled Talen's chest, and she donned her best, fierce grin.

Etty and those with her continued forward, an unstoppable force. They paused only long enough to put two bullets in the heads of every fallen stained they passed.

Talen turned her attention back to the larger fight, picking off stained as she dashed from one spot of cover to the next. When she stopped to reload yet again, she wiped at her face to clear some sweat and found her hand came away red with blood. She ran her hands over her face and winced when she touched the right side of her brow. It only seemed an inch or so long, and from the angle, had been the result of a shot bouncing up from her coat.

Sparing only a few seconds, she checked herself for anything else. By the number of holes in her pants, a few shots had missed her legs by bare inches. Unfortunately, one caught the edge of her calf, leaving a furrow. The flow of adrenaline had kept her from feeling it. Unfortunately, seeing it now broke the dam. A burning throb radiated from her calf, spreading to her leg, and sapping the strength from her muscles.

I ain't got time for this.

Gritting her teeth, she willed her trembling leg muscles to still. When they calmed and the discomfort slid to the back of her senses, she walled off the myriad of minor injuries now making themselves known.

She came back to herself just as, above the fray, the Cumulus sailed into view. A fresh torrent of gunfire and dwarven railgun shots rained down.

Talen scanned the battlefield for the preacher, but didn't see anyone who stood out. Her chest tightened, and she clenched her jaw, biting back and snarl of frustration. She hoped maybe he'd been killed when she wasn't looking, but she didn't think she had that much good luck left. Odds were, he was hiding out in the church.

"Knights, to me!" someone shouted. "We'll rout these Yankee bastards!"

A tall man in a fancy gray uniform stood behind a hastily-built rampart. It seemed odd he'd take the time to dress for the fight, but Talen had seen dumber things. His black hair streaked with white at the temples, but his bushy goatee seemed as dark as his soul.

A few stained hooted as they hurried over to join him.

It seemed safe to assume this was General Forrest. His reputation as a skilled tactician seemed lacking, considering he left his flank exposed, even if only to Talen, who remained hidden from view.

She leveled her right-hand iron and made to slip from shadows.

Forrest stood, took aim and shouted, "Show these nigg—!"

A torrential downpour of lead rained from the Cumulus, shredding him and his men. They jerked and stumbled as—seemingly everyone on the Cumulus's deck—unloaded on them.

Talen could only gape in pure, stunned awe as the deadly rain reduced most of the slavers to piles of nearly unidentifiable gore. For a half a moment, she wondered if she'd assumed wrong about this man's identity. From what others had said, she'd been expecting some masterfully fearsome genius. But then, she'd heard the same thing about Custer, and he'd also proved to be a pompous, overconfident, imbecile.

She blinked away her surprise to find a few had survived the onslaught. She rolled her cylinder to a different load, stepped from the shadows, and fired.

A fireball leapt from the barrel, struck the cowering, dying men, and exploded. Some flew into the air, others slammed into the wall. All of them screamed in pain as they died burning.

Regrettably, Forrest, and at least one other man, didn't move or scream, they just burned away.

Before long, the surviving stained found themselves pinned down in a crossfire between Netty's fighters and Talen's friends in the woods. The Cumulus's continuing barrage from above turned the square into a killing field. Even stained couldn't stand up against that level of fire.

Not wanting a surprise appearance from the preacher, Talen left her allies to finish off the stained. She made for the church. To be safe, she took the long way around to keep clear of the righteous slaughter.

As she went, Talen could still hear the phantom chorus singing above the gunfire and screams of the dying.

Glory, Glory, Hallelujah
His soul goes marching on.

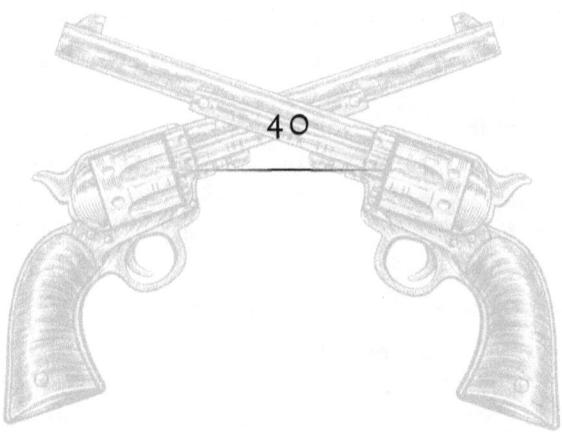

40

T alen took a moment to reload and listen at the rear door of the
church. There didn't seem to be anyone on the other side, but
with so much sound and fury nearby, she couldn't be sure.

Standing off to one side, and putting a brick wall at her back, Talen
turned the knob and pushed the door open.

Nothing happened.

A quick peek around the door's edge revealed a small, dark room, and
no one in sight.

She dared another glimpse, a little longer this time. It looked to be a
kitchen, and empty.

Still in shadow, with irons leveled, she stepped inside and made sure
no one hid, or lay in wait. She only found three very small cubby holes
containing nothing but spread out, threadbare blankets over tattered
bedrolls. A child might fit, but an adult would need to fold themselves
damn near in half. Judging by the large footprints worn into the sides of
the nooks, that had, in fact, been the case. Her blood boiled, and she
wanted nothing more than to see the person responsible die screaming.
Hopefully them being empty meant the occupants had run off when the
opportunity presented itself.

Continuing on, she approached the far door. It had no latch and led to
a narrow, open space. If she had to guess, it was to keep the kitchens separate from the main building in case there was a fire.

There would be tonight, but a breezeway wouldn't be enough to save the church.

Passing through the open space led to still another door, also unlocked. Whether ignorance or arrogance, Talen didn't know, but she appreciated it either way.

This door opened onto a dining room, a rather extravagant one at that. It was smaller than either Bennfield's or Perkins's but no less opulent. A chandelier filled with dozens of unlit candles hung above a massive polished table. A dozen intricately carved and padded chairs sat even spaced around it. A cabinet holding fine dishes and glassware sat against one wall. On either side of the chandelier hung a pair of feather fans which appeared to be operated by a cord along another wall.

Imagining some poor, ragged, and likely starving, Black soul forced to silently work the fan as the rich white folk feasted further stoked Talen's fury. It took her a moment of concerted effort to calm enough to keep from destroying everything in the room.

How could Wilfred, Harriet, Margaret—or anyone even a shade darker than lily white—worship the same god as these slavers?

She let her bewilderment shift to anger and indignation, stoking the already-burning fire in her heart.

To her right, another door led out, but as she went to it, something about the room twigged her brain as off. She turned and studied the opposite wall.,

Nothing but wood panels and paintings

She turned in a slow circle, looking over the room as a whole.

Whiles she couldn't place what exactly, some about it just felt wrong.

Part of her said to let it go and continue on. The uneasy twisting in her stomach however argued that something terrible lay just beneath the well-polished veneer of this room.

After a few seconds, she still didn't see anything. Her chest tightened more and more with each wasted moment. While she stood here, innocent people fought and died in the town squ—

Was the room too small? Hurrying back out the way she'd come, she stepped into the breezeway and turned to the outside of the building. It sure as hell looked bigger from the outside. To confirm, she poked her head back in. Sure enough, the dining room stopped a good six feet before the exterior wall.

It might be possible the space got used by a room she just hadn't found yet. However, she clearly remembered the trap door, and the repugnant room it hid, in the farm they'd cleared just a few days ago.

Talen went back into the dining room and, careful not to make a sound and also still mind her surroundings, began examining the wall in question. It had no door—at least no obvious one—so she started at one corner. Moving slowly, she ran her hands over the smooth surface, tapping lightly and listening at intervals. A few feet from the opposite corner, Talen found a very small space between the panels. Another gap appeared a few feet farther down, but otherwise all the other panels sat flush to each other.

She pushed against the panel. It gave a bit, but didn't open.

A solid kick would probably take it down, but Talen didn't want to risk alerting anyone.

She checked, but couldn't find any catches or such on or near the door. However, a large landscape painting hung in the middle of the wall. She tried to look behind it, but it seemed to be held fast somehow. Just before her patience expired, and she just ripped the damn thing off, it pivoted. A small click sounded a few feet away, and the door swung inward a couple of inches.

She pushed it open, happy to find it swung silently, revealing a short, narrow hallway that led to another room. As soon as Talen stepped through the threshold, the fetid, sour stench of human filth near knocked her over.

Her stomach lurched and her throat tightened. She turned away, took several slow breaths, and managed not to empty her guts onto the floor.

After wrestling the nausea into submission and wiping tears from her eyes, Talen turned back to the entryway. Carefully carved runes and sigils set along the doorframe glowed in soft purple.

Must be some sort of charm to hold back the stench so as not to ruin the appetite of the diners.

That notion nearly sickened her more than the stench.

For an instant, Talen debated whether or not she really wanted to see what foulness Thompson kept hidden away. In the end, she didn't have a choice. The fact Thompson wanted to keep it secret gave her plenty of reason enough to keep going. More than that though, there could be, and likely was, one or more people bound by some detestable craft who needed help.

Or a merciful end.

Steeling herself for the worst, Talen took the last few steps.

The only light came from the wan moonlight shining through a few small, high windows.

Six bunks, each three tall, lined the walls, leaving just enough space for two people to stand in the middle of the room. In each of the bunks lay a silent, still form. No surprise, all Black. Three women, the rest men. Not a one of them could more than twenty. Two might've barely in their teens.

Their chests rose and fell in a regular, slow, steady rhythm, but otherwise seemed entirely unaware, save for the anguished scowl they all wore. None had any clothing above the waist, and on each, just above the heart, sat a palm-sized stone, carefully carved with intricate sigils.

Elven sigils.

No. No Elven crafter would be so clumsy in their etching. She narrowed her eyes, peered closer, and tried to make out the crude, human approximation of Elven script. Despite her keen vision, the ineptly etched letters proved hard to read.

An instant later, her heart dropped and shattered inside her chest, making it difficult to breathe. Though her knees threatened to buckle, she managed to keep standing.

Talen knew the stones, despite never having seen them before. However much she might wish she had it wrong, the thin tendrils—not unlike what connected the quiet ones to their stones—that ran from these talismans out through the wall told her she wasn't.

"Siphon stones," she whispered.

The elves, after suffering brutal defeats at the hands of the other eldar, had grown desperate. Ironically, the desperation came from elves' inherent toughness. While very few actually died in battles, those fights did result in huge numbers of injured. The numbers quickly outpaced the available energy for healing prayers. So, they sought out another source of energy, a more direct one. Healthy elves, specifically those not trained as warriors, volunteered their own vitality. They crafted stones that would work in pairs. One set for a giver, and the other for the receiver. The literal life force of one to would be siphoned away and given to the other.

Like most of the detestable crafts, the stones had been made with the best of intentions. However, darkness moves by inches, not miles. In far too short a time, prisoners of war replaced the willing volunteers. Soon after, innocent hostages joined the acceptable list of donors, willing or otherwise. Inch by inch, the elves lost their way. In time, the injured numbers no longer required such extreme measures. However, Talen's people found the stones didn't just heal, they could empower those already in good health, granting them extra strength, speed, or vitality.

A cold shiver slowly clawed its way up her spine. With this many stones, Talen didn't know if she could win this fight. Hell, she didn't know if an entire army could. Stories passed down from the Eldar War spoke of how terrible even a single stone made a warrior.

Thompson had eighteen, and she doubted he shared the power with anyone else.

Obviously, she needed to destroy the stones, both to save these poor people but also to break Thompson's ability to feed on them. However, as soon as she destroyed the first, he'd know. No chance she'd be able to destroy them all before he came running.

Her mind spun as she tried to come up with any other options. Even if she did the unthinkable and killed all these people, each spell iron only held eight loads. Somehow, she didn't think Thompson would wait for her to reload before coming at her.

Even if that would work though, she'd never accept it as an option.

At the least siphon stones, unlike the geas stones, instantly released their victims once deactivated. They'd be weak—a side effect of having their life forces drained away—but they'd recover eventually. Unfortunately, there'd be no getting back the years taken from them. They would, however, be able to live out however many they had left. She refused to take that from those who'd lost so much already.

She needed to find another way. One that would, at least, save these people, and as many of those outside fighting as possible. Her own survival didn't matter. If she died, she'd die fighting for the right thing.

That's when the solution came to her, and it hit like a kick to the chest.

"I can't do it alone," she whispered, and almost fell to her knees, though she wanted to scream in anger.

Not just in frustration at realizing something so obvious, but also what it meant. She didn't just need one or two people to help, she needed a score. Some, probably most, of whom, wouldn't survive. To someone on the outside looking in, it'd seem like a ridiculous worry. Countless people outside this church, even now, risked their lives. Many had already fallen, and more would before the fighting ended.

But they fought that fight for themselves, and those trapped in this town. Talen would be asking them to lay down and die for her. To buy time. They'd be literal cannon fodder, throwing themselves in Thompson's path to keep him from getting to her.

How could she ask that of them?

Why did she have to?

She was a shadow warden, damn it! A two-gun witch! She'd fought entire companies of soldiers. Brought in some of the most dangerous stained imaginable. Hells, she'd even stood against dwarven leviathans.

It's not fair!

It should be her standing between darkness and the innocent, not the innocent between her and the darkness her people made possible. She'd spent centuries honing her skills, becoming a righteous weapon against the darkness, not them.

But you were never alone in that fight, her mother's voice said, inside her head, or maybe her heart.

When you fought the soldiers, her mother said, *you had your sisters and the Oceti Sakowin by your side. Even when you hunted stained for the humans, you always had Gaoth there. And when you stood against Elizabeth Tuller, the dark caster that violated every law of magic you'd ever been taught, Wilfred and Margaret were with you.*

Talen gritted her teeth and wiped at her eyes. She knew it was all true, but it didn't make it any easier to accept.

And I'm with you, my daughter. I always have been, and I always will be.

Talen drew in a slow breath. "I love you," she said, almost inaudibly. She didn't know if it actually was her mother speaking from the other side. It could've just been Talen's heart speaking on her mother's behalf. In the end, it didn't matter. It didn't make any of it less true.

Less than a minute had passed since Talen had come into this dank little room, making it a minute wasted on pointless contemplation. She had work to do, grim as it might be.

The knot in her stomach didn't untie, rather it turned to a heavy, cold stone. She'd carry that weight for the remainder of her life, however long or short that might be.

She turned on her heel and silently left the church the way she'd come.

The sound of gunfire had slowed significantly, thought it hadn't stopped entirely. She spared only a quick glance at the remaining stained —a couple dozen at most—as she ran in search of Wilfred and Alice.

The square had become a blood-soaked, corpse ridden, wasteland. Bodies, or just pieces of them, lay in shredded piles or on their own. The air hung heavy with the smell of blood, powder smoke, and acrid fear. Between the cacophony of gunshots, people screamed, or cried out for their mothers. Many of them stained, but not all.

Talen walled off her heart in a vault of cold stone and kept looking.

Etty and hers had apparently joined up with Wilfred and Alice's volunteers. All of them hunkered down behind bullet-riddled buildings or random debris. They all focused their fire on a pack of stained holed up in a cluster of buildings. Unfortunately, many had taken refuge in the bank, its solid stone construction serving as a veritable fortress.

Wilfred and Alice, no surprise, huddled together near the vanguard of the attack. Maggie popped into view, just long enough to fire a couple of shots from a repeater, before ducking back down. A tremor of anger and aggravation shook the fortifications around Talen's heart. They kept up a steady stream of fire, holding the stained's attention, as others looted bodies for ammunition.

In that moment, the sad brevity of their lifespans made them appear as children to Talen. She'd spent almost twice the years a human would live just training to be a warden. Even Wilfred, despite the gray in his hair, lines on his face, and wisdom born from a harsh and brutal existence, had only lived a fraction as long as Talen. Maggie, fierce and determined as she might be, huge repeater in her hands, looked damn near an infant.

All of them, candles burning out far too quickly. And now, Talen came to extinguish them even sooner.

Pushing it all from her mind, Talen went to them, crouching low to stay behind cover, and slipped from the shadows.

"What the hell is she doing here?" Talen asked, gesturing at Maggie.

Alice nearly jumped out of her skin. "Sweet Jesus! When did you get here?"

"Just now. And who gave her a gun?"

"I got it myself off one of the dead," Maggie said, a scowl settling on her face.

"She just turned up," Wilfred said.

"I snuck off the ship when no one was looking," Maggie said.

"Well then you can damned well sneak back on," Talen said.

Maggie glanced up at the Cumulus still hanging overhead. "How you reckon I do that? I left my wings on board."

Wilfred chuckled but stopped when Talen shot him a glare.

"This ain't your fight!" Talen said to Maggie, ready to hurl the kid onto the deck of the airship.

"The hell it ain't!" Maggie said. "I had to watch those around me do horrible things, and weren't nothing I could do that'd make a bit of difference. Now I can!"

"Ain't exactly no place for her to go," Wilfred said.

"We've kept her with us to make sure she stayed safe as could be here," Alice said. "I get what you're feeling, but I was about her age when I ran, and not much older when I signed up to fight in the war."

"That don't make it right," Talen said.

"No, it doesn't," Alice said. "But if you look about, there's a lot of that going around."

Talen wanted to argue, but she couldn't, and it infuriated her. Worse still, none of them had time for this debate. As if to punctuate the point, a few shots struck a nearby wooden post.

All of them ducked, and Talen flinched away from a spray of splinters.

"This conversation ain't over," she said to Maggie.

Maggie smiled. "Yes, ma'am." She took aim and fired a few shots.

"I need your help," Talen said to Alice and Wilfred.

"The preacher?" Wilfred asked.

"Yeah." Talen explained the situation with the stones.

Wilfred nodded. "So you want me to undo them while you hold the preacher's attention?"

Alice glared at him. "You sure as hell ain't doing it alone."

"Neither are you!" Maggie said.

Talen, Alice, and Wilfred all shot her a look that quieted her instantly.

Talen turned to Wilfred but couldn't meet his eyes. "You can't undo them."

"Then I'll do it," Alice said. "I ain't a crafter."

Despite being wrapped in stone, Talen's heart started to crack. "They don't work like that," she said. "Only the person who set them can shut them down. Otherwise, they got to be destroyed, and mundane weapons won't do it."

Alice scrunched her face. "So, you're saying you need *us* to keep the preacher busy while *you* can take care of the stones."

"Yeah," Talen said. "But soon as I start breaking them, he's going to want to come for me." She swallowed. "You can't let him 'til I'm done."

Wilfred and Alice looked at each other and then back to Talen.

"And?" Wilfred asked.

"I'm confused. What exactly is the problem?" Alice asked.

Both Alice and Wilfred stared at Talen with genuine confusion. She shouldn't be at all surprised that neither hesitated to step up and do what had to be done. That didn't stop it from tearing at Talen's heart all the same.

Alice's expression softened in apparent understanding. "I see. You're saying he'll be a tough one?"

"Like nothing you've seen before," Talen said.

"Worse than Elizabeth Tuller?" Wilfred asked, only a hint of fear in his eyes.

Even that sliver of fear wrapped Talen's chest in a vise. "By a good measure. I don't know for sure how the stones will be working for him, but he'll be strong and fast. Probably heal from whatever you do as soon as it happens."

"Don't know about fast," Maggie said, "but near every service, he'd lift these big, heavy rocks to show how strong he was." She made a face. "Said his faith in God and the truth or something was the reason."

Alice looked from Maggie to Talen, smiled, sighed, and shrugged. "Okay."

Talen stared back at her for a moment. "I don't think you understand—"

Alice laughed. "You think this is the first time I'll be wading into a fight I ain't expected to survive? When this is done, we'll share stories over some of Draven's whiskey."

Time seemed to freeze around them. Talen's heart filled with love, respect, and admiration. Reverence, even. As cruel as some humans could be, others could be twice of selfless and compassionate. Her heart swelled, shattering the confines she'd wrapped it in. The warmth of affection and esteem spread through Talen's body and soul.

She just stared at that beautiful, remarkable woman.

When time resumed flowing, Talen leaned forward and kissed her.

Alice kissed back.

The taste and feel of her lips, the touch of her hand on Talen's face, could not be confined by something as mundane or ordinary as words. In that stolen moment, she found a spark of hope.

When their lips parted, Alice's eyes fluttered open and she smiled. "God damn, that was certainly worth the wait."

"If you two are done," Wilfred said, fighting back a grin, "I reckon we best get to work."

"Done for now," Alice said.

The look she gave Talen sent a hot shiver of hunger and desire down her spine, but she drew in a breath and pushed it aside, for now.

"Now you go on and get back to the stones," Alice said. "We'll pull together some others and make a racket so you know you can set to work."

"I'd see it as a kindness if you didn't dawdle," Wilfred said, smiling his ever-present smile.

Talen clenched her jaw to hold back the tears from her breaking heart. She pulled him close, kissed his forehead, and then each cheek. "Good luck, both of you," she said, nodding at him and Alice. She pinned Maggie with a hard glare. "You find someplace to hunker down well away from that damned church, you hear me?"

"Yes, ma'am," Maggie said, unhappily.

"Swear to me," Talen said, putting some heat in her tone. "There's enough folk going to hear their kin ain't coming home. I will not have Jacob and Mary be among them."

Maggie turned to Alice and Wilfred, but found no support. "I swear."

"Go on," Wilfred said to Talen.

Reluctantly, and with some wetness in her eyes, Talen slipped wrapped herself in shadows and sprinted back to the church.

It took some effort to push her worry aside and focus on what needed to be done, but she managed. Despite knowing the layout of the church, she entered it with caution, keeping low and behind cover when possible. No way of knowing if Thompson had an eye piece, or even needed one.

When she reached the dining room, she didn't go immediately to the hidden chamber. Instead, she went to the door she hadn't opened before, and pressed her ear to it.

With the gunfire much reduced, she could just make out the sound of someone talking. It sounded like a prayer, but farther off than just the other side of the door. She cracked it and peeked through to find the adjacent room empty too.

Opening the door all the way, she scanned the room. Like all the others, no candles or crafter lights burned. This one appeared to be a parlor or sitting room. Again, the extravagant décor seemed excessive for a preacher or a church. All this opulence confounded Talen. Power and destruction typically interested stained more than money or material wealth. And yet, damned near the entire town contradicted that wisdom.

The door on the opposite side of the room was opened onto a study or library. Assuming she lived through this, Talen would be sure to give it a good once-over for any other stolen relics before burning the place to the ground.

A second door, halfway down the wall on her left, was closed. From the sound, it led to the church proper. Though still muffled by walls, she could make out the words more clearly. Someone—presumably Thompson—prayed loudly, almost a shouting rant.

Admittedly, Talen didn't know much about human religions, not modern ones anyway, but these prayers didn't sound like any she'd heard before. This raging bluster didn't even carry the pretext of mercy and forgiveness, it just called for cruelty and iniquity.

Hell, Thompson didn't even seem to be asking for nothing. Rather, he shouted to God his eagerness to kill any unbeliever that stood in his way.

Talen had to at least give him credit for being honest about it all. Not that it'd stop her from ending him.

A door opened at the far end of the church, and her stomach tightened.

"Well, I'm guessing you'd be Preacher Thompson," Alice said, louder than necessary.

"I am but a vessel for the Lord," Thompson said in a cold, deriding tone. "A shepherd leading his flock."

"Since you've been hiding in here," Alice said, "you might not have noticed, but your flock is all dead or dying."

"Or soon will be," Wilfred said.

"Vengeance is Mine, and retribution," Thompson said, loud and clear. "In due time their foot will slip; For the day of their calamity is near, and the impending things are hastening upon them!"

"I do believe he called us retribution," Alice said.

"It do sound that way," Wilfred said.

"Never take your own revenge, beloved," Thompson said, "but leave room for the wrath of God, for it is written, 'Vengeance is Mine, I will repay,' says the Lord."

Despite her every instinct and desire to kick the door open and lay into Thompson, Talen turned and sprinted to the hidden chamber. She told herself she wasn't running away, and while true, it sure didn't feel that way.

Talen found Thompson's bound victims just as she'd left them, silent and still, their life energy slowly draining away on filaments of foul magic.

As she considered her options, Talen wished she'd paid more attention to the lessons on the detestable crafts. She couldn't burn the stones without risking the innocent people in the room, and potentially all those keeping Thompson distracted. A force blast seemed the logical choice, but would she need to do one at a time?

She imagined the blast not hitting right and sending one or more stones flying, and then having to crawl about to find it while her friends tried not to die.

Could be she could make a hole, pile them in, and shoot at close range. But what if the magic from her iron didn't manage to destroy them?

The weight of each passing second pressed down on Talen more and more, further fueling her doubts.

"Damn it! Stop thinking and do the deed!" she said to herself.

Starting with those on the highest bunk, she gently lifted the stone away. Just touching the cursed thing sent waves of stomach-twisting nausea through her, but she fought them back. She pulled the wretched charm away, but a second thin thread of magic trailed back to the young man.

Talen paused and listened for any sudden raging from outside the room.

None came.

Not daring to question further, Talen kept going.

Unfortunately, she didn't have enough room to lay them all out. So, after collecting the charms, she piled them together, and set a single stone off by itself.

After covering the faces of the unmoving victims with the scraps of blanket she could find, Talen drew her right-hand iron. She took a steadying breath, poured magic into it, and took aim.

Despite there being less than a foot between barrel and stone, anxiety and fear set her hand to shaking.

"Mother, please let this work," she said softly and then closed her eyes, turned her head away, and pulled the trigger.

Force slammed into the earthen floor with a thump, followed instantly by a sharp crack.

Even before she opened her eyes, Thompson's rage, his hatred-filled scream, echoed through the building, nearly shaking the walls.

Not wasting a precious second, Talen took another stone, placed it on the powdered remains of the first one, aimed, and fired.

Another bellow sounded from the church proper, followed by the sound of splintering wood, and a heavy thud.

A barrage of gunshots sounded in reply.

As quick as she could, Talen destroyed one stone after another.

Thompson's roars became more frantic and furious with each stone's destruction, followed by more gunshots

Then the brave, doomed volunteers started screaming.

The sharp, pained, and desperate cries tore at Talen's soul.

Tears poured from her eyes, having nothing to do with the growing cloud of pulverized stone filling the room, and made it hard to see. When her right-hand iron went dry, she switched to her left and continued her work. All the while, struggling to ignore the horrific noises coming from the church proper.

Her left-hand iron ran empty, so Talen put the second to last stone in place and set to reloading both irons as fast as her shaking hands could manage.

Weeks passed in those few seconds.

When the cylinders were full, she didn't holster either iron. Instead, she aimed one at each of the remaining stones, and fired.

The building really did shake then, but Talen paid it no mind. She glanced over and saw the victims stirring, but they still seemed too weak to move.

"I ain't got time to explain," she said to them as rage filled her, screaming for retribution. "Stay here and someone will be back to get you in time."

She didn't know if they understood, or even heard her. She took half a moment to chide herself for not bringing anyone along to tend to these people. Unfortunately, she couldn't do anything more for them just now.

Gritting her teeth, and with irons still burning, she turned and ran.

The time, at last, had come for her to get into the fight.

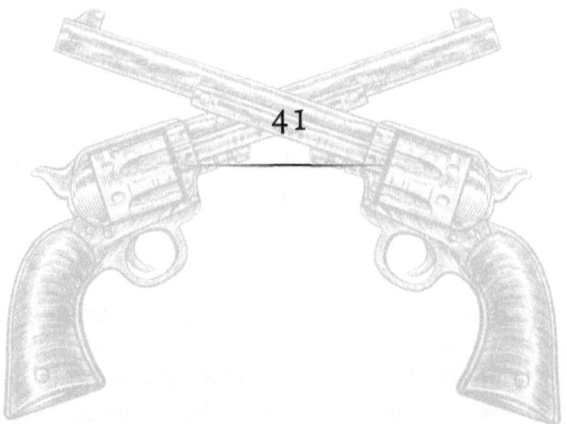

41

T alen's focus narrowed. Fury powered her legs as she rounded the corner, and bolted through the dining room. The door to the church, along with a section of wall, lay in the sitting room.

She didn't slow, just pivoted, and sped into the church.

Thompson had his back to her as he swung a pew bench like a cudgel. Several others lay broken and splintered around the massive church.

Talen heard the gunfire but could only see Thompson in her tunnel vision. She hurled herself at him, driving her shoulder into his spine with all the strength she could muster.

As she connected, his back bent and cracked. The force driving him face first down to the floor.

As they slid along the polished stone floor, Talen shoved the barrel of her right-hand iron against his skull and pulled the trigger.

He twisted at the last moment and her shot obliterated a bench and section of floor instead.

Talen tried to tumble away, but he moved faster, and drove an elbow into her face.

Stars danced behind her eyes. For a lingering moment, she floated weightless and senseless through air. She crashed into a pile of debris, and back to reality. Reflexively, she rolled to her feet and darted to one side just in time to avoid a massive chunk of wood hurled at her.

"Foul creature!" Thompson screamed. "You cannot stand against the Lord!"

Her vision returned just in time to see the preacher's eyes, entirely black, lock on her. The roiling darkness she'd seen around the other stained seemed as nothing compared to what surrounded Thompson. It reached out like the tentacles of some nightmarish monstrosity all around him, for several feet.

Though she couldn't smell it, Talen felt the rancid, fetid corruption to her core, like a greasy film that wouldn't wash away. The crystal in her belly burned with such a sudden, fierce heat that she worried it might set her shirt ablaze.

Time slowed and Talen's vision opened enough to take in the whole scene. She couldn't see Wilfred or Alice anywhere, but a handful of nameless volunteers from the Cumulus lay on the floor, unmoving. Nearly a dozen others fired down from the three rows of balconies above. Ghostlike shadows moved in Talen's peripheral vision, vanishing the moment she tried to look at them.

Gunshots struck Thompson's back, making him jerk, but otherwise, he hardly seemed to notice.

"You think destroying the physical can stop a spiritual warrior of God?" Thompson asked as more shot peppered his back. "Your people might've found hints, but I am God's prophet! I am the one with whom he chose to share his entire truth and to usher in a new world of his glory!"

Revulsion and fury churned in Talen's chest, a brief fight for dominance, but found common cause in a desire to wipe Thompson from existence.

She fired her left-hand iron, sending three balls of lightning at him.

Thompson sidestepped them like casually lobbed stones. He laughed, and two of the tendrils surrounding him lashed out at her.

She turned and leapt away.

One missed her entirely, tearing through debris and sending it flying like the tossed toys of a petulant child. The other landed square on her back. She slammed to the floor so hard it drove the air from her lungs. She tried to suck in a breath, but it took several tries before her body complied.

Yep, he's worse than Tuller.

Before she could recover, it wrapped around her, squeezed, and tossed her like a ragdoll.

She tried to tuck and roll, but landing amid a pile of broken benches made it useless. Her back and shoulders cracked as they bent to their limits. Thankfully her coat prevented any of the snapped pieces from impaling her.

Her chest anyway.

A flash of near blinding agony radiated from her left leg as a sizeable piece punctured it, just below the knee, narrowly missing the bone. Inertia tore the wooden shard free as it carried her on, bouncing and tumbling.

Her vision went white for an instant and her ears rang when her head struck something hard.

Once she, and the rest of the room, stopped moving, she tried to scramble away, but her leg screamed in protest. Instead, she just flopped over and tried to push herself back as Thompson came at her.

Somehow, she managed to keep hold of her irons through all this. She took aim, but before she could pull the trigger, Thompson blurred and was on her.

One of the dark tendrils lashed out and batted the irons aside. The blow knocked them from her hands, and skittering across the floor. A second twisting mass of corruption seized Talen around the neck, lifted her from the ground, and squeezed.

She punched and clawed at the foul manifestation as her legs kicked at the empty air. Desperation fueled her muscles, but she would've had more success kicking a redwood.

Thompson sneered, his eyes black pools of swirling corruption. "Thou shalt not suffer a witch to live."

The iron grip around Talen's neck tightened, and everything went dark at the edges. Panic set her heart to pounding, and she looked around for something, anything, to turn the tide. She only found the ruins of a lost battle.

Another lost battle.

That's when she finally spotted Wilfred, unmoving, and partially covered in debris, his left arm bent at an unnatural angle. A few feet away, Alice, bloodied and bent, still gripped Draven's railgun in her right hand.

The rumble of dwarven leviathans and the screams of her dying sisters reached across the years from Whitestone hill.

No. Not again.

A fresh wave of indignation surged through Talen and she redoubled her efforts against the darkness choking the life from her. Bending and twisting, she tried to press the crystal in her belly to the corruption made manifest. However, when did manage to get a leg over it and tried to leverage her body up, the writhing darkness became incorporeal and her leg fell through.

And yes, somehow, the section gripping her throat remained as solid as iron.

Her lungs burned for air, and everything grew darker.

A sad, regretful peace settled over Talen. With calm acceptance, she closed her eyes.

Mother, I'm coming home.

"Let her go, asshole!" someone shouted and a series of gunshots split the air.

Thompson jerked and bellowed in annoyance rather than pain.

Talen opened her eyes and saw Maggie standing defiantly, levering a new round into her repeater and firing again.

"You shall stand up before the gray head and honor the face of an old man," Thompson said, "and you shall fear your God. I am the Lord."

"You're a son a bitch is what you are." Maggie didn't budge, she just kept shooting until her rifle ran dry.

When it clicked empty, Talen's heart broke at how entirely she'd failed the child.

Thompson turned and began striding toward Maggie.

She threw her empty rifle at Thompson and looked around for another.

"If there is anyone who curses his father or his mother, he shall surely be put to death," Thompson said.

"Damn right I cursed him," Maggie said. "And I curse you too, you shit stained rot!" She found a revolver, took aim, and started firing. As she backed away, she neared Alice.

After some less than gentle nudging with her foot, Alice blinked dust from her eyes. After half a heartbeat, without pausing, or bothering to get up from the ground, she started shooting.

"Rise and fight," a strange voice in Talen's head said, oddly calm and even.

The last of her strength evaporated. Talen couldn't even manage the will to find more. Every part of her hurt, even her slowing heart ached with every beat. "I got nothing left," she said back. "I failed her. I failed them all."

"You are inviolate protector," the voice said. "Imbued you with purity. No corruption can stand against the fire of it."

On the edge of death, Talen saw again the stained farmhouse burning, and the corruption fading from the land around the flames. Warmth, life, and power flowed from the crystal and into her body, drawing her from the encroaching darkness. It occurred to her just then that she'd been holding back the crystal's power without even realizing.

With an effort of will, she stopped resisting. The gentle stream became a flooding torrent. Strength and power filled her aching, exhausted body.

The burning in her lungs vanished, as if she'd taken a deep breath of cool, clean air just after a rainstorm.

Every ache and pain in her battered body faded away.

Her vision cleared.

Thompson, his face illuminated with a searingly bright light, stared at her in wide-eyed shock. After half a moment, his expression shifted, twisting into a sneer of genuine pain.

More gunshots sound from behind him, and he jerked a couple times as, presumably, bullets peppered his back.

The light grew more intense, and the roiling darkness around him recoiled. He shrieked in pain and hurled Talen across the room.

She hit the floor, tumbled, and slid, but if it hurt, she didn't notice.

A defiant anger and vaguely familiar energy surged through her, powering her to her feet. Her leg almost buckled, but she managed to stay upright.

Talen glanced over to Maggie and Anne. Both gaped at her.

In their eyes, Talen finally understood two things.

First, neither anger nor rage fueled her. Oh, she despised Thompson and all he'd done. She hated the slavers. But that hate wasn't what got her back to her feet just now. That strength came from love, from compassion, and from hope. Love of her friends and found family. Compassion for all the innocents who suffered indescribable cruelties. And hope that, even in the face of overwhelming evil, she wouldn't stand alone.

Second, the white light now filling the church and causing Thompson to hesitate didn't emanate from the crystal. It came from her. The light, the magic, the power entrusted to her by elementals suffused her entire body, and it caused her to shine like a star in the night.

Thompson bared his teeth and lashed out again, but he seemed to be moving slower.

Talen smacked away the tendrils, her hands wrapped in beautiful, blue-white light.

Thompson hissed in pain, and the darkness recoiled again. "No! I am the truth and the way!"

Talen limped toward him.

"I am His chosen vessel!" Thompson said and swung at Talen with his actual fists.

"I've had about enough of that, rot." Talen slapped his fist aside and punched him in the face.

He growled and swung again, and again.

Talen blocked and dodged most, but her injured leg slowed her.

Thompson's fist slammed into the side of her head and literally rattled her brain, staggering her senseless for half a heartbeat.

A second blow landed in her stomach with enough force to not just push the air from her, but also lift her from the ground a couple of inches.

Again, no pain as such registered. More strangely though, the inability to breathe for a moment or two didn't bring the usual panic. She just noted it, as if observing these things in someone else.

Instinctively, she stepped back, avoiding a haymaker that might've taken her head clean off.

As the swing whiffed by, she regained her senses. Bending low, she drove her fists into his kidneys. Despite being fueled by love, Talen allowed herself to hope the organs ruptured.

Thompson doubled over and tried to move away.

Talen took the opportunity to drive an elbow into his nose. It broke with a satisfying crunch.

Thick, black blood poured out and covered his lower face. He roared in rage and unleashed a flurry of blows, almost too fast to see.

Again, no pain, but she couldn't resist the sheer force of the impacts. Neither could she afford to keep getting pummeled like this. Feeling it or not, her body could only take so much damage. As if to prove the point, a single, sharp throb erupted from her wounded leg. The magic running through her quieted it, but not before the leg gave, and she went to one knee.

Thompson's fists passed over her head, and threw him off balance, but he took a step forward and caught himself.

"Let's see how you like it." She drove her fist into the side of his knee, dislocating it with a wet pop.

"Kick his ass!" Maggie shouted.

Thompson swung down to hammer Talen's head.

She caught his fist, stood, and pivoting, heaved with all the strength she could summon.

He sailed bodily across the room and crashed into a pile of shattered pews.

"Talen, catch!" Maggie shouted.

She glanced over and saw the girl holding her irons.

Maggie tossed them one at a time.

Talen caught them, turned, and took aim at Thompson just as he got to his feet. A torrent of power poured into the irons. The spellfire burned so brightly it extended beyond the runes and sigils, engulfing the entire spell iron.

Thompson flung pieces of broken pew at Talen.

She ducked and dodged them, as she looked him up and down for a weak point.

He faced her and bellowed, an unholy howl that rattled the windows.

A smile crept across Talen's face and she couldn't keep herself from taunting him. "Here I thought you were going to be tougher than Elizabeth Tuller, but *she* went down harder than you."

Thompson charged forward.

Talen fired.

As expected, he dodged to the left. A force blast sailed past him harmlessly, punching a hole in the far wall big enough for Gaoth and Joseph to step through, side by side. In so doing though, he stepped right into a blast of artic air.

Fog swallowed him and the temperature inside the church plummeted to below freezing.

Talen didn't wait and gave him both barrels again.

Twin trios of blue comets blasted through the vapor, revealing his frost-covered face. The starburst loads connected and exploded in a blinding shower of sparks.

He didn't even stumble, just grunted in annoyance and swatted blindly at the air. When the embers settled, he took a wide stance, as if inviting her to try again. "Foul witch! Your petty magics can't stop me!"

Talen obliged. She rolled both cylinders and took aim again. Between his legs. "Wanna bet?" She fired, one iron an instant after the other, giving them as much power as they could hold.

As hoped, Thompson didn't bother to dodge.

The two force blasts hit home, one right after the other.

The impact folded him in two, driving him into, and then through, the wall.

It might've been wishful thinking, but Talen could've sworn she'd heard a wet, squelching sound just before he went through the wall. However, she didn't have time to savor the petty notion, however gratifying.

She chanced a quick glance over her shoulder.

Maggie watched with wide eyes and a huge grin from behind some debris.

Alice, however, had gone still once more.

"Check on her, Wilfred, and the others," Talen said to Maggie. "If they're alive, do what you can to help. I'll be right back."

Maggie nodded.

Talen limped over to the hole Thompson had made and stepped out of the church, irons still shining like the sun.

The preacher lay on the ground, gasping and whimpering, bent double. His hands covered his balls, or more likely, where they used to be. Around his hands, a growing, dark pool of blood soaked his trousers.

Talen tried to think of something to say. Some answer to his evil and the bullshit he'd spat at her. Nothing came to mind, so she took aim and started to pull the trigger of her left-hand iron.

But she stopped short. The swirling corruption surrounding Thompson had withdrawn. Just a little. And only around his face, and the spots on his shirt where starburst had burned through. In those spots, a faint, dirty gray glow shown through.

Utterly flummoxed, Talen just gawked for a moment. Her gaze shifted to her hands, and the pure white light surrounding them. Understanding dawned on her then, casting away ignorance like the morning sun washes away the night. Just like she'd managed to wash away at least part of Thompson's stain.

"I'm a damned fool," she said. If she didn't have a bad leg, she would've kicked herself.

Thompson spit black blood and stared at her with pure, rancid hatred.

She doused both irons, holstered the left, and knelt down over Thompson. She reached out with her left hand, still wrapped white magic.

"Your dead will live," he said. "Their corpses will rise. You who lie in the dust—"

Talen stopped listening and extended her fingers to touch him.

Thompson grabbed her wrist and tried to push her away. He would've had more luck stopping a glacier.

Her fingertips touched the bare skin just over his heart, exposed through a burned hole in his shirt.

A rush of power flowed into him from her. As powerful as a storm. As unmovable as a mountain range. As vast as a fresh water ocean some called a lake.

The undulating corruption surrounding Thompson began to burn off, evaporating into nothing. The last of the darkness that filled his eyes seared away last. Only fear remained behind.

"What have you done to me?" he asked, his voice shaking with terror.

"I reckon I healed you," Talen said. "And ain't no one more surprised by that turn than me."

"No!" he shouted and swung at her. A slow, weak, entirely unstained human swing.

Talen almost pitied the man as she slapped his hand away and got to her feet. Almost.

"You think this will stop me?" Thompson asked. The winces of pain with every movement undercut his sad bravado. "You cannot stop the truth of the Lord! I will return and—"

Talen sighed in either pity or contempt, she couldn't decide, then lit and fired her right-hand iron.

A pulsing green sphere shot from the barrel and vanished into Thompson's chest.

After a moment of nothing happening, he laughed and struggled to his knees. "Awake and shout for joy," he said. "The earth will give birth to the departed—" He convulsed and grabbed at his chest, his eyebrows drawing together.

Talen limped back a step and waited.

He reached out for her with a hand that had turned to a gnarled collection of branches. Eyes wide, he opened his mouth, but green fire filled it. More magical flames emerged from his chest and quickly engulfed him. As his body bent and turned, he tried to scream, but only a pathetic gurgle escaped.

Panic took hold as his feet and legs twisted, turning to roots that immediately sank into the earth. Slowly, though not slow enough to Talen's thinking, his body swelled and grew. Flesh turned to bark and wood, as he transformed into a tree. Like the stained Talen had used the Gaia load on before, Thompsons' face froze into a gnarled knot.

Unlike him though, this was no nightmarish, twisted mockery of a tree. Rather, it grew into a huge, majestic, utterly beautiful, oak. At its heart, a blue-white light burned and pulsed. With each beat, threads of white light spread out, filling the creases in the bark, and eventually reaching the tips of the highest branches.

As what could only be the pure magic of an elemental filled the tree, it straightened and grew, and grew, and grew. In a few heartbeats, the trunk spread to four or five feet across. The branches reached well above the church, leaves sprouting and opening, the veins of them filled with light. When the tree had finished growing, the magic flowed down the tree and into the earth itself.

A weariness like Talen had never felt washed over her and her knees wobbled from the sudden, immense weight of the night. Every ache and pain that had been quiet moments ago now screamed. The exhaustion even reached her brain, leaving her unable to do anything but hurt.

She gritted her teeth, let out a sigh, slumped against, and then slid down the church wall. Setting her dark right-hand iron on the ground, Talen pulled her shirt away. The crystal had dimmed to only a soft, faint glow. When her head swam, she remembered her leg. After tearing a strip from her shirt, she wrapped it around the wound, tied a knot, and braced herself. Biting down hard, she cinched the knot as tight as her broken body could manage. The sharp, searing jolt soon faded into the veritable sea of hurt that her body had become.

She closed her eyes and let her head fall against the stone wall. The strange irony of a life spent as a warrior, only to now become a healer, and one who couldn't heal herself, settled over her. As it did, she became increasingly aware of a long litany of injuries she'd missed. Several ribs were cracked, if not broken. Her battered left shoulder protested every movement, even breathing. A couple of fingers were dislocated, and she suspected her left wrist had broken at some point. Not to mention the no-doubt countless bruises and cuts covering her body.

"At least it's done," Talen said.

"It is," someone said, from the darkness. "I admit, I didn't see that coming. To be honest, I'm not even entirely sure what it was you did."

Talen snatched up her right-hand iron, filled it with magic—which now seemed a meager soft glow compared to a moment ago—and leveled it.

An elf woman stepped from the shadows, leading Gaoth.

Talen's brain seized at what she saw.

The woman stood an inch or two taller than Talen, with hair several shades lighter green, but grown long and twisted into a single braid. The markings on her dark brown skin were more complex, but covered less of her face and neck.

When her addled brain finally made some sense of the impossibility standing before her, Talen's heart near burst with shock and joy. "Neia? Is it...is it really you?"

"It is, little sister," Neia said, a thin smile on her face. "And no, you aren't dead. I'm not here to lead to you the mothers."

"What are you doing here?" Talen managed to ask. "*How?* I saw you die."

"That leviathan shell did nearly kill me," Neia said and traced faded burn scars along one cheek. "I was left buried, so I waited and healed. By that time, the soldiers and dwarves had gone." One side of her mouth twitched. "I found Tintreah, not just dead and broken, but butchered. Not knowing what else to do, I started walking, following the tracks. I walked for weeks before I managed to steal a horse. Then I rode as fast as he could manage back home, and... Well, you know what I found."

"Mother's mercy." Talen's heart broke, managing to exceed all the pains wracking her body. Her throat tightened. It'd been hard enough for her to lose their people, but if she'd lost Gaoth too, Talen couldn't imagine surviving that.

"Nothing but charred corpses."

"I'm so sorry," Talen said, tears running down her cheeks, and struggled to get to her feet. "I thought I was the only one! If I'd known, I would've waited for you. Searched for you!" She stumbled forward to embrace her sister. "Thank the mothers!"

Neia pushed her away, knocking her back against the church wall.

Talen winced in pain and stared in stunned confusion. A heartbeat or two later, a cold chill ran through her and she looked at her sister. "Neia, what—"

Neia drew her spell iron and leveled it at Talen.

Talen's brain struggled to make sense of what was happening. "What are you doing? Have you lost your mind? It's me!"

"Me?" Neia asked, her face twisting into a mask of rage. "Have I lost *my* mind? I'm not the one that has taken up with humans and a dwarf! A *dwarf*, Talen! How could you?" Her spell iron lit with blue fire.

There, amid the sea of pain and confusion, Talen could finally seize onto something that made sense. "I know what you're thinking." Talen lifted her hands. "I thought the same, but Draven ain't like that. Lots of dwarfs ain't. See, what they did caused a schism and—"

"I don't care!" Neia shouted, her hand shaking, and the spell iron flaring. "They slaughtered us! They butchered my horse!" She covered her face with both hands.

Talen reached out for her sister, desperate to help or at least offer some small comfort. "Neia, please, let me—"

Neia pointed her iron at Talen again and glared. "But that wasn't enough. They had to take more, so they went to our home. Our home! They let the humans defile and burn our mothers and children!"

A cold fist clenched Talen's heart. "Neia, I was there," she said, her own hands shaking. The tears running from her eyes blurred her vision. "The dwarves weren't, just the humans. Red—"

"You were there?" Neia asked, her expression softening. "So, you fought them?"

Talen stomach dropped and her chest tightened. She swallowed and looked away. "No."

Neia's expression became utter disgust. "No? What do you mean no?"

"Mother made me swear to hide," Talen said, pleading. "She said the fight was already lost and—"

"Stop!" Neia said, the dancing spellfire on her iron flaring up again. "No! I didn't want to believe my eyes when I saw you fighting with and for humans. Fighting alongside a dwarf. But now, to hear you stood by and watched them slaughterer our people? How could you? How did you not throw yourself from the cliffs?"

Talen couldn't say anything. Fact was, she'd asked herself that question more than once. The hate, loathing, and disappointment in Neia's eyes near broke Talen.

"We used to fight side by side against corruption," Neia said. "Now you've taken up with a dwarf, and humans? The very people that feed and grow the corruption that will end this world!"

Talen opened her mouth to say something, anything, to make Neia understand, but something in her sister's eyes brought her up short. Realization finally hit Talen like a physical blow.

"No." Her already weak knees gave out, and she fell to the ground. "No. No, no, no. Please, tell me it wasn't you. Say it weren't you what gave the *Malihane Carid* to that *juarchian* filth!"

Neia scrunched her face in confusion. "Of course, it was me!"

"What?" Talen asked, the tears flowing like a river now. The entirety of the world seemed to be crumbling around her. "Why? We're shadow wardens! We swore to protect magic, to destroy corruption, not spread it!"

"We did, and we failed, sister," Neia said, genuine sadness in her tone. "We tried, but the humans are a plague. They spread like wildfire, destroying everything in their wake. If they aren't ended, they'll spread their rot across the world, killing it, and all the pure magic in it."

Talen opened her mouth.

Neia waved her away. "And don't tell me about the *Oceti Sakowin*. They're just as defeated and lost as we are. Even if they do survive, which I doubt, they're still human. In time, they'll be overcome by the same cruelty and malice that consumes them all."

"I don't understand," Talen said, pleading. "You're figuring on saving the world by destroying it?"

"No!" Neia said, her eyes wide and wild. "By giving the humans the power to destroy themselves! Don't you see? The only way to stop the tide of rot that they'll bring, is to speed it along, so they kill themselves off before they destroy the magic! Once they're gone, the surviving elementals can heal the world and restore it. Like when the fires swept through the redwoods, opening the seeds and letting new growth take root!"

"The elementals gave me the power to heal rot!" Talen said and gestured at the tree. "Look! There's no corruption there! I burned it from that *shanzi fetsuian*. Can't you see?"

"I see a single tree in a sea of rot." Neia shook her head. "Even if you did what you say, you think you can do what elementals can't? You think you can purge a world of rot?"

"I don't know," Talen said. "But I do know that magic is fueled by life. If your plan succeeds, who'll be around to see it?"

"No one living deserves to see that new world," Neia said, her tone sad. "We failed, over and over. First by creating the detestable crafts, and again in our futile attempt to destroy corruption. We don't deserve to survive any more than humans or dwarves. Might be new life will come with that world. If it does, I hope it does better than we did."

"Sister, so long as we draw breath, we ain't failed," Talen said. She lifted her shirt and showed Neia the crystal. "I done lost hope too, but I found it again. The elementals saved me! One put this crystal in my belly to save me from corruption." She pointed to the tree. "Others gave me the power to stomp that preacher and clean what had to have been as stained a soul as ever walked this earth. It's not too late."

Tears spilled down Neia's cheeks, and she shook her head again. "We can't know what the elementals want, but I envy you your hope. Even if it is misguided and pointless. You really don't see that there's no way to win this fight, do you? That you're just delaying the inevitable?"

"Might be I won't," Talen said and swallowed. "But our duty, our promise, was never conditional on the assurance of victory. Just cause we might lose don't mean we give up. It sure don't mean we turn on everything we believe."

"That kind of hubris is the heirloom of our people, dear sister," Neia said, her expression going hard. "We thought ourselves the very pinnacle of wisdom and understanding, but we were wrong. So very wrong. Remember, the detestable crafts were Elven make, or adopted by us so quickly they might as well have been. No, I'm finally seeing past the lies and self-delusion. I spent years trying to think of another way, but there isn't one. There's only one path forward. Your way might win some battles, might even save some." She motioned to the tree. "Like you did here. But my path is the only one that leads to winning the war."

Talen wracked her brain for words, any words, to make Neia see sense. But when she looked into her sister's tear-filled eyes, she knew there weren't any. Neia was lost. The grief and pain had been too much. It had broken her.

Talen didn't see the telltale miasma of corruption surrounding her sister, but the dark magic must've found another way to get to her. Whisper its lies and convince her to venture down this dark road. She cursed herself for wasting the magic on Thompson, but maybe she had enough left to help Neia.

Talen tried to tap into the crystal, but found it near empty. She gritted her teeth, tried to draw out what little she could find, and reached her hand to Neia. "Sister, please. I ain't got much left, but let me try and heal you."

"Heal me?" Neia stared at her for a moment, clearly not understanding.

Talen managed to get back to her feet, hand still extended, and nodded at the tree.

Neia looked from the tree to Talen and back. "Heal *me*? You think I've gone stained?"

Talen couldn't stop herself from laughing at the lunacy of the question. "You're working to spread corruption!"

"How do you still not understand?" Neia shouted. She turned away and grunted in frustration. When she faced Talen again, her expression had gone stoney but tears ran down her cheeks. "Come with me. Join me and I'll show you. If we're together, we might even succeed in time to save some of our sisters on the reservations."

All strength left Talen's body and her arm fell limply to her side. She wept unapologetically, tears matching her sister's. "I can't."

"If you don't stand with me," Neia said, a hard sadness in her voice, "you stand against me."

Talen drew her left-hand iron and dropped it to the ground next to the right. She lifted her hands and met her sister's eyes in one last, desperate plea. "Then you best kill me now, sister. Send me to our mother, cause I can't go with you."

Neia's mouth twitched and her hand shook.

Please, Mother, show her the way out of darkness.

Neia drew in a slow breath and lowered her iron. "I won't kill you, sister. I can't."

This glimmer of hope gave Talen the strength to smile a little. She opened her mouth.

"I'd hoped it wouldn't come to this," Neia said. "I wanted you to see for yourself, but you won't. It's okay, I'll help you see." She turned her iron on Gaoth. "You just haven't lost enough."

Talen's heart stopped, but instinct took over. She snatched up both spell irons and leveled them at Neia. "Sister, put the iron down. Please. I'm begging you."

For some reason, Gaoth didn't react, he just stood there in a daze.

"What did you do to him?" Talen asked.

Neia used the brief distraction and moved fast, damned fast, surging forward. She kicked at Talen's wounded leg.

Talen bit back a scream as searing pain surged through her body, and she crumpled.

Neia cracked her spell iron barrel across Talen's broken wrist.

Talen briefly went blind from the pain and dropped her left-hand iron. She tried to bring her right-hand iron around, but Neia seized it, twisted and pivoted her hips, leveraging the iron away.

"You were never as fast as me," Neia said and tossed the pilfered iron out of reach. "Even when you weren't beaten to a pulp."

Talen lifted her empty hands in surrender and bent double, prostrating herself. "Okay. I'll go with you. Just don't hurt him. He ain't got no part in this."

Neia shook her head. "You might come along, but you wouldn't be able to see. Gaoth has a part to play. I am truly sorry for it though." She aimed the iron at his head.

"Gaoth, run!" Talen said and threw herself at Neia's legs.

Neia stumbled back and slammed the barrel of her iron across Talen's head.

Light exploded at the edges of Talen's vision and she crumpled again. When she looked up at her old friend, he just stared through her, as if not seeing her. "What did you do to him?"

"I'm not a monster," Neia said. "I worried it might come to this, so I gave him something so he wouldn't die afraid or feel any pain." She stroked his mane. "That's a mercy Tintreah wasn't given. I know this'll hurt, but I'm afraid there's no other way."

Talen grabbed for Neia's legs again. "No, please!"

Neia didn't budge, she just took aim and—

A shot rang out.

Neia hissed in pain as blood exploded from her hand. The spell iron fell to the ground.

Maggie stepped into view, repeater aimed at Neia. "You so much as twitch, I'll split your skull, hear me?"

Neia actually laughed. Her mouth twisted into a cruel smile as she gripped her wounded hand in her good one. "I suppose I can see why you like some of them, dear sister," she said, attention locked on Maggie. "Were you not a child, I'd happily rip you to pieces."

Maggie swallowed but didn't waver.

Neia looked down at Talen. "Savor this victory, sister. Keep to your hopeless fight if you must, but stay out of my way. Interfere with my plans again, and the long span of no elf having killed another will end as abruptly as our people themselves did." She turned back to Maggie, winked, and vanished.

Maggie's eyes went wide. She swung her rifle back and forth, scanning for a target.

"She's gone," Talen said, tears still spilling down her cheeks as a vast, cold emptiness spread through her. A twinge of gratitude lingered though. Thank the mothers Neia hadn't been more determined to see Gaoth dead, because she damned well could've—

"You sure?" Maggie asked, still not lowering her rifle.

"Yeah," Talen said. "I'm sure. She's well and truly gone."

"All right. If you say so," Maggie said. "Come on then. Let's get you up." She took hold of Talen's good hand and pulled her to her feet.

Talen stood and stumbled to Gaoth. From the look of it, Neia had given him a dose of dream weed. It wouldn't cause any lasting problems, but it'd be a day or so before he was back to himself. Through the emptiness, relief washed over her, and she hugged his neck as tight as she dared, pressing her cheek to him.

"I'm so sorry," Talen whispered, her tears soaking his fur. "Please forgive me."

Maggie gathered up Talen's irons and holstered them for her. "Looks like your sister grabbed hers when she run off."

Talen didn't answer, just held to Gaoth. She'd never won a fight and lost so much in the winning.

"Wilfred and Alice are alive," Maggie said, after a long moment. "They ain't feeling too good, but they're alive. In fact, most of the folk in the church are. Reckon preacher must've lost interest when they stopped moving. There's broken bones and such a plenty, but that's it."

"That's good," Talen managed to say. While she did feel sincere relief that her friends were okay, the cracks in her heart grew wider and wider, threatening to swallow her whole.

After another long, silent moment, Maggie put her hand on Talen's shoulder. "Come on. Fighting is done and the Cumulus is setting down. Reckon you need to get looked at."

Talen didn't protest, but only because she didn't have anything left inside. She followed Maggie, leading Gaoth around the church, and back to the town square where the Cumulus slowly descended.

Bodies littered the ground, mostly white faces, but more than a few Black ones too.

Talen hardly noticed. She just held to Gaoth, determined to never let him go.

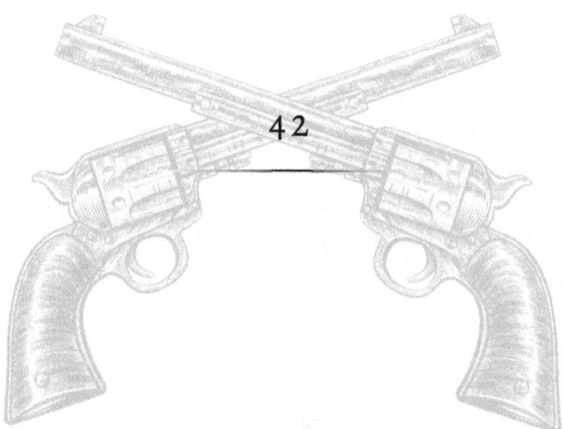

42

Talen refused treatment or to leave Gaoth's side, at least until he'd recovered from the doping Neia had given him. The way she saw it, plenty of others needed help more than her. Besides, it felt right to hurt physically with her heart and soul torn to shreds. However, when her friends pointed out how badly she was bleeding, Talen agreed to let Frieda bandage her up properly.

The following day, Gaoth had returned to normal and practically dragged her off the ship to heal. She went along, not wanting to refuse him anything, and spent the next two days under the sun and moon in constant prayer.

Gaoth never left her side.

By the third day, she'd recovered enough to function, though she'd need another few days before she'd be fully healed.

Physically, at least.

She had no idea how long it'd take for her heart and soul to mend, or if they ever would. At least the crystal in her belly had refilled and once again shone like a star in the night sky. Though it provided only a small comfort.

Over the next several days, they scoured the remaining small farms for anyone who'd managed to avoid the slaughter and freeing the last of those held in bondage. They saved scores of enslaved, but not at all.

Each corpse and living victim utterly lost to one of the detestable crafts left another scar on Talen's soul.

They also found nearly a dozen kids. Maggie tended to them all. Thanks to her, they all went to sleep with as few tears as possible.

No one even suggested heading north until everyone who could be saved had been. When that day finally came, everyone took time to mourn those who'd been lost—either in the fight for freedom or at the hands of the slavers. However, they also rejoiced, celebrating those who'd survived.

Talen spent that time alone with Gaoth and tending to the horses that still needed extra care.

Most kept their thoughts regarding the slaver's kids to themselves. However, on one occasion, a few suggested leaving the children behind. Talen didn't have the desire or wherewithal to deal with such talk. She stepped into the middle of the discussion and simply made it clear that anyone who tried to offload the kids would need to go through her.

It never came up again.

Maggie had apparently told Wilfred, Margaret, and Draven what had happened at the church, or at least what part of it she'd seen. They'd nearly reached New York before Talen could bring herself to tell them everything herself. She didn't say much beyond the telling of events. The others mostly just listened and offered what little comfort they could. To their credit, they gave Talen her space.

When the Cumulus returned to Harriet's home, Talen stood by silently as Delia reunited with her mother, brother, and even her father who'd been found in one of the outlying farms. They all thanked Talen, Delia hugging her tight.

Talen just nodded, forced a smile, and told them no thanks were necessary. Even so, a twinge of warmth and hope echoed from the shattered remains of her broken heart.

The entire town turned out to help the new arrivals find places to stay, and settle into their new lives. By the time the sun set, an impromptu party had broken out. Talen didn't join in, but did watch the festivities from a distance. It surprised her how much it fed the spark of hope still burning inside her, shining out in defiance of the darkness. Almost as much it surprised her that the spark still burned at all.

Talen couldn't help but think of Neia. Maybe if she could see this—all the love and joy, hope in the face of brutality—she'd understand. Hopeless or not, some fights needed fighting.

"Might be we'll lose the war, sister," Talen whispered to herself, watching the smiles and laughter of those so recently bound in chains. "But if this is what winning battles looks like, I ain't never going to stop fighting. And I ain't giving up on you."

A while later, Alice found Talen and sat down next to her. "You doing all right?"

"Nope." Talen turned to her and managed a feeble smile. "But I expect I will be in time."

"You did a good thing."

"*We* did a good thing."

Alice chuckled. "Oh, don't think I won't take my share of credit." She put her hand over Talen's. "But we couldn't have done this without you. I don't know what happened to you at the church, but a blind man could see it was something terrible."

Talen opened her mouth.

Alice lifted a hand. "No, ma'am. It ain't my business. You told those who needed to know, and I ain't the least bit offended I wasn't among them. I just wanted to make sure you understood just how big a thing you did, for a whole lot of people."

Talen squeezed her hand. "I'm glad I could help."

"And here I thought I was going to have to smack you when you tried to downplay what you did," Alice said, smiling.

They sat together in silence for a while as people danced and sang.

"I know there ain't going to be more than that kiss," Alice said. "Not right now anyhow. When the time comes that you're healed from whatever happened, if you're so inclined, you know where to find me."

Talen turned to her. "I do."

Alice lifted Talen's hand, kissed it, and then stood. "You take care of yourself. When you don't see fit to do so, be sure to let Wilfred, Margaret, or Draven do it for you."

"I will."

"Promise?" Alice asked, arching an eyebrow.

Talen smiled despite herself. "I promise. A year ago, might be I'd have argued with you, but I ain't the same I was then." She let out a breath. "Won't the same in another year neither."

Alice gestured to the party. "Lots of folk won't be either." She turned and left without saying another word.

The next morning the Cumulus made ready to deliver the children to Draven's friend. Harriet came on board to see them off.

She shook their hands. "Can't thank you all enough."

"We were happy to be able to help," Wilfred said.

"But sorry our help was needed," Margaret said.

Harriet nodded. "Amen. But until it ain't needed no more, I'll take comfort in knowing good folk such as yourself are ready to step up."

"Speaking of," Wilfred said and passed Harriet a leather covered box with a pamphlet on top.

"What is this?" Harriet asked.

"Wireless telegraphy machine," Wilfred said. "Draven made it, but as I'm flying with her directly, I ain't got need for it no more. Thought maybe you would."

Margaret tapped the pamphlet. "These are the instructions on how to use it."

"I thank you, kindly," Harriet said. "But don't wait for a telegraph to come back and visit. You all are welcome anytime."

Talen just watched in silence. Despite everything, she still felt hollowed out and numb inside.

"If you don't mind," Harriet said, "I'd like a private word with Talen."

Margaret, Wilfred, and Draven nodded, made their final goodbyes, and went to tend to other tasks in the cargo hold.

Harriet walked over to Talen, put a hand on her cheek, and met her gaze. "I can see you paid for the freedom of them folks. More than most."

Talen opened her mouth to protest, but Harriet silenced her with a look.

"I don't know what you paid," Harriet said, "but I can venture a guess. I can connect things, and I do see in your eyes the same pain and regret I saw in my own mirror for a long time."

Talen furrowed her brow. "I don't—"

Harriet's granite expression softened, and her eyes turned a little sad. "I tried to save my sister Rachel, over and over. But she died in chains before I could. Her children got sold off to different farms." She let out a slow breath and wiped at one eye. "Got the rest of my family out, but I couldn't never save her."

Talen stiffened, and her heart twitched in sympathetic shame.

"It don't help you feel no better, but the truth is, we can't always save everyone."

"Respectfully, ma'am," Talen said. "This ain't quite the same."

389

"It never is," Harriet said. "Everyone's song is a little different, but that don't mean the tune ain't similar. All I'm saying is, if you spend all your time crying for those you couldn't save, you'll miss seeing the joy in them you did." She glanced over Talen's shoulder at where Wilfred, Margaret, and Draven stood talking. "And not all of them you saved was bound in chains."

Even the trickle of shame, gratitude, and damn near every other emotion, seemed a torrent inside Talen's hollowed out soul. She just swallowed and nodded.

Harriet wiped a stray tear from Talen's cheek. "You keep doing what you're doing, and don't let no one ever tell you it ain't enough." She motioned to the remnants of last night's party with her head. "I know a whole lot of folks who will tell you it most certainly is."

"Yes, ma'am."

Harriet left, and soon after, so did the Cumulus.

That night, Talen managed to talk more about what happened with her sister. Margaret, Wilfred, and Draven listened, offering support, and sympathy; and more than a little whiskey.

"Any notion what her plans are?" Wilfred asked.

"Not a one," Talen said.

"You think she had anything to do with Elizabeth Tuller?" Draven asked.

Talen shrugged. "Could be, but I don't think so. Neia gave Thompson the means to do terrible things and corrupt plenty of magic, but ain't nothing in the *Malihane Carid* to explain what or how Tuller and Thompson could do the things they did. That's something new."

"How did she get him the book anyway?" Margaret asked. "I don't imagine Thompson, or anyone in that town, would've been open to treat with an elf."

"I reckon she used the glamour stones we were all given," Talen said. "Same as I did in Chicago and Boston."

"Right. Of course," Margaret said.

"So, what's next?" Draven asked, refilling hers and Talen's cups.

Talen took a drink. "First, we get Maggie and the other kids to Mr. Hicks. After that, I reckon we see what the dwarves mean to do about the bounty crystal facilities. Then, I got no idea."

"There is something bigger at play here," Wilfred said. "Tuller was disturbing enough with what she could do, but Thompson was a whole 'nother level of bad. Everything I know about magic says he shouldn't have been able to do what he did. Stained or not."

"Didn't seem to stop him," Talen said.

"From what you say," Wilfred said, "sounds like you did a fair bit of law-breaking yourself."

Talen's hackles raised, and she had to bite back some choice words at the implication. Rather than snapping, she just furrowed her brow. "What the hell are you talking about?"

Wilfred eyed her. "You said your hands shone with magic when you was slapping away Thompson's—hell, I don't know what to call them—stained tentacles?"

Talen just sat there, stunned silent. In the moment, she'd been so focused on not dying, she didn't have time to think on it. After, well, everything that happened with Neia sort of occupied all her thoughts.

"I vote for calling them something else," Margaret said. "Anything else, please."

"That weren't really the same thing," Talen said, but everyone, including her, could hear the lie to her words.

"What aren't you telling us?" Margaret asked, eyeing Talen's face.

Talen told them what happened with Thompson, how she'd purged the corruption from him.

"Mother of God," Margaret said.

"Holy shit," Wilfred and Draven said at the same time.

Margaret glanced at them and turned back to Talen. "Well, I for one am more than a little relieved to know we have an opposite to those dark casters on our side."

"It didn't help Neia none," Talen said. "If I'd just killed Thompson outright, I'd have had the magic in me to heal her instead."

"Are you sure you could have?" Margaret asked, her tone gentle. "Sounds like you gave it a good try and it didn't work so well."

"And," Draven said, "at the risk of upsetting you, are you sure Neia is really gone stained?"

"What else could it be?"

Wilfred and Margaret looked at each other.

"What?"

"I know you want to believe she didn't choose that path on her own," Margaret said. "That some outside force compelled her to do it, but…"

Again, Talen had to fight back the urge to argue and defend Neia. But she couldn't stop the cold ball of dread from forming in her stomach. "But what?" Talen asked, but already knew the answer. Even if she didn't want to see it.

"But even if that was the case, she'd still have to *choose* to turned stained," Wilfred said.

Talen opened her mouth to protest, but couldn't think of anything to say.

"And if she isn't stained," Margaret said, "isn't that a good thing? Doesn't it mean, however misguided she might be, she still refuses to give in to dark magic? Seems to me that suggests there's at least some hope of reaching her and changing her mind."

"I reckon so," Talen said and took a drink. "Suppose it just made me feel better to think she weren't acting on her own, and that all I had to do was burn the stain from her like I did Thompson, and she'd be back to the sister I knew."

"Unfortunately," Margaret said, putting her hand over Talen's, "I suspect that, like you, the person she was died with her people."

"I expect you're right," Talen said. "Sure hope I can save her though. Cause I damn sure don't want to have to stop her instead."

"Whatever the case," Margaret said, squeezing her hand, "you won't be alone."

Wilfred took Talen's other hand. "You will not."

"You ain't got no third hand," Draven said, tapped Talen's cup with her own, and took a drink of whiskey. "But you know I'm with you too."

As she looked at her friends, her new family, Talen didn't so much feel better, as start to believe she could, eventually. It still didn't sit right with her though, like she had no business smiling, or laughing, or even being happy when her sister wandered lost in such a dark place. Rather than letting that thought consume her, something she would've done last year, she used it as motivation to ensure, one way or the other, her sister would come out of the darkness.

"I love you," Talen said to them all.

Two days later they set down in the hills of northern Tennessee and met Dino Hicks. An older man, with a head of long white hair, and an even longer, bushy white beard. His eyes kind eyes had a sparkle to them that made Talen like him instantly.

He greeted everyone with a smile and a handshake.

Though taken a little aback by the number of children, forty-eight in total and—apart from Bennfield's babies—ranged in age from two or three to fourteen or so, his smile never wavered. Neither did his eagerness to do all he could. He promised he'd take every child and care for them until he could find them a proper home, however long it took.

In a rare bit of good luck, Dino had two newly calved cows, so the babies would have milk. Hany had stayed in New York with a son well beyond nursing. Talen hadn't asked, but she felt safe in assuming Bennfield had killed Hany's baby to ensure neither of the twins went hungry. While not a mother herself, Talen knew no woman could nurse three children herself.

When Dino assured Talen that he had a network of trusted men and woman who would help as needed, Maggie volunteered her help as well.

Talen got the impression that she, Mary, and Jacob would be staying with Dino for good.

At Harriet's insistence, they gave Dino one of the bags of gold coins lifted from the train. He tried to refuse, more than once, but as soon as he learned Harriet Tubman herself had told them to give it him, he got a little teary-eyed and accepted it.

"I promise I'll make good use of it," he said, wiping his eyes.

"I don't think Harriet would've insisted if she didn't believe that," Talen said.

"She did have some rather nice things to say about you," Draven said.

Dino's eyes went wide. "What? No, that can't be. I only met her one time and—"

"You clearly made an impression," Margaret said.

It took more than a few trips, but they got all the sleeping children into the bunkhouse Dino had waiting. When they finished, as Draven said her goodbyes to Dino, Talen walked over to Maggie who stood off on her own.

"I ain't got words to thank you," Talen said. "You saved Gaoth."

Maggie smiled and shrugged. "Weren't nothing really—"

"Yes, it was," Talen said. "He's my oldest and closest friend. All I have left of my people. And when I couldn't save him, you did. I won't never forget it, nor you."

"I'm sorry, real sorry, about your sister," Maggie said.

The scene tried to play out again in Talen's head, but she managed to push it away. Even so, just the flash of it hit like a physical blow. "Thank you. Me too." She looked around at the farm. "This is a nice place, and Dino seems real nice too."

Maggie's grin lit up her eyes. "Yeah, he does," she said. "Mary and Jacob already like him, but that might be because he gave them each a sweet when he didn't think I was looking."

"I hope you'll all be happy here. They deserve it, and so do you."

Maggie scowled a little. "I suppose. Just wish I could've done more or done something sooner." Her frown deepened. "All them people, mammas, daddies, even children, treated worse than nothing, and I didn't—"

"There weren't anything you could've done," Talen said. "Except maybe get yourself killed. It ain't right, but you did something when it would matter." She nodded over at the house. "And I expect you'll have your hands full correcting them kids of their thinking on Black folk."

Maggie scoffed. "Hell, that won't be nothing. Ain't a one of them I can't whoop. I'll make them see the right of things."

Talen couldn't stop herself from laughing. "You know, I bet you will."

Maggie looked a little awkward for a moment and turned away. "I know it's kind of a little kid thing to ask, but would it be okay if I gave you a hug?"

Talen raised her eyebrows. "It's a little kid thing? Hell, I was about to ask you the same thing."

Maggie beamed.

Talen knelt down and opened her arms.

Maggie threw her arms around Talen's neck and squeezed hard enough to hurt.

"You saved me first," Maggie said. "Saved Mary and Jacob too."

"Guess that makes us even then."

"Nah, there's three of us," Maggie said. "Gaoth is just one."

Talen chuckled. "But he's bigger than the three of you."

Maggie giggled.

The happiness and pure, unbothered delight of her laughter was a balm to Talen's battered heart. For just a moment, all the pain vanished, and she felt the same joy.

"I suppose that's true." She pulled back but didn't let go. Her expression turned sad, and her eyes filled with tears. "Will I see you again?"

Just like that, heartache returned, if of a different flavor than before. While she'd always been protective of children and anyone innocent or helpless, Talen had never much cared for kids in general. Until now. Her eyes got watery too, but she smiled. "You absolutely will, that's a promise."

"Okay." Maggie hugged her tight again. After a moment, she let go, stepped away, and wiped her eyes and nose with a sleeve. "See you later then."

A maelstrom of pride, happiness, hope, sadness, and heartbreak roiled in Talen's heart. As much as she'd miss the girl, she also knew Maggie belonged here. "See you later."

Maggie hurried off, threw her arms around Margaret and then Draven. Wilfred stood patiently by, waiting his turn. Maggie turned to him and offered her hand. He clearly would've liked a hug as well, but he just smiled and gave her a firm handshake. Dino tried to convince them to stay the night, but it was agreed he had more than enough house guests already, all of whom would be waking in the next few hours.

The Cumulus lifted off, and Draven set course for the Granite Halls, a trip that would only take a day or so. Talen went below and set about seeing if she could recreate what happened with Thompson. She suspected that even if Neia wasn't stained and didn't need healing, Talen would need every advantage she could get in the fight that would follow.

ACKNOWLEDGMENTS

My deepest gratitude goes to all the fans and readers who supported Two-Gun Witch so much and gave me the energy to write this sequel. Thanks to the Knights of Powhatan: Kenda and Mike; the Knights of Olney: Dustin, Stephanie, Parker, and Lyla; the Loughrey clan: Casey, Geoff, Geofferson, Delaney, Callahan, and Maguire; and the newly formed Mattis coterie: Kristin, Rodney, and Molly. Thanks to my stalwart sidekick, Ed (my book, which means you're the sidekick) and his podcast (Geek History of Time) compatriot and pun master, Damian. Special thanks to Nicole Kurtz for her review and feedback. Thanks to my editor Venessa for weathering yet another book with me. To Dino (aka book Santa) you earned that tuckerization a hundred times over.

And last but not least, thanks to John and the Falstaff team of misfits for your faith and efforts.

ABOUT THE AUTHOR

Bishop O'Connell is author of the American Faerie Tale series and the award-winning novel, Two-Gun Witch, as well as a consultant, writer, blogger, lover of kilts and beer, as well as a member of the Science Fiction & Fantasy Writers of America. Born in Naples Italy while his father was in the Navy, Bishop grew up in San Diego, where he fell in love with the ocean and fish tacos. After wandering the country for work and school (absolutely not evading mind controlling bunnies), he settled in Richmond VA, where he writes, collects swords, revels in his immortality as a "visionary" of the urban fantasy genre, and is regularly chastised for making up things for his bio. He can also be found online at A Quiet Pint (aquietpint.com), where he muses philosophical on life, the universe, and everything, as well as various aspects of writing and the road to getting published.

Blog – https://aquietpint.com/
Facebook - https://www.facebook.com/AuthorBishopOConnell
BlueSky - https://bsky.app/profile/bishopoconnell.bsky.social
Instagram - https://www.instagram.com/bishopmoconnell/
Amazon Author Page - http://www.amazon.com/-/e/B00L74LE4Y

ALSO BY BISHOP O'CONNELL

Two-Gun Witch

An American Faerie Tale series:
The Stolen - Falstaff Books
The Forgotten - Falstaff Books
Three Promises - Falstaff Books
The Returned - HarperVoyager

FRIENDS OF FALSTAFF

Thank You to All our Falstaff Books Patrons, who get extra digital content each month! To be featured here and see what other great rewards we offer, go to www.patreon.com/falstaffbooks.

PATRONS

Dino Hicks
John Hooks
John Kilgallon
Larissa Lichty
Travis & Casey Schilling
Staci-Leigh Santore
Sheryl R. Hayes
Scott Norris
Samuel Montgomery-Blinn
Junkle
Vickie DeSantos
Quincy J. Allen
Allison Charlesworth

Thank You for Supporting Independent Publishing!

We believe that you should be able
to read your books, your way.
That's why this Falstaff Books
print edition includes a digital copy
at no additional cost!

Just scan the QR code with your device,
follow the directions on Prolific Works,
and enjoy!
You can also join our newsletter when prompted,
and never miss an awesome Falstaff Release!

WWW.FALSTAFFBOOKS.COM

www.ingramcontent.com/pod-product-compliance
Lightning Source LLC
Chambersburg PA
CBHW020524110726
47899CB00004B/1231